Andy Livingstone was born on New Year's Day in 1968 and grew up with an enthusiastic passion for sport (particularly football) and reading. An asthmatic childhood meant that he spent more time participating in the latter than the former and an early childhood encounter with *The Hobbit* awakened a love of epic and heroic fantasy that has never let him go. He is a press officer and former journalist and lives in Lanarkshire, Scotland, with his wife, Valerie, and two teenage sons, Adam and Nathan. He also has four adult stepchildren, Martyn, Jonathon, Melissa and Nicolas, and four grand-bundles-of-energy: Joshua, Riah, Jayden and Ashton. He can be found on Twitter @markethaven and at his website, www.andylivingstone.com

Hero Born

ANDY LIVINGSTONE

Book One of The Seeds of Destiny Trilogy

HARPER
Voyager

Harper*Voyager*
An imprint of HarperCollins*Publishers* Ltd
1 London Bridge Street
London SE1 9GF

www.harpervoyagerbooks.co.uk

This Paperback Original 2015

First published in Great Britain in ebook format by Harper*Voyager* 2015

A catalogue record for this book
is available from the British Library

ISBN: 978-0-00-812067-2

Set in Sabon by Born Group using Atomik ePublisher from Easypress

Printed and bound in Great Britain

For Valerie

Prologue

'When hope is dying, we crave inspiration. And at that hour, we look to heroes.'

The storyteller paused. The ensuing silence spoke as eloquently as the lack of comprehension on the face of the boy behind him. Just moments before, the young voice had cut through the first haze of dusk, stopping him in mid-pace.

'There aren't really any heroes, are there?' It had been a simple question, a challenge born of childish bravado. But the storyteller could no more leave that seed of doubt behind him than a dog could ignore the scent of a rabbit. It was not his nature. Instead, he must plant a seed of his own.

He drew the sounds and the smells of the early evening deep within him: the wheat in the surrounding fields stirred by the breeze; the vestiges of the cooking fires; the heavy musk, the stamping and the grumbles drifting from the stables; the lazy drone of the insects and the cries of the birds seeking them one last time before handing the predators' dayshift over to their nocturnal cousins.

It was a land basking in the contentment of peace, when heroes were not needed. When heroes were forgotten. There are some who say that peacetime is a curse; that we only appreciate what we have to fight for. He had grown to see much truth in that in recent years. Although he would never welcome a return to even the slightest of the horrors he had witnessed on these and other shores, still he marvelled at, and despaired over, the human spirit's desire to dismiss and trivialise that which it did not see for itself. And, therefore, to lower its guard.

It was the mind's greatest defence against terror turning to madness. It was also its greatest weakness if the cause of that terror were ever to return.

Still the storyteller paused, fewer than a dozen steps from the village hall. The weakening autumn sun was setting behind him. That was the way he liked it. Inside, the villagers would be waiting, packed on benches around the concentric circles dug down into the ground, galleries that focused on the stage below in unconscious and incongruous mimicry of the gladiator pits of the southern continent. The world over, people desired performance, whether the blood was in the words or on the earthen floor.

It was an oppressively atmospheric arena. And, tonight, it was his arena.

He would enter with the sun behind, a silhouette in the doorway framed by the deep amber rays. And so the performance would begin. The performance of a master craftsman, and one who loved his art. They would share that love, for they always did. That was what fed his soul, what pulled him from village to village, town to town, day after day, night after night, telling after telling.

He turned, a smooth and balanced movement. Three boys sat on a broken plough propped against the wall of the black-smith's workshop. The largest, slightly older and perhaps trying to impress, stood up awkwardly but with determination.

Clearly deciding that failing to understand the storyteller's reply rendered the man's words irrelevant, the boy pressed on. 'You must know that. It's just all stories to entertain people, isn't it? You add things into it and make it more exciting. You make one person amazing to make it a better story. Admit it.'

The storyteller cocked his head in curiosity. What sunlight was left managed to reach far enough into his deep hood to reveal wry amusement. 'Is that really what you think?' His voice was soothing, measured and cultured, with a foreign hint to his speech.

The boy was defiant. 'I asked you first. Tell me you admit it.'

The man smiled. 'What I think is irrelevant; it can be dismissed. But what I know is different. It is fact, and can never successfully be disputed.

'And I know that there can be heroes.

'They are born, but often the potential they possess never meets with the circumstances that offer it release. Indeed, often when those circumstances arise, there is no one who happens to be there with the qualities needed to face them and triumph.

'A hero's light is always shining, but it is most bright when the world around is in its darkest hour.

'And so, occasionally, perhaps just once in several lifetimes, fate allows the circumstances and the one person to coincide. And when that occurs, the hero is born.' The smile became a grin, and he crouched before them, beckoning them closer.

'Picture it: there is a battle, a vast battle, and the fate of a nation rests on its outcome.' His voice lowered, drawing them in. 'There is no glory, there is no honour, there is no chivalry: it is horror, it is terror, it is screaming and dying with your face pressed in the mud and the boots of friends and enemies trampling you as your tears run into the mire: it is war. And in the midst of the mayhem, there is an island of order: a group of men moving with calm assurance through the carnage. They use their weapons with the economy and efficiency of master craftsmen, with a skill born of years of surviving where others have perished, despatching all in their path as they move steadily and irresistibly towards the leader of the host opposing them. And at their head strides a figure, of no special height, of no special strength, hair plastered black on his face by the grime of battle and his pale eyes fixed, unwavering, on the enemy leader. His sword, a curious black blade, is in his hand, but he swings at no foe. He walks directly at the leader, and the men with him follow, and still they kill all in their path. And the leader turns, and notices them. He pauses as his eyes lock with the stare of the figure bearing down on him, then barks an order and the forty men of his personal guard, the finest warriors of his huge army, turn to meet the small band. The one at their head, eyes locked only on the enemy leader, seems oblivious to the death confronting him. The men beside him roar and run past, closing with the élite guards. Despite the overwhelming numbers, they clear a path for the bare-headed youth. The leader, a great champion of his people, tall and broad-shouldered, his blond hair oil-slicked back from his angled, handsome features, cradles his great war axe in his arms. The merest gesture of his head restrains his guards. He studies the youth, and laughs. He enjoys his sport. With contemptuous ease, terrifying skill and more speed than the eye can follow, the heavy axe swings up and slices down at the centre of the youth's head. But, with all eyes on the flashing weapon, almost imperceptibly the youth sways. He turns, the axe missing by the width of a blade of grass. The youth continues to spin, his movement as fast as the axe itself had been. Even before the axe has embedded itself in the turf, his sword has flashed in the sunlight and he finishes his turn, facing the leader once again. It takes a moment for all to realise that the leader is not as he was. His head is spinning over his guards. It bounces once, and rolls, coming to rest face-to-face with a dead farm boy who had left his parents that morning full of ideals to fight the evil of the man now facing him in the mud. A silence has fallen over this small part of the battlefield, an unreal island of hush amid the clamour of men straining to kill one another, and the youth starts walking again, between guards too confused by the inconceivable to know how to react. As word spreads of the leader's death, so also spreads panic and fear, and his army starts to flee the field in disarray. The youth ignores them. He walks, still, to the body of the farm boy and the head of his former foe. He kneels and, oblivious to the tear running down his cheek at the sight of the dead boy, no older than himself, he closes the eyes of the lad so that, even in death, he need not look upon the face of evil.

'Then he stands and, looking neither one side nor the other, walks from the field, to be where only he knows.'

The storyteller rose, and smiled gently, an amused glint in his eyes. 'So tell me: would it not be a terrible shame if his story were not to be remembered? Say someone knew such a hero and knew that the deed just recounted was not even the greatest of his achievements. Such a man would be bound by his conscience to tell his story, would he not?

'So that is what I do.'

The boy's resolve faltered under the storyteller's piercing gaze. 'Do you mean that you knew such a man? It is all actually true?'

The man turned to the waiting doorway. 'Oh, yes. And you should thank your gods that it is so.'

Now the curious one, the boy stepped forward. 'Why is that?' His companions stood silently, drinking in the man's words as much with wide eyes as with their ears.

The storyteller started forward. 'If you want to know, then step inside, and let the story begin.'

He unlatched the door and pulled it so that it swung slowly open as far as it would go. A haze of smoke drifted into the opening and mingled with the sun's rays as he stepped into its midst. A hush settled like a blanket over the packed interior. From deep within his hood, he stared slowly around the waiting faces, before starting down the stairs.

He murmured softly to himself, 'Indeed. Let the story begin.'

Chapter 1

He stumbled, just enough to tip him beyond the point of balance. He knew there was no stopping the fall. There never was, these days. And he knew to brace himself against the impact would be too much to ask of old bones. Instead, he dipped and turned his shoulder, hitting the ground rolling. Instincts that once saved him on the battlefield and in the duelling circles now served to save brittle bones. Momentary pride at avoiding injury gave way to irritation at the irony of the comparison. His roll had left him with his cheek pressed against the cold flagstones of the floor, the breath punched from him, and wishing he could somehow move himself forward to a time when the pain coursing through his shoulder might have dulled to a throbbing ache. Maybe he could lie here until then. The floor was cool enough, respite from the searing heat of the balcony he had been escaping when he fell. He twisted, enduring the sharp sting from his shoulder in favour of a more comfortable position on his back. He could easily lie here, watching the dance of the dust in the single shaft of sunlight that entered the gloom of his chambers. There was plenty of it to watch, after all. The layer was thick on the floor, as it was everywhere else in his sparse

7

rooms, and the area around his fall was swirling with it. Pity it had not been thick enough to cushion his fall. Why not just lie there? His two criteria for a successful fall had been fulfilled: break nothing and do it when no one was there to see. Why not lie there, indeed? What else did he have to do but watch the dance of the dust? He sighed, and brushed a long lock of white hair from across his eyes to allow him to better see the dust. Hair that had once been not white, but as deep brown as the soil under the freshly watered plants in the garden far below his balcony. Hair that had once been held in place by more than just the plain leather strap that bound it now. His eyes hardened at the thought.

No.

This was no way for one born to rule to behave. To give in. To be found.

He levered himself onto his front, gritting his teeth against the pain, and gathered his knees under him. Slowly, he raised himself to his feet.

'Always get back up,' he growled. 'Always.'

Carefully, he moved to the full-length mirror at the far side of the room. He drew himself erect, and looked the image in the eye.

'If I never see you again,' he said, 'be sure that the last time we met, my head was held high.'

****

The boy stumbled, then went down hard as several larger bodies hit him in close succession.

His cheek pressed into the hard-packed dirt, the precious bundle of rags clutched to his chest, the wind knocked out of him and the shouts of opponents and team filling his head,

8

he wished he could somehow move himself forward an hour when the game would be just a pain-fuelled memory.

One of the large boys lying on top of him pushed his face harder into the ground and seemed to read his thoughts. 'Why don't you just give up, little boy?' he snarled. 'Give us the head and in minutes we can all be off enjoying the Midsummer Festival.'

He cursed the stubborn pride that never seemed to let him back down; a trait that had done him more harm than good, but one that he had found as hard to change as it was to fathom. *Not pride, stupidity*, he corrected himself. He desperately wanted to give his antagonist a smart reply. Instead all he could manage was a suggestion as to where the boy could stick his suggestion. Not exactly witty, he supposed, but it would have to do, as his face was, predictably, pushed into the earth again.

'Have it your way,' the youth smirked as several of the village boys pulled him away. 'Next time we'll hit you so hard they'll need to scrape you off the ground to take you home.'

Climbing to his feet, still slightly winded and unsteady, he believed them. He felt a hand on his arm, and looked up to see his older brother, a tall lean boy, built for both strength and agility, universally popular and everything his smaller sibling wished he could be. But where the pair contrasted physically, they shared a quirky sense of humour: something that had made them easy, and inseparable, companions throughout their childhood. Inseparable even on the sporting field: with only eleven months between them, they had been born in the same year and were therefore of an age to play in the same fixture of the annual apprentices' game.

The tall boy half smiled. 'Enjoying being a punchbag today, are you, Brann?'

Brann grinned. 'I am used to it.' He started to move back towards the rest of his team, then stopped. 'Callan, call Gareth over, will you? We have a few seconds before we restart and I have an idea.'

Under normal circumstances, Brann would quite happily avoid Gareth whenever possible. The apprentice blacksmith tended to determine the worth of his peers by their strength and size: a formula that left Brann firmly at the bottom of his popularity stakes and meant that the small boy was usually treated with little more than contempt... on a good day. But Gareth was also the leader of their team and so, unfortunately, Brann faced the uncomfortable prospect of speaking to the oaf face-to-face. Spitting out some stray dirt and rubbing his bruised shoulder, he was reminded that there were worse things in life.

Gareth skidded to a halt beside him. 'This better be quick – and important. If we don't start now, we'll have to hand the Head over. What is it, runt?'

Maybe it was stupid, Brann thought. It would be easier just to let them get on with the last few minutes of the game and be done with it. But he could not stand the thought of not knowing if it would have worked or not.

He looked up. 'I've had an idea.'

Gareth snorted. 'I knew it was a waste of time. There are no "ideas" in this. You take the Head, get it passed them, go up the cairn and put it the basket. That's it.' He turned away. 'I knew I shouldn't have bothered with anything the feeble runt had to say.'

Brann grabbed at his arm in desperation. 'No, wait. It is not complicated.'

Gareth wheeled round, his look dangerous. 'Are you saying I'm stupid?'

Self-preservation and general love of life just managed to overcome Brann's temptation to answer with the truth. Callan stepped in quickly. 'Of course not. He is saying it will not take long to explain it.'

Gareth sighed. 'What is it, then? And hurry up.'

Brann took a deep breath. 'Look, we cannot batter through them. Too many of them are too strong, or too quick, or both. And they are organised. Once they get set in place, we've got no chance of getting through them.'

'So? We know that. Spit it out, man.'

'So we have to try something else.'

'But there is nothing else. All that anybody has ever done in this game, we've tried today.'

Callan smiled slowly. 'But that does not mean we have to do just that, does it? If we do something new, they will not be ready for it.'

The two tradesmen appointed to enforce the few rules the game possessed had started to shout across to them. Gareth stood up. 'We've got to get on with this. If you have anything of value to say, say it now, and quickly.'

'Right.' Brann took a deep breath. 'This is it. Pretend I am injured, and that is why you are over here just now. Restart the game, and work the Head round to the other side of the cairn.'

'And?' said Gareth.

'And throw it over here.'

'Throw the Head away? Are you mad? We might as well tell them we'll put it in the basket for them.' Gareth was disgusted.

But Callan grinned and slapped the ground in glee. 'Not if we get it over the cairn. There will be no one here.'

'Except him,' Gareth grunted in acknowledgement. 'I know I'm slow, but I get there eventually. Is that it?'

Brann shrugged. 'That's it.'

Callan looked at Gareth. 'Are we going to try it?'

Gareth unceremoniously shoved Brann back to the ground. 'Not just try. Do. There is no way we're going to lose to those towny scum.'

Brann felt the baking earth pressing against his face again. *Gods, I hope not*, he thought. *Please don't let all of this be for nothing.*

The dark-haired man stumbled, slightly, as the crowd jostled and surged with excitement.

He moved, but only in the manner of one who allows himself to be moved, just enough to regain his balance and then brace himself. Somewhat in the manner of an experienced warrior, an observer might think.

But no one was watching him. All eyes were fixed on the game unfolding before them as they shouted themselves hoarse. The man, too, watched the sport intently, but there the similarity with his fellow onlookers ended. He stood, silent and impassive, absorbing every detail. And finding more of interest than he had expected.

He had seen more spectacular sport in cities near and distant, from the magnificent gladiatorial arenas of the sun-hardened Empire far to the south, where decadence was masked by a veneer of civilised laws and customs, to the tracks where humans and animals raced, sometimes even against each other, in the more fertile lands at nature's border where sensible weather stopped and the short sea-crossing began to these rain-drenched islands. Lush and green they may be, but damp and miserable they were, too. He had grown up in a land where the winters were cold, deadly cold, but at least it was honest cold that you could clothe yourself against.

Here, the insidious damp worked its way past however many layers you piled on, and seeped into your bones, setting you shivering with an unhealthy regularity.

Which was why he was thankful that his work had brought him here during what must be their meagre summer. A scant few weeks of blue skies and heat that were welcomed with joy and appreciation by the locals but that, to a foreigner, were more of a taunt: here is what the rest of the world gets for much of the year.

And what lay before him was no grand arena, but a field of short grass and hard earth outside a market town in name and function only compared with the larger and more grandiose – but, if truth be told, more lacking in soul – settlements farther south in these islands; it was in truth a glorified village of no more than a thousand or so residents, although a suggestion to any of the inhabitants that it was anything less than a town would be met with outrage and suggestions of lunacy.

Heavy rope, dyed bright red, lay on the grass to mark out a circular area, around a hundred and fifty paces across, and along that boundary the roaring and beseeching crowd was gathered, three, sometimes four, deep and jostling each other as much from excitement as from their attempts to gain a better view. In the centre of the area stood a cairn of large rocks, roughly the height of three men and at least ten paces across the base, with a battered wicker basket (apparently a veteran of many such a contest) sitting at the peak.

The action raged around the cairn. As far as the impassive stranger had been able to determine, the idea was to scale the cairn and place a tightly bound bundle of bright-coloured rags, apparently weighted by rock or metal in its centre, in the basket. Two teams competed to do so: one defending

13

the cairn while the other attempted to break through and scale the rocks. Rules seemed few, and were therefore easily deduced. The team in possession of the rag-bundle, which was around the size of a man's head, attacked the cairn relentlessly until the defenders managed to wrest the ball from them – at which point the team's roles were reversed.

Tactics seemed only slightly more numerous than rules. Either a player, or group of players, would attempt to force a breach in the line of defenders through brute force by becoming a human battering ram, or one player would dodge and weave his way as far forward as possible, usually aided by team-mates who would try to block, often violently, the defenders' attempts to reach the carrier. If the player with the bundle looked as if he were about to be caught, he would try to hand it over to a colleague to allow the attack to continue. If, however, the player was caught by the defenders, or if the bundle of rags was intercepted or snatched, the fun began. An almighty mêlée would ensue, with players from both sides piling in to try to retrieve the rags in a maelstrom of flailing limbs and frantic dives.

If the attackers retained possession, the attack would resume immediately if possible or, if they were under pressure, the rag-bundle would be fed back to a deep-lying player to allow them to regroup; the defenders would not venture too far from the cairn for fear of exposing gaps in their tight-knit ranks.

Were the bundle of rags to be won by the defenders, they would be able to break immediately for the cairn. As soon as such a battle for the rags began, therefore, several attacking players would position themselves between the defenders and the cairn so that, in the event of a turnaround, they would be able to slow down such a break until their colleagues could reinforce them. In positioning themselves in this precautionary way, however, the numbers competing directly for the bundle were then weighted in favour of the defenders, so turnarounds were fairly frequent as a result.

And, as far as sport went, it was brutal. There appeared to be no limit to the amount of physical violence that could be used to advance one's cause, save blatant attempts to seriously injure an opponent, such as biting or gouging. Kicking, punching, butting and the pulling of any available limbs seemed perfectly legitimate, and even encouraged.

And so it had continued, for almost an hour. The pace was fast and relentless, and the silent stranger was forced to admire the fitness of those who could maintain such efforts continuously at that level for so long. It was even more impressive, given their age: the players, numbering fourteen in each team, looked to be aged near enough fifteen years; probably final-year apprentices, he guessed, if their apprenticeship system conformed to the usual set-up.

A shorter-than-average boy had been hit hard by two much larger opponents, crashing to the ground and only just managing to hang onto the bundle by clutching it to his chest and curling up like a threatened animal until his team-mates could come to his aid.

A heavy man, in the apron of a baker, cheered beside the stranger and jostled him again in his excitement.

'Apologies, my friend,' he bellowed, 'but that's their weakest link down again. It's only a matter of time before we win.'

The stranger looked round. 'It is nearly over, then?'

The baker nodded. 'You haven't visited before, I guess?' The town was boosted by travellers of all sorts throughout the spring and summer as traders brought this year's wares, hunters trailed back and forth from the hills with fresh game and those who preferred to seek a new horizon every day made full use of the better weather; and every year brought most of the same old faces and a smattering of new ones. 'Yeah, it's nearly over. The score is tied, and the time's up. There must be a winner, though, so the game plays on until the next basket is scored.

'All we have to do is get the Head off them and we've as good as won.' The man noticed the stranger's quizzical frown. 'The Head: it's what we call the rags they fight over. They say it was an enemy's head they used hundreds of years ago when the game started.' He snorted in amusement. 'It is slightly more civilised now. That was when it was played between the two villages in the valley. These days we are a prosperous town and they are still a village but still they seem to think they have a chance of beating us. Anyway, having that wee runt on their team is like being a man short for them. The others in the village team have given everything to get it to this stage, but that's all they've got. Next time the runt has the Head, we'll get it back. He gets knocked down every time.'

The warrior looked at him coolly. 'True. But every time, he gets back up.'

The baker nudged him one more time, unconsciously taking himself one large step closer to an early death. 'Nah,' he grinned with relish. 'The little runt is staying down this time. We are a man up now. It's all over for this year, mark my words.'

That warrior turned to him as far as the tightly packed throng would allow. 'This happens every year, then?'

The baker looked at him directly for the first time. His eyes moved over the carefully trimmed beard, the clothes and boots that spoke of efficiency as well as expert tailoring, where wear was obvious but tear was minimal, and the obvious quality of the longsword, dagger and boot knife, and his manner became more respectful. Or, at least, as respectful as an oaf such as he could manage. Even the L-shaped scar on the warrior's cheek failed to diminish the impression of breeding. He nodded.

'Every Midsummer's Day, for as long as anyone can remember. The game takes place between this town and Twofords, the village further up the valley. Final-year apprentices show what they can do and, for the last decade or so, ours have shown they can do it better. The same again this year, as you can see.'

'Because you've got more apprentices to choose from?'

'Because we are better than those hicks from the village, of course. Class shows.'

The tall stranger nodded towards the game. 'It is close so far. And not over yet.'

The baker grinned arrogantly. 'It's over. Believe me, my friend, it's over all right.'

The warrior's eyes darkened at the term of address. He returned to his gaze to the small figure lying alone as the action moved around to the other side of the cairn. There was something about the boy that nagged at him. Something to do with the fact that… He smiled. 'He always gets up.'

The baker looked at him. 'What was that?'

The warrior smiled. A cold smile, but a smile all the same. 'Oh, I was just thinking that you are right. One way or another, it will all be over soon.'

Despite the noise saturating the air, Brann began to feel strangely detached as the action moved around to the other side of the cairn. The nature of the game meant that the players were always in one mass, all involved in one concentrated area. As a result, shouts of encouragement and instruction to team-mates, grunts and roars to prepare themselves for moments of impact and yells of abuse towards the opposition made for a constant roar.

To suddenly be set apart from that immediate clamour left him with a distant sensation. Insignificancies caught his attention: an ant crawling past his nose, twisting and turning as it explored its way about its own world; the heat of the hard-packed earth; the feel of his legs pulled tightly into his chest; the shape of a lone cloud against the deep blue of the sky. It was as if, in the absence of the immediate noise of the contest, the whole world had gone silent. With a wrench, he forced his concentration back to the game, berating himself for letting his mind drift.

Slowly, partly in the hope that no one would notice, and partly to give the impression of still being injured, he rose to his feet. He tried to look shaky, but felt certain that it was the most unconvincing and embarrassing display of acting that anyone would have seen. Instead, he bent over, resting his hands on his knees for support.

He risked a glance at the crowd nearest to him. Most were craning their necks to try to catch a glimpse of the action at the other side of the cairn. Some, however, had seen him stand and were shouting various forms of abuse at him.

That will be the good old townsfolk, he thought, wryly. *Such sophistication from our larger neighbour.*

His gaze was caught by the incongruous stillness of a tall man, dressed in black and with dark straight hair caught back in a serviceable ponytail that hung beyond his shoulders. He was impassive, an island of calm in the tempestuous sea of the crowd. For a moment, pale, calculating eyes locked with his, and Brann's concentration was almost distracted again.

A nod of the man's head directed his attention to a dark speck arcing over the cairn, growing rapidly as it headed towards him.

The Head!

Slapping his thigh in annoyance – and grimacing when he hit a bruise – Brann moved to his left, trying to judge where it would land with a hesitancy that stemmed from years of knowing that his inability to throw with any effectiveness was exceeded only by his inability to catch.

He edged sideways, his eyes fixed on the object, knowing that, once it had landed, every second would be vital to him – and suddenly, and uncomfortably, aware of the world around him. On the edge of his vision, figures moved rapidly around the cairn. He did not dare take his eyes from the multicoloured bundle of rags. He was terrified of making a mess of what, only a few moments ago when he had been explaining his idea to the others, had seemed so simple.

And, most of all, he became aware that the silence that he had imagined in comparison to the noise of the game had become reality. In a sport where possession was paramount, the ball was only ever carried or thumped firmly into the hands of a team-mate; to lob the Head even just a few feet to a colleague, and risk losing it to the opposition, was unthinkable. To launch it nearly forty yards, as the crowd had just witnessed, was madness on a scale that had stunned the baying, bawling crowd into a shocked hush.

And the sight of that very object dropping towards a solitary, small, hesitant figure who, just moments before, had been curled up, insignificant and apparently useless merely added to the stunned disbelief of all those watching, regardless of where their support might lie.

The realisation of that silence was the worst thing that could have happened to Brann. He had, until then, been nervous merely about catching the Head. Now he also felt hundreds of eyes glued to him; most willing him to fail, others desperate for him to succeed. In many ways, it was the latter that placed more pressure on him.

In the last few seconds before the Head landed, one vision after another flashed through his mind – each one a different version of his failure. His mind raced so fast, everything else seemed to be happening at half speed.

Spinning lazily against the clear blue of the sky, the Head took an eternity to drop. The boys running towards him looked as if the air had become as thick as water. And his own legs felt as if he had two of the boulders from the cairn tied to them. Brann wished it would never land, that he could just walk away and leave it all to someone else who could do it so much better than he.

The Head hit the ground, and rolled. He stared at it, scared to move for it, to try to grab it and miss. It hit a stone and spun across in front of him.

Instinctively, he reached out and caught it. And the silence was shattered. The crowd roared. The players accelerated in alarm. His eyes fixed on the cairn, Brann ran.

Thoughts of weariness and aches were gone. Movement at the edge of his vision forced him to glance away from his target. The faster members of the opposing team were closing on him, arms driving and faces contorted with effort and aggression as they strained to block his path. He glared intently at the cairn, then back at his opponents. He might just make it. Forcing his knees to rise, his breathing loud in his ears, he pounded forwards.

Then, with the cairn just a dozen strides away, they were upon him. A figure flew at him from the right. Without pausing to think, he jammed his heel into the dirt and almost came to a halt. The boy, arms flailing, staggered in front of him, trying desperately to change direction. Brann swerved slightly to his right and ran behind him. Another opponent, only feet to his right, thundered at him, aiming to bowl him over. He was too close to avoid. Instinctively, Brann dropped to one knee, taking the force of the attack on his shoulder. He barely had time to tense, bracing himself, before the larger boy's momentum bent him over Brann's back. Driving down with his legs, Brann forced himself to his feet, flipping the boy into a somersault.

'Forward. Must go forward,' he muttered over and over. 'Don't stop moving. Must go forward.'

As he started moving, another opponent was upon him. Roaring – either in fury or anticipated triumph, it was impossible to tell – the boy thundered at him, this time from the left. All that Brann could do was drop his left shoulder and half twist, taking the hit on his shoulderblade. The impact started to turn him, and he continued the movement, rolling around the boy and leaving him sprawling.

He stumbled, regained his balance and looked up to find he was just three paces from the foot of the cairn... with a smirking, round-faced mountain of a boy, arms outspread, waiting right in his path.

Despair struck him savagely – but, just as savagely, a blur of movement saw Gareth strike the boy with his shoulder at full sprint, launching him into the air and, more importantly, out of Brann's path. A hand grabbed the back of Brann's tunic and heaved him forward.

'Time to move, I think,' Callan's grinning face suggested beside him. Gareth's huge right hand blocked another opponent in the chest with such force that the boy was left sitting, dazed and winded, in the dirt, while Kevern, the village's apprentice baker, grabbed another by the hair and dragged him over backwards. The way was clear.

Breathing so deeply and rapidly that it hurt, Brann forced himself forward and, with Callan half-dragging him, he started to scramble up the cairn, the bundle of rags clutched tightly in his left arm as his right hand grabbed frantically at the rocks.

He reached halfway. The basket was only a few seconds from him. Something brushed against his leg and he turned. One of the town's players, his face twisted by desperation, was right at his heels.

To look back had been a mistake and, too late, Brann realised it. The boy used the wasted second to climb the extra few inches and, as Brann hurled himself forward and upwards, his pursuer reared up, clasped both hands above his head and smashed the double fist into the centre of Brann's back. He slammed into the cairn, a cry of pain bursting from him with the force of the impact. All he could do was clutch the Head to his chest with all the strength he had left while the boy grabbed him from behind in a bear hug. Callan tried to prise the boy from him. Brann glanced down. His team-mates were lined around the foot of the cairn, trying with the last of their energy to keep the town players at bay but, as he watched, two town boys broke through the thin rank of defenders.

His voice hoarse, he tried to shout to Callan but managed only a croak. 'Take the Head.'

'No,' Callan yelled. 'It's your basket. I'll get him off.'

'It is their basket if you don't take it now,' he shouted back, finding his voice.

Callan started to object, but he knew it was true. He looked at Brann, took a deep breath and nodded. With a sudden movement that took his opponent by surprise, Brann rolled onto his back, trapping the boy momentarily beneath him. Callan nodded again, grabbed the rags and bounded the last few feet to the top. He briefly held the Head two-handed above him, and glanced around at the crowd. With a sudden grin, he slammed the Head into the basket.

The Twofords villagers, accounting for barely a quarter of the crowd, broke into a roar that started suddenly but seemed to go on forever. The townsfolk shouted in shocked anger or merely stood in stunned disbelief.

Rolling to one side, Brann freed the boy beneath him. Taken aback by the sudden end to the game, the lad sat up, swore once at Brann and started to climb down the cairn. Too tired to respond, Brann laid his head back against the rocks and stared at the blue of the sky, listening to the celebrations drifting over to him from one small part of the crowd.

Callan's face appeared, blocking his view. 'It worked!' he yelled. 'I don't believe it. It worked!'

Brann smiled. 'I don't believe it, either. I couldn't even think while it was all happening.' He laughed, an intoxicating mixture of joy and amazement racing through him. 'There just seemed to be bodies everywhere. Going at high speed. And doing their best to dismember me.'

Callan grabbed him by the front of the tunic, pulled him into a sitting position and enveloped him in a solid hug. 'Well, thank the gods they couldn't manage it, little brother. Mind you, they would have had to catch you first. You were dodging like a demon out there. It would have been easier to catch Kevern's father's hens.'

Brann grinned back at him. 'It's amazing what desperation does for your agility. And sheer terror, too. I just made it up as I went along.' He grabbed Callan by the arms and shook him. 'But we won!' he yelled.

Callan laughed, a sound born of pure joy. 'Let's go see the oldies,' he suggested.

They descended the cairn rather more easily than they had climbed it, and started across the deserted field. Most of the townsfolk had drifted away already, shocked by a result they had never considered to be a possibility. The pair's younger brother and sister tore across the grass towards them, with their parents following behind. Brann had thought that he barely had the strength to walk, but he suddenly found himself running towards them, laughing loudly in a release of tension and joy. As the children met in a maelstrom of grabbing hands, dancing feet, and exultant laughter, the adults caught up. Their mother joined the celebration, her slim figure slipping easily between the cavorting children and her long blonde hair swirling in their faces as her easy laughter mingled with their celebrations. Brann and Callan looked to their father, standing to one side, watching the situation with his habitual dour appraisal.

He nodded at the two of them. 'I would have preferred you to have won it conventionally. Trickery like that is not my style. But you worked well together, as brothers should. And after a dozen years of defeats, a win is a win. So well done.' He turned to leave, and called over his shoulder, 'Don't get carried away with celebrating. We'll be waiting with the wagon outside the town gate at six o'clock. If you don't want to walk home, be there.'

The boys watched his retreating back until he was out of earshot.

'Don't you sometimes wish we had the sort of father who would go now and enjoy himself? You know, go and get blind drunk and lose control for once,' Brann murmured.

Callan frowned, and Brann remembered his brother's short-lived dalliance with Ciara, the tanner's daughter, when he had talked of seeing first-hand the effect on a family of a man who habitually returned home of an evening after turning to too much ale to relax at the end of a working day.

'No,' he stated emphatically. 'No, you don't.' His face brightened. 'Anyway, did you hear that? He actually said, "Well done." We are indeed honoured.'

He nudged Brann and, laughing, the boys turned back to the rest of their family.

In the sparse remnants of the crowd, the scruffy baker stood shaking his head, unable to accept what he had seen. 'It can't be. It's not possible. And that little runt? What a fluke.'

The black-clad warrior's eyes narrowed in a faint show of amusement. 'He used three things: his head, instinct and determination. A powerful combination… if channelled properly.'

The baker turned away, his expression dark. 'I still say it was luck,' he muttered, trudging away.

The warrior looked back at a small group far out on the field, as the subject of the brief conversation was enveloped in his family's hugs.

'If it is channelled properly,' he repeated softly. 'May the gods do so, little one, and you could make your family prouder still.'

Chapter 2

He started awake, eyes wide, searching for danger. His right hand was on his left hip, reaching for a hilt that had last lain there more years ago than he could remember. He snorted in derision. His reactions mocked his infirmity.

He needed air. He rose stiffly, moving slowly past the brazier that was his barrier from the starkly chill night air. He slipped between the heavy drapes and onto the balcony, his skin prickling at the cold and the strands of his hair shifting against his shoulders at the merest touch of the soft breeze. Once that hair had demanded so much more of the wind or the gallop of a horse to lift it and when it had, it streamed like a banner behind him.

But times change, and men with them. Fight that change, and you lose. That much he had learnt. But observe the change, and you can use it. That much he was realising.

He returned to bed. But he did not sleep.

****

Brann laughed loudly and battered the ground like a drummer.

'Yes, yes, yes!' he shouted, lying back on the grass of an undulating hillside above Twofords.

Callan sat up. 'I take it you are still a touch happy about the game,' he said. 'Last night's celebrations not enough for you?'

Brann laughed again, exuberance bursting from him. 'Nothing will stop me feeling like this, ever. I will remember yesterday for the rest of my life.'

Callan smiled. 'Oh, it was good all right. I'll give you that. Did you see the townies' faces? If they had looked any more sick, old Rewan would have put them down like the animals that are too far gone for him to heal.'

Plucking blades of grass, Brann nodded. 'They just didn't consider that losing was possible. How could they be prepared in any way for something they had never even thought about?' He laughed delightedly. 'That's what made it so wonderful.'

Callan stretched. 'Oh yes, life is good. You'd better believe it, little brother.'

He stiffened, staring past Brann, his voice suddenly harsh. 'Please tell me I'm seeing things.'

Brann twisted round squinting in the direction of Callan's pointing arm. To the left side of the village, two fields separated it from a small wood. Beyond the trees lay one of the pastures where the village's sheep occasionally grazed. There were no sheep there today. There should have been no movement. But there was. Sunlight glinted off metal, flashes of brightness that drew attention to the figures spread out across the field and moving with purpose in the direction of the village.

'Armed men,' said Callan, confused. 'What are they doing?'

'Maybe they are the king's men, doing a check or a patrol in our area, or something,' Brann offered hopefully.

Callan rose to his feet, shaking his head. There was urgency in his voice now. 'No. Why not use the road then? They are using the woods as cover to get as close as they can without being seen. This is bad.' He started to run down the hill, shouting over his shoulder, 'Come on. The wood won't just hide them – it will slow them down, too. If we hurry we can reach the village before them.'

The pair raced down the slope with the reckless abandon that only youth can make successful. They covered the ground in massive leaps and skipped over rocks in a way they had done many times before but this time, instead of the infectious excited laughter that usually accompanied it, their faces were set in grim determination. They reached the bottom of the hill and used their momentum to carry them on at speed as the ground levelled out into another of the village's pastures. At the far side, they splashed through a stream and scrambled into a loose thicket of bushes, knowing that, when they emerged on the far side, they would be among the first houses.

Callan slowed down and turned. Crouching, he caught his breath as he waited the few seconds that Brann needed to catch up. He grinned, a sight that was as familiar to Brann as his own reflection. 'We did it, little brother. We are ahead of them. Those bastards will find that we "soft" villagers can fight. Our men outnumber them, and they will be ready because of us. Come on, little brother, let's go and be heroes!'

Abruptly, Callan jumped several inches off the ground. He returned to his crouching position, before sinking slowly to his knees. Brann was used to his brother's light-hearted antics, but was still caught by surprise and burst into laughter. But Callan was not laughing. His grin had gone and his expression had faded into a glazed look. His eyes were just as blank – the first time Brann had ever seen them without a sparkle.

Brann's laughter caught in his throat. Moving forward was an effort, as if the air had turned to treacle. He felt detached, as if he was no part of what he was seeing. His head swam and he had to force himself to start breathing again.

His brother tilted slowly sideways, then fell forwards. Brann forced himself to move and lurched into a kneeling position, catching him just before he hit the ground. Callan's head turned, pressing his cheek into Brann's arm and revealing the end of a short feathered shaft just above the back of his neck. Brann had been on enough hunts to recognise a crossbow bolt when he saw it. Dark blood seeped rapidly from it, dripping from Brann's arm and starting to form a pool beside his knee.

Brann was vaguely aware of two figures around twenty yards ahead of them. If Callan had kept running, he would have blundered right into them. For a long moment, however, he was unable to force his eyes away from his brother. When he did turn his head – slowly and feeling as blank as Callan looked – he saw two men crouching in the undergrowth. One, holding a spent crossbow and wearing a garish red scarf on his head, started towards him but, as the crash and barely restrained curse of a falling man came from the wood, the other man grabbed the first and dragged him away. In seconds, they were out of sight, and the occasional receding noise suggested they were not remaining close. In a surreal moment, Brann was left, in the warmth of a glorious summer day, with the sounds of nature returning around him, holding his brother as Callan's life dried into the hard earth beside him.

'No!' he screamed. 'No!' he implored to the gods, throwing his head back and roaring at the sky. 'No, no, no don't do this!'

Another muffled curse and increased movement from the nearby trees jolted him back to reality. His screams had been a signal to the incoming men that caution was no longer needed.

He needed to move for his own sake as much as the villagers', but his screams had also been heard among the buildings and concerned village folk began to move towards the source of the sound. They were greeted with the sight of Brann, his tunic and breeches soaked with blood, emerging from the bushes. His chest heaved with sobs and he was raggedly gasping breath from shock and the effort of dragging his brother's limp body at his side with all the strength left in his arms. A stunned hush fell as the close-knit community stopped on either side and watched, in shock, the boy's determined progress along the dusty track between the houses. The invaders were gone from his head. All except one thought had left him. He was taking his brother home.

The silence couldn't last. A woman screamed, breaking the spell, and the air was instantly filled with the sounds of horror and grief, mixed with calls for the boys' parents. As Brann neared his home, his father emerged from the mill door, his heavy black cloak in his hands, but dread etched in his face. He saw his sons and his legs almost gave way beneath him before he caught himself and stumbled quickly to them. He gently, almost reverently, took Callan into his arms, cradling his son's body like a small child, the cloak forgotten in the dust at his feet. Relieved of the weight and with his determination not needed anymore to lend him strength, Brann sank to his knees, sobs bursting from him savagely. His father's features crumpled into sorrow – it was the softest emotion Callan had ever seen from him – and he pulled his eldest son's head into his shoulder. As he did so, a man in the surrounding crowd noticed the crossbow bolt and realised that this had not been the terrible accident that all had initially assumed.

His cry cut through the assembly. 'To arms! To arms! We are under attack! Defend yourselves!'

The villagers scattered, men scrambling for whatever could serve as a weapon and women rushing their children to any place of relative safety they could find. Brann and his father were left alone before their home. The man stood, hunched with deep grief, belying the fact that his build was a combination of that of his older sons, with Callan's height and Brann's broad shoulders. He slowly fingered the end of the wooden shaft and raised his head, just in time to catch sight of the men emerging from the wood at a run. His eyes darkened with rage and he rounded on the boy sagging on the ground before him.

'Get off your knees, boy,' he snarled, the fury that was in every syllable flowing through his muscles and drawing him erect as he pulled his dead son close into him. 'Go!' he roared. 'Go away. Now. Go. Away. From. Here.'

Brann staggered backwards under the force of the rejection, almost falling. 'Go away!' his father bellowed, and Brann spun and ran from the words. He could understand. Callan had always been the perfect son. Why had the gods not taken him instead? If he thought that, why would his father not? But the words still stabbed through him with a viciousness that no amount of logic could prevent.

He ran, swerving away from the approaching men into the very bushes from which he had so recently emerged. He ran from everything: from the sight of his brother, drained of life; from the wild men charging his village waving swords and axes; from the noise of the screaming women; and, most of all, from his father's words.

Another, smaller stand of trees lay near the thicket. Pausing as he reached their cover, he looked back at the village. Heavily armed men were fighting with the locals, but were finding that a daily routine of farming and hunting had honed muscles and reflexes that – when combined with spears and bows designed for tackling wild boar and wolves, and scythes and hammers wielded by those who used them every day for a living – provided formidable opposition.

His gaze drifted mechanically to his home, the tidy mill beside the river. His father was fighting in the doorway with the four of the raiders, thrusting and swinging grimly with a hunting spear. As Brann's empty gaze fell upon him, he inevitably succumbed to the pressure and fell back into the building. The four men poured into the mill but reappeared a few moments later as smoke began to spill from the door and nearby windows. Two other houses were already on fire, and the wooden mill quickly joined them as the blaze took hold. As the raiders started to fall back, villagers raced to the mill as if trying to rescue those trapped inside, but were beaten back by the intensity of the flames.

Suffused with emptiness, Brann's blank stare watched his life disappear as effectively as his home as the fire consumed it and his family. Overwhelmed by despair and dismay, he turned to flee from the destruction of everything and everyone that meant anything and everything to him... and ran straight into a meaty hand that slammed solidly into his chest, knocking him abruptly onto his back. Dazed as much by recent events as by the blow, he looked up to see a leering face under a garish red bandana looming over him. Amid foetid breath, words drifted down to him. 'Thought we'd lost you, boy. So good of you to come running back to us. Lovely to see you again.'

Hard hands grabbed him by the arms and jerked him to his feet. Quickly and expertly, his wrists and ankles were tied and a heavy bag was dragged over his head, letting in little air and less light. He was lifted with apparent ease and carried a short distance before being slung face down over the back of a horse.

He had no interest in what was happening to him. All he could see was his brother's corpse, his burning home and his father's raging rejection. The horse moved off at a canter. His light-headedness grew. What little light the hood allowed receded, and all went black.

Chapter 3

He shivered. It was cold in his rooms, though the sun had risen high. It was always cold, now. Built to keep out the heat, the design took no account of the heat that the elderly crave once the cold starts to set into their bones. He shuffled towards the balcony, lured by the sunlight. He scanned the floor for dangers under the dust. He had had his fill of falling for a lifetime, no matter what little of that may be left to him. He watched the dust kicked up by the slippered feet poking out from under his ankle-length shift. Dry dust. Lifeless dust. He grunted. Just like his skin. But it had not always been so. Not like this. Far from this.

The heat hit him like a hammer. He had reached the balcony. It was too hot. And bright. He grunted again, the closest he could manage to humour at the irony. He forced himself to endure it, and gripped the heavy balustrade, the sun casting ornate shadows through the carved stonework onto the plain grey of his shift. Squinting against the glare, he peered beyond the gardens, past the high white walls, to the dusty flat area beyond, the sand hard-packed by generations of feet. He saw a rider, galloping in triumph, sword gleaming high as he circled the area, acknowledging the roars *of the crowds. Royal crimson lined his billowing cloak, and crimson of another sort soaked into the dust beside the body slumped in the centre of the arena, a riderless horse standing disinterestedly nearby.*

His eyes were wet. The sun must be particularly bright today. He blinked to clear his *vision, and the scene faded. It seemed so, so long ago. It was so, so long ago. Who benefitted from memories? Would they give strength to failing muscles? Would they ease aching bones? Would they turn white hair brown?*

He turned and shuffled back into the cold, taking care not to fall.

* * * *

Brann shivered and spluttered as he was wakened by ice-cold water thrown roughly into his face. Sitting up, he tried to open his eyes but, before he could focus on anything, his stomach heaved and he vomited violently over his legs and lap.

A raucous laugh blared in his ear. 'There we go,' a voice as rough as his treatment sneered. 'If I had a gold piece for every time that happened, I'd have my own boat by now.'

Another voice answered him. 'Can't have him going on board like that, though, Boar. Captain won't thank us for attracting disease, and so on.'

The first voice was irritated. 'I think I know what I'm about after the years I've had doing this. Better than someone like you who has never done it before. I don't need you to tell me.'

'Like when you released the horses we had taken as soon as we got here?'

The man gave a dismissive snort. 'We don't need them any more, do we? They could have been noisy and given away our position.'

The other voice was scornful. 'If anyone was close enough to hear horses whinnying, we would be found anyway. Our position is much more likely to be given away by a couple of riderless horses roaming around. And where was your vast experience when you shot the other boy?' he snapped. 'All we were looking for was food and water. Others were taking what few slaves we need. Did you know what you were doing at that time?'

'He would have seen us,' Boar grumbled, although he seemed too wary of the other man to react with any aggression to the withering criticism. 'I had to do it or they would both have raised the alarm.'

His companion's tone was contemptuous. 'That is not true, and you know it. We saw them coming and they were going too fast to notice us. If you had moved just a few yards into the heavier bushes when I told you, they would never have seen us.' His voice dropped to a low, threatening level. 'You know what I think? I think you enjoy it. I think you like the killing, just for the sake of it. And you saw the chance for it with the attack on the village. Just like you enjoy the misery of the slaves you take. Well, I don't care who you sailed with before: you are with us now. And it will stop when you are with me, because the next time it happens you'll know what it feels like to be on the receiving end, and you'll have my sword to thank for it.'

'You better not be threatening me,' Boar objected hotly, but it was obvious that his tone carried more bluster than menace.

The first man was unconcerned. 'Take it how you will. But if you know what's good for you, you will remember it.'

'Anyway,' Boar objected, trying to salvage some pride, 'you have taken as many slaves as I have on this trip, as many as any of us have.'

The first man paused, and when he spoke his voice was heavy and low. 'That may be true, but none of the rest of us approaches it with your relish. It may be the way of the world in some parts, but not where I come from. If a man's fate is to be a slave, so be it, but I would prefer not to be a part of fulfilling his destiny, thank you very much. All but you will be glad when we are free of this cursed contract at the end of this trip. Then, if you miss your slaving, you can go back to the pirate ships you came from. Though I'm guessing that whatever reason made you leave them and turn up when our Captain was recruiting might just still apply. What do you think?'

Boar fell silent. Whatever he thought, if anything, was kept to himself. The other man's voice moved closer to Brann.

I should feel rage, or grief, or something… anything, Brann thought. He had just listened to a description of his brother's death – and the futility of it. But, instead, all he felt was emptiness. The feeling seemed to grow from a lump in his stomach and spread through every part of him, leaving him light-headed and almost dreamlike. A hand grabbed his tunic between the shoulderblades and hoisted him to his feet. His vision started to clear, and he shook his head as if to try to help his eyes focus more quickly as his feet sank a fraction into rough sand.

He already knew he was beside the sea – the crash and hiss of waves breaking and soaking back into the beach and the heavy salt air in his nostrils had made that obvious from the start. He may have felt completely disinterested in his surroundings, but that did not mean that he was unaware of them.

Rough fingers gently prised at his hands. He looked down and realised he was clinging to a bundle of black cloth, his

37

fingers clamped about it and his arms grasping it tightly against his chest.

The voice of the man was soft, soothing, almost caring. His surprise at the tone caught his attention. 'It's all right to let go. You'll get it back, don't worry. The gods know you may be glad of it. It's not so warm out on the water.'

Brann looked at it. His father's cloak, heavy, black and with a vertical rip near the hem at the back. His mother had urged him to look for a new one when they visited the town for the ball game, but he had resisted. For reasons he never explained, he loved it, and insisted on having it repaired instead. That must have been where he had been heading when he saw his two sons, only one of them alive. In his grief, he had dropped it. And in his grief, Brann must have picked it up. He had no idea why. He had no memory of even doing so. But he had it now. His only link to what already seemed a distant life. And he was not about to give it up.

The man eased at his fingers again. 'You were the same last night. Nothing I could do short of breaking your fingers would let me get that from your grasp, even when you were out cold.' Brann tensed, gripping it tighter to him. He sank back to the ground, his knees drawn up protectively in front of him. 'I don't want it, boy, fret not. I have my own, and so, if you're interested, does Boar. I was only going to stow it safe on the horse last night, and now I just want to keep it dry. It is no use to you wet and you need a wash. But we have little time, so if you don't let go now, it's going in the water with you.'

This time he did not try to prise Brann's fingers from the material, but simply held out his hand. Brann, staring only at the hand, slowly placed the cloak in it. The bundle was dropped on the ground at his feet.

The man grunted and stared at the boys around. 'I keep my word,' he said. 'You'll get it back.' The instruction to the boys sitting beside it was clear, but they were too cocooned in their own misery to care.

Brann was hoisted to his feet once more. It was fortunate that the man was still grasping his tunic: as soon as he was pulled upright, his knees buckled and his vision began to swim once more. He was half-led, half-dragged into the shockingly cold water and, in only a few paces, he was thigh-deep. He thought the cold of the water might clear his head; it did not, it just left his legs numb.

Abruptly, the hand let go. His legs, with a lack of feeling now added to the weakness, gave way. Before he could even register that he was falling, he crashed into the water. This time, his head did clear. The anonymous hand grasped him again and pulled him up before he managed to swallow too much of the sea. He spluttered, the salt water making his stomach lurch again but, this time, he resisted being sick.

The hand held him up while its partner roughly rubbed his face and clothes with water to clean them. He could force himself to stand under his own strength, and he helped to wash himself. He staggered slightly in the swell, but determination let him catch his balance.

'A little fighter, are you?' the voice said. 'We had to dunk most of the others four of five times before they came to. Keep it up and you might just survive all this.' *All what? Who were these people? And who were the 'others'?* Through the blank apathy in his head, the questions nagged him. But, because of that cold indifference, the answers were not so plain.

He wiped the water from his eyes, the manacles hindering even the simplest of movements. He blinked several times before his vision cleared. He caught his breath at the sight of the man beside him in the water: a mountain of leather, weapons, shaggy black hair and even shaggier beard. As he reached over to start dragging Brann back to the beach, his cloak moved to reveal a lean, muscular build; the cloak, worn over his multitude of weapons, had created a false impression of bulk.

'I'll manage,' Brann croaked, staring down at the water.

The warrior laughed again. 'We'll see. Keep that attitude, and you might just.' He slapped Brann casually on the back, almost launching him face-first into the water. 'Anyway, you're clean now, and awake. Enough of this idle chatter. Get back ashore with the others.'

Brann waded back to the beach, where five bedraggled figures huddled together for warmth and, probably, comfort. A quick glance told him no one else from his village had been taken. A quick glance born of cold curiosity, it was, but no more; he found he didn't care whether or not any of the faces were familiar. Four of them, boys of around his years, were hunched in dejection. His gaze held on the fifth figure: a rangy youth, little more than his own age, with a shock of unkempt and probably untameable black hair that sat every way except flat, the thick tendrils exploding like dark flames from his head. Everything about him seemed angular, from his craggy face to long arms that hung, all bones and corded tendons, and from wide shoulders to legs that seemed as if they would have the co-ordination of a new-born foal. Despite wearing nothing but a rough tunic, he seemed oblivious to the damp chill that was forcing shivers into the others, and he exuded an indefinable strength that ignored the impression given by his gangly build. Most curiously, while the rest of the group exhibited a predictable mix of dejection and shock, he merely stared around him, as if nothing untoward at all had taken place. On closer inspection, an aggressive intensity burned in his glare. It burned, but its fire was cold. The sort of look that Brann had spent his life avoiding. He had preferred to spend his time among those with open personalities, with friendliness that brought none of the intensity or false posturing of those who felt they had to be aggressive in life to hold the respect of others. He had preferred those with personalities like his brother's. He forced his emotions back into numb emptiness, pushing back the grief that threatened to surge through him.

A second warrior – presumably the one called Boar – comparatively shorter than the first and this time genuinely broad, crouched beside them, smirking and enjoying their discomfort and dismay with obvious pleasure. At the sight of the smirk, memories of foul breath flooded Brann's senses and he massaged the bruise on the centre of his chest. Even without the sight of the red scarf on the man's head, he would have known he was looking at the man who had murdered Callan and rage and fear rose in equal violent measure, threatening to make him vomit again. Pushing the emotions deep down and locking them away, Brann stumbled the last few steps from the water, a receding wave dragging at his feet and, guided by an unsubtle shove from behind, he joined the group. A chain was looped quickly through his manacles; he saw that it ran similarly through the bonds of the others, linking them in simple, but effective, fashion.

He sat, watching, listening, but still feeling detached, as if he were not a part of the scene. Two of the boys whimpered softly; the rest, despite their differing demeanours, were silent, staring down at the sand in their collective misery and despair. Only the dark-haired boy looked up, his burning gaze locking for a long moment with Brann's. Then he nodded at him,

41

once, and looked ahead once more. It seemed appropriate to his situation that the one with the character he would normally avoid was the one who had connected with him. He spat the remnants of salt water into the beach between his feet. What did it matter? What did anything matter now?

Strangely, Brann felt lucid, to a heightened level. He could understand the reactions of the others, but not his own. Although distant, he was coldly logical, absorbing everything around him with frank clarity. He was an emotional boy (his father had often chided him for letting his heart rule his head, in the days before he had so quickly rejected him and sent him running into the clutches of the men who had murdered his brother) and it was an alien experience to find himself as he was now, without fear, nerves, anger, despair, horror: all of the feelings that he thought should be overwhelming him.

Instead, he felt a calm assurance with, perversely, a tinge of bitter amusement. *Perhaps this is how you feel when you accept you are going to die*, he mused. *Or maybe I can't be hurt any more. Or maybe both.*

His mind turned back to Callan, replaying the images of his brother's death. It must have happened so quickly yet – at the time and, now, in his mind – it seemed to take an eternity. Then, as a misplaced background to that picture, he saw his home ablaze, with his family inside.

Why am I not crying? Where is the pain? he asked himself, over and over. It seemed as if the boy he had been was a stranger, as if he had awakened beside the sea a new person.

You're not you any more. You can't afford to be. Face it, this is what you've got from now on. Get used to it. A hint of an ironic smile twitched one corner of his mouth, a distant relation of the broad grin that had always sprung so readily to his face. *Oh, gods, I'm going mad. I'm talking to myself like an idiot.*

One of the boys tried to speak, failed and cleared his throat. He tried again. 'It's freezing. Can we not have a fire?' He indicated a bundle of wood and dry leaves that had been piled together just a few yards further up the beach from them.

Boar cuffed him roughly across the side of the head, knocking him into the sand. 'Keep it shut, maggot,' he snarled. 'Speak again and you'll get worse than that.'

The taller man inserted a foot under the boy's shoulder and lifted him until the youngster took the hint and sat himself up once more.

'Don't lie down, boy,' he growled. 'It's damp. You'll only get colder.' He looked back across the beach. 'There will be no fire. We're not exactly wanting to invite guests to our party, are we? Don't worry, you'll be dried off soon enough.'

His burly companion grumbled, 'You talk too much, Galen. Leave them alone – they're nothing but your next wage.' His voice turned mocking. 'You sound as if you're starting to care for them. First rule of slavery: they're nothing but pieces of meat.'

Galen grunted and turned away, walking to the edge of the sea and staring out across the waves. 'Where are they?' he hissed, exasperation heavy in his tone. He jerked round, his hand reaching for the crossbow slung across his back. Dunes separated the beach from the land beyond, and movement there had caught the edge of his vision.

Boar rose from his crouch with an exaggeratedly casual air and glanced lethargically across the sand. 'It's only Barak,' he said. 'You are a jumpy old woman.'

Ignoring him other than to murmur, 'Better jumpy than dead,' Galen walked towards the approaching figure, a small wiry man but no less festooned with weaponry than his two comrades. Boar spat forcibly and muttered unintelligibly.

Brann guessed it was not a compliment. He also noticed that, whatever Boar had said, he had waited until Galen had moved beyond earshot before passing his low-pitched comment.

Barak reached Galen before the tall warrior had moved more than a dozen paces from the group and skidded to a halt. He nodded a greeting to the other two. 'Light the signal,' he said simply in a hoarse voice. 'They'll be round the headland in minutes.'

'Not before time.' Galen crouched beside the firewood and, in seconds, had sparked it to life. A trail of smoke quickly reached towards the clouds.

Barak looked at the bedraggled group chained before him. 'An extra one.' It was said as a statement, but it was clearly a question.

'Boar,' Galen said, without looking up.

Barak grunted, obviously needing no more explanation.

Boar roughly dragged the chain upwards, effortlessly pulling two boys clear off the ground. Not wishing the same treatment, the others stood by themselves as quickly as cramped legs allowed. The burly warrior barked a harsh and unpleasant laugh and started to pull on the chain to lead the captives to the edge of the sea. 'Time for a lovely voyage, lads!' he cried, revelling in their anguish. 'Bet you never thought you'd get the chance to see distant shores and exotic lands.'

A ship, sleek and nimble, swept around the narrow rocky peninsula that formed one side of the bay. Its mast bare of sail, it cut through the water, driven by a single bank of oars on either side that rose and fell in perfect time to a relentless drumbeat. As it pointed itself directly at the smoke, Boar dragged the captives into the water, while Galen – who had kicked sand over the fire as soon as the ship had responded to the signal – and Barak kept pace at either side.

A double-beat of the drum was followed by a barked shout of instruction and the oars reversed their stroke for three long sweeps, churning and foaming the water and seeming to stop the craft almost immediately.

The wading group had reached deeper water and started, in their haste, to lose their footing. Brann, spitting out an unwelcome mouthful of water, looked ahead to see archers gather in two small groups at the prow and stern. Galen shouted urgently to the boys, 'Kick your legs. We'll pull you along. Just concentrate on keeping your faces above the water.'

None of them wanted to go to the ship, but the consequence of defiance was drowning. As if to inadvertently prove the point, one of the boys, obviously not a swimmer, panicked and started to thrash in the water, dropping quickly beneath the surface. With a pointed lack of haste, Boar moved over and dragged him up.

'There's always one,' he moaned. 'Why can't you pathetic farm boys all make sure you can at least float?'

He grabbed the back of the spluttering boy's tunic and held him clear of the water. For all of the man's obnoxious traits, Brann could not help but marvel at his brute strength. *It's just a pity about the 'brute' part of it*, he thought. All three of the warriors seemed oblivious to the weight of the host of weapons encumbering each of them as they swam, but to have the ability, as Boar was casually demonstrating, to support a mostly grown boy with one hand at the same time was more than impressive. Brann resolved that, for as long as he was in this predicament and in Boar's company, he would keep quiet and try not to attract attention. Where Boar was concerned, the only consequences seemed to be harmful ones.

A net was thrown over the side to help the swimmers from the water. Hands reached down to pull them aboard, and the three warriors followed in an instant, hardly out of breath. A hoarse voice bawled 'Row!' and, as the drum started to sound, the three men on each oar bent their backs. With a beauty in its precision, the oars on each side rose and fell in a single motion and the ship seemed to leap forward.

As they picked up speed, a party of around a dozen horsemen, each with a short cavalry bow held ready in his hand, thundered onto the beach, drawn by the smoke of the signal fire. Brann realised why Galen had smothered the flames as they were leaving: it had seemed like a waste of time when the men were otherwise consumed by urgency but, in dissipating the tell-tale smoke as, unknown to them, the riders had been closing, he had made it slightly harder to pinpoint their exact location and had bought them precious time. If they had still been in the water when the men had arrived, they would have been as soft targets as there could be. He harboured no notion that the horsemen would have bothered about the boys in the water if they had a chance of striking back at any of the hated raiders.

Several of the horsemen leapt from their mounts even before the animals had come to a halt and, with the speed of professional soldiers, nocked arrows and let fly. The ship, however, had already cleared the range of the short bows and the volley dropped short.

With a shout and a gesture, one of the riders stopped the bowmen, realising the futility of the action and thinking, perhaps, of the cost of arrows and a quartermaster's ire. Several of the group hurled furious insults at the retreating boat, their cries just audible above the creaking of the oars, the slapping of water against the hull, the grunting of the rowers and the thumping of the drum. Within seconds, they could be heard no more.

Galen stood at the rail, staring impassively back at the shore. 'Soldiers,' he said in a low tone. 'A whole squad. See how quickly they came to the fire, lads?' He nudged with his foot the boy who had complained. 'Now you know why you stayed cold.' He threw down a bundle of towels onto the deck beside them. 'Now strip. Dry yourselves.'

Several of the boys looked hesitant at the thought of disrobing in public. Galen chuckled. 'There is no modesty at sea. Dry yourselves or you'll sicken. Don't worry – I'll let you keep the towels until your clothes have dried.'

Their sodden garments were taken and hung on a line near to the captives. The sun was beginning to climb in a sky that was largely unencumbered by clouds and, with the added help of the sea breeze, it would not be long until they could dress once again.

The ship hit deeper water, and Brann began to notice the feeling of the slow rise and fall as it rode the swell. A shout from the stern prompted several men to busy themselves with unfurling the sail on the single mast. Once the fresh wind caught in the canvas, causing it to flap and crack for a few moments before it swelled forwards, the drummer banged twice and a square-headed man with close-cropped grey hair bellowed, 'Ship oars!'

With a rumble surprising in its brevity, the long oars were dragged on board and fastened into position. The rowers stretched muscles, settled more comfortably on their benches and caught their breath after the burst of hard exercise. The short intense nature of their effort had not allowed them to gain a second wind and, in the manner of men who knew not when their services would be called upon next, they seized without hesitation the chance to recuperate.

Brann sat on the deck and huddled against the other captives in the broad aisle that ran between the rowers. He hugged his knees to his chest, staring down at the planks of the deck. The wood was worn smooth, but was solid and tight-fitting; even that small detail suggested a quality ship, expertly crafted and carefully maintained. The easy confidence and efficiency of the men aboard, and the quality and condition of their weapons and clothing, added to the impression that he was among anything but a rag-tag group of outlaws and bandits. These were professionals, skilled and experienced – and Brann was unsure whether that was a good or a bad thing.

On one hand, he felt that his safety, while not admittedly at an all-time high, was more assured with such men in terms of avoiding either a shipwreck or harm at their hands than if they had been drunken unscrupulous oafs. And cleanliness and hygiene would lessen the chances of disease.

Alternatively, chances of escape would be virtually non-existent among captors such as these. They knew what they were doing and, in the case of Boar and most probably many of the others, had done it many times before. Whatever they were, they were good at it. Whatever their intentions for him – and, with a start, he realised that he had not even thought that far ahead – he was sure they would achieve them.

He was, to his surprise, not sure that he even wanted to return to his village, to the scene of the brutal deaths of everyone close to him. What was there for him to go back to, other than pain and grief? But where else did he have to go? His mind spun furiously. Shaking his head violently, he ran his fingers through his hair in anguish and confusion.

A pair of black boots stopped in front of him, breaking both his gaze and his whirling thoughts. A voice, cultured but anything but soft, said, 'Welcome aboard. I assume none of you is a sailor. You have a morning to become accustomed to the motion of the ship, and to put your clothes back on. Then you will eat. Whether you feel like it or not.'

Brann looked up. 'Why are we here? Where are we going?'

The tall man's dark eyes locked with his and Brann's stomach lurched with nerves at the intensity of the gaze, the first strong emotion he had felt since his capture. The man's expression flickered, surprise momentarily evident. Brann cursed himself. A man like that would not be accustomed to being interrupted. So much for keeping a low profile.

'You will find out soon enough. We have almost a full cargo now, and we are heading for port after just one more stop.' He turned to go, then paused. 'Rest assured, you will have more to concern you now than a ball game for apprentices.'

He brushed spray-soaked hair away from an L-shaped scar on his cheek, and returned to the rear of the ship.

The morning dragged by in a daze. At first, the movement of the ship caught Brann's fascination. He'd known it would rise and fall, but he had never envisaged the rocking, both from side to side and front to back – or any combination of all of them. In the absence of any notable activity (with the wind filling the sail, the rowers were still taking the opportunity to doze and, of the crew, only the helmsman and a lookout remained in view) all he had to fill his attention were the noises – which comprised the creaking and groaning of wood and rope, the occasional sharp crack as the sail flapped, sporadic snores from the rowers and a soft whimpering from one of the boys beside him – and the sensation of movement. He tried to play games to relieve the boredom, predicting the combination of movements that would come next, or whether the boat would roll to the left before it rose. But it did not take long before he lost interest in that, also.

One of the boys retched, his body jerking forward and jangling the chains. Brann was relieved that at least he did not feel any sickness from the motion of the ship. Two of the boys spoke to their miserable and pained companion, trying, without success, to comfort him. It appeared from the conversation that the boy had nothing left in his stomach to vomit, having been brought over the course of a night and a day to the coast by captors who had lost all of their rations – and one of their number – in a fierce skirmish along the way. The boys had been left with Barak while the men left again to search for provisions, intending to meet up with the ship further up the coast. When Galen and Boar had arrived with Brann, Barak had left to find a vantage point to watch for the ship.

Brann watched the trio dispassionately, still feeling a detached onlooker. He was well aware that he was in the same situation as the other five, but still felt different from them in ways he could not rationalise, as if none of it was really happening to him, as if he were watching a performance by one of the groups of travelling players who would periodically visit his village.

'Get a grip on yourself,' he muttered angrily to himself, slapping his thigh as if to waken himself from a dream. *You won't find a way out of this unless you accept it is real*, he thought.

The boy had stopped retching, and his comforters had fallen silent again. Now that the distraction of another in need was over, the captives were left to face their own misery once more, their hunched shoulders and hanging heads speaking more eloquently of their emotion than any words. And with the little tableau finished for Brann, he cast around the ship for anything else that could hold his interest.

A few warriors had returned to the fresh air of the open deck and were tending to their weapons, cleaning and oiling them to protect against the effects of the salt water and anything else that may have attached itself to them in their use over the past day. Those weapons that were not worn about their persons – and these seemed few, Brann thought wryly, considering the host of swords, knives and axes that festooned the men – such as spears, crossbows and bows, were carefully wrapped in lightly oiled cloths. Brann noticed, however, that even these wrapped weapons were never far from the warriors' reach. Most of the men seemed to be from the same tall, powerful race as Galen, their pale skin beaten and scoured by the gods knew what sort of violent weather, by rain and wind or sun, by howling sandstorms or driving hail and lashing salty spray, until it matched the faded leather of their boots in consistency and colour. The remainder, few as they were, were from a variety of other origins, but they all had at least one thing in common: they were not men who would be caught unready.

The monotony was broken by the return of the boys' clothes, but only briefly. Brann turned his attention to the rowers, sprawled against each other and whatever part of the ship was available as they took advantage of the chance to rest.

Brann had heard of ships that used rowing slaves, and had imagined such men to be huge muscle-bound hulks, selected for their stature and with their bulk increased by endless days of heavy toil. Instead, these men were of all sizes, but with a uniform leanness rather than being over-laden with bulging muscles. True, they looked strong enough – the ease with which they had handled the large unwieldy oars had been testament to that– but it seemed more of an adaptable strength that could cope equally well with short bursts of power or long stretches of steady rowing.

It seems obvious when you thing about it logically, he mused. *I just never had reason to think about it before.*

The ringing of a moving chain as one of the oarsmen shifted position drew his attention to their feet. The rowers sat in threes, and each man had a manacle on his left ankle with a short chain reaching from it to a ring at the other end. Under each bench, another chain ran, passing through each of these rings. This chain was anchored to the side of the boat at one end but, where it reached the aisle, it was linked by another ring to a long chain that ran the length of the ship.

The wild-haired boy beside Brann noticed his interest in the chains. 'Clever, is it not, chief?' he said, his voice as cold and flat as the sea around them. It was a statement of fact, not admiration. 'Simple, but clever.' The boy regarded him with a cold dispassion and Brann looked into the palest of blue eyes. They did not bore into him as the dark stare of the man with the L-shaped scar had done: instead, the intensity in this gaze was behind the eyes, a cold fire that burned within, never raging nor dying. There was something about him that suggested an older perspective on life. Perhaps it was his physical calm amidst the dejection of the other boys.

'What do you mean?' Brann asked. His voice was as low as his spirits and the aggression in the boy's gaze indicated a temperament that he had always found irritating, but he welcomed any conversation that broke the tedium.

The lad nodded with economy of movement towards the rowing benches. 'The chains. It is an old enough system, but it works, so why change it?'

'What system? Surely they just get chained up and they row. That's it.'

His companion shook his head slightly. 'Simple, but not quite that simple.' He spoke in short bursts, as if uncomfortable saying any more than was strictly necessary. It was so much in keeping with his appearance that Brann almost smiled. 'My father rowed. On a galley bigger than this. An Empire one with three banks of oars. Until he escaped and tried farming instead.'

Brann's eyes came alight. 'Escaped?'

The pale eyes flicked his way. 'Don't get excited,' he said. 'It took more than a decade for the chance. Six tried; he and one other made it. That's better than normal. We face a life of slavery.' He snorted. 'The son follows the father's trade.'

'So that's what they mean for us? Galley slaves?'

The untameable hair quivered slightly as the head shook in reply. 'Not right now, and not for you. Look around, chief: any spaces on the benches? It will be the slave markets of the Callenican Empire for us. A little lad like you? May be lucky and get a nice position as a house slave. Someone like me...' He indicated his large ungainly frame, and shrugged. 'People look at an oaf like me and think of heavy labour.'

'Not all heavy labour is on a ship,' Brann pointed out.

The boy spoke deliberately and patiently. 'We will most likely finish in Sagia, the capital. They will look for a quick sale and Sagia holds the biggest slave market. There are no mines or quarries there. The farms are worked by families. The city is a port, so the work revolves around shipping. The Dockers' Guild controls the jobs onshore, so all that's left is a bench on some ship. If I'm lucky, I'll get a watertight one.'

Brann looked more closely at him. The boy had noticed, and deduced, much in a short time. And he had knowledge that extended the width of a continent further than the half-day's walk that had been the limit of Brann's world until the day before. He could prove to be a valuable ally if they were ever to spot a chance to escape. 'You know much about these distant places. Your father?'

'Do you always ask so many questions?'

Brann grunted. 'Only when I don't know so many answers.'

The youth considered this, and nodded. 'That's fair enough. I was put to sleep each night with stories of his time at sea. Never thought I would get to see it for myself.' He turned away and stared over the rail at the choppy blue-grey waves.

Emotion surged in Brann, taking him by surprise and forcing him to fight it hard. Somehow, what his companion left unsaid was more touching than if he had poured out his heart. For the first time since he had returned to consciousness, Brann felt empathy for another – and realised that he did not even know the name of the person who had awakened it. Unnerved by the combined power of grief, loss and fear, and lest it would overwhelm him, he forced the feelings back down, quickly re-establishing the cold, hard barrier. If he could not confront the emotion, it was better to avoid it. And, anyway, he was a little intrigued by what the youth had started to explain beforehand. Unlikely as it seemed, he was finding that he wasn't quite so irritated by the boy's personality as he had thought he would be. It was intense, but there was comfort in its straightforward logic.

'What did you mean about a system?' Brann ventured. 'To do with the chains,' he prompted.

The youth nodded at the rowers. 'They are slaves... but valuable slaves. They do what they do, well. Their bodies have adapted to it. And, if they are rowing, the warriors can be warriors. So the warriors take care of the rowers. Do you see what I mean, chief?'

Brann nodded. He felt hollow, as if nothing really mattered but, under current circumstances, he had time to fill and he was at least learning about his surroundings. Despite the logic in the boy's dismissal of any chance of escape, that course was exactly the one he intended to follow at the first opportunity, and the more knowledge he gathered about his captors and surroundings, the more likely he was to spot, or even create, such an opportunity. 'I understand what you say,' he said, 'but what has it got to do with the chains?' The chill eyes looked at him. 'Sorry. More questions. I know. You must be tired.'

'If I was tired, I would sleep. But I'm not. You have a question, I have the answer, and we both have the time.

'At times, the chains need to come off quickly. A sinking ship, or an attack with hand-to-hand fighting.'

Brann was puzzled. 'Why then? So they can be protected from harm?'

The boy shook his head. 'Well-treated slaves are better staying with the masters they have. The alternative is to risk worse with someone else. If the attack is by pirates, the alternative is worse. So, in such times, they fight beside the crew and, when it is over, return to the benches. At sea, this is accepted.'

Brann considered this. 'I count sixty rowers, and about twenty-five or so crew. Once the fighting is over, could the slaves not...?'

'I know, chief. Could they not overpower their masters?' He shrugged. 'They need each other. And you have seen these warriors: weapons are their life. If the slaves did overcome them, it would be at terrible cost. And they would always be fugitives, hunted by those who would fear other slaves encouraged to follow suit. So why risk it? Anyway, after fifteen years at the oars, a galley slave is freed. They reckon you have deserved it if you live that long. The longer you row, the closer you are to that.'

Brann's eyes narrowed. 'So why did your father take such a risk to escape?'

The boy stared over the sea once again. 'A valid question, chief. His circumstances changed. His ship was taken by pirates. Several slaves were tortured and thrown overboard to show the consequence of defiance. So he reasoned his situation had worsened. Yes, he had little more than two years of his fifteen left, but pirates tend not to adhere to that arrangement. They work their slaves till they drop. They can always pick up more. A small group saw an opportunity. It was a slight chance, but desperation drove them. He made it; all but one of the others did not. But they were under a death sentence anyway.'

He flexed his shoulders and arched his back against the effects of sitting still. 'So, the chains. Do you see the two long chains that run fore to aft – front to back? In emergencies, the crew can unfasten those chains at one end and pull them through to the other. Each set of rowers can then pull out the chain that runs under their bench, linking their individual chains. They are completely unfettered in seconds. And, you will notice that the long chains running up the aisle not only run through the rings on each bench's chain. They pass through several metal rings that secure hasps set into the aisle. Those hasps are for hatches into compartments containing weapons for the slaves. So, when the long chains are pulled free to let loose the slaves, they also give access to the weapons. The slaves can be unchained and armed in moments.'

Brann's face clouded as a thought struck him. 'These men don't seem to be pirates, yet they have taken us as slaves. Surely they *are* pirates.'

'Not all who take slaves are pirates. In the Empire, and the southern lands still more dusty, slaves are a part of life. They are traded and valued just as a horse or a sword or a house would be. These men here are seafarers, chief, and northerners mostly. They will be engaged by a slave-trader to fetch him goods to sell. On another day they would be transporting passengers or goods to a market or to a buyer's estate.'

A warrior strolled down the aisle, checking the chains had not become tangled and kicking the occasional one. Brann looked at the legs of the men nearest him. 'So, if I understand this properly, they can remove an individual rower by unlocking his manacles, or all three on a bench by unclipping them from the main chain along the aisle. So it can work for all of them or just one at a time, or almost any number in between.'

The boy almost smiled. 'You seem to understand. But still I see confusion in your eyes.'

Brann nodded. 'If there is such a special relationship that the slaves can be released and even armed if need be, why chain them up at all?'

'Trust extends only so far, chief.' The eyes burned with pale fire into his. 'A wise man leaves as little to chance as possible.' He shrugged. 'And, in any case, it is expected. They are slaves. As, now, are we.'

Brann grunted. 'Thank you for reminding me. For someone who is of few words, you speak at great length.'

'I speak when I can offer something of value. Otherwise, I prefer to listen. Thus I learn what may be valuable. And you know more of your situation, which is no bad thing.' His expression never yet wavered. 'And it passed the time.'

Brann snorted, irritated by the reminder of his predicament. 'At the moment, passing time is like passing water. I don't particularly want to have to do either but, if the need arises, I'll let you know.'

He was fixed with a curious stare, the head tilted to the side. 'I would make the most of being able to pass time, chief. At the moment, it is the only one of the two for which you control the opportunity to do it.'

His childish pomposity was brutally exposed for what it was by simple logic. 'I'm sorry. You didn't deserve that. It was kind of you to explain it all.'

'Kind?' It was only one word, but his tone was such that a speech could not have better conveyed the boy's confusion. 'You asked questions, I answered.'

Brann felt his mouth turn into a half-smile, as if it were an awkward movement. 'One last answer, then: your name.'

'One last answer for now. I feel you will have more questions over time. My father named me Gerens.'

'And mine, Brann.'

'Right you are, chief.' The boy clasped his hand in a formality that was as comforting as it was incongruous in their situation. 'I feel it is good to meet you.'

A voice boomed above them, making them both jump. The fat warrior, Boar, stood over them.

'Up, maggots,' he roared, rattling the chain so violently that several of them flinched – a reaction that seemed to please the oaf. 'Those who can walk, get to the stern. That's the bit at the back. Your food is there. Those who can't walk will be dragged by those who can.' He sniggered at what obviously passed for humour in his warped mind and thumped back up the aisle, leaving them to follow in whatever manner they could manage.

The sorry little group began to rise, some slower than others as cramped legs objected to movement. As they did so, the boat lurched, causing them to fall against each other. Brann was knocked from his feet and fell painfully against the end of a bench. He banged solidly against a sleeping rower, a burly bald man with an incongruously bushy black beard, but the man's slumber was so deep – or he cared so little about a slip of a boy falling against him – that he merely wriggled into a different position without waking.

As he did so, a hard object poked into Brann. Instinctively, the boy's hand slid forward and found the handle of a knife, tucked discreetly into the waistband of the man's breeches. Before he could think, he had grasped the bone handle, pulling it smoothly with him as he rose, and secreting it within his sleeve while he pretended to hold his stomach in pain. By the time he did think about what he had done, and about the unbelievable folly of doing so, it was too late to undo it.

Two of the boys were helping up the one they had earlier comforted while he had been retching, and the rest of the group had managed to stand and were waiting until all were ready to move off. Brann mingled with them as they shuffled forwards, using their tangle of chained limbs to conceal his movements as he slipped the blade into his own belt under his tunic, not so much out of a desire to keep the knife but more for reasons of keeping it better hidden until he could secretly dispose of it. His heart pounded as he came dangerously close to panic. He cursed his idiocy and tugged his tunic down, even though it was already more than adequately covering the incriminating object. With each pace, he could feel the metal digging into him and, with each dig, his stomach lurched and churned with tense fear.

He cursed himself. Why had he done something so stupid? Why? He had taken the knife automatically, his hand moving before his mind considered the idea. If it were found on him, the best he could hope for would be that his death would be quick. The rower he had taken it from had been courting that risk also but, whatever his reason for doing so, it was immaterial now – the risk had passed to Brann. Yet he could not get rid of it at the moment without being caught. He would just have to remain alert for an opportunity... and he prayed that moment would come soon.

They reached the rear of the ship. A steep stairway led up in front of them to the raised area and two closed doors faced the group, one set either side of the steps. Before them a small table bore bread, cheese and water. The boys hurriedly grabbed some of each, and forced it down. With the exception of Gerens, who wolfed it down with all of the relish but none of the manners normally reserved for a finely prepared banquet, not one of them had much of an appetite, but they had no idea when they would next eat. So they ate.

Boar clambered clumsily down from the area above. 'Through the door,' his voice boomed. The boy at the front of the group reached for the nearest latch.

It was hard to believe Boar could shout any louder – but he did. 'The other door, fool! If you step into the Captain's cabin, you'll spend the last two seconds of your life thinking about your mistake. Now move before you die of stupidity.'

The sorry group passed through the other door, discovering another steep set of stairs – almost a ladder – leading down below deck level. They found that the chain linking them was just long enough, if they were careful, to allow them all to climb down one by one.

'Keep moving, maggots,' Boar said, his voice relatively quieter but no less bullying.

The boys shuffled along a short corridor dimly lit by a single lamp, passing doorless portals that let them glimpse the rooms inside and, Brann realised, would allow any occupants to exit rapidly if necessary. No light burned in the first room they passed, but Brann was just able to make out the figures of those warriors not on deck who were grabbing, like the slaves above, the chance to sleep. The next room seemed to be used as both a kitchen and storeroom and, like the first, was in darkness. Dim light did come, however, from the room that lay straight ahead, which seemed to be their destination.

Boar confirmed it. 'Straight ahead, maggots. Keep going. Welcome to your new home.'

They stumbled towards the room, steadying themselves against the walls that were conveniently close on either side. As they neared the doorway, Brann could see two rows of faces, all belonging to boys of around his age, lined along the walls to each side of a long narrow area, staring at the newcomers. Boar shoved them roughly towards the room.

'In you go, maggots,' he growled gleefully. 'We'll get you chained up with your new friends. You couldn't ask for better quarters – it's clean, dry and there's even a latrine.' He indicated a bucket beside the door. 'If you're good, we might even empty it now and again.' He sniggered, once again finding himself highly amusing, although Brann suspected that this was not the first time he had produced this particular witticism. The whole procedure bore the hallmarks of a routine that the fat oaf thoroughly enjoyed.

As the boys started to file into the room, an eldritch screech burst from a room to their right. They stopped in terror. Like the others, Brann's attention had been drawn by disconsolate curiosity to the room that was to be their temporary home to such an extent that he had not noticed this other room, let alone its occupant.

The scream started again but, this time, words could be made out. 'Bring him to me! Bring him now!'

The man with the L-shaped scar stepped from the room. 'Hold them there, Boar,' he said. His order was unnecessary: the captives were rooted in terror, each hoping desperately he was not the subject of the ear-splitting demand.

The voice started again. 'The little one. The little one at the back.'

Brann's breathing froze and his chest constricted in fear. The tall man nodded to Boar. 'You heard Our Lady,' he said simply.

'Yes, Captain. Right away, Captain,' Boar said, the whine of his deferential tone a stark contrast to his previous bullying bluster. He knelt and hurriedly released Brann's manacle.

The Captain waved Brann forward. 'Come,' he said, leading the way into the room as Boar resumed ushering the remainder of the group to their original destination. Gerens cast a look in Brann's direction, his eyebrows raised. Brann knew that the boy was as mystified as he, and shrugged in reply. His initial fear had subsided greatly, mainly due to his emotionally dulled state of mind and the belief that his situation could not, conceivably, deteriorate to any great extent. Maybe he was taking Gerens's implacable logic to heart.

The room was more shadows than light. Two candles flickered shapes on the walls, a worrying hazard on a ship, Brann thought, where all other light was provided by oil lanterns that were sturdily constructed and designed to avoid spillages. The Captain was standing beside what appeared to be a pile of rags. Assuming this to be the source of the voice, Brann continued towards it and stopped several feet short, unsure what to do.

The words did, indeed, come from the rags. 'Come closer, boy,' it said. It was the voice of an old woman and now had, to his surprise, a gentle tone, almost kindly. The most astonishing thing about it was not the dramatic drop in volume, however, but how normal it sounded. He had expected a mysterious whisper or, at least, a demented growl. Certainly not something that sounded like a benevolent grandmother.

'I don't always screech, you know. Terrible sore on the throat, so it is.' She laughed, softly. 'But it surely catches people's attention, so it does. It catches their attention. And it does me no harm to have a certain reputation. I like to keep them on their toes, so I do. Unpredictable tends to work well in my profession. Mad and mysterious, that's me.' She laughed again, almost a giggle this time. 'Just you remember that, little one, when they ask you what I said. And they will ask you, so they will. So tell them I was mad and mysterious. Mysterious and mad. And terrifying. Terrifying is good, so it is.'

She coughed, a dry, dusty old sound. 'Come closer again, boy. I will not bite. No teeth, see: makes it difficult, so it does.' She laughed again.

Brann shuffled forward, beginning to make out her wizened face: sunken, watery eyes amid protruding cheekbones and creases upon creases. White hair hung limply, held in place by a thin gold chain that dangled an assortment of charms across her forehead; they jingled musically at the slightest movement.

His foot brushed against something, causing a slight rattling sound. The Captain had been standing, silent and still, while she spoke but, at the noise from the floor, he flinched with a sharp intake of breath.

The old lady was, however, more calm. 'Mind the bones, boy, mind the bones,' she said equably.

Brann looked down with a nervous jerk to see a selection of small rune-engraved bones (animal or human, he did not know – did not want to know) lying scattered on the floor. One of the candles had been placed to cast light on the area, but he had been so intent on the woman's face as he walked forward that he had stumbled right into the macabre relics.

He drew back in horror. Stories abounded about the folly of incurring the wrath of women like this. Call them what you will – seeresses, witches, wisewomen, earthmothers, oracles – it did not do to cross them. No one knew for sure if tales of mysterious retribution held some truth or were exaggerated fancy but, by the same token, no one was willing to take the risk of testing the theory. To anger them was a bad idea, but to touch, and therefore sully, the individual tools of any of these women, whether it be bones, animal entrails, embers of a fire, sacred stones or any one of myriad other objects, dead or alive, that were their means of divining anything – from the future, the weather or the chances of crops failing or cows calving to the prospects of armies triumphing or women conceiving – was sacrilege.

And he had just stood on top of them.

But the old woman did not cast a spell. She did not fly at him with talon-like nails scratching at his eyes. She did not even scream.

She chuckled.

'Calm down, child, calm down.' The charms strung across her forehead tinkled delicately as she leant forward and gathered the bones from the floor in one long-fingered, sinew-ridged bony hand with a quick and well-practised sweep of the other. 'My fault, so it is, my fault. Forgot they were there when I called you nearer, silly me. Not to worry: not in use just now, are they? No, no, just bits of creatures that long since ceased to need their outer shell in this world, so they are. Nothing more, nothing less.'

Her eyes grew distant, her voice low and heavy. 'When they are in use, though, it is different. Then, they are alive; alive and so very powerful.' She opened her hand to reveal the bones and stroked her fingertips across them. 'Oh yes, so very powerful.' The hand snapped shut, and her head jerked up, as if she had abruptly awakened from a dream. Her eyes focused on his once more and her voice grew gentle again. 'No harm done, is there, little dear? No need to fret, no need at all.' She laughed softly.

Brann was unsure how to feel. He had seen his home set ablaze with his family inside and his brother brutally slain just feet from him; he had been dragged away from everything and everyone he had ever known; he was a slave bound for a future that only the gods could predict in a place he could not envisage; his immediate future was to live, cramped with others like him, beneath the decks of a slave ship under the total authority of a bullying oaf; and now, in a dingy, musty, gloom-laden room, watched by the most quietly menacing man he had ever met, he had trampled all over the sacred bones of an ancient crone who was held in fear and reverence by the battle-scarred crew who shared a ship with her. And her response? To sweep aside those relics as if she were a grandmother brushing away crumbs on a table.

Yes, indeed, he had no idea how to think. He continued to feel nothing. His head was light, and he swayed slightly as he stood, arms hanging limply by his sides, staring blankly at her.

She patted the now-clear floor in front of her, a soft sound. Disturbed dust swirled in the faint candlelight.

'Here, sit,' she said, her voice as gentle as the tap on the floor. 'Sit, before you fall.'

He realised as she said it that his head was spinning more than he had realised, or cared. He stepped forward slightly to the indicated spot, his movements clumsy and his senses deadened, feeling as if time, for him, were moving slower than for those around him.

She patted the floor again, twice. He sat, cross-legged like a child, so close to her that his knees brushed her robes.

'Look at me, boy. Look at me.'

He lifted his eyes to hers and was locked into her gaze. His consciousness seemed to be drawn by her and his mind felt as blank as his emotions. He was aware of her eyes but, beyond that, he saw no more: not the Captain, watching silently; not the dancing flames of the candles; not her robes, many and smoke-thin; not the skin stretched across her face, as fragile-seeming as her clothing; only her dark, dark eyes.

He was aware of her voice but gone was the creaking and groaning of the ship, the calls and footsteps from above, the coughing and whimpering from the neighbouring room, even the faint sound of his own shallow breathing. All he could hear, all there was to him, was her soft, mellow, soothing voice.

'A melancholy right into your bones, you have. Much have you seen, so you have, that should never have passed before such young eyes, and much will you go through again, of a weight a babe should never have to shoulder. But you must release, so you should, you must release – the smallest kettle or the largest volcano must obey the same laws: neither can be sealed, for the force within will only grow and the release will be worse and not of your choosing. So let it out, boy, let it out or it will fill every part of you, and it will leave room for naught else within you. It will destroy you and those you hold close.'

She stared at him in silence, waiting impassively for the emotion to burst from him.

But it did not. A solitary tear gathered at the lip of one eye before slowly drawing a silver line down his cheek. His face, as blank as before, looked back at her, his gaze still locked with hers.

She sighed heavily, and shook her head slightly. 'It is deeper than I feared. As deep, perhaps, as that consuming you, my Captain. So many questions waiting to be asked, pain like a thousand blades, a yearning that tears you asunder but, for now, nothing but emptiness of the soul. Not today will it be filled, for better or worse. Not today and not tomorrow.' She sighed again, a mournful sound. 'So sad, in one so unprepared.'

A shadow of a smile drifted across her lips. 'One answer, though, there is. One answer to a question not yet asked. Know this: not your fault, no, it is not your fault. Remember that, my dear, remember that you could have changed nothing. When fate draws a map, man must follow it, so he must. Man has no choice but to follow it.'

She took his hand in both of hers, stroking the back of it gently. 'Have peace, now, little one, have peace. Go, now; eat and sleep. Best thing for you, so it is. When in doubt, return to the basics of life. Eat and sleep.'

Still clasping him in her grasp, she reached with her other hand and, with surprisingly soft fingertips, gently wiped the tear from his cheek.

She froze. Tensing, with a sharp hiss, she gripped his hand so violently that his attention was snapped away from her eyes. He looked questioningly at the Captain who, silently and intently, nodded Brann's attention back to the old lady.

Slowly, almost tentatively, she drew her hand away from his face and lifted it to her mouth. The moisture on her fingertip glistened in the candlelight with a magical air. She touched the single tear to her lips and, tentatively, brushed her tongue against it.

A scream of pain wrenched itself from her. With her back arched, her body jerked upwards. Her eyelids fluttered erratically, her pupils rolled up, and she began to moan, a low drone that filled the room with an uneasy dread.

The Captain nudged Brann with the toe of one boot. He looked up. 'Listen carefully, boy,' he cautioned. 'What she says, you will hear once, and once only. When she returns to us, she will know nothing of what passes her lips. So listen carefully.'

Brann returned his attention to the old woman. She was mumbling without pause, a stream of incomprehensible sounds that ran into each other. At best, what she was uttering was a monotone of gibberish. What was there for him to listen carefully to?

Her grip on his hand redoubled, and the moaning stopped. She became still, eerily still. Her eyes opened, wide and unblinking, and she stared directly at him. There was silence. Bran realised that he had stopped breathing, and forced himself to draw in air. His hand was in considerable pain, but he dared not do anything that might disturb her.

She spoke, her voice that of a young woman, clear and strong.

'Paths you will travel, in many a realm,
You'll be blind to the journey, trust to Fate at the helm,
But you'll know you are standing in Destiny's hall
When heroes and kings come to call.'

68

Her eyes rolled up once more but, this time, her lids shut peacefully. Her grip eased and her hand slipped from his. With a long, dry sigh, the tension seemed to flood from her and she relaxed, almost sagged, where she sat.

She opened her eyes, and saw Brann massaging his aching hand. Taking it gently in both of hers, she lifted it gently to her lips and kissed it softly.

'Apologies for the pain, my dear, many apologies,' she said so softly that he had to strain to make out the words. 'I know not what I am doing at my special times. I have no memory of my words or actions, no memory. I have only an echo of the memory, a picture in smoke, and the more I try to grasp it, the more it fades.

'But it does leave me with a feeling, so it does. Like a tracker with the indent of a footprint, after the foot has passed. I cannot see the person, but I see clues to the person in the footprint, so I do, I see clues in the footprint. And what I see is your fate lying heavy on your shoulders. Yes, heavy it will lie.'

Brann felt himself sagging as despair plunged down upon him. She took his hand again. 'I know, young one, I know. You have faced so much in a short time, and you are living so much more. Destiny has a habit of arriving slowly. When it comes, you think it is suddenly bursting through the door, but most times it has been building, and making you stronger all the while.' She patted his shoulder. 'Do not despair. When fate visits you, your shoulders will have grown stronger to bear it.'

Her hand drifted down and brushed against the knife hidden under his clothes. He tensed in fear, but she merely smiled quietly, and her eyes narrowed in amusement as they met his.

'You already show me a hint of the man you will need to be. Be careful, and it will serve you well, so it will, it will serve you well. Be complacent and, well… you live in a dangerous world, so you do. We all act sometimes without knowing why; only in later times do we see the significance. Do not be over-hasty to rid yourself of that which may be the saviour of your life. That is all I will say.' She traced a finger down his cheek. 'Take care, little one, take care. It would please me to see you prosper. Yes indeed, it would please me.'

She patted his hand: a simple but surprisingly reassuring gesture. 'Now I must rest, so I must. And so should you. Go now.'

She lay back on cushions that had gone unnoticed in the gloom, her features disappearing into deep shadows where the clutter blocked the candles' meagre reach. The Captain gestured to Brann to stand up. Despite a stiffness in his legs, he did so quickly and followed the tall man, who had started from the room without a word. In the corridor, they found Boar. The Captain headed for the ladder leading to the deck and, without turning, said, 'Put him in with the rest. Make sure he has food and drink.' Boar barely had time to acknowledge the order before he was up the ladder and out of sight.

'You heard the man,' Boar rasped. 'What are you waiting for?'

Brann stumbled into the small hold, realising how exhausted he was. Boar gestured towards a space beside Gerens, where Brann would originally have been installed had his progress not been interrupted.

Boar grunted, 'Better late than never.' He smirked as his gaze passed around the small room, crammed with pale and harrowed faces. 'You're mine, now. Don't you forget it. Especially you, late boy.' His foot flicked out and nudged

Brann's side to indicate the object of the comment. 'Don't you be getting any ideas about being special just because the old crone shared her ramblings with you. You're all the same, now: all maggots under my boot.' He used that very boot to emphasise the point again, but this time it thudded into Brann's ribs in a full-blooded kick. The boy cried out before he could stop himself, and curled up, praying that the fat bully would go away.

But Boar was still speaking, enjoying lording it over his captive audience. 'Remember, you are our pay-day. So eat and drink when it's given to you, and keep yourselves clean. I don't want to go home to my wife with my pay short just because any of you fall sick.'

Brann was unsure which was the worse thought: the idea of what it must be like for some woman to be married to such an obnoxious oaf, or the image of the sort of woman who could place Boar in a state of fear.

Boar reached into a heavy canvas bag and produced a loaf and a hunk of cheese. Breaking off part of the bread, he threw it and the cheese into Brann's lap, before picking up a wooden bowl. He leant back out of the doorway to fill it from a barrel of fresh water that stood in the short corridor.

Setting the bowl down beside Brann, he grunted. 'Make the most of the bread and cheese. Fresh food don't come your way very often at sea. But you maggots weren't the only things we brought back from our fun ashore.'

He turned away and snorted hugely in amusement, the noise lasting the length of his passage to the ladder. The sound would normally have blunted Brann's appetite, but not today. The appearance of the food in his lap had awakened a hunger that had been lying dormant until now, but had re-emerged with a vengeance. He picked up the cheese but, as he chewed

71

it, his arm drooped and the food fell and rolled against Gerens's leg. Gerens turned to see Brann slumped, deep in slumber and snoring gently.

Gerens carefully wrapped the remaining cheese in as clean a rag as he could find and picked up the bowl of water. Lifting Brann's head upright, he touched the rim of the bowl to his lips. In a reflex action, Brann drank.

A boy close by sniggered, nudging the lad beside him. 'Look,' he snorted gleefully. 'He's trying to get him to wet himself.'

Without looking up, Gerens said darkly, 'I am trying to keep him in health. But if you favour sport of that sort, wait until you sleep yourself and I will see what I can arrange.'

The laughing stopped. The boy looked at Gerens. 'Why do you help him?'

Gerens shrugged. 'I feel like I should. So I do.' His stare swept onto the boy. 'Are you saying I should not?' The boy shook his head, but Gerens had already turned back to Brann and helped him to two further swallows. In a lower voice, he spoke again. 'That will do, chief. Enough to keep you going. Any more, and those fools will have their entertainment.'

As he put down the bowl, Brann mumbled in his sleep. It was almost incoherent, but Gerens could just make it out. 'Thank you, mother.'

With a hint of a smile, the boy replied softly, 'Thank the gods you did not say that loudly enough for the others to hear. I do not know which of us would have suffered more if you had.'

On deck, hours later, the slow, steady drumbeat was muffled, for sound carried further at night and it was not generally wise at sea to advertise one's presence unnecessarily. It also helped any of the crew who were managing to rest, to do so.

The night was clear, the stars sharp, the large moon bright enough to give visibility to the horizon, the sea peaceful and – most relevantly – the breeze gentle, so the oars were needed to maintain their progress, albeit at a reduced rate. Every third bench was rowing, while the others slept; the remaining slaves would follow suit in two further shifts, so that all would be able to rest for the majority of the night.

On the raised deck at the stern, Boar broke wind violently. 'There,' he declared. 'That's what I think of those maggots in the hold.'

The steersman grunted, glad he was upwind of the foul oaf, who smelt badly enough without the aid of flatulence. 'That's what you think of everything, Boar.'

The fat man spat over the side. 'Nah, these are the worst ever. We'll be lucky to clear our wages this trip. And there's one wee runt thinks he's better than us, away chatting to the old witch below. He'll be the first I break, wait and see. He's no better than Boar, that's what he'll learn.' He spat again.

'Would it not be better to keep them healthy, Boar? You know, keep them looking good for the market,' the steersman suggested. 'More money for us. Better idea, no?'

Another voice spoke from the shadows. 'And a better idea to show more respect for Our Lady. Would that maybe help, Boar?'

Had there been more light, it would have been clearly visible that the colour had drained from Boar's face. The steersman, without being able to see it, knew it to be so nonetheless, and smiled his amusement.

Boar spluttered. 'Yes, Captain. Good idea. I mean, sorry, Captain.' He regained his composure, such as it ever was. 'Got to catch some sleep, Captain. Better go below. G'night.'

'Another good idea, Boar,' the Captain said evenly. 'Good night.'

Boar stomped off. The deck was silent again, but for the soft drumbeat and the creaks and splashes of the oars. The steersman broke the silence. 'Why do you keep him, Captain? Few skills, too many weaknesses, potential for trouble. You know that if you want his throat cut and him dumped over the side there will be no shortage of volunteers.'

The tall, black-clad figure looked at the veteran warrior. The man was one of his oldest companions and an astute reader of men, although this assessment of Boar had hardly taxed his talents in that respect.

'I know, Cannick, I know.' He sighed. 'And you know he is not the sort I would normally choose, had I the choice. But also you know that circumstances do not, these days, allow me to be over-particular. And you know men well enough to understand we have been lucky with the standard that fate has, mostly, given us.'

Cannick spat over the side. 'We have been lucky, Einarr.' The Captain did not stir at the use of his name. 'From the first campaigns I fought with your father as young mercenaries who needed only the promise of gold and excitement to turn our faces towards lands we had never even heard named before, to the time when your grandfather's death called your father back home, I served with men good and bad. Sometimes the bad are the ones you want more at your back in a fight; some of the worst have saved my life. But some of the best have stood by me when the worst have run, and your father was the best of those. When disease robbed me of my family and someone else's war took my home, I had nothing. I was freed by the worst of fates to determine my own path, and I could have gone anywhere.

But the path I chose was to your father's home, because all have their benefits, but the best have the benefits that sit most comfortably on your shoulders.

'These men you have here, you have indeed been lucky to find signing up with you. All are true, most are good men and all will stand by you. All except one. He is as rotten as I have come across, but we are in a dirty business. Everyone in this business expects to get his hands dirty, but there's always a need for someone who will shove his hands in shit without a second thought.'

The Captain sighed. 'We have indeed been lucky with them, Cannick. You and Our Lady downstairs are the only ones I trust with my name, but these men I trust with my life. They are capable in combat and are generally a good bunch of lads, caught, like us, in something we'd rather not have to be a part of, had we the luxury of choice. Which is why I wonder why we need a man like Boar. He is different from the rest of us: he belongs in this life. If truth be told, he enjoys it.'

'You are right, old friend,' the veteran warrior agreed, his gaze lingering on the moonlit horizon. 'And that is exactly why he has his uses at the moment – because he belongs in this life. We are in it, whether we like it or not, and we need men like him to make it work until we can be rid of it. But you are right: he does enjoy it… too much. His use will continue until fate decrees that it should stop. He will push someone too far one day, he will become too much for someone, and it will be surprising how quickly his advantages become less important to us. In the meantime, though, you need to treat him as you would a fighting dog – keep him on a short leash and watch him carefully until the times arise when he is of use. Do you know what I mean?' Cannick smiled again, but this time grimly. 'But I do hope I am around to see it when the gods decide he has outlived his usefulness.'

The Captain looked at him. 'As usual, you are right. But, as for the last, who will be their tool, I know not. I only know it will not be me. I will kill a man in battle without hesitation, but I will not end a man's life merely because I do not like him. However, when his end comes, I am sure it will be of his own making and we will not need to prompt it. He is good enough at that himself. And, when it does happen, I will trust that the gods have indeed decreed it, and who am I to judge against their decision?'

'Who indeed, boy, who indeed?' Cannick said softly as the tall dark figure descended the ladder and made his way forward to check with the lookout, as he did every night at this time, before retiring to bed.

The Captain reached the prow and held himself steady beside the warrior on duty. The ship reared up at the front into an ornate figurehead of a blue-painted dragon, rearing in silent fury to the height of two men and half as much again. On the back of the head was a small platform that was only a few feet higher than the raised area at the stern; but even just a few feet made a difference in the distance a man could see over the waves.

The lookout was expecting the visit. 'Just one thing, Captain,' he reported, pointing. 'A ship to port, keeping close to the horizon.' He pointed almost due east, back towards the land. 'It has been there a while. I would have called you if it had got any closer, but it has kept its distance and I knew you would be coming by at this time anyway. It's closer to the coast so it may just be a fishing boat. Thought I'd better mention it, though.'

It was not unusual to see other ships at sea – this was a well-used area, after all – and it normally sufficed to keep a wary eye on other vessels until they passed out of sight. 'That's fine. Watch it closely. Have me wakened if it does get closer before dawn. And pass on that order to your relief.'

The Captain returned to the stern, stopping at the base of the ladder. 'Steersman, one degree towards the east. There's a ship out there, to the west. See if it has matched our change of course when the sun comes up, after you have rested.'

'I can see the shape, now you point it out,' Cannick confirmed. 'Thank the gods for the light nights; in a few months we wouldn't have known it was there at all.' He squinted. 'Couldn't have said it was a ship, right enough. Lookout has good eyes.'

The Captain paused as he opened the door to his cabin. 'We may all have cause to be thankful for that before long. Pass on the orders when you are relieved. And if any of the men come up on deck, send them back below and tell them I said they should get as much rest as possible. Best to be ready.'

He was in his bed in moments; the advice on rest applied to him, too. But sleep did not come as quickly. He lay, his eyes fastened on the ceiling but seeing nothing but the faces of an old woman and a frightened boy. And a phrase rang, over and over, echoing in his mind: 'When heroes and kings come to call...'

In a dark, damp, crowded room below the Captain's cabin, a boy, confused, battered in body and mind, numb shock his only defence against unbridled terror and despair, slept the deep, dreamless sleep brought only by utter physical exhaustion.

But had he known the day that lay ahead of him when he woke, his eyes may never have closed in sleep at all.

Chapter 4

They were coming, he knew that. No messenger had forewarned him, but living for years, so many long years, in a world limited to the dust and gloom of these few chambers perversely had brought with it an acute sense of the wider place around him. Servants and retainers moving about their daily routines around his quarters, unseen beyond his doors but betrayed by their soft murmuring and quiet tread, created a rhythm that needed only the merest change to attract his attention. He had listened.

At first, there had been abject dejection that his existence had descended to such banality but, before long, there was a resurgence of the curiosity of his youth, the voracious appetite for information that had been far more the reason for his success than the chilling ruthlessness for which he had been known to the public eye. He became absorbed in the noises, the movements, the rhythms. Over time, the changes, and not just the routine, brought understandable meaning and, bereft of any distractions, he had become adept at reading that meaning. And it had helped the hours to pass.

From time to time, they would come for him. When they remembered that he could be of some use. And they would be surprised at his knowledge of the world outside his chambers.

*Not of the movements of servants – such trivialities were so
far beneath them that they had no interest in that class other
than knowing that the required services had been performed
even before they realised they were needed. No, their surprise
would be at his knowledge of the machinations of court politics, and even of the swirling currents of affairs within and
between nations. But, then,* he *had never seen servants and
their movements as trivial. Not in the sense that he had appreciated them, of course, but rather in the sense that every one
of them was an opportunity to be exploited: the wine-bearer
waiting behind the pair of nobles deep in conversation; the
ostler helping an ambassador dismount while he dropped his
impassive visage and ranted, safe from the gaze of the court;
the handmaiden in the bedchamber of the visiting king's wife;
the concubine in the bedchamber of the visiting king. He had,
in previous decades, made it his business to know by name
every servant in the palace. Few of those were still in service,
but enough remained to paint a picture of the world near and
far. Whenever he was summoned, he revealed only a fraction
of what he knew – it went against the grain to do otherwise
– but he gave them enough to engender a sense of wonder, or
suspicion, at his knowledge; he cared not which, he enjoyed
both. They concealed their surprise, of course, but he had spent
too many years reading other men to miss the glimpses of their
true feelings. He had so few moments of genuine pleasure any
more, but these times were counted among them. He, too,
would never reveal such emotion, but he was well-practised at
concealing it, and they were mere novices in reading it. And
an air of mysticism was always handy.*

*Nevertheless, as he left them, they would always see him
as their fool. And he would always see them as his puppets.
And he despised them for both.*

Unseen knuckles rapped softly at the door. They had come to summon him to the court. He rose and grunted acknowledgement. By the time the servant entered the room, the smile that had played around the corners of his eyes had been replaced by his familiar cold mask.

He was ready.

****

Shortly before dawn, the Captain woke from a fitful sleep. Sitting up, he pulled on his boots and shirt and reached automatically for the sword from lying beside him in the bunk. Some old habits refuse to die. He buckled it on as he left the room and, in moments, was below deck.

He hesitated. Even after all these years, he felt a touch of nerves before entering her presence. Taking a breath, as Brann had done only a few hours before, he walked in. He stood, looking down at the bundle of rags, unsure if he should wake her. As he watched, however, he gradually became aware of her face, eyes unblinking, staring calmly back at him.

He jumped. Slightly.

'Think you I was unaware of you, boy?' she said softly. 'Much use to you I would be, were I not even able to notice your approach. Much use indeed.'

He bowed his head, a faint smile twitching the corners of his mouth. 'Apologies, my lady,' he said. He was about to continue, but she pre-empted him.

'Want to know what the day brings, do you? Want to know of approaching others?'

His eyes narrowed. 'You know the other ship?' he asked.

She shook her head slightly, the charms tinkling gently. 'I see many things, my boy, ships, weather, mortal spirits among them, but I recognise the identity of no ship but this one,' she said quietly. 'But sometimes I cast the bones for myself, not just when you ask, so I do. Today I did. And so already I know of others approaching. Would you know more?'

He nodded, once. 'I would, my lady. As ever, anything you can tell, I would know.'

The bones were lying on the floor in front of her. With a surprisingly deft sweep of her arm, she caught them up and cast them in a single movement. They rattled to a halt and, without taking her eyes from them, she reached to the side and drew one of the candles closer. 'Danger approaches, twofold,' she said.

He stiffened. 'Two ships?'

She shook her head. 'Specific, it is not. But men or weather, all that approaches means this vessel harm, so it does. Take care, so you should.'

'We have few friends in this world, and none out here in this sea,' he murmured. 'Is there anything else?'

She poked one long finger at two of the bones, staring intently at them. She brushed the other relics aside, as if to concentrate on the pair. Silence hung heavy as she stared, unmoving. The Captain checked himself, feeling the urge to hurry her, but knowing the futility of doing so.

She nodded once, as if now sure of something that she had suspected. 'Yes,' she said. 'There is more. If conflict there is, I cannot say the outcome, neither I can. Conflict will swing many ways, at the whimsy of fate and the decisions of men. But one thing is clear: if you fight or if you run, you will lose some in your charge. How many, and who, is down to you. Down to you, it is. But this much is clear: men will die today.'

He cursed the capriciousness of Calip. Why could the god of luck and chance never allow anything to be straightforward?

She spoke again, her tone final and dismissive. 'I see no more. Take care and think clearly, so you should. Think clearly as you battle nature and man. Perhaps you can use one against the other.'

'Use them to fight or to run?'

'I see no more,' she repeated, sweeping up the bones and watching them as she fiddled with them absently. 'Take care, boy.'

He thanked her, and turned to go, his shadow flickering in the candlelight. As he reached the doorway, he stopped, his fingers tracing the scar on his cheek as he stared, his eyes on the floor but his mind clearly elsewhere.

Without looking up, she murmured, 'Something else bothers you?' She almost sounded amused.

He turned. 'It does, and that you well know.' He could have sworn that she smiled in the dim shadows. 'The boy. What is it about him? What did you see, and why did he affect you so? Why does it trouble me? I cannot rid my head of it.'

She shrugged, a strangely normal-looking gesture from one such as her.

'I saw what I said, and I said what I saw,' she said simply. 'I know it troubles you, as it troubles me and it troubles him, so it does. Do not forget that: it troubles him, most of all. It is never pleasant or easy to be introduced to your destiny, even if you know not what it will be. Especially if you know not what it will be. Just knowing it is there, that a choice awaits you, is not welcome for anyone, let alone one so young.'

He crouched in front of her, a move that was almost imploring. 'But who is he? Is it good or bad for us that he is here? What will he do? What should I do?'

She laughed, quietly and briefly. 'Who he is, is less important than who he will be, so it is. And good or bad for us, depends on him. And what he will do, will be his choice, so it will. And what should you do? Nothing. Nothing that you would not do otherwise, had you not heard of any destiny. Do not free him, if you would not otherwise free him. Do not speak to him if you would not otherwise speak to him. His destiny is not yours to influence, not yours, no. If his fate is now to be a slave, so be it. If there comes a time when you would use him otherwise, so be it. Cera will sit in the Hall of the Gods and spin the thread of his destiny accordingly, so she will. She will spin as she spins for all of us now and before and all who ever will be. She will spin, she will spin, she will spin, and we all must accept our place on her tapestry.'

She cocked her head to one side and looked at him in amusement. 'But why ask me of him, when you have the boy on your ship that you can ask yourself?'

He stood. 'As ever, you are right. Apologies, my lady. I am thinking so deeply about it, that I cannot see the most simple truth. I thank you, as ever, for your assistance.'

He made to leave once more, but her voice stopped him. 'Take care of him, while you have him. Tomorrow, especially. And take care of yourself, Einarr.'

He froze. Without turning, he said, 'I will do my best – on both counts,' and left.

Brann stirred and, as memories flooded back, he jerked into a sitting position, discovering that he had acquired new aches from his awkward sleeping position to add to those from his journey draped over the back of a horse. At first disorientated, he peered around the cramped hold at the sleeping boys. The last of the drowsiness left him, and he reacquainted himself with his surroundings, examining the room and its inhabitants in the detached way that was becoming so familiar that it had almost moved to his subconscious. Almost. He felt sure he would never truly be at ease with the feeling of separation.

Discovering a hard lump under one leg, he fished out the cheese in its rag covering. Remembering the way that Boar had thrown it down, and noticing the careful way it had been wrapped, he guessed that Gerens had stored it for him. He silently thanked the sleeping youth beside him, still not quite sure why the brooding, in many ways intimidating, youth had chosen to take him, to whatever extent, under his protective wing. His hunger overwhelmed his thoughts, and he wolfed into the food. He noticed the bowl on the floor, and greedily gulped down the water. It was lukewarm, but it still tasted sweet and precious. He leant back against the wall, and the hilt of the stolen knife dug into the small of his back, reminding himself of his folly. Fear swept through him and he cast about for somewhere to dump it, but the room was so bare of all but sleeping boys; it would surely be found, and that could mean the death of all of them.

He pulled out the knife and twisted it in his fingers. A cold melancholy sank over him, and he ran a thumb along the sharpness of the blade. The death of all? Or the death of one? With interest, he found that the prospect of death did not concern him, one way or another, but the ease with which it could be achieved fascinated his darkly dispassionate mind. He ran the keen edge across his wrist. The slightest of pressure, the least of effort, the simplest of movements would be all it would take to make the most momentous of impacts of a life.

The approach of unmistakable footsteps jerked him back from his introspection and he shook his head, thrusting the thoughts back down, buried alongside his suppressed emotions. As quickly and quietly as he could manage, he slipped the knife once again into his waistband and curled up on his side, closing his eyes in the hope of avoiding Boar's attention.

It was in vain. A heavy boot in the small of the back, no more than two inches from the knife, made him yell in pain.

'Morning, maggot,' Boar said with satisfaction. 'Time to get up. For some reason, the Captain wants to see you.'

He unfastened Brann's manacles from the chain on the floor and, grabbing the front of his tunic with one hand, hoisted him to his feet. His knees immediately buckled and he fell back to the deck.

Boar grinned maliciously with the few teeth he possessed. 'Better get the legs working. Easier to walk than be dragged – especially on the ladders. Mind you, more fun for me that way.' He laughed, amused at his own wit.

He grasped the back of Brann's tunic again and, lifting the boy's torso from the ground, started dragging him along the short dusty corridor, his legs trailing behind him. Mindful of the comment about the ladders, Brann forced his stiff limbs to move and scrambled until he was upright.

'There you go,' Boar smirked. 'Got you walking again, didn't I? Can't say I'm not good to you.'

Thinking it unwise to offer any reply, Brann climbed the ladder and waited at the top for Boar's massive form to emerge. The huge oaf pointed him to the door of the Captain's cabin, and knocked on it three times. At the sound of a voice from within, Boar opened the door, pushed Brann through, and followed him in.

'You wanted the boy, Captain,' he said.

Rising from behind a simple rough desk that seemed, to judge from the remains of a meagre meal left from the night before, to double as a dining table, the Captain moved towards them.

'That will be all, Boar,' he said, dismissing the man.

Alone with the man responsible for the loss of everyone and everything he held dear, Brann stared at him. He should have been overwhelmed with rage, or terror, or hatred, or all of these. But all he felt was a dull resentment, as if the world he was in was unwanted but unreal. He stared blankly at the Captain.

The subject of his stare drew a chair up to the desk and gestured to Brann to sit. Placing food in front of the boy, and nodding in reply to Brann's questioning look, he said, 'Yes, eat. It is just the leftovers of some bread and cheese from last night, but I am guessing you have not seen much food these past couple of days.'

As Brann launched into his second breakfast of the morning, the Captain sat down opposite him.

'Slowly, slowly,' he cautioned. 'If you throw it back up, you would be as well not bothering to eat it.'

Brann forced himself to take the advice. He felt conscious of the man staring at him, as if he were assessing him, and looked up at him. What could the man tell from the way he ate? Why watch him now? Feeling that he had no way of knowing the answer, he shrugged slightly and returned to the food.

For a few long moments, the sound of his eating was the only noise in the room, and as Brann became aware of it, the noise seemed to become louder with each bite. The tension was eventually broken by the Captain.

'Apologies in advance,' he said. 'You will find me blunt. Too many years in the company of professional men who expect orders and know nothing of small-talk.' He stood up, and spoke abruptly. 'I am wondering what you made of what Our Lady said to you.'

Swallowing a mouthful of bread, Brann said, 'Your Lady? You mean...?'

The Captain cut in. 'The old woman below deck, yes. She is our wise woman. She reads the bones, as you saw, helping us prepare for changes in the weather or...' He paused. 'Or other things.

'But the vision she had with you – I have never known it before. That reaction, the strength of that trance... I have never known it to be like that.'

'Maybe she has not been well,' Brann suggested, noticing that the ship had started to rise and fall more violently. 'The movement of the ship, sea-sickness, and things like that.'

The Captain laughed, a natural sound that was startlingly at odds with his grimly efficient appearance. 'Oh, boy, if only I had your innocence around me more often. No, no, she has been at sea, with us and many others before us, for at least seventy years now – well, seventy that we know of. No, that reaction was something different, and powerful. Do you remember what she said?'

Brann nodded, not realising that he had stopped eating. 'I cannot forget it. Do you want me to repeat it for you?'

The Captain sat down again. 'No need. I, too, cannot remove it from my head.' He leant back, running his hands through his now-unruly black hair.

Hesitantly, Brann asked, 'Do you know what it means? All this talk of destiny and suchlike? Is it real?'

'That you can be sure of,' the Captain nodded. 'If she says it, it is real – in some fashion or another. She sees future possibilities, but what actually transpires depends on so many things: random occurrences, decisions – considered and intuitive – of many people, twists of fate, the whims of the gods, and on, and on. So she cannot say what you will do, only what you will face. So, whatever happens to you, at many points you will have to decide what path to take. And one of those decisions, one of those paths, will be one on which hangs the fate of others. That she knows. What that decision will be, may not be decided yet – it may change several times according to the way your life goes between now and then.'

He sighed, then leant forward, his eyes boring into Brann as if gauging his reaction. 'Everybody faces decisions on a daily basis. But in your case she knows that one moment of great import will come – and when she speaks of that, she speaks of importance to a great many people. Who are you? What is it that you offer? That you *can* offer? What are you?'

Brann felt himself go still. His tone was as dull as his feelings. But there was bitterness in the truth of the words. 'I have no family. I have no life of my own. Your men saw to that. You made me what I am. I am nothing.'

An edge crept into the Captain's voice, but too slight to tell whether it was from frustration or anger. 'That may be your fate now, but according to Our Lady, it is not how you will be in time.'

Brann felt sick at the thought, lurching in an instant from a complete lack of care to overwhelming waves of emotion. It seemed as if the world was closing in on him, and he felt very small. Tears started to well up.

The Captain moved around the table and patted his shoulder, awkwardly. 'If you want to, cry. Let it go. It is shock – you have been through much, and it will take a while to get over it, as she told you. If you want my advice, try to let it out – but not in front of the others. Weakness is not a good thing to show around here, but I guess you have worked that out for yourself.

'I have worked with many warriors in my time, so I have seen many people go through what you are feeling just now. Some find it helps to take one day at a time. Treat everything you do as the most important thing in your life and devote yourself to it until it is done, then move on to the next.' He laughed briefly. 'You may end up an obsessive, but at least you'll get through the days.'

Brann, however, did not cry but instead finished the last of the food and caught his plate as it threatened to slide from the table. The rising and falling of the ship had now been joined by what felt like a sideways buffeting, giving a distinct feeling of being tossed about by a playful giant.

'Did something bad happen to you?' he asked, taking a deep breath as if sucking his self-control back inside him. 'Is that how you know what to do?'

The Captain stopped, his face set grimly. 'Another piece of advice, boy. It is seldom beneficial to your health to pry. Try to avoid doing so.' He grunted. 'Anyhow, that is all. I merely wanted to make sure that you did not say anything to anyone – and I mean anyone – about Our Lady. The less that people know about her, and the more mystery that surrounds her, the more she is revered, or feared... and the better it is for her, for me and for the ship.

'And it will be better for you, too, not to talk. You will find that, when someone is the subject of a prophecy, good or bad, small or great, it tends to breed jealousy and resentment. At the very least, others will never look at you for the person you are: you will just represent the prophecy to them.'

He walked to the door and shouted for Boar. Brann cast a look around the room, realising that he had been so intent on eating that he had never bothered to examine his surroundings. It was basic: a wooden bed, the desk and chairs, a long chest large enough for weapons and clothes and, curiously among the bare efficiency of the rest of the cabin, a small bookcase. He could not make out the titles of the books, but they looked both well-read and cared-for.

Then Boar had him gleefully back in his clutches and prepared to drag him roughly from the room, squeezing his arm so hard that Brann caught his breath.

'Hope you don't mind me holding so hard, only we don't want you to fall over in the storm, do we?' he growled happily at the boy. Brann thought that he would rather fall, but felt it wiser not to suggest it to Boar.

Before they could leave the room, however, a bell started to ring. The Captain froze in the doorway, holding one hand out behind him to tell Boar to stay where he was. A warrior skidded to a halt in front of the door, as others tumbled from below decks, weapon-bearing belts in their hands rather than having wasted time buckling them on until they could determine the nature of the alarm.

'Pirates, Captain!' the warrior shouted above the noise of the sea and the bell. 'To the port side, and closing fast.'

'How did they get so near?' the Captain yelled back. 'I gave strict orders to watch them and rouse me if they approached.' He paused, and his eyes narrowed. 'To port?'

The warrior wiped his soaking long hair away from his eyes and, with a practised hand, tied it behind his head as he spoke. He nodded, confirming the Captain's suspicions. 'That ship was a decoy, Captain. It moved closer, then dropped away. Then closer, then away, all the while to make us wonder. While we watched, the other one crept up on the other side. With no lights and dark hull and sails, they managed to stay under cover of the waves as they rose higher, whipped up by the storm as it came in from the wide sea, and fast with the wind behind it.'

The Captain nodded curtly. Whatever the reason, and no matter his anger at himself for allowing them to be duped, they had a situation to deal with. It had been admirable sailing, whoever his foe was, and if their fighting in any way matched that level of skill, they would have a job on their hands.

'Get to your position,' he shouted. 'You too, Boar. You,' he pointed at Brann, 'stay here.' He slammed the door shut. Brann raced over to it and opened it slightly. He was damned if he was going to miss whatever was going on. His right hand went instinctively to the hilt of the knife at the small of his back. Then his common sense took hold and he realised how ineffective the small weapon would be in anything that was about to transpire. Very quickly, however, his foolishness was overwhelmed by his curiosity, and he returned his attention to the scene unfolding beyond the door.

The Captain was roaring, 'Cannick! Cannick!' The old warrior appeared at his side. Despite having finished his shift at the steering oar only two hours beforehand, the Captain could see he was still one of the first on deck. 'What's the situation?'

'Pirates, Captain,' Cannick shouted. 'One hundred yards out, and closing fast. Not enough time to arm the slaves. The other ship is not immediately within dangerous range, so I've readied the men for any attack from the one side, and I've sent the archers to the bow to oppose their crossbowmen.'

The Captain assessed the situation in a sweeping glance. 'We cannot afford to arm the slaves, anyway; we need them to keep us steady in these waves. In any case, this weather will see that there will be no boarding unless we are defeated first. No one could successfully cross to another ship in these conditions if they had to face armed men to do so.' His eyes swept around the ship. 'Good, Cannick, well done.'

'So why attack?' Cannick was confused. 'Pirates steal. If they can't board, maybe they won't attack.'

'Look at them, they are attacking. They will be close in minutes. The time for wondering is by. If we stop to wonder why, all we will know for sure is how we are to die.'

He started to climb the ladder to the platform at the back of the ship. Without warning, he reversed his decision and dropped back down beside the veteran.

'Cannick, change of plan. Bring the archers to the stern.'

Cannick was astonished, but masked his expression instantly. 'All six of them, Captain?' he shouted. 'What about the enemy's crossbows? It gives them liberty to loose untroubled, if ours are not giving them something to think about.'

Although he was voicing his misgivings, he had already signalled to the archers, who were by now running towards the stern.

The Captain looked at Cannick. For anyone else, questioning his orders would have brought a harsh penalty, but this war-hardened old man had taught him most of what he knew about battlecraft. He started to climb the ladder again, shouting back over his shoulder, 'I don't want stalemate. I need to win, and fast.'

He knew it was a gamble, but he had no choice. Most, if not all, pirate ships were bigger than his and more heavily armed, and usually with some sort of artillery. Reaching the rail, he saw that this one was no exception. The heavy ship was indeed closing fast, and its crossbowmen were readying in its bow. At the stern, however, was mounted the real threat: a springald – a huge crossbow-like weapon that had been swivelled towards them. It was pointing, it seemed, straight at him; they always seemed bigger, he thought, when they were aimed at you.

The Captain turned to the drummer. 'Signal reverse stroke, for three strokes, then resume.'

The order was obeyed instantly. As he had hoped, his ship had slowed slightly – not enough to lose its momentum, and therefore control, in the stormy waters, but enough to cause the other vessel to overshoot slightly. They were still facing the springald, but at least the change had altered the part of his ship that the fearsome weapon was aimed at, and the pirates would have to decide whether to shoot at a target other than their first choice or go through the process of unlocking the springald's mounting, reaiming it and locking it down again before letting loose its missile – which, particularly given the tossing conditions, would buy them some extra time. He fervently hoped it would be the latter.

As if to mock his tactics, the springald loosed with a chilling twang that could be heard above the storm, arcing the giant bolt at the mast. It struck the furled sail, ripping it, and carrying on into one of the benches. Screams rang out: not of pain from those hit, but of horror from those around them, hardened men as they were. The two rowers who had been struck had died instantly, and horrifically.

The archers had arrived beside him. 'Aim for the steersman,' the Captain shouted. 'Start as soon as they are in range.'

One of the archers replied, 'That would be now, Captain.'

They let loose their shafts immediately, desperate to end this as soon as possible after witnessing the destruction wrought by the giant bolt. Probably through luck, considering the movement of the ship and the high wind, their first volley flew towards its target, with one shaft catching the steersman square in the throat as he turned to look their way. The force of the blow flipped him backwards, and he disappeared into the sea.

The Captain shouted, 'Shower arrows on anyone who comes to take over. Until they do, feel free to target the weapon.'

The springald's crew had taken cover when they first saw the arrows fly but, under the persuasion of a huge man with a bared cleaver-like sword, they had quickly reappeared to reload the weapon, furiously cranking back the wire and slotting another bolt into place. Bellowed orders saw them lower its aim. Having witnessed the effect of their first attempt, they were abandoning the difficult shot at the mast and aiming for the rowers directly this time. It was a quick adjustment to make, for the vertical angle could be altered without unlocking it; although the mechanism allowed it to slide back to absorb some of the energy and reduce the chance of it ripping up the deck to which it was bolted, the massive power it released meant that it had to be anchored against lateral movement. As four arrows flew towards them, the men around the fearsome device took cover again but at that time a pirate could be seen running in a crouch for the swaying tiller and the archers switched their aim back to the steering arm and, as they did so, one of the men operating the springald took his chance to dive at the murderous weapon and hammer at the release mechanism.

Perhaps mercifully, the rowers were facing away from the other ship. Again, those killed never knew that it was coming. The devastation at that short range was, however, horrific. The huge arrow smashed directly into two benches and ploughed into the side of the ship, taking a chunk of the wooden wall with it into the heaving sea.

Three men died instantly. Another two had their heads bludgeoned and shattered by an oar whipped around by the passing missile. Incredibly, no one else was injured. The bolt had been eerily precise in its destructive passage. The ship's drummer, well aware of the need to keep the vessel pointing into the maliciously relentless waves, beat relentlessly, bellowing at the rowers to keep working to maintain their position. Fortunately, and almost unbelievably, their discipline held in the face of such horror. They knew they had no option: to stop rowing would mean death in either case, from the sea or from the pirates.

The Captain had only glanced at the impact, his attention solely focused on determining the damage to his ship, for the moment at least. If it had been mortally holed, he would have had no option but to change his tactics and attempt to board the pirate vessel. In the current stormy conditions, that was a move that could sink both ships.

One of the archers turned to him. 'Should we go for the springald, Captain?' he shouted. 'We can't afford too many more hits like that.' The Captain shook his head. His opposite number on the pirate ship was no fool and had quickly seen his ploy and, although the enemy crossbowmen themselves had been slow to react, they had clearly now been ordered to make their way aft as quickly as the conditions would allow.

'If we do not get lucky soon, you will have their crossbows to worry about as well,' the Captain yelled back. 'Concentrate on the tiller.'

The archers had long since abandoned ordered volleys, and were now loosing as fast as their ability allowed, with arrows being shot before the previous ones had landed. Many were being carried adrift by the blustering wind, but enough were reaching the area of their target to give them hope.

The crew of the springald, however, were busy reloading, and the crossbowmen were nearing the stern. The replacement steersman crouched low, determinedly holding course; the Captain could not help but admire his courage. Behind the group around the springald, a man was trying to push past. The Captain stared through the driving rain, and saw a large shield in the man's arms.

'Shoot faster,' he yelled. 'They are bringing protection for the steersman.'

As he shouted, however, the instruction became unnecessary. An arrow – ironically one blown slightly off course – struck a metal fitting on the springald. It careered at a sharp angle and streaked a few short yards before spearing into the chest of the crouching steersman. The deflection had robbed the arrow of much of its speed, so it did not strike as hard as the one that had launched the previous steersman into the sea. Nevertheless, it was instantly obvious that it was a fatal blow.

Without any control, the ship started to drift into a turn. The crossbowmen had reached the stern, and one realised the danger and started to throw himself at the tiller. He was too late. The life had run from the steersman and he was slumped on the arm of the tiller, turning the ship completely broadside to the massive waves. The desperate man hauled him to the side and wrenched round the steering arm, but he must have known it was already an impossible task.

It was over in seconds. Three massive waves in quick succession smashed into the wallowing vessel, both swamping it and rolling it to a critical angle and allowing water to pour over the side. For a moment, the stricken ship started to right itself, but the water already on board and the waves that continued to batter from the side, and fill it further, left it lying at a steep angle on its side with the stern slightly raised, and low in the water. Even the thunderous din of the storm could not mask the noise of everything above and below its decks that was not fastened down – and much that had been – crashing towards the lowest point. What they could not hear, but what was even more critical to the stricken ship's fate, was the noise of the sea rushing into the vessel through every available aperture now open to it, as well as a few that the forceful water had opened up for itself.

It remained at that angle briefly until, without warning, it slipped quickly and quietly beneath the surface. Eight or nine pirates could be seen, when the weather allowed, bobbing in the water, although three were dead already.

One of the archers turned to the Captain, nocking an arrow to his bow. 'Do we shoot them or bring them aboard, Captain?' he asked.

His face impassive, the Captain stared for a moment at the figures in the water, then shook his head.

'Neither,' he said abruptly. 'They seal their fate when they sail as pirates: no captain would risk the lives of his crew by taking on board any of those murderous scum. And we have used more than enough arrows already because of the weather and the need for fast action. The sea will take care of them, soon enough.'

He turned to call for Cannick, and found the veteran already standing attentively a few yards away. 'The other ship?' the Captain asked.

'Gone, Captain,' Cannick said. 'They started closing in when they saw their friends attack, but then held their position, not wanting to risk anything in this weather, I guess, and waiting to pick up the pieces when we were finished. As soon as they saw the other ship go down, they disappeared the way they had come.'

His leader nodded. 'I expected as much. They could be close enough to see it sink, but not close enough to see how we did it. If they had known how lucky we were, they maybe

97

would not have left so quickly. But people like that only fight when they think the odds are heavily on their side.' He smiled coldly. 'The gods were kind to us today.' He looked at the seven bodies on the benches. 'To most of us, at least.'

Cannick nodded. 'Indeed, Captain. Indeed. And for those others, it was quick. The only good death is a quick one.'

The Captain was watching as the bodies of the dead rowers were unchained and, unceremoniously but with quiet respect, were committed to the tossing sea. Others worked to take down the torn and flapping sail, clear the wreckage and patch up the damage until proper repairs could be carried out. Without turning round, he said, 'I can see you have got the tidying up under control, Cannick. Just make sure the steersman and drummer work together to keep us afloat. We are damaged and have a bit of rough weather to deal with. We can yet follow the fate of the pirates.'

As he started down the ladder to the deck, he shouted, 'Once the waves die down, give me a full damage report, on ship and people. And alert me at once, of course, if we have any more uninvited guests looking as if they want to taste our hospitality.'

Cannick grinned. 'Of course, Captain.'

As the footsteps started down the ladder, Brann eased the door shut and moved back into the cabin, trying to look innocent. As he sat down, the knife prodded him and he realised he had passed up a perfect opportunity to secrete it in the Captain's cabin. Frantically, he scanned the room for a hiding place for the weapon, but the footsteps outside the door told him he was too late. He dropped back into the chair, resuming his attempt at innocence, as the Captain entered and sat on the edge of the desk, easing off his boots, pouring sea water from them into a nearby basin.

Without looking up as he peeled off his sodden, woollen boot linings, he said: 'Did you enjoy the view?'

Flustered, Brann floundered for an answer. 'I... I don't know what you mean.'

The man's eyes narrowed in amusement as he walked across the room to hang his sodden and dripping cloak from a peg behind the door, his steps steady and assured despite the violent and unpredictable tossing of the ship. 'Remember, boy, and continue to remember: it is my job to know everything that happens on this ship – and to notice everything. You would not have been able to see all of our little encounter from the doorway of this room, but you would have seen enough. And do not bother to deny it. Hell's demons could not have stopped me looking, had I been in your place.'

Brann shrugged. He did not know what to say.

The Captain stared into his eyes, his gaze intense and penetrating as if he were trying to probe Brann's thoughts. 'How do you feel?' he asked at last. 'It cannot be something you will have witnessed very often.'

Brann fidgeted with his cuff, dropping his gaze to the floor. 'I don't know how I feel. Ever since your men killed my family and burnt our home, ever since Boar put a bolt through the head of my brother an arm's length away from me, ever since I was *enslaved*, I have felt cold and emotional, opposites at the same time. Most times it feels as if I am just looking at things and working them out, but occasionally, without warning, I feel that I am about to burst into tears for no reason.' He glanced at the Captain. Seeing his face impassive, he continued. 'But when I saw all that, I was just numb, taking it all in and trying to notice everything. I was not scared, but I was not brave either – I just felt as if I was no part of it, as if nothing would happen to me.'

He shook his head in confusion. 'But I should have been scared, and I should have felt sick when I saw what happened to those rowers. Anyone would have.' He looked up at the Captain. 'But I didn't. Does that mean I am evil? Those men were torn apart, and I felt nothing. Am I evil, now?'

The Captain put a hand on his shoulder, as awkwardly as he had done earlier. 'No, your mind has switched part of itself off because of all you have experienced. You could not have coped with the emotions created by even a fraction of what you have had to face, else you would have gone mad. It is too much, so your mind protects itself. You will learn quickly about everything you see, because you will analyse everything without emotion cluttering your thoughts.' He moved to lean heavily with both hands on the desk, staring at the dark wood but seeing something far from the dim cabin. He sighed. 'But we all need our hearts as well as our minds, so you will open yourself up again in time and, by then, you will be tougher and better able to deal with the more unpleasant side of life. Be careful. All men have a darkness within them, and a light, in differing balances. But if you create a void within, the darkness may fill it completely before you begin to let light back into your life once again. At the moment, you may not like your situation, but whatever point you are at in your life, the present is the only reality. You can work to change the future, but not the present. If it is your fate at the moment to be a slave, it is not my place to question the will of the gods, and neither is it yours. That is the belief of my people and, among the many races I have met in my travels, I have not found a reason that can invalidate its simple truth, so it will do for me. As it would serve you well, also.'

'I understand that, but there is another thing I do not understand.' Brann's brows were furrowed. 'I was told that the rowers were prized slaves, that their well-being was important to the ship. Yet those who lost their lives while sticking to their duty were just dropped over the side, like rubbish. How can you expect the others to give their all if that is how those men were treated?'

The Captain smiled. 'Your feelings may have been put on hold, but you have been thinking about what you have seen. That's a start, at least. And I can see how it would appear to you that way. But these men live in a hard practical world. Had those men been injured, we would have done all in our expertise to save them, or at least to ease their suffering. But they were dead. And what were we to do with the bodies? Store them on board to attract disease and serve no purpose? Quick clean disposal was right. They had no family here, and the gods already know them, so what would be the point of a ceremony when we are already battling a storm? The men they were in life will determine their passage to the next world, not prayers offered on their behalf once they are already travelling that road. To conduct ceremonies would merely delay us when it is folly to hang around at the scene of a fight. These men understand that. This is the world we live in: one where practicality helps you survive and sentiment kills you. This is the world you now live in, too. Remember that, and you will learn more quickly how to stay alive.'

The Captain moved to the door and sighed wearily. 'If we can manage it without interruptions this time, I will have Boar take you back below. And, if anyone asks what passed between us, it is none of their business. If they persist, tell them to ask me about it. I do not expect they will do so.'

He opened the door and shouted for Boar. Before the fat bully appeared, the Captain turned to him. 'And tell them I scared the hell out of you. After all, like Our Lady, I have a reputation to protect.'

The door closed and Brann was left standing on his own. At first, it seemed strange that he, a captive, should be left unattended, but then he thought, *Where could I go?* Footsteps approached, and his stomach knotted at the thought of Boar. Sure enough, his fear was borne out as the lumbering giant enjoyed bouncing him against every wall and sharp edge he could find on the way back to the hold.

As Boar fastened Brann back into the chains, he knelt beside him and leant close over him. The smell from his body or clothes – or both – was overpowering.

'Don't you be thinking you're the Captain's pet, maggot,' he snarled, and Brann flinched as he realised that the smell of his breath was even worse. 'You're mine, and mine you'll stay.'

As Brann jerked back from the stench, Boar mistook the reaction for fear. Satisfied that he had achieved his goal, he grinned, showing the few rotten teeth he had left. 'Good. Remember that, or I'll have fun reminding you, maggot.'

He stood with surprising agility for one his size – Brann reappraised his opinion of the proportion of the man that was blubber – and made his way, laughing, back up the dim corridor.

Gerens nudged Brann. 'I see you have made a friend there,' he said dryly.

Brann sighed and leant back. 'Oh, Boar and I, we get on great,' he replied. 'You know, the sort of relationship where he makes my life even more of a misery than it already is, and I dream of killing him.'

A boy nearby spoke up. 'You would have to join a queue for that. Remember, you have only had it from him for a day or so. Some of us have been here for more than a week.'

For the first time, Brann looked around the small room. Fatigue had driven curiosity from his mind when he had been brought in previously, but now he wondered if anyone else from his village, or even the town, had suffered the same fate. A quick glance, however, determined that he had the dubious honour of being alone in being brought on board from his valley. 'What is it like?' he asked the boys. 'What happens to us?'

A second boy snorted. 'Nothing, and that's it. We are just left here and fed occasionally. The exciting times are when you get your food and when you use the bucket there, because those are the only parts of the day that you do anything other than sit on the one spot. Apart from once a day when they take us up to walk up and down the deck for a while to keep strength in our legs. Can't sell us if we can't walk, can they?'

The first boy barked a hoarse, humourless laugh. He was thin, almost skeletal, with sunken eyes that disappeared into shadow in the gloom and was, Brann realised as his eyes adjusted to what little light was afforded them, at most two or three years older than himself. His laughter turned to coughing and the boy cleared his throat before adding, 'Sometimes they even stop us talking if any of them are trying to sleep. As if it was not boring enough already down here. But forget *your* questions. Why were you taken up there? And what in the gods' names was going on?'

Brann shrugged and made an excuse that he had been asked about the land around his village in case the raiders ever wanted to pay a return visit.

'I hope you didn't tell them,' the thin boy snarled. 'Bastards.'

'Not enough time,' Brann said, and recounted the attack by the pirates, telling as much as he had seen and embellishing the rest. After the excitement of the tale wore off, the others

103

around him were silent as it dawned on them that their fate could have been even worse.

'I don't know what I would have preferred,' the thin boy said. 'Drowning or being captured by the pirates. Suddenly boredom seems much more attractive.'

A slight, tousle-haired lad with an angelic face at odds with a voice that was deep in anticipation of the man he would become, but layered with the harsh tone of the adolescent he still was, butted in. 'What about the old woman? What did she want with you?'

Brann shrugged. 'No idea. She thought I was someone else. Who knows what she wanted?'

The thin boy stared at him, his eyes narrowing in suspicion. 'Seems strange to me. I think you know more than you are saying. You'd better not be holding out on us, boy.'

Gerens turned his dark glare on the boy. 'What do you mean? Did you hear the way that woman screeched when they took him in there? Made my blood run cold, so it did, and I was in here. Would you have liked to have shared a room with her? And how do you fancy being marched about in the gentle care of Boar? I know I'd rather be here. Would you have traded places?'

The boy grunted, coughed raspingly and lay back to doze, and the hold fell silent. The musty room was filled only with the creaking of the ship, a noise that was becoming so familiar to Brann that, most of the time, he was no longer aware of it. He leant back himself; he was exhausted again. It was not too long since he had slept, but he assumed the tiredness was due to the effects that the Captain had talked about. He tried occupying his mind, counting the lines of the grain in the floorboard beneath him but, before he had got far, he had drifted off to sleep once more.

He wakened twice and, each time, managed to eat a little. On one occasion, the captives were talking, but he lacked the energy, or will, to do anything more than idly listen before drifting back off to sleep. From what he could hear, the others were the product of raids further north up the coast. It made sense: the ship's destination would be far to the south, where countries with the slave markets lay, so they would always be headed in that direction after each raid; were they to work their way northwards as they raided, they would be increasing the distance they had to run if anything went wrong, and would be leaving enemies between them and their haven.

The third time he wakened, it was as a result of being shaken roughly by Gerens.

'At least look as if you are awake, chief, even if you don't feel it,' the youth murmured in his ear. 'Boar approaches – you could tell his tread a mile off. And I would guess it is better not to give him the chance to wake you himself.'

As if to prove his point, Boar appeared in the doorway and casually kicked a sleeping boy in the guts. The boy awoke, coughing in pain, and Brann was thankful for the timely advice and the fact that, for some unfathomable reason, Gerens seemed to have appointed himself to watch over him, like a savage but attentive guard-dog. Still clutching his stomach, the boy lurched to his feet; he was one of several who had previously learnt the folly of staying down long enough to allow Boar a second kick.

'Captain wants seven of you upstairs now,' he growled, unfastening those nearest the door – the six in Brann's group, and the next one along. He stood them in the corridor and looked along the line. His gaze stopped when it fell on the boy who had been sick when they first came aboard. While most of the others had adapted to the movement of the ship – in fact, some, including Brann, had actually found that it lulled them to sleep – the lad had continued to be ill without respite, and looked as weak as he must have felt.

Boar snorted in derision. 'Captain asked for the seven most recent, 'cause he wants the ones who haven't been weakened by all the sitting around you maggots do. But you,' he prodded the sick boy in the chest with a force that rocked him onto his heels, 'you won't do, will you? Pathetic little worm.' He shoved the boy back into the room and fastened him back to the chain, taking instead the next one available: the thin boy who had spoken to them earlier.

'You'll do,' he grunted, dragging him from the room. The boy could hardly walk, but he forced his legs to work, mindful of the sort of 'helping hand' that Boar was likely to offer. The huge oaf, his constantly moist lips glistening in the lantern-light, peered into their faces, his foetid breath causing more than one of them to cough. 'You'll all have to do, won't you?' he sneered.

He pushed them to the ladder, and they climbed into the blinding sunlight. The storm had passed and a stiff breeze was filling the large sail. An older warrior walked over to the little group as they stood, squinting and shivering. He looked them over and stared at Boar with piercing blue eyes.

'This the best you could do?' he asked. Brann recognised from his voice that he was the one the Captain had called 'Cannick'. He had seemed to be the second in command on the ship, and close to the Captain.

Boar nodded. 'Just what the Captain wanted. Can't bring better than I've got, can I?'

Cannick turned away from him. 'That you can't, Boar, that you can't.' He examined the group again. 'Anyway, they are not your concern now.' Noticing Boar's glower at the edge of his vision, he added, 'Do not worry, we should be filling the gaps for you soon enough. We may as well make use of the room in the hold and, more importantly, we need to fill our quota so we can be rid of this contract as soon as we can.'

Boar grunted something unintelligible – and probably obscene – and stomped off. Cannick stared again at the little group.

'As you may have heard,' he growled, 'we had to deal with a little incident. What you will not know, however, is that we are short of seven rowers as a result. Those of you who can manage to count further than the limits of one hand will have noticed that there are seven of you. Work out for yourselves what happens next.' He grinned. 'Your pleasure cruise is over, boys. Now you start working for your crust – at least, until we can pick up some others more physically suited to the task. And, rest assured, you will work.

'As you can see, there are three rowers to a bench. You will be put, mostly, in pairs with an experienced rower as the third member of the bench. The final one of the seven will, obviously, be with two existing rowers, but do not think that equates to an easy ride – you will just have two people to nag you rather than one.

'Now, I know some of you will be looking at the condition of the men already there, and at the state of yourselves, and noticing a little difference. You may be feeling a little puny. There is a good reason for feeling that way: you are.' They were indeed feeling more than a little inadequate compared with the lean, muscled men who were taking the chance to rest while the repaired sail did their work for them.

Cannick continued, 'You may also be wondering at the wisdom of putting two of you with just one rower. Why not put two existing men to one new one to maximise the pulling power on each oar? It is simple: it would be too easy then for the one of you to let the two other men do all the work. Even if you were trying, you wouldn't be trying as hard as you would if you felt that your efforts, or lack of them, would always be evident. If you pull your weight, however, it will not only help the ship, but it will help you, for you will develop physically more quickly. And do not worry about whether you are strong enough to cope. Rowing is more about technique and stamina than brute strength; keep pushing yourselves, and you will be surprised how long you can keep going. And it *will* get easier, believe me. You will pick up the technique quickly enough – it is not complicated.' He paused, a mischievous glint developing in his eyes. 'Oh, and do not worry yourselves about the crew coming down too hard on you if you are not trying hard enough. We will not need to. Your fellow rowers will let you know soon enough. I advise you not to let them down.'

He gestured one of the warriors forward. 'Galen will allocate you to a bench. Pay attention to what he tells you, and listen to the rower you are placed with. It is the easiest way to learn, so take the chance.'

With that, he wheeled away to attend to some other matter. Galen looked them over and slowly shook his head.

'I understand what Cannick was saying,' he said. 'But I do not share his confidence that putting two of you with only one rower is wise.' He sighed. 'But I suppose we have to fill the spaces, and cleverer men than me have decided how it is to be done. It is up to you to prove them right and me wrong. Let's go.'

He started to lead them off, but spun back as a thought occurred to him. The group bunched up at the sudden stop, and he took the chance to lean in close and speak quietly. 'One other thing, and I will tell you of it before we get into earshot of the rowers. What Cannick said about your effort was right. He has more experience than the rest of us combined, and he has seen more... let's just say, "incidents" than he probably has cause to remember.'

He nodded towards the rowers. 'These are hard men living a hard life. Just do not mess with them. Keep in mind that accidents happen at sea, and that you do not want to be one of them.'

He started off again and the seven, who had grown ever more nervous with each instruction or word of advice, followed him towards the front of the vessel. Brann watched the tall warrior, moving with a grace and assured balance that was unusual for a man of his size. It was strange: he did not like Galen – how could he? – but at least the man was fair to them and, whatever the reason for it, he seemed to care about their health and well-being. So did Cannick and the Captain; in fact, Boar, who most closely fitted any preconception that he might have had of slavers, seemed to be an exception on this ship. But what surprised him was that he did not hate them. They had murdered his family, destroyed his home, turned him into a galley slave and were intending to sell him in a slave market. On top of that, they were slavers: people who were abhorrent to normal folk. Yet, try as he might, he could not make himself hate them.

Why? Maybe he had nothing left in his life, and he was clinging to any crumb of kindness that fell his way. *Or maybe I'm going mad*, he thought with a smile.

Galen had noticed the smile. 'I see you still have spirit, boy,' he said. 'Either that, or you are monumentally stupid.

109

Either way, make the most of that smile. You are not likely to have the energy for another one for a while.'

They had stopped at the front of the ship. A group of warriors was waiting there, and one of them had started unlocking rowers from their chains at the boys' approach.

The men and boys were quickly rearranged over the front benches on each side of the aisle according to Cannick's instructions. Brann noticed that two of the benches looked new. It would have been there that the missile had struck, and he shuddered at the thought.

As they were assigned their positions, Brann realised that, while the warriors around them appeared to be lounging casually, their hands never strayed from their weapons and their eyes were watchful. The crew and slaves may have an understanding, but these were men who took no chances. They appeared more like professional soldiers than the lowlife vermin that he would have expected slavers to be.

Brann stayed close to Gerens, in the hope that he would be paired with the closest thing to a friend that he had at the moment. It worked. Galen pointed to the pair of them, ordering curtly, 'First two, in here. New boys nearest the side, rower nearest the aisle. That way, the one at the end who effectively controls the oar will be the one who knows what he is doing. That does not mean you boys can catch an easy ride – those who do not share the burden will soon be reminded of the need to do so by those around them.'

This was the third time that the boys had heard this last piece of advice, but Brann guessed that, on this occasion, it was being said for the rowers' benefit. He felt glad that the grim men he was sitting among knew that the boys had been warned, so they would not feel the need to inform the newcomers of the fact in their own fashion.

Brann and Gerens were placed with a lean, bald rower with staring eyes and swirling tattoos painting symbols and unfamiliar script across most of the exposed parts of his body, including his scalp. His smooth skin and lean build made it hard to determine his age, but Brann guessed he was at least old enough to be his father. Brann found himself wondering if he had pointed teeth and spoke in a hiss. He just seemed the sort.

The tattooed man stared at the boys appraisingly – something that was becoming familiar, but no less uncomfortable. He grinned. 'Grakk,' he said. 'And you are?'

Brann was disappointed: both Grakk's voice and teeth were perfectly normal, if respectively a little guttural and stained. And, despite the strong accent, his speech seemed, even in those few words, to be cultured and eloquent, entirely at odds with his appearance and proving the rashness of Brann's initial assessment. On reflection, though, his reaction turned to relief – the unkempt hulk of a rower on the bench in front of them was berating the red-haired youth and his companion purely on the grounds that he had been landed with a couple of puny farm boys through no fault of his own. And his threats of what would ensue if they even thought about slacking were decidedly unpalatable, to say the least.

Brann and Gerens introduced themselves and Grakk – in a formal gesture that was as incongruous in the setting of the rowing benches as it was from one who, despite his refined speech, did still resemble a nomadic savage – gripped their hands and nodded his acknowledgement of their meeting.

'Do not expect frivolous conversation,' he informed them. 'Observe diligently to learn, and work to your utmost to make use of what you learn. Here, as in life, learning is everything. In that fashion, we will all prosper. In the meantime,

111

appreciate what is in front of you.' He stared intently at Brann. 'It is indeed a glorious day. Now, however, I will sleep.'

With that, he curled up on the floor in front of the bench, closed his eyes and, in moments, appeared to be sound asleep.

They looked at each other. 'I believe we may be lucky in our companion,' Gerens said solemnly.

Before Brann could reply, the shaggy-headed rower in front of them turned round. 'Yes and no, boy,' he growled in clipped accent. 'Yes: you did not get me, and I am not as well-spoken in my instructions as he just was. No: the last man on these benches who crossed him had his throat slit from ear to ear by the morning. Left a terrible mess, it did. Of course, nobody knew who did it. It couldn't have been any of us rowers, could it? We have no means of doing something like that.' He grinned malevolently with around half the teeth that his mouth should have contained. 'Do we? Sleep well tonight.'

The pair stared at each other again. They looked down at the gently snoring Grakk, and back at one another. 'Well, chief,' said Gerens with a shrug. 'It's something to bear in mind.'

Brann stifled a giggle, the tension that had knotted his insides all of his time on the ship exaggerating his reaction. He was sure that Gerens had meant it without any humour, given that the boy's dark delivery had not wavered in the way he had said everything since their meeting. It mattered not. He was unable to totally prevent the giggling, and he bit on his sleeve in an attempt not to draw unwelcome attention to himself. Despite himself, he found that he was starting to like Gerens. His dark, practical approach to life was consistent, and consequently dependable. Brann tended to think things through, to be sure he was making the right decision; sometimes, however, it was necessary to cut to the simple truth of a situation, and Gerens was certainly the master of that approach, which Brann found, under the current circumstances, comforting. As was the boy's unfathomable decision from the moment they met to make it his mission to take Brann under his protection. Unfathomable, but, under the current circumstances, there was no earthly need to attempt to fathom it and all that was left was to accept that it was extremely handy. Handy, and comforting.

The laughter subsided, and he wiped the tears from the corners of his eyes. The boys sat quietly for a while, mindful not to disturb any of the rowers around them – especially the large one in front of them – who had followed Grakk into slumber. Their tattooed companion looked as if a raging thunderstorm would not waken him, but they felt it wiser not to risk it.

The thin boy turned around, taking care not to wake the rower on one side of him or the sallow boy on the other. 'Since we're all in the same boat...' Brann manfully resisted the urge not to giggle again. 'Sorry.' He smiled weakly. 'Since we're all in the same situation, I think it would be better if we all get on. Whatever went on between you and the old woman is not my concern. And your friend was right: I am glad it is not my concern. Any attitudes from down below could maybe be left in the hold, yes?'

Gerens shrugged and nodded. Brann, as the main target for the comments in the hold, felt awkward in his company and was more reticent about accepting it so easily. But he saw no advantage in showing open hostility; better to accept him on the surface, and be wary underneath. The smoother things ran among them, the easier it would be to cope with their ordeal. At the very least, it was one less thing to worry about.

He nodded as well. The youth introduced himself as Pedr, a metal-worker's son from a small coastal village. He was taller than Gerens, but gangly and skinny in the way of boys who had grown rapidly in height; he had not yet filled out to match it, if ever he would. He was talkative, and strong of opinion and, although that could prove irritating at times, his chatter – kept low to avoid disturbing the frightening rowers on each of their benches – at least passed the time.

After what seemed like hours but could only have been, according to the sun's progress, little more than half-an-hour, the large drum at the stern let out three thunderous bangs. With a start, Brann realised that Grakk was sitting beside them – he had gone from sound sleep to ready alertness so quickly that the boy had not seen him move from the deck.

Every one of the rowers was in position – obviously the drumbeat had been a signal to action. Flexing his arms, Grakk confirmed it. 'Make yourselves ready. We will be commencing rowing,' he said simply.

'Straight away?' Brann asked, alarmed. Now that the moment had arrived, he suddenly felt the weight of how little he knew about the activity that would be his life for the gods only knew how long.

Grakk looked at him for a moment. 'If it were "straight away", you would be rowing already.' Brann blushed. It was indisputable logic, and obvious. Grakk grinned. 'When the drum bangs three times, as it just did, you will prepare yourself. When the drum bangs twice more, you will extract the oars. Understand?'

Brann nodded, taking in the simple explanation with wide-eyed attention as if he were listening to the most complex of instructions. 'Yes, I understand,' he stammered.

Galen strode down the aisle. 'We row in fifteen minutes,' he shouted. 'First of all, the first two benches nearest the bow on each side will practise getting their oars in and out, for the sake of the new lads. The oars are the big wooden things by your side, by the way, just in case you hadn't noticed.'

Brann realised with yet more embarrassment that he had been overwhelmed by so many other things that he had not even noticed the single most important object in his new life. As the smallest on his bench, with the shortest reach, he had been placed closest to the side, where the swing of the oar would travel less. He looked to his right, and saw the oar lying flush with the side of the boat, at a slight angle. Its lower half extended out through the side of the boat via a hole that was currently sealed with a waxed wooden plug cut to fit precisely around the stowed oar to prevent sea water from splashing in around their feet or, in the case of Grakk and several others that Brann had seen, around their bodies when sleeping. The length of shaft inside the ship lay on top of the oar from the bench in front of him, and was strapped securely in place. The shaft itself was not straight, as he had expected, but had been crafted with a shallow double-curve around halfway along it to allow it to lie snugly against the boat both inside and out.

Gerens saw him looking at the oars. 'On some ships, chief, they pull them completely on board, but there is not enough room on this one for that. My father used to make me wooden models of all sorts of ships when I was little. I never suspected I would find myself sitting on the real thing.'

Galen returned from the other end of the ship, where he had been explaining to the rowers what was going to happen. He spoke again to the boys. 'Now you have had a chance to look around, listen to me. There are two things to notice: one, a plug with a handle and, two, a strap beside you holding in place the oar for the bench in front of you. You can see that the same strap extends over your own oar as an extra safeguard.'

Both Brann and Gerens looked closely at the oars. These details had not, of course, been possible on childhood models and, from this stage onwards, Gerens was as much a novice as Brann. Where the strap held the oar in place, a wide, wooden ridge protruded around the oar by the width of a man's hand; it stopped the oar slipping through the strap and, when the oar was in a rowing position, it would prevent the shaft from sliding out into the water. Looking closer at the ridge, Brann could see that a curved slot had been carved out of it to allow the oar lying on top of it to nestle against it securely. Brann determined to take care to ensure that the oar was the right way up whenever they were stowing it – as the one closest to it, he assumed that he would be held responsible if anything went wrong at that point, and he was determined not to draw attention to himself for any reason, let alone for causing problems.

'Two more things,' Galen continued. 'Those nearest the side will be responsible for undoing the strap on the oar for the bench in front of them. And, if you look at the oars again, those astute minds of yours will have noticed that the oars sit on top of one another in a way that means that they must be lifted out in a particular sequence. Now, where do you think that sequence starts?' He looked around the nervous faces. 'Yes, you guessed it: it all depends on you. The other oars cannot be positioned for rowing until you lads take yours out. Not that I want to put you under any pressure, newcomers, but you will not be popular if you fail to get it right.'

116

He clapped his hands. 'So you had better switch on now, because you have ten minutes to perfect it. When you hear the double drumbeat and the order "Oars!" you act. Immediately. The one in the middle of the bench pulls the plug and the one nearest the side releases the strap for the bench in front. The exception is the bench nearest the bow on each side – you have no one behind you to free your oar. So, in your case, the one nearest the side will jump back over the bench – don't worry, your chains will stretch – and free the oar for your bench. The middle rower will, meanwhile, be freeing the oar for the bench in front, and the rower nearest the aisle will, you will find, have already pulled the plug, so to speak.

'The one who is behind the bench will now be jumping back into his place, sliding the oar forward and swinging it over his two companions as he does so. The other two will tend to help him to swing it round into position, because you will find that you very rarely trust someone to avoid the back of your head when you have a chance to get your hands on the oar yourself and help it over.

'As soon as your oar has cleared out of the way, the next will be swung out, and so on. So you must get it right, and you must be quick, because you will be holding up the whole boat otherwise. It is not hard, but until you have done it a few times, it will seem daunting. So, now we are going to do it a few times.'

Intent on avoiding being branded inept, Brann listened with wide-eyed attention, straining to take in every word. But as soon as the large warrior had finished speaking, he realised that he could remember not a single word.

However, with Galen talking them through the process, and with the experienced rowers helping to guide them, the boys managed the procedure without over-much clumsiness, starting slowly and building up more speed by their fourth and fifth attempts. Brann was surprised by the oar – despite the fact that its size and its need for strength lent it weight, it was so well balanced that it was easily manoeuvred, even by a boy as slight as he. After falling ignominiously when he tripped over the bench in the haste of his first attempt to get to the strap behind him – causing much merriment among the watching rowers – he began to manage the sequence of taking out and stowing the oars, and even started to enjoy himself. Especially since, when he had fallen, he had taken the opportunity to slip the damn knife from his waistband and ram it point-first into the underside of his bench. There would still be danger if it were discovered, but at least it was not directly attributable to him any more. The sense of relief lifted his spirits and he attacked his work with increased vigour.

He was also surprised at the shallow angle needed for the oar to dip its blade into the water, until he realised how low they were sitting in the vessel. The area below decks was under both the Captain's cabin and the part immediately forward of that, where the deck was stepped higher, while the rowers were sitting relatively close to the waterline – hence the need for the plugs in the holes when they were not rowing. When the oars were being used, Brann assumed, they would just have to endure the discomfort of any water that made its way in around their feet.

'Right, that will have to do,' Galen called. 'Catch your breath before we try rowing. Make the most of the rest – believe me, you'll need it.'

Gerens wiped the stinging sweat away from his eyes and squinted at Brann. 'Well, at least you gave them a bit of entertainment.'

Brann grimaced, rubbing his shin ruefully. 'True,' he agreed between heavy breaths. 'But I'd rather do it a little less painfully.'

Brann turned to Grakk. 'How did you think we did?'

Grakk recognised the eager sincerity in the words, but did not allow it to soften his assessment. 'You are still too slow,' he said evenly.

'Oh, right,' Bann said, crestfallen. 'Have you any advice for us?'

Grakk's gaze never flickered, nor did his neutral tone. 'Try not to fall over.' A glimmer of a smile did play around the corners of his mouth, however.

'Thank you,' Brann said. 'But I think I managed to work that one out for myself.'

The tattooed rower ignored the comment. 'Listen to me, and listen carefully. You are trying too hard. Admirable in its intent, but not helpful in its execution. As in life, technique is all; without it, power is nothing. When we row, I will control the movement of the oar. You will follow that movement and add to it what effort you can. Nothing more, nothing less. Do you understand?' They nodded. He pointed to the bench in front. The boys saw that it was solid at the back from the seat to the floor. 'You will observe that the benches are open at the front for storage and, indeed, for those rowers who can fit there when the weather deteriorates sufficiently to warrant it. However, more pertinent to us just now is that they are closed at the back to allow you to brace your feet when you are rowing.' Oblivious to, or perhaps ignoring, the boys' open bewilderment as they still struggled to equate his barbaric appearance with his cultured speech, he placed his feet against the back of the next bench and mimed pulling an oar. 'You will push with your feet and pull with your arms.

119

Understand?' They nodded again. Grakk looked doubtfully at the length of Brann's legs. 'You will perhaps require to devise an alternative method.'

Brann was ready with a cheeky retort as he bridled at the slight on his lack of height, but the intense stare from the tiny pupils amid yellow-green irises that showed white all the way around reminded him of Grakk's less-than-savoury reputation. The hesitation allowed common sense to block his hot-headed reaction, and he realised that Grakk was being coldly practical, rather than insulting. He chided himself: until recent events, he had been particularly slow to anger, and he was not finding much to like in the surly temper he seemed to have developed. It was not so much an increase in that emotion, but rather a lack of any desire to hold back in expressing himself. He was caring little about anything, including the consequences of his actions or words, and it was only tempered by his desire to avoid injury, or worse.

He nodded, not knowing how he could address the problem of reach, but aware that he must address it if he were to put in enough effort to avoid being seen as a slacker. That was the last outcome he wanted; he had long since decided that the best way to survive – and to find a way out of this nightmare – was to draw as little attention to himself as possible.

The drum banged twice with insistence, interrupting their conversation, and a shout of 'Oars!' rang out. Brann hesitated, then remembered with a start that everyone on his side of the ship was waiting on him to carry out the order. Grakk already had the plug removed, and Gerens was working on the strap. Galen, who was still beside them, bellowed 'Now!' in his ear and he jerked into movement, scrabbling over the back of the bench and throwing himself at the strap as they had practised.

120

His hesitation had been for the merest of moments, but he was furious with himself as he saw that it had allowed the equivalent benches on the other side to start moving the oars ahead of them. The new rowers swung their oars into position in what they thought was a quick time – and then watched in astonishment as, with a thunderous rattle, the rest of the oars slipped into place in a sequence so rapid that it took their breath away.

'Now you see how it should be done,' Galen bawled. 'You have something to aim for next time.' They felt severely inadequate.

The drummer let out another double-beat and Brann felt himself being pulled forward as Grakk, in perfect unison with the other rowers, readied the oar for the first pull. Almost immediately, the drum sounded again and, as one, the oars dipped into the sea and pulled smoothly through the water. Remembering Grakk's advice, Brann tried desperately to reach the other bench with his legs but found, as Grakk had predicted and as he, within himself, had really known, that the distance was too great. By now, even though the drummer was setting a slow pace, they were completing their second stroke and Brann, off balance and edging forward on his own bench, found his arms being pulled back and forth by the oar rather than adding any effort to the movement. Grakk glanced across at him. Brann blushed and, starting to panic, felt tears of frustration welling up. In desperation, he placed his feet flat on the deck and pulled back with as much strength as he could muster. The effort lifted him off the bench, and he found that adding his body weight to the pulling motion allowed him to compensate in part for not being able to brace himself against the other bench. He started to incorporate the movement properly into his rowing action and Grakk, satisfied that the boy had adapted to the situation, turned back without expression.

Using his technique for a few strokes, Brann felt that the work was not as strenuous as he had expected. After around fifteen strokes, however, he realised that his opinion had been premature. His hands were burning, his legs were quivering and his back felt as if it would never again straighten. Even arms and shoulders built on a daily routine of lifting and carrying heavy bags of grain and flour felt as if all reserves of strength had drained from them. His breathing became searing in his chest and so loud in his ears that it would have rendered the creaking, splashing, grunting and drumming inaudible if his concentration on merely maintaining his movement had not already blocked out all outside distractions.

Sweat ran in a series of rivulets down his face, enough of it easing into his eyes to make them sting and forcing him to squeeze them tight shut; he did not need them open anyway to perform the repetitive and all-consuming motion as he forced everything he had into keeping his arms and legs moving and preventing his feet from slipping on the deck.

His arms began to seize up and he began to lean back further with each stroke to compensate for the reduced arm movement. In doing so, his back quickly grew more painful, but he forced himself on, mindful of his ignominious start to the exercise. Time seemed to stand still as he focused entirely on repeating the movement over and over again. His head was swimming and his breathing ragged, and he felt that the only thing preventing him from passing out was the thought of the other rowers' reaction to such a sign of weakness.

The rowers stopped. He had been so intent on keeping going that he had not noticed the drumbeat to signal the cessation. Galen's voice rang out. 'Ship oars and stow.'

The oars were drawn in, in sequence. Without instruction, the rowers in the last few benches before the boys slowed their action to allow the exhausted newcomers to bring in their oars without too much panic or mishap.

Squinting through stinging eyes, Brann attended to the strap with difficulty. His palms were raw and burning and his fingers were unwilling to move from the shape they had formed when gripping the oar. He wondered, as he slumped against the side of the ship, too exhausted to do anything other than gasp for breath, how long it would be before the skin was rubbed right off his hands. After several long moments, he found the strength to wipe the sweat from his eyes, but the effort did little to clear his blurred vision and he sat still, waiting for his head to stop spinning. To his surprise – and gratification – Gerens looked almost as exhausted as he felt. Obviously physical strength counted for little when those muscles were faced with such unfamiliar activity. Gerens started to slump against Grakk, but a baleful stare from the rower changed his mind rapidly and he collapsed instead against Brann.

'That was the longest half-hour of my life,' Gerens gasped. Brann could only nod weakly.

Galen strode towards them. 'Well, lads,' he said jovially. 'Not bad for ten minutes' work.' Brann and Gerens stared at each other, aghast. Grakk looked amused. 'We will take half-an-hour's rest, then another ten minutes' rowing. After another break, we will build up to fifteen, then twenty.' He caught the identical horror-stricken expressions of the new rowers around him. 'Think yourselves lucky that you have started on a day with a following wind, when we can use the sail to fill in the gaps and make up for the slow pace you are setting. If we had needed to row all day, you would not have enjoyed the luxury of being broken in gently, and you would just have had to find a way to survive.'

He passed a small earthenware pot to Brann. Inside was a pale paste. 'Take some, then pass the pot to the other new boys,' Galen instructed. 'Smear it on your palms and fingers and let it dry in after each session of rowing for the first week. After that you'll be fine.'

He headed back up the aisle, chuckling at the looks that had sprung to seven faces when he had revealed the short span of time they had rowed. It had not seemed possible that they could have seemed more stunned, but they had managed it.

Grakk turned to his companions. 'You,' he looked at Gerens, 'worked hard.' Brann's breath caught in his throat as the staring eyes turned his way. He had let them down. 'Your start was deplorable, but the fault was not yours – we will attend to that. Do not concern yourself. You also tried hard; I like that.'

The boys nodded weakly. Grakk indicated the paste in Brann's hands. 'Do what the man said. It will work. It is made from the sap of a tree that grows in my homeland. It is mostly utilised for its soothing qualities, something I am sure you will appreciate at this time. But what you will find even more useful over the coming days is that, with regular application, it also aids the toughening of the skin. It is one of my country's two main exports. One day, I will tell you of the other.' Without another word, he slipped to the deck and sat with his back resting against the bench. Gerens rolled his head around to look at Brann, and started to say something, but gave up as the effort became too much and, eyes closed, flopped back against him. Brann was left pressed against the side of the boat by his weight, with little option but to remain there – not that he had any intention of doing anything more strenuous than breathing in any case. His spirits had been lifted, however, by Grakk's unexpected approval. If they put in the effort, the tattooed rower seemed willing to offer them consideration and, however long Brann's ordeal at the oar lasted before he could escape, it seemed as if he might survive it. If he could survive the effort of today.

The break seemed too short. When the order came to row again, they felt as if their stiff limbs would be unable to move to their full extent. Within a few strokes, however, the boys were surprised to discover that their muscles were easing enough to allow them proper movement after all.

And so the day progressed. They rowed and rested as Galen had said, six times in all, during the three hours until lunch – then repeated the programme in the afternoon, but in reverse, easing down to the shorter periods of rowing at the end of the day. During the second stint of rowing, Gerens, and then the others, had noticed the technique that Brann had been forced to adopt and copied it, still pressing their feet against the bench in front that they, unlike Brann, could reach, but also lifting themselves clear of their own bench as they pulled back. The men beside them said nothing, but exchanged glances, their expressions eloquent enough to demonstrate that, while they noticed the physical difference in the contribution the newcomers were making, it was the attitude that mattered more to them. They were showing that they were eager to maximise their help. Whether that effort was born of natural character or fear of the rowers, they did not care – it was enough that it was there. The new rowers would quickly grow stronger, but only if they worked. And, already, they were showing that they wanted to do so.

By the time dusk settled over the sea, the trainee rowers had barely enough energy to eat. Encouraged or, in some cases, forced by the men around them, they took the food but, immediately afterwards, every one of the seven was slumped and sound asleep. The men around them were amused – it had been a light day's work for them, as they were used to periods where they needed to row for hours with breaks only for meals and, for a few minutes, for water – but no more than amused. Each one of them could remember, even over a distance of, in some cases, a decade or more, their first day on the rowing bench.

The boys were awakened at dawn by a drenching of shockingly cold water. Spluttering, Brann and Gerens jerked up to find a chuckling Grakk watching them with interest.

'Good morning, young fellows. That is both your wake-up call and your daily wash. Rub it over you,' he grinned, vigorously rubbing over himself the water that had also been thrown over him. The boys gaped at him, still gasping for breath. All along the aisle, warriors were hurling large buckets of water over the rowers, although none of these seasoned men was still sleeping by the time that the water had reached their row.

'We are blessed with plenty of fresh water just now,' Grakk explained, noting their confusion at the profligacy with the precious resource. 'When there is plenty, we wash. It keeps the salt off the skin, and the sun will not burn as much. Although this may not seem quite so relevant in the feeble sunshine, remember this especially if you ever row in the waters around the coast of the Great Southern Empire. Here, on certain days, the sun can be hot, but not compared with there. There it can murder men.' He gestured to remind them of his previous instruction. 'Go on, young chaps. Rub the water over you. It will not harm you, you know.'

The boys copied him as well as they could. As he did so, Brann shifted on the bench and his foot knocked against something. He looked down to discover a wooden block nailed to the back of the bench in front. He glanced across and saw Grakk watching his reaction with interest.

The man nodded at the block. 'For your feet, boy with short legs. One should not fret about problems, but should look at how they may be addressed. We are defined not by the mistakes we make, but by the reactions we have to them; not by the problems we face, but by the solutions we find to them. In life, learning is everything.'

Gerens looked impressed. 'I like that. Did a great philosopher come up with it?'

'Absolutely,' Grakk nodded, his face and tone solemn. 'Me.'

Brann tried his feet against it, and found it to be a perfect distance. 'Did you do this?' he asked Grakk.

The rower shrugged. 'Me?' he said innocently.

Brann pushed on it again, miming an oar stroke and wincing slightly as his aching muscles objected. Despite the pain, it felt good to be able to follow the correct movement. 'How did you manage it?' he asked in astonishment.

Grakk shrugged again, holding up his manacles. 'Did I say that I was responsible for it? I am chained up, am I not? I could not wander away and fetch tools.' He grinned mischievously. 'Perhaps Boar misses you. Perhaps Boar did it.'

Brann snorted. 'Yeah, and maybe I am a mermaid. You did it, or had it done, though the gods alone know how.' He smiled. 'Thank you, Grakk.'

Grakk just shrugged once again, and turned away, slipping onto the deck to sit in his customary position against the bench. Try as he might, however, he could not hide the fact that the boy's appreciation had pleased him.

The day passed with the periods of rowing increasing further, as they did the following day, and the one after that. The days, and then the weeks, ran into one another and Brann found himself silently thanking Grakk with each stroke of the oar. The addition of the block, although a simple measure, made a huge difference to his contribution and he was able to improve at the same rate as the other six. Soon the newcomers had settled into the routine. Oars were unstrapped and swung into position – and stowed away again – almost by second nature, and almost as quickly as the other rowers. The work was still exhausting, but Brann was surprised how quickly he had become used to it, despite the increase in the amount of rowing, day by day. He was still drained at the end of every day, and sore at the start of the next, but he managed. After just a few weeks of the activity, he found that, once he settled into a rhythm, he felt as if he could row all day. And he soon found that the physical activity helped him to avoid the morbid and morose thoughts that dogged his quieter moments. Thoughts of his family, of his home, of his brother, of a life now distant.

The days drifted past, merging into one another. Brann found, curiously, that the repetitive nature of the rowing did not bore him, as he had expected it would – and as it might have done previously. Instead, it was soothing, a physical activity within which he could lose himself from his recent horrors. It suited the change in his character: as time passed, he found himself becoming more withdrawn, contrasting starkly with the gregarious, outgoing, cheerful child he had been before. He now preferred to observe others, rather than join in their conversations. He did not lack interest in what was being said, but rather listened intently, becoming watchful of everything spoken or done around him, feeling almost analytical about his surroundings. Gerens's companionship was comfortable, and Grakk seemed satisfied with the continuing levels of effort shown by the pair and seemed, as far as they could tell, to be warming to them – although it never manifested itself overtly in any way beyond occasional words of advice or, even more occasionally, of approval. Brann's two companions were not among the great conversationalists on the benches and, for that, he was grateful. He had wondered if they would think his reticence rude, but as they proved to be of few words themselves, it did not seem to be an issue.

And so they rowed on, and Brann rowed with them. Even the brief interlude when they put a party ashore to seek replacements for the seven of them who had been brought from the hold, rowing out of sight and returning the same evening to retrieve the men and their captives, had proved little distraction for the boy. He had seen the bedraggled and bewildered group brought on board but, although he knew vividly what they were experiencing, he felt little empathy; he felt little at all, other than a need to fulfil his duties and sleep.

They travelled south, and then – as far as Brann could reckon – roughly east before turning south again. It took them, he guessed, around six weeks, although it was impossible to be even close to accurate. The ship moored in a port that Brann neither knew the name of, nor cared. What did it matter? The boys from the hold were led, blinking and staggering, to the dockside and were taken away, a chain of head-bowed misery and bewilderment. Brann and his six companions readied themselves to follow them, but, when Cannick returned to the ship, he conferred briefly with the Captain before approaching the young boys on the benches.

'You lads are no longer our guests, but are now residents. A new contract has come our way, so we have sold the delivery of those other boys onto some other captain, who will complete their journey south to the slavemasters who commissioned this. This port is a staging post rather than a market, so we can't buy any strapping oarsmen of experience to replace you... so we all lose out. We are stuck with you puny boys, and you miss out on the sunshine of the Empire. Welcome to our happy family.'

As Cannick's boots banged back down the gangplank, Brann turned to Gerens. 'Why change to a new contract? What's the point?'

'Money.' Gerens looked at him. 'Isn't that always the point? They can make more with several short trips in the time that it would take to sail to the Empire and back.'

Brann looked over the rooftops of the low buildings in the port town, his eyes towards the south. 'I would have liked to have got closer to these slavemasters. I have a score to settle with them on behalf of my brother.'

Gerens snorted. 'Brann the Avenger.' He stretched his back, trying to ease several weeks of combining intense activity with cramped rest. 'You can forget that. Every slave has thought of that, brother's death or not. Never happens. Even if you succeeded, which wouldn't happen, you would die anyway.'

A cold laugh burst harshly from Brann. 'What would that matter? I have nothing anyway. At least I would have achieved something.'

'You would have achieved nothing.'

Grakk opened his eyes but refrained from uncurling from his position on the deck beside them. 'Your friend is correct. You would be seeking revenge on a system, a way of life, not a single man. The rest is just a series of actions, reactions and consequences over countless time and people. What we call "life". That is what killed your brother. That, and Boar's crossbow.

'Think to your own life. What has happened, has happened. Those who are gone, are gone. You are here, and this is your life. These men are not the worst masters you could have. The blood of the pirates they took this ship from is still in the timbers, but so is the blood of many a slave who served under that previous crew. Be thankful you were not on these benches last year. But these men, they are more used to ships rowed by freed men. We are still slaves because they can afford to feed us, but not to pay us as equals. And because, for us, that is what is.'

Gerens stood and spat over the side into the still water of the harbour. 'I told you. Money.'

The new cargo – non-human, this time – was brought on board in crates and was stowed below decks, presumably in the small hold that had so recently been a very temporary home for Brann. Gossip spread around the rowers that the cargo was linen cloth from Qotan, far to the south, and that the merchant needed it delivered as soon as possible to a destination called Cardallon on the east coast of somewhere called Salaria to avoid reneging on a deal that threatened to ruin his business. Brann reflected that, weeks previously, such news would have held no interest to him. When your world was restricted by metal links to the few rowing benches around you, however, the gossip was high entertainment.

As the last of the food and fresh water was brought on board and the mooring ropes were cast off, however, it was clear that the nature of the cargo had meant nothing more to the men at the oars than passing curiosity – it mattered not to them what the ship carried, for the oars would rise and dip the same way regardless.

Now he knew what he was.

He was a galley slave.

Chapter 5

The high-backed chair felt better than he would ever let any of them know. He'd had it moved to what he considered the perfect position: close enough to the balcony to give him a fairly widespread view; but at just the right angle that it was always in the shade. He'd had them put it there shortly after he moved – was moved – into these apartments, and he'd never seen the need since to have it any other way. He sat there when he needed to think. All of his days now, he had time to think, but the occasions when he needed to do so were fewer than he liked. But since he had returned from his summons, he had been blessed with such a time. During the discussion, he had given and received, but he had taken from it far more than he had offered – he had been careful about that, as ever. It was part of his nature; he had learnt it longer ago than he could remember.

So there were stirrings in the north. There were stories of incidents unusual even among the ungodly practices of the barbarians. The debate had turned to matters of greater import: trade with near neighbours, the forthcoming Empire Games; a slowing in the supply of slaves. Condescendingly, they had enquired his opinion on the machinations of the *near neighbour's court. His opinion must have been valued, or he would not have been there. But it would not do for them to give it openly any credence. Far more acceptable to make it look as if it was an unfortunate necessity to give the past its place, a consequence of manners more than anything else. The matters in the north were treated with disdain and disinterest: would the mighty elephant pause to wonder about the squabbles of the ants around its feet as it passed?*

But the matters in the north were precisely what the fools should have found most interesting. They presented an opportunity. And if the fools failed to realise that, then they allowed the chance to exploit the opportunity, in an altogether different way, to fall to him.

He sat in his chair. He envisaged possible scenarios. He predicted outcomes for each, and he thought of possible scenarios ensuing from those outcomes. And so on.

And as he plotted, he felt young again. And he sat, his eyes on one scene while his mind watched another. He smiled. The chair felt good.

****

They retraced their passage north, and Brann became more watchful.

He knew he was heading in the direction of his home and it was simple logic that, if he were to escape, it would be best to do so with as little distance as possible to have to travel afterwards. How he might escape, though, he had no idea, for the chains were solid and the men who watched over them were as hardened professionals as he could imagine. But he could not prevent himself from thinking that, somehow, a chance would come.

On the first day out of the unnamed port, Galen walked among them. 'Well done, lads,' he said. 'You have adapted well, and under more pressure than you deserved. But that is life in the world outside your cosy little villages, and you have learnt a lesson. Just make sure you keep learning it, and do not slack off, thinking you are old hands already – if the men you are sitting with made you shoulder an equal share of the effort, you would know all about it. I do not know how much longer you will be needed here, but you have this voyage at least to contend with, so keep up what you have been doing and you will do all right.'

Brann was sure that they had been contributing latterly more than Galen was admitting, but guessed that the warrior was concerned that they would become blasé and felt that it was better for the boys that they were warned in advance by him rather than 'advised' afterwards by the rowers around them that they could have been trying harder. In any case, the relentless rowing had begun to alter their physiques already – all of them came from a rural background and had been fairly fit and strong to begin with, but the work at the benches had toned their muscles and broadened their shoulders and backs, and was continuing to do so. This had combined with their adoption of Brann's rowing technique to mean that, Brann suspected, they were contributing more than Galen would wish to say.

In the meantime, however, the wind had picked up behind them and the sail was unfurled. Once it filled, the oars were drawn in and Brann reached under the bench, drew out his father's cloak that now also served as a blanket or towel as necessity demanded, pulled it over him and, in the manner of sailors and soldiers around the world, dozed off without hesitation.

The ship travelled north, with the coast just beyond the horizon to their left, for around four weeks, as the two boys' combined reckonings agreed. They dropped anchor one cloudy morning in a small bay that was deserted but for a small road leading through lofty sand dunes fringed with whispering long grasses. As the crates were taken ashore, the rower in front of them turned to say that he recognised the cove from his time on a previous ship. It was hidden from any approach, by land or sea, until you were almost upon it, he said, and as such was one favoured by smugglers. Since the current business was legitimate, however, they agreed that it must have been chosen on this occasion for convenience, for its proximity to the village that was the cargo's destination.

That having been decided, they settled down, as usual, to rest, having rowed through the night, and were soon lulled into grateful slumber by the gentle slaps of the water on the hull and the repetitive hiss of the waves on the loose sand of the beach.

Brann wakened late in the morning as a buzz of unrest ran around the ship. The small party who had been detailed to carry out the mundane delivery task was returning, and it was clear that all was not well. Three of the four men were pulling the small handcart that they had used to carry the crates, and they were moving in the manner of men who wanted to be back among comrades as soon as possible. As they drew closer, it could be seen that the cart bore the fourth man, who appeared to be still alive, though barely.

The order was given to ready the oars and they edged the ship as close to the shore as they could without risking becoming grounded. The men dropped the handles of the cart and pulled the injured man into the shallows, dragging him on his back and keeping his face clear of the water as they waded with a ferocity that bordered on panic. They neared the ship and were forced to swim, with two of them supporting the injured man. Their sense of urgency was infectious and ropes were thrown to them to help speed their progress. The move was justified as, in a scene that eerily mimicked the time when Brann's group had been brought aboard, a group of riders stormed onto the beach. This time, however, those on the ship were not so nonchalant: the vessel and the swimming men were closer to the shore and, more importantly, within arrow range.

Brann's side of the boat was closer to the riders, and he felt distinctly uncomfortable at the thought that he might be expected to sit and wait for arrows to fall. As if reading his mind, Grakk – and the rowers on each bench down that side of the ship – reached across and flipped up a thick, square board attached to the inner side of the vessel by a pair of hinges. As he lifted it, a pole swung down from underneath and he used it to brace the board so that it angled upwards and inwards.

'I don't believe it to be heresy to say that we cannot rely on the gods' good grace to watch over us all of the time. A little protection from arrows never goes amiss,' Grakk explained dryly.

Brann had caught only a brief glimpse of the riders before the protective board had been raised. But he had seen enough to catch his breath with fear – hard black masks, distorted into the most ghoulish of faces, could not conceal a malevolence that somehow radiated from the eyes of the masks and the hoods of the crimson cloaks. Peering between the boards – the folly of the move did not occur to him until later – he saw the swimming men approaching, disturbing terror etched into their battle-hardened faces.

The swimmers were only a few yards from the ship, two of them holding their companion's head above the water as they dragged him and grabbed for the ropes. Several riders had scrambled from their mounts and arrows arced towards the frantically splashing men, spearing into the water with a plopping sound that seemed ridiculous in contrast to the dire danger they posed. The ship's archers replied in kind, but the movement of the ship in the choppy shallows made their task much harder than that of the men on the beach who, in any case, seemed oblivious to the peril, so eager were they to draw blood from their prey. The sound of their eager snarls and guttural words speared across the water, adding a macabre element to an already nightmarish scenario.

An arrow struck one of the swimming warriors square in the back, and he stiffened, his eyes wide, losing his grip on the wounded man before sinking face down into the water. The third swimmer unceremoniously pushed his lifeless body clear and, grabbing his semi-conscious comrade, he dragged on one of the ropes and helped to pull him the last few feet to the ship. The three were pulled quickly over the side near to the bow and, even before they were fully on board, the order was given to start rowing. The rowers were only too happy to comply and the ship leapt forward, picking up speed as they gratefully angled away from the beach. A scatter of arrows followed them, most falling short. Two reached the ship, thumping into the aisle between the rowers, and one embedded itself, quivering, in the board above the bench in front. Brann, Gerens and Pedr paled in unison, and redoubled their efforts. The seasoned rowers, however, seemed unperturbed and worked impassively, as if there was little more to contend with than a few irritating flies. The ship surged forward and, in the space of surprisingly few strokes, they were out of range of the bowmen.

The Captain, who had come to the bow, regardless of the danger, to oversee the efforts to bring the men on board, turned to Cannick. 'Tell the drummer to set a more sensible pace, and have the steersman head us over the horizon while we deal with this.' The veteran nodded and strode back up the aisle.

As they adjusted to the slightly slower drumbeat and moved steadily out to sea, Brann flicked glances over his shoulder at the group behind him. The two men who had been swimming were exhausted, but unscathed. They sat, heads thrown back and eyes shut, dragging air into heaving chests as water formed an expanding puddle around them.

Their companion was faring less well. A warrior tended him, apparently a medic from the efficient and assured way that he was approaching the task. The man's breathing was shallow and irregular, and his eyelids fluttered. Blood soaked the front and left side of the heavy tunic and leather jerkin that were being cut from him, despite any cleansing effects that the sea may have had. He lay still most of the time, but occasionally convulsed with a cough of pain.

The Captain crouched beside the wounded warrior and the man working to save him, watching the medic's examinations intently. The blood-soaked man convulsed once again and coughed twice, a rough, guttural sound. Blood, ominously frothy, bubbled from his lips.

The medic paused. He looked up at the Captain and gently shook his head, but the black-clad man had already determined as much for himself. He stood, and gestured to the medic to do the same, unsure if the wounded man could hear them if they stayed close. 'Just make him as comfortable as you can,' he said quietly, his face tight as if he were trying to mask his emotions.

The medic nodded and took a couple of small leaves from a pouch at his waist. He rubbed them between his fingers until they crumbled, and placed the fragments on the stricken man's tongue. Within seconds, the warrior had calmed noticeably and his breathing became more even as his eyes unfocused. The medic caught Brann's gaze and said, 'Not long now, boy. But at least he will feel no pain.'

Brann felt horror and fascination simultaneously. He was unable to tear his attention away from the tableau beside him. The warrior's breathing became slower until Brann realised that it had stopped altogether. Brann rowed on, unsure of his feelings.

The medic closed the dead man's eyes and moved beside the Captain, who was standing, hands resting on the side of the ship, staring at the receding coastline. 'Captain,' he said softly. 'That's him.'

The tall man took a deep breath and nodded without shifting his gaze. Ostensibly, he appeared to betray no emotion, but he was close enough to Brann for the boy to see his fingers tighten on the rail until his knuckles stood out white. He stood like that for several long moments and Cannick, who had quietly come forward after having been busy at the stern, stood back from him, watching attentively. The Captain loosened his grip and slapped the rail once with both palms, as if to close an event.

Without turning, he said, 'Cannick, give him to the sea, please.'

If the grey-haired veteran was surprised that the Captain was aware of his presence, he did not show it. He quickly and quietly organised the medic and another warrior to remove the dead man's weapons – a ready supply of good-quality arms was essential to survival on a ship such as this – leaving him with only his sword for the passage to the afterlife. They wrapped him in a canvas sheet and tied it tightly around him. Once they were finished, and without a pause, they slipped the body over the side and into the sea. One man traced in the air the symbol of Akat-Mul – his culture's name for the god of death who was both guard and guide on the road to the afterlife – and it was done. There was no ceremony, there were no words of remembrance; each man had his own memories of both of their comrades who had died, and his own thoughts at this time. As warriors, they gave, and asked, no more.

The Captain turned to the two men who were left from the party that had gone ashore.

'Tell me,' he said.

Both men started to speak at the same time, and stopped. They looked at each other and the younger one nodded to the other, deferring to his more experienced companion, a stocky man of average height whose black, heavy beard was criss-crossed with the hairless lines of at least half-a-dozen scars.

'It was pure bad fortune, Captain,' the exhausted man started, shaking his head. 'The worst fortune. There seems to be some minor war in progress. The whole area is crawling with soldiers. We found our way to the village without a problem, but we were ambushed by a scouting party just short of it. We did not manage to kill them all, but the one who survived looked as if he would die of his wounds soon enough so, not wishing to linger onshore any longer than we had to, we left him dragging himself away and headed into the village to make the delivery. Unfortunately, the dying man chose not to oblige, and we spotted him upright and managing a fast stumble, so we did not want to waste any time in case he raised help. By this time, Erik was forced to admit that the injuries he had sustained were worse than he had wanted to say, and we had to use the cart to bring him back. The rest you saw, and we made it here.' His face tightened. 'Not soon enough for Erik, though, was it?'

The Captain nodded. 'You could not have done more. Hakar, too, in taking that arrow was just running out of the luck we all rely on every time we fight, no more. There is no blame on your part. Get some food then rest as long as you want.' He paused. 'You delivered the goods, though?'

The man nodded. His leader started towards the stern, but was stopped by the warrior. 'Captain, there's more.'

His exasperation at not having been given the full story was magnified by the feeling of having watched two of his men die. 'What is it?' he snapped. Then he saw the pain in the man's eyes as the stocky warrior found it a struggle to begin. 'Take your time, Egil,' he added more gently.

'We delivered the goods to the village, but not to the merchant,' he started hesitantly.

The Captain frowned. 'That is not good. We took on a contract, and if we want to work, we have to fulfil our duties to any man who is relying on us to keep his business alive.'

Egil grunted. 'I don't think he has to worry about concluding this deal, Captain.'

The tall man frowned. 'The village was empty?'

The man shook his head. 'Of life, yes. But death – oh, it was full of that. Every person had been slaughtered. *Every* person. The entire village. Men, women, even the tiniest children.' He shook his head, clearly shaken. 'I've never seen its like, Captain.'

His leader looked at him sharply. 'Never? You have seen much over the years, Egil, with me and before, that none of us would care too much to talk about. Are you sure?'

The warrior stared up at the Captain, his eyes haunted. 'Oh, I am sure, my lord.' Brann started. He had not heard the Captain referred to as nobility before. But he concentrated on keeping his rowing normal, hoping to draw little enough attention to his eavesdropping so that he could continue to listen.

The warrior eased himself to his feet and spat viciously over the side as if trying to rid himself of something distasteful and disgusting. Staring over the waves, he continued, his voice low. 'It was brutal. No, worse than brutal. We have all seen things, as you say – the gods know, we have all had to do things we would rather wipe from our consciences, because we have had no option. That is the way of the warrior, like it or not. But this...' He paused, his breathing heavy as he struggled with the effects of the scenes in his mind. The Captain said nothing, not wanting to pressurise him. The warrior slapped the rail, as if angry at himself for losing composure. He cleared his throat. 'It was savagery, pure savagery. Beasts would not have left such a scene, never mind men. These people – nothing more threatening than farmers, merchants and their families, mark you – these people had been ripped apart. I mean, literally, ripped apart.'

The younger warrior must have been struggling with the same images, but the sound of them put into words was too much for his self-control and he lurched to the rail and vomited.

The Captain frowned. 'You usually have a stronger stomach than that, Philippe. You are not a newcomer to combat.'

The man hung his head, though it seemed more from the weariness of carrying such heavy memories than any hint of shame at his reaction. 'This was not combat, Captain. This was not even a one-sided massacre, or mass executions. This was the scattered remains of people whose flesh had been torn from them, whose limbs had been ripped away, whose heads had been pulled – not cut – pulled from their shoulders. And...' He started shaking violently. 'And the babies, they... they...'

The shaking increased and Egil gripped him by the arm. In an almost tender gesture, the Captain laid an arm around his shoulders and steered him towards the stern. 'Go see Cannick,' he said softly. 'You need food and rest, and we are going to be at sea for a while, now, so – weather and pirates allowing – you will have a chance to enjoy both.' He nodded to the medic to accompany the man and watched his heavy-footed progress to the door that led below decks. He turned to Egil. 'What was he trying to say?' His voice had lost his tenderness, and was as coldly grim as the north wind. 'I am sorry to subject you to this, but I must know what you saw if I am to decide our course from here.'

'I know, Captain, I know,' Egil said, his voice as bleak as his lord's. 'But it was like arriving in hell, with all its evils, and then discovering that all that you found there was just an anteroom before the doors opened to horrors beyond our imaginations.' Avoiding the Captain's eyes, he stared across the swell of the sea; it was incongruously peaceful compared with the scenes that were being described. He fixed his gaze on the sparkling swell, speaking in tones that were forcibly measured.

'The men had died trying to protect the women and children; that much was obvious from where they fell. The women had been rounded up, and taken into a large barn, a grain store that was only about a quarter full: a solid enough building with rough stone walls. They threw ropes over the beams above and tied them to the women's wrists, hoisting them until only their toes supported them. They slit their bellies, letting their entrails spill out. But they knew the women would not die at once. They did not wish them to, although the women must have prayed for the release of death.' He paused, his voice cracking slightly. He cleared his throat. The Captain stared at him in silence, his face a tight, blank mask. 'Because they brought in the babes and killed them before their mothers' eyes. They took them, little ones of five years or so, right down to mites that could not even crawl, and the bastards swung them by the ankles and dashed their heads against the wall. Some of them were smashed over and over, far beyond what was needed for death. They just dropped their little bodies at the foot of the wall and went for another one. The pile was as high as my chest.' His voice was cracking again, but he ploughed on unaware, lost in the story that had been so easy for the party to read from the aftermath of the slaughter. 'Can you imagine what it must have been like, Captain? Horror more than any of us could understand was still on those women's faces when we found their bodies hanging there. And think what the little ones must have felt like, those who could see what was coming their way.'

The Captain put a hand on his shoulder. 'You have seen too much, Egil. More than any man deserves to. Get as much rest as you need. And come to see me any time you need to.'

The man turned slowly and directed eyes filled with pain at the taller man. A single tear had traced, unnoticed, a trail down the grime on his cheek. 'That's not even the worst of it, Captain,' he said, his voice a hoarse whisper. He gripped his leader's arm. 'Do you know what they did when they were finished? Do you know what we found? On the floor, facing

144

the women, were the remains of food and drink. They sat there, Captain, and they ate a meal. They ate and watched the women die, watching these women who had just been forced to witness the slaughter of their infants. They enjoyed it, Captain, the bastards actually did it for fun. Can you see that?' He wiped his brow with his sleeve and shook his head in disbelief. 'Can you believe that? Some of the women must have died from blood loss, or maybe their hearts gave out. Others had their throats cut – I don't know if they wanted to make sure they were dead before they left, or if they just got tired of the screaming. Either way, the only mercy of the day was that none of them survived to live with those memories. Some mercy that, is it not, Captain?'

His leader gently prised the warrior's fingers from his forearm. 'Let us hope that the gods are helping them now more than any man could,' he said softly.

Egil cleared his throat. He still spoke quietly. 'The gods... that's the thing. It was a scene of sickening horror, but it was methodical, ordered, like something religious. But no god I know would accept offerings such as those.

'We sent their souls onwards as best we could. We fired the barn, giving them a pyre, but the smoke alerted those who had destroyed the village. We knew the chances were high that it would, but we could not leave those people like that.' His voice was stronger as he insisted, 'You do know, Captain, that I did not run back to the ship because I feared these savages. It was only that the numbers were uneven, and vastly so. Our deaths would have served no purpose.'

'I know well that you are no coward, Egil. You will never need to convince me of that,' the Captain said softly.

The man's tone was fierce. 'I am not trying to convince you of my courage, Captain, but my desire. I want to find those who did this, and I cannot do that if I die. I want to hunt them down and send them to the hell they must have sprung from.'

'We will, Egil,' the Captain promised. 'You need not worry about that. I know you will not be able to rest until you have done so, and Philippe, too, but you will have to content yourself with the thought that it will happen in time. What you have seen places a burden on us, and not just in terms of retribution on behalf of those villagers. They will not be the only ones who have suffered at the hands of these savages, and if these people are riding about in confidence with so many soldiers in the area as you say, then there is something going on of a grander scale than we can attempt to address. We must speak to others. No, your revenge must smoulder for now, but be assured that it will be satisfied. Be certain of that.'

His hand on the veteran's shoulder, he walked him towards the stern, speaking to him quietly as they went.

Not long afterwards, the wind picked up and they shipped oars. Brann was left with whirling images of horrors filling his mind. Even after, at dusk, he drifted into a fitful sleep, the pictures haunting him, invading his dreams.

The next morning, he was shaken awake by Cannick.

'Captain wants to see you,' he said simply, in a low growl. He unlocked Brann and led him slowly to the stern. He supported the boy by gripping his arm above the elbow, as Brann found that his legs, used only to the movement of lifting himself up and backwards when he rowed, seemed so soon to have forgotten how to walk.

The Captain was sitting behind his desk when they entered. He told Brann to sit in the seat that he had occupied the last time, and indicated to Cannick that he could go.

'I will get to the point, boy,' the Captain said bluntly. 'I know you heard some, or maybe much, of what was said when the men came aboard yesterday. You, and those beside you, could hardly fail to hear, so close were you to us.' He stared intensely at Brann. 'Tell me what the oarsmen talked of last night. I need to know what fears and rumours may take their attention away from instant obedience. There are times when the timing of the rowers' work keeps us all alive and, if there is a situation that may affect that, I need to deal with it now.'

Brann shrugged. He saw no point in lying and, indeed, even had he wished to do so, he doubted if he could withhold the truth for long under the glare of those piercing eyes.

'They know little,' he said, his voice blank. 'There was a massacre, and that's really all that was discussed. The other rowers seem to have seen fighting before, so didn't seem to think it was worthy of any more talk than that. Because of where I sit, I heard more, but it wasn't really something I wanted to gossip about. I heard what they did to the people,' he paused, 'and the children. I saw how it had affected the man who was telling you. I know something is going on there that involves soldiers and the people that did these terrible things. I know the village that you were meant to deliver the goods to was wiped out,' he paused again. 'And I know you felt horror at what they said.'

'Anything else?' the Captain asked.

'Only that you are going to do nothing about it.' He shrugged again, and stared at the floor. 'But why should you?'

The Captain frowned. 'Meaning what?'

Brann hesitated, but knew he had started to say something that he must now finish. 'Meaning that it seems little different from what you did to my village.'

The Captain's hand slammed down on the table, causing Brann to jump. 'It was very different,' the Captain hissed violently. 'You would do well to remember your place, boy. If you can count, three of my men came aboard with you. Whoever attacked your village, it was not us. And whatever their reason, it was not my orders. What happened to your brother, what has befallen you, these are unfortunate in your life. But they are fate. Fate happens. Fate is what will happen. Fate is what has happened. We merely craft what we can of the life fate gives us, however long that lasts.' He scooped two gambling cards from the desk and slammed them onto the tabletop in front of Brann. He leant in close, his voice intense. 'You play the hand you are dealt. To dwell on the cards you would have preferred is to allow others to play theirs before you. And then you have surely lost, whatever the cards you hold.'

He stood and walked to a small window at the rear of the cabin, staring out in a manner that suggested that he saw nothing of the scene that lay in front of him. His hand strayed to the scar on his face. After a long moment, he sighed and ran his hands through his hair.

'I will tell you this, boy,' he said quietly. 'And not because I owe you anything, nor that you deserve anything. But because knowledge arms us and ignorance kills us, and I will not let you die like...' He turned away. His voice was almost a whisper. 'Like others.' He ran a hand through his hair and stared at the wall. Brann could see the side of his jaw where it clenched for a long moment, then relaxed abruptly as the Captain faced him once more. 'And because you, like everybody else, should be aware of something more than the few miles of countryside around the village you have grown up in. I suspect that you have never been out of your valley before now.'

He returned to his seat and, rather than the upright, alert manner in which he had sat before, he slumped into it, staring at the ceiling.

'So, I will tell you basically where you live, which is as good a place to start as any. The Green Islands, so-called because the amount of rain you get allows nature to flourish more than anywhere else known to man. Though how you don't drown or die of misery, I will never understand. I have lived in ice-bound cold, blistering drought, and everything in between, and to everything I have become acclimatised other than that accursed incessant rain.' He snorted, though it was unclear whether it was dark amusement or climate-induced disgust.

'Anyhow, two islands lie one to the north of the other, separated by a narrow stretch of sea; at some points it is only around two or three miles across. The northern island, as you will perhaps know, is Alaria. It stretches around two hundred miles, north to south, and roughly one hundred miles across its broader southern coast. Its neighbour to the south, Cardallon, measures maybe double each of Alaria's dimensions.

'Your village is in a small valley around halfway up Alaria, an hour's ride from the east coast. Your island is a kingdom, but many of your people do not even realise it. The king rules, and has contact with community leaders, but he really has an easy job.

'Those in the south are not interested in coming north and, because yours is a single kingdom, there are no neighbouring factions jostling for power. All that the king must do is to ensure that everything is running more or less smoothly, and so his duty is really just to be administrator-in-chief, and nothing more.

'If it were not for the weather which, as you will know well, changes between glorious and miserable more frequently than any man should have to endure, with more emphasis on the miserable end of the scale, it would be idyllic and an attractive target for other monarchs looking to expand their territory. But the weather puts them off, understandably, as does the fact that this climate tends to produce men who are hardened both physically and in spirit. Even the farmers in your country can offer a hard fight.'

Brann flushed with anger and pain at the memory, surprised by the short flash of emotion he had thought he had lost the ability to feel, but the Captain had not noticed. He continued, 'The southern island was once under one ruler, but split several hundred years ago into three kingdoms, Ragalan, Salaria and, unimaginatively, Westland.

'By and large, through marriage and politics, they managed to live with each other and trade, content to be lucrative. Every generation or so, however, some king or other tends to forget that war is bad for business and dreams of the perceived personal gain that would come of uniting the island under one ruler once more.

'To date, no one has managed to do so since the original split, and the three kingdoms have remained as such. In the meantime, this set-up maintains an undercurrent of distrust and intrigue that extends to civic leaders, and this occasionally produces a challenge to a king from within his own borders, either through an assassination attempt or a full-blown military uprising.

'This latter option is what may be going on at the moment in the area we have just visited. Either someone is trying to take over, or has done so already and is flexing their muscles to establish the sort of regime that they wish.

'The problem is the level of brutality that you heard described. Horrific as it is on that scale, it also has wider implications that reach beyond the borders of even this island.

'Our Lady downstairs also seems to think that it holds some serious import. All that she could shed on the matter was that she saw fire, darkness, fear, sorrow and pain hanging over the country. That may sound pretty vague to you, but in her terms it is a fairly specific prediction.

'In any case, when a situation is affecting what looks like such a large area, anything we do to avenge slaughter, no matter how horrific, in one village will be inconsequential. What is more use is carrying the information to those who are in a better position to assess it and its consequences on a more wide-reaching scale.'

He swung his legs down from the desk and stood up. 'There, your lesson is over for today. Any questions?'

Brann shook his head. The Captain's eyes narrowed as he stared at the boy, as if trying to fathom his thoughts.

'Not so talkative this time, are you?' he said after a few seconds.

Brann shrugged. 'I have changed,' was all he said. It was not cheeky, or defiant – merely a simple statement of fact.

The Captain walked to the door but waited before he opened it. Brann had stood, ready to leave, his manacles clanking as he moved.

The man said, 'You may find that you change back. Not totally: you will always carry a bit more hardness with you, but maybe that is not a bad thing.

'Maybe you will not change back, but most do: the gods know we all do things out of character now and again, so do not let any setbacks worry you overmuch.'

Brann had already been surprised at the length, and content, of the conversation. Early on he had felt strongly

151

that the Captain had been struck with a need to unburden himself in some way, and faced with an unthreatening – and, in the grand scheme of things, irrelevant – companion, Brann guessed the temptation to take this rare opportunity had been too much for him. He had hardly opened up his soul, but he was clearly talking more than he was used to doing. Perhaps he now regretted saying so much; perhaps not – but either way Brann was left with no misapprehension that the conversation was over.

The Captain opened the door and nodded to the waiting Cannick. Without another word he turned back to the desk and let Cannick lead Brann back the length of the ship to his bench. Most rowers were still sleeping, but those few who were awake did not show any interest in the sight of him being brought back from the cabin.

He sat back in his place. Gerens was sound asleep, lying to his left on top of the bench. Grakk was in his customary sleeping position, curled up on the deck in front of the bench. He opened one eye as Brann was fastened back onto the chain, said nothing, and went back to sleep.

There was a peaceful, golden, almost magical haze as the sun came up, but there was still a sharp edge to the soft breeze, so Brann pulled his cloak about him as he leant against the side of the ship. The words of the Captain filled his head until he dozed off, suffusing him with images of a bigger world that he'd always known must be there but had never previously thought – or had to think – about.

The wind dropped early during the next day, and the rowers worked for several hours. Brann welcomed the effort even more so than usual. Normally, even if the wind was up, they rowed for a period every day to keep the men at their peak in terms of fitness and technique. Sometimes, if there was a strong forecast from the Lady below decks for wind the next day, they would row at night and sleep through the daylight hours, as they had done for the first three hours during the night after heading directly away from land, and away from the scene of such horror.

As his fitness and strength grew, Brann had come to enjoy the exercise: it passed the time, and there was a sense of purpose and satisfaction about it that he could not previously have imagined from something to simple and repetitive.

When dusk threatened to fall, around an hour after they had stopped rowing for the second time that day, and while the rowers were starting to eat, a ripple of murmurs rolled along the benches from the stern. A broad rower two benches away turned around and said simply, 'Halveka', before returning to his meal.

The two boys turned to Grakk. Gerens asked, 'What does he mean? Who is Halveka?'

'Not who, but where, ignorant lad,' Grakk chided him. 'Your eyes are open but do you see nothing? Until now, we have ever sailed due north or due south. But now we head northwest.

'They are taking us to their homeland.'

Chapter 6

The servant girl was there, he could feel her presence behind his chair. But he had not heard her enter.

He had started from his doze at the knowledge she was there, but the slow reaction irked him. Yet another sign of deficiencies that, like bad houseguests, had arrived unbidden and unwelcome and outstayed their welcome. Except that these guests would never leave. There was a time when a shadow could have slipped through the drapes at his balcony door and he would have wakened from the deepest slumber and had knife in hand before the intruder was more than a few paces into the room. There were times when this had been the reason why he had been the one standing over the corpse, reversing the intruder's vision of that particular tableau.

Those times were gone. But he was still here.

'Fetch me water, girl.' He was always thirsty when he woke.

No water was brought. No answer was given. But there was a voice, soft and dry as the sand blowing across the tiles of the balcony floor.

'Be ready.'

He started. It was so close it could almost have been whispered right into his ear.

154

'*I will come. Ere then, think as only you can think. Be as only you can be. Be ready.*'

The arms of the chair let him heave himself up and around, barely catching his balance. His breath ragged, his eyes leapt around the room.

He was alone.

But he knew he had not been.

****

They rowed frequently for three days, as the winds were light. Brann did not mind: it also meant that the sea was fairly flat, which was good because he was feeling distinctly uneasy about being so far from land.

The fourth day began eventfully. A huge roar and a raucous commotion below deck was followed by bellowing and cries of pain that sounded young enough to belong to the boys in the hold.

Grakk looked at the two boys, the slight narrowing of his eyes the only indication of his mischievous humour. 'Boar, I believe, has discovered sea water in his sugar. A taste for sugar, has our Boar. Always has some on board and keeps it in his precious sugar jar. Never shares, never trades it for anything. Boar, you understand, is partial to his sugar.'

'And someone has put water in it?' Brann asked. The boys were finding it easier to become accustomed to the technique of rowing than to the incongruity of Grakk's appearance and his speech, although they found that it lent him credibility: cultured words from an apparently barbaric source somehow seemed, with their unexpectedness, more profound.

The roaring and banging were continuing below. The warriors on deck at the stern were almost dancing with suppressed laughter. Grakk nodded at them.

'I wonder if you can guess who?' he said.

'Much as I detest Boar, it is a bit childish, isn't it?' Brann said. A snort from Gerens and a glance at his expression indicated that he found it grimly amusing. Brann reflected briefly that almost anything connected with Gerens could be described as grim.

Grakk was also amused. 'Rowers have rowing to fill their time, and afterwards, our priority is to replenish our energy, so we eat and sleep. Warriors have little to do, even less when they are at sea for many days. Boredom brings out the child in everyone, regardless of their age and station in life, I have found.'

He nodded towards the stern again. 'A rower up there heard talk of it, and word soon spread around the benches. The warriors will only be surprised that Boar took more than one day to find out. But then his mind has been preoccupied with the fact that this is his last voyage with us. It seems our Captain has decided Boar's particular skills no longer enhance our capabilities.'

The noise below decks, surprisingly, managed to increase. Brann was only glad the captured boys had been sold on; he didn't like to think of what might have happened had there been ready targets for Boar's rage.

'Perhaps they have misjudged how much this would affect him,' he suggested. 'He must have been worrying about returning home to tell Mrs Boar that he'd lost his job.'

Gerens spluttered and Grakk almost smiled.

The door at the stern exploded open and Boar, a picture of all-consuming fury, emerged like some vast sea monster seeking prey.

He cast about and glared up at the raised section of deck, where the warriors were a picture of innocence and forced nonchalance.

'Something the matter, Boar?' one of them asked, and several of the others turned away quickly to study the horizon intently. Boar growled something unintelligible and turned away, starting to stalk down the aisle. The merriment evaporated quicker than spray off the deck on a hot day.

'Boar suffers from an affliction known as cowardice,' murmured Grakk. 'He is well aware that the warriors are responsible, but he will not challenge them. He seeks an easier target now to assuage his fury, and logic will not play a part. Be wary. The Captain will not tolerate Boar injuring a rower to the extent that a rower cannot row, but Boar knows well how to hurt you without incapacitation. Do not catch his eye.'

Brann looked down at his feet, needing no second instruction to avoid Boar's interest. The huge fat man was now halfway down the aisle, and was muttering to himself in dark anger. The words grew louder as his fury sought a target.

'Who did it?' he growled. 'It was one of you maggots, wasn't it? I know it was. Who was it?'

His voice had reached a shout, now, and the benches trembled as his thumping step passed. Brann was trembling also.

The furious man reached the front and could go no further. He roared wordlessly. He turned and found the seven boy rowers in front of him. His breathing heavy, he stood for a moment, glaring at heads that were steadfastly staring at feet.

Brann heard the raging man's breathing grow louder as his heavy footsteps slowly approached behind him. His stomach, already knotted with nerves, lurched as his nose caught the overpowering smell of the man, an aroma that he had thought had passed from his life with his move to the rowing benches. He held his breath, hoping that Boar would pass on.

But he did not.

157

'You,' he growled hoarsely, so close behind Brann that his breath was hot on the boy's neck. 'Oh, yes. I should have known. The boy who thinks he is special. So clever, aren't you? You think you can play a trick on Boar, and get away with it, don't you? Well it's not a trick. And you can't get away with it.'

He was so close now, bending over the boy, that his nose, dripping with sweat, pressed repeatedly, repulsively, terrifyingly against the back of Brann's head.

Brann was quivering, visibly. He stared harder at the floor, hoping that Boar would have his say and go away. But he knew that he would not.

Boar was working himself evermore into a frenzy, so Brann stammered a denial, hoping that the man would accept logic. Still staring down, he said hesitantly, 'But I have been chained here for days. It could not have been me.'

Boar, however, was not for accepting rational argument. He wanted a target, and an easy one... and he had found it.

His fury had reached a level where he could not even form speech. With a frustrated howl, he cuffed Brann on the right side of his head, knocking him roughly into Gerens. Much as he was trying to show no weakness, Brann could not help grunting as the blow landed. His head was left spinning, and it took a moment for his vision to return.

The men on the raised deck had stopped laughing, aware that the situation had turned serious. They knew that if any of them tried to intervene, Boar was so far beyond reason now that a full-scale brawl was likely to develop. Injuries and, possibly, death could ensue – not just for the warriors, but also for the rowers chained nearby who would be unable to avoid swinging weapons. And casualties among warriors or rowers would not go down well with the Captain. Already they had young boys making up the numbers. Any further reduction in the number of experienced slaves could affect their control of the vessel.

The only course of action with any chance of success was for someone in authority to intervene, and one man was already hurrying below to fetch Cannick. Another felt that this would take too long, and had started for the Captain's cabin, much as they wanted to avoid involving him in what was a chain of events begun by their trivial joke. All they could hope was that smacking Brann would have assuaged Boar's anger enough that he would now limit himself to kicking parts of the ship.

Boar loomed over Brann, his fury exploding from him in a bellow as he managed to formulate words once again. 'You think Boar is stupid, don't you? Don't you? But Boar has seen you, visiting the Captain and the old witch.'

Brann was too terrified to point out that he had been escorted on each of these occasions – and once by Boar himself.

The huge slaver, scarlet-faced and spraying spittle over the terrified boy, had reached a frenzy of irrational rage. His voice high-pitched, he screeched, 'It was you! I know it was you. Nobody touches Boar's things. Nobody touches Boar's sugar. Nobody!'

He hauled Brann up by the neck of his tunic and, in one astoundingly quick movement, let go and hit him back-handed on the side of his head. Brann battered against the side of the ship and rebounded onto the floor. Head ringing, he knew then he was going to die.

Grakk leant over and hissed at him, 'Stay down. Play dead.'

Brann found that his head had cleared surprisingly quickly, however, and he felt strangely calm. He was aware of where he had been hit, but – for the moment – felt no pain. And he felt with certainty that if he lay down, Boar would continue to beat him to a bloody pulp, such was his spiralling fury.

He forced himself back to his feet, but was felled again by a full-blooded punch that came down from above and struck him on the top of the forehead. He let his knees buckle to lessen the blow but still crashed again to the deck. A hiss of intaken breath rose from the benches as, to a man, the rowers assumed his neck had been broken, replaced by a gasp of surprise as he obeyed the instinct that screamed at him to start climbing back to his feet.

He glanced up to see where the next blow was coming from. Boar was casting about for anything that he could lay his hands on that would do quicker damage and stop the boy relentlessly getting back up every time he hit him – once down the boy would be at the mercy of his gleeful bloodlust.

Brann reached under the bench for leverage as he started to pull himself upright again. His hand brushed against the stolen knife that he had jammed point-first into the underside of the bench.

He wrenched it free and stood warily, hiding it against his loose trousers. He was unsure what he would – or could – do with it, but it seemed better to have it than be empty-handed. He was well aware, though, that if Boar saw it, he was likely to become even more savagely violent.

Breathing heavily, he watched as Boar spotted a hand-axe, forgotten when the dead warrior had been stripped of his weapons and consigned to the sea. With a howl of delight, Boar seized it and turned back to Brann.

The Captain burst from his cabin and took in the scene at the other end of the ship in an instant. 'Boar!' he shouted, his voice slicing through the air like an arrow. 'Stop this now!'

But Boar was oblivious. With a roar, he lurched at Brann, swinging the axe down from high on his right. It was cutting directly for the side of Brann's neck, and would have cleaved into his chest – had he not swayed back instinctively at the last moment.

The axe smashed down into the bench, embedding its edge in the wood and slicing the end from Gerens's little finger where his hand was resting on the seat. The boy shouted in shock and clutched his hand to his chest as Grakk dragged him away from the madness.

The Captain, Cannick and two warriors were sprinting down the ship, weapons drawn. They would be on them in seconds, but Brann knew that it would not be soon enough.

Laughing manically now, Boar pulled the axe from the bench as if it were a toy and, without a pause, swung a sweeping back-hand stroke that would behead Brann in an instant.

Without time to think, Brann stepped forward, closer to Boar, and smashed his forearm, supported by his other hand, into Boar's solid arm. He could not hope to stop the force of such a blow, but he did manage to deflect it upwards just enough for it to pass a fraction above his head.

Boar's arm swung up high to his right. He was unbalanced, and surprised, and his front was completely open to an attack that he never imagined would come. But it did.

Brann, his arm still numb from deflecting Boar's swipe, put one foot on the bench and lunged forwards. In an action that was almost a punch, he stabbed the knife into the front of Boar's throat. Undefended and unexpected, the blade plunged in to the hilt. Unfettered and unexpected, an animal roar burst from his throat, carrying with it his pent-up fury at his brother's death.

161

The surprise of the blow over-balanced Boar further, and he toppled backwards, incomprehension widening his eyes. His hand started to reach for his throat, but Brann was still gripping the hilt. The chain attached to Brann's ankle had reached its limit and pulled him also from his feet, snatching the weapon from the wound.

Boar crashed to the deck, as did Brann, but with considerably less noise. Blood fountained from the wound and the knife fell from Brann's grasp and slid across the deck. Grakk reached down and, as the Captain skidded to a halt beside them, casually flipped it over the side of the ship.

Inspecting the area around his feet, Grakk said, 'Merely some rubbish lying on deck, Captain. Some people are so very careless.' He looked up. 'Someone could get hurt.'

'Indeed,' the Captain said, dryly. He cast a cursory look at Boar's body, and turned to Cannick. 'Get this scumbag off my ship, and have the mess cleaned up. And have the medic see to the boys' injuries.'

Brann rose to his knees, his throbbing arm clutched to his chest. He stared at the corpse, at the face staring skywards from a pool of its own blood, but seeing only his brother's face, drained of colour and life, still expecting the look of surprise to be replaced in an instant by the familiar and irresistible grin. His roar of release had released little. The cold returned to his stomach; spread up to his head. In a solitary concession to the situation, his body started to shake.

The Captain faced the benches, and raised his voice. 'Let this be a lesson to all of you,' he called. 'The deck is a dangerous place: it is unsteady and it is slippery. Nasty falls can happen, as in the case of poor Boar, here. Learn from his folly.'

The message was clear – the matter was closed. The Captain turned back to Cannick and, low enough that only the veteran warrior could hear, he said, 'See to the boy. I think he's had enough of the deep and meaningful heart-to-hearts. Keep it short and sweet, but make sure it doesn't push him over the edge.'

The older man cleared his throat, then seemed to change his mind and turned to follow the orders. The Captain's hand on his arm stopped him. 'What?'

'The boy, Einarr.' His voice and eyes were soft. 'He is not...'

'Don't,' the taller man snapped. 'Don't say his name.'

Cannick nodded. 'My apologies. I shouldn't have mentioned it. I know that.'

The Captain's tone was more controlled, but there was still tension in the words. 'You do know that. And I know well enough myself who this boy isn't. What I don't know, is who he is, or will be. And until I do, maybe even more so when I do, I want you to do as I say. Will you do that?'

Cannick nodded. 'I will see to the boy.'

He organised two men to dispose of Boar's body, and in moments they had unceremoniously tipped him over the side. The fact that it was done with no preparation of his corpse and no pause for reflection was significant. Compared with the reverence that had been afforded to the disposal of the last warrior to die on the same spot, the difference in attitude was vast and said much of the level of respect and affection, or otherwise, that his comrades held for him.

With a large splash, Boar was gone from their lives. As the two warriors dragged a bucket in the sea and rinsed away the blood, Cannick squatted beside Brann. The medic, already working on Gerens' finger, moved slightly to give him room. Brann was sitting on the bench, his back against the side of the ship. His knees were drawn up to his chest and he was hugging his shins.

The old warrior noticed that he was shivering violently, and that he was fighting hard to hold back tears. Cannick spat on the deck and, without looking up, said conversationally, 'First kill?'

Brann nodded, and looked at him as if he were mad even to contemplate that his answer could be otherwise.

Cannick grunted, ignoring the boy's expression. 'Don't worry, he was worthless scum. More than a few around here would have been glad to take your place.'

His voice low and expressionless, Brann said, 'I can't stop shaking. I was fine when it was happening. Everything seemed to happen so slowly, even though I knew it was actually fast.' Cannick looked up sharply, as if that statement had betrayed something significant about the boy, but Brann did not notice. 'But now,' he continued, 'I can't stop shaking and I feel like I'm about to throw up.'

Cannick shrugged. 'Nothing unusual in that, boy. Your body got fired up to deal with the danger, and it doesn't realise you've stopped yet, is all. Anyway, better to be shaky now than when you had to act. Believe me, many a grown man would have frozen in fear faced with that lunatic.' He stood. As if it were an afterthought, he said, 'And, by the way, if that proves to be more than a one-off performance from you, you have got something special. I have seen, trained and fought beside and against a lot of men, so I know what I see. You should remember that. Don't rely on it. But be confident about what you can achieve.'

Leaving that thought hanging in the air, he walked off. The medic, having tended to Gerens's finger and given him a handful of leaves from his pouch of herbs to chew on, which seemed to relieve the pain, turned his attention to Brann. He was particularly astounded that there appeared to be no great damage from the blow to the top of Brann's head, the one that all watching had assumed had broken his neck. When he expressed his astonishment, however, Brann's explanation was simple: when you grow up accustomed to heavy grain sacks unexpectedly falling on you from above as you play in your father's store or, when you grow older, as you help him with his work, you quickly develop a natural reaction that instantly rolls with such a blow and cushions it rather than taking the full force. It was merely a remnant of what already seemed a distant former life. His other questions were answered by the boy absently and, satisfied that there was no serious physical damage – and quietly amazed at the fact – the medic moved on to other duties.

Cannick's words played around in Brann's head and, after a while, began to take effect. While still shaken by the experience, he found himself reliving the incident, movement by movement, in his mind's eye. He found it hard to believe that, faced with an axe-wielding monster like Boar, he had survived with barely a scratch. What was more, he had killed the brute, armed with nothing more than agility and a fairly small knife. If it had been suggested to him beforehand that the outcome of such a confrontation would result in a victory for the small boy, he would have laughed at such a ridiculous notion.

But it had happened. And he was the small boy. He coughed to stifle a giggle at the relief of being alive, and pondered the idea planted by Cannick that he might have a talent for such things.

But that was ridiculous. All of his life, he had tried anything to avoid any sort of confrontation. *You just desperately wanted to stay alive*, he thought to himself, *and you did what you had to do to survive. Don't get carried away or you might not survive the next time.* For he had found that, whatever your talent, there was always someone out there more talented than you. And meeting a more talented carpenter, or singer, or runner, or blacksmith wasn't too likely to be the death of you. So, if his talent did lie in that this violent direction, he was fairly sure it wasn't a direction he wanted to follow as a career choice. If he was granted the luxury of choice.

Though it may come in handy, on occasion.

For the moment, though, he felt a sense of importance. The attitudes shown to him in the aftermath of Boar's death had clearly indicated approval of the outcome. And, while he was slightly uncomfortable at the thought of being the subject of attention and gossip, another part of him was enjoying the feeling of having done something worthy of admiration, and in front of so many watching eyes.

Whether he had achieved it by talent or accident, he decided that he may as well enjoy it while it lasted. In the eyes of one man, it lasted for barely a day. One of the rowers, a bald man with a bushy black beard, was brought to the prow to help with a repair to the damage caused by Boar's wildly swinging axe. He had been, Grakk informed the boys, a carpenter before being enslaved – a useful man to have aboard. Maybe too useful, as he was likely to spend much of the rest of his life on the ship, even after old age rendered his rowing days at an end, but at least then he would receive payment in return for his services.

As he worked, the carpenter moved gradually closer to Brann. The boy thought it was coincidence but, as the man shaped a piece of wood beside their bench, he spoke in a low voice without looking up from his work, and quietly enough that the attendant warrior was unaware. 'That was a fortunate time to find a knife, boy, was it not? A good strong knife it was, too.'

Brann blushed, becoming aware that this was the previous owner of the blade he had stolen on his first day aboard. He stammered, 'I can't really remember where it came from. It all happened too fast.'

The man paused, examining the edge on his tool. Brann had no idea what it was called, but it looked deadly enough and it was obviously in the dextrous hands of a man skilled in its use. He continued as if Brann had never spoken. 'It looked a very good knife to me. In fact, it looked very similar to one I lost quite recently.' He paused, and looked directly at Brann. 'As recently as the day you came aboard, actually.'

He tested the edge of his tool against his thumb. 'Do you know what we do to thieves where I come from?'

Grakk casually brushed some stray sawdust from the bench. 'Of course, you will recall also that you are not where you come from?' he said casually. 'And you will recall that the knife performed a good deed? And you will recall that the outcome of this good deed was welcomed by all on board?' He turned and met the carpenter's gaze calmly. 'So you will remember to forget the knife, I am sure. Unless, of course, you would prefer to take your grievance to the Captain over the alleged theft of an illegally possessed knife?'

The large rower at the bench in front of them turned round. 'Grakk is right. The boy is an upstart, and he got lucky, but you are better off to have lost both that fat slimeball and the knife from your life, than to still have them both around.'

The carpenter glared at Brann and spat over the side of the ship, before finishing his work without a further word. He was taken back to his position shaking his head and muttering something about a tattooed freak and his little puppy. But he

167

had been left in no doubt that the matter should be dropped, and he was not so foolish as to cross such strong opinion among the rowers. Justice and retribution were rare among them – but rare because, when they did come along, they were brutal and quick. He preferred to live out his days, if possible, even if they were as a slave.

Brann allowed himself a smile and, for the first time since he came aboard, he felt his spirits lift. A slight lift, but one nonetheless. *I still can't believe it was me that did that to Boar*, he thought. *But I did, didn't I?*

Gerens saw his expression. 'Welcome back to the land of the living, chief,' he said with his dark smile. 'And you made it with all of your fingers intact.'

'Gerens, I am sorry. How are you?'

The boy shrugged as if it was of no consequence. 'I still have most of that finger. And I am still alive. As are you. I would prefer that to having ten full fingers and an empty space beside me on the bench.'

Brann smiled.

The incident, terrifying as it had been, ironically proved to be exactly what Brann had needed. Visions did flash back regularly into his head, making him shudder with horror at what might so easily have been. And the ease with which the axe had sliced through Gerens's finger, and the thought that it had been aimed at decapitating him, did make him rub his neck absently as he mused – though he tried not to – on the way that the short fight could have (and logic would say, should have) finished if fortune had not fought alongside his cause.

But Calip, with all his fortune and whimsy, had sided with him. And Boar had not managed to separate his head and his body. And he knew that the result had not just been due to luck. He had seen Boar's movement, and acted against it; he had spotted an opening, and had exploited it. Both actions had been instinctive, but they had also been deliberate, and the thought that he had defeated such a fearsome opponent sparked pride in himself.

He kept the feeling to himself, certain that it would not be well-received by his colleagues on the benches, but the pride was the spark that started the return of his spirit from the place in which he had buried it. It was still stored deep within him, and would not return quickly, if at all fully, but the start was made.

Several days later, Gerens nudged him from behind as he stood, stretching out his chain and leaning on the side of the ship, staring out over the waves. The wind was constant and in their favour, so the rowers had been left to their own devices – such as were available to them – for the best part of the morning.

'You are doing it again, chief,' Gerens said, nudging him a second time.

Brann turned around, and swung his arm in a wide sweep to ward off a third nudge.

'Hey, mighty warrior!' Gerens said in mock alarm. 'Try to remember I'm not a fat raging madman with an axe, will you?' In terms of Gerens's sense of humour, this was close to raucous hilarity, and Brann was forced to smile.

'What was I doing again?'

Gerens nodded out over the sea. 'You had left us for a while. Your head was miles away. You have done it many times recently, and it had come to the stage where I either mentioned it or threw a bucket of water over you. And I have no bucket of water.'

Brann had the feeling that Gerens's humour did not extend to this comment, and strongly suspected that there was a chance he would actually have carried out that alternative. 'I was thinking of my village,' he said, sitting down on the bench. 'I was wondering who was still there that I knew, and what they were doing right now.'

'And if they were thinking about you?' Gerens asked.

Brann nodded, turning to stare out over the choppy waves again. He clenched his jaw in an attempt to contain the surge of emotion that that simple admission had provoked.

Gerens solemnly regarded him. 'Of course they think about you. Every day, there will be somebody who thinks about you, and every time a figure approaches the village, they will catch their breath at the thought that it might be you. There will always be some who have a certainty within them that you are alive and who pray regularly for you to return – because it is not a case of "if" you will find your way back to them, but "when".'

Brann looked at the boy, wondering at such wisdom and certainty from someone who was only the same age as he was. Even if it wasn't true, it was a consoling thought.

Noticing the quizzical look on Brann's face, Gerens shrugged. 'I have seen it before. I am not the first to be taken from my village. We are – we were – close to the coast and two boys were taken a couple of years ago. Two families, two different backgrounds – and one reaction. The one that I described to you, the same each time and with each family. And not just the family, all those about us. Everybody hears about such things happening but they never think it will happen in their village until it does. So the whole village feels the effect.

'So of course they will miss you. After all, you miss them, don't you?'

Brann smiled at him. 'You are right.' He wiped a sleeve across his eyes. 'Thank you, Gerens.' He looked across at him. 'You know, I'm glad I met you here. You've helped me more than you know.' That was one of the few advantages of the way his mind was working at the moment: things that would have been awkward to say in the past just seemed to spill from him with no restraint.

The dark gaze turned his way. 'To be accurate, I've helped you more than you know.' He shrugged, and turned to look again over the water. 'But pay it no heed. I did it by choice, so you owe me nothing.'

'To be accurate in return, I suppose I owe you a finger.'

The corner of the taller boy's mouth twitched slightly in the faintest amusement. 'To be accurate, a bit of a finger. And the least useful finger at that.'

'How is it now? The rest of the finger.'

'Fine.' He flexed his hand into a fist then stretched the fingers out straight again, the daily renewed bandage held up for inspection. 'That medic is skilled. And it will make me interesting, in a way.'

Brann grinned. 'Yeah, 'cause you merge into a crowd so well as it is.'

Gerens shrugged. 'That depends on the crowd. Some yes, some no. But you're right. Some less well-to-do crowds may contain many who have more than a fingertip missing.'

'Do you never think that it could have been worse? That it could have easily been more than a fingertip that you lost? Does it never make you shudder?'

'Why?' Again the stare, betraying not a flicker of emotion, as still and pale as a corpse. 'Why would it? It was what it was. Where's the use in worrying about what might have been, but wasn't? That's about as stupid as worrying about what might happen, when you don't know what will. Better in both cases to deal with what is there, now – that's what

171

requires your attention, and the rest serves only to distract you from it.'

'Fair point,' Brann conceded. 'Did you learn that from someone special?'

'Absolutely,' Gerens nodded, his face and tone solemn. 'Me.'

An amused snort came from the blanket that covered the curled-up form of Grakk behind them, and Brann laughed.

'Anyway, whatever you say, every time you look at your finger with a bit missing, remember that I owe you for the missing tip.'

Gerens shrugged, as if it were nothing more than a trifle, and the pair stared quietly over the waves, comfortable in the silence, until the order came to row again, around an hour later.

The wind stayed gentle for the next few days and the rowing was constant during the daylight hours, with short breaks only for lunch and either side of that meal, in mid-morning and mid-afternoon. It was, however, set at a pace that would have been exhausting at the start of their time on the benches, but which now seemed only slightly more vigorous than normal.

After what seemed like close to a week, they rowed into fog.

'We are approaching the end of this journey now,' Grakk advised them. 'Coastal fog,' he explained succinctly.

Brann was fascinated, and impressed. 'I didn't realise you could tell the difference between different types of fog.'

Grakk smiled slightly. 'I am sorely tempted to sound clever and continue the pretence. But I am not really as clever as that.' He nodded in the direction of the warrior at the prow, staring intently into the mist. 'Do you see the lookout? He has a horn. These people only ever use a horn in fog when they are near land.'

Gerens spoke up. 'When they blow it, they listen for a horn blown in response from the shore to guide them into a safe harbour. Some say these men can even hear land in a faint echo from the horn call, but I do not know if that is true.'

'Why do they only use the horn near land?' Brann asked. 'Why not out at sea where they might bump into another ship?'

'If they are near land,' Gerens said, 'they know roughly where they had been heading for – in fog, what they don't know is exactly where they are. But they know enough to be fairly sure that it is a friendly place.

'Out at sea, however, you don't know who you will come across. And in general, you assume that everyone at sea is unfriendly until you know otherwise, so it doesn't do to draw attention to yourself if you can avoid it. And the chances of bumping into another boat, in the vast area of the sea, are pretty low.'

Grakk grunted, 'Enough talk. Retain what strength you puppies have for rowing. You may find yourself working through the night, if we are close to land.'

Two warriors walked past, one carrying a bunch of long slender poles. They quickly fitted them together, feeding the sections forwards ahead of the ship as they did so. Once the constructed rod extended almost half the length of the ship ahead of them, one of them fitted the end into a stand that his companion had slotted into a hole in the deck to brace the end of the rod so that the entire length arced ahead of them and dipped its tip into the water to a depth equivalent to the height of two men.

Brann glanced, puzzled, at the activity. Grakk grunted in annoyance. 'Stop looking so curious. Your expression makes it impossible to refrain from explaining. The rods are for...'

173

Brann cut him off as realisation dawned. 'For rocks!' he said, triumphant at not needing help from the pair beside him – for once. 'They would rather splinter their pole than the boat.'

Grakk nodded without looking across. 'Joy of joys. The boy is not as stupid as it would otherwise seem.'

Brann smiled at him. 'Learning is everything.' He earned a smile in response.

Afternoon turned to evening and then early night and, as Grakk had predicted, the drummer kept the slow cautious beat going, and they kept rowing. The lookout had started to blow the horn – an eerie, mournful sound in the stillness of the fog – as dusk had fallen. He listened intently between calls, trying to hear either a response or the sound of waves breaking against rocks or sand.

After a long hour of horn-blowing, which Brann had started, strangely, to find both irritating and soporific, two shorter blasts of a similar horn replied through the fog and darkness. The fog had, through its obliteration of sight and sound, enveloped them in a feeling of complete solitude, as if the gods had transported the ship to a separate place where they floated in emptiness. The sound of another noise floating across the water jolted Brann back to reality, making him jump violently in the process. Grakk looked across, a smile twitching the corners of his mouth, but said nothing.

They altered their course slightly to aim at the noise, and shortly afterwards they heard the sound of waves breaking gently against a beach. Brann felt excitement at the prospect of seeing land – any land – again after so many days at sea and had to fight the urge to pull harder at the oar. The beat of the drum, still cautious as they edged forwards in the hope of avoiding rocks above or below the surface, seemed torture to the boy, even though he knew well the good sense in playing safe.

The horns continued their conversation, the lookout on the boat blowing a single note, and the reply coming each time as a double blast. The lookout paused as he was about to blow again, peered into the darkness, and shouted to the Captain, who was standing at the stern, beside the steersman.

Brann could not make out the cry over the creak of the oars, but many others did, and excitement rippled along the benches. Curious, he craned his neck around as he pulled back and, at the edge of his vision, he saw the cause of the excitement: two fires flickered through the fog, directly ahead.

The Captain called a reminder to the drummer to keep the beat steady, but in a few short minutes it was immaterial as the order was given to cease rowing and ship oars. As they fastened the shafts into place, the ship nudged alongside a simple wooden jetty.

Brann jumped again in surprise, not having noticed their approach to the land. The basic wooden structure that they were now bumping against appeared surreal in both the suddenness of its appearance and in the fact that he was looking at something solid after so many days with only water to fill his vision.

Ropes snaked from the darkness and were quickly tied in place, although Brann noticed that the men doing so kept low as they worked. He glanced up and down the ship and saw warriors crowding along the side of the vessel with arrows nocked to bows and swords drawn.

The rowers were flipping up the wooden boards that had saved them from the arrows the last time they had been beside land. Was this an attack on the local people, or were they just being cautious? Either way, Brann wriggled down against the thick wooden side, anxious not to become an unfortunate statistic.

Cannick strode down the ship and stood waiting at the prow. Words, deep and powerful, rang out from the shore. If a bear could speak, this would be its voice. 'Who enters the harbour of Lord Ragnarr at this hour?' it bellowed.

'Einarr, master of the *Blue Dragon*, is here to taste your hospitality,' Cannick roared back, his voice no less impressive.

'You are not he,' the voice called. 'If he would seek hospitality, he should show himself.'

Cannick's brows drew together. 'And you are not Ragnarr,' he shouted. 'So where does that leave us?'

A roar of laughter erupted from the man on the shore. 'It leaves us with a pair of masters who are not careless with their safety, and who will doubtless live longer to lead their men as a result.'

Torches flared along the jetty and a huge man, enveloped in a bearskin and carrying the biggest war axe that Brann had ever seen, stepped forward into the light. The axe, despite its size, was cradled casually in his arms. Everything about the man exuded vastness: even the hair and beard, yellow-blond and shot through with grey that almost created a shimmer in the spluttering torchlight, dominated his head to the extent that his face was practically an afterthought. Six other warriors, who would in other company have looked large, could be seen holding the torches.

'Welcome to Ravensrest, domain of Ragnarr, in the lands of Sigurr,' he said, more quietly than a bellow but no less grandly than before. 'I am Ulfar, first warrior of Lord Ragnarr. All aboard should step ashore now.'

The Captain strode forward. 'I knew you well, Ulfar, from happier days,' he said.

The man-mountain bowed his head slightly. 'And I, you, my lord, of course. I hope you know what you are doing, returning here.'

The Captain dropped smoothly onto the jetty in front of Ulfar. 'I hope so, too, my friend,' he replied, as the pair embraced strongly. Brann was glad that it was the Captain, and not he, who was in the undoubtedly eye-watering grasp of such a hug.

'Look at you,' Ulfar exclaimed, doing just that. 'You have not aged a day in the decade since you were last here. A runner is already on his way to inform Lord Ragnarr of your arrival. He will be delighted, as I am, to see you – but as worried as I am for your safety.'

'No less cautious than I about it, be assured,' the Captain replied. 'May my men come ashore?'

Ulfar nodded. 'As I said, all must come ashore, men and slaves alike. Those are my orders for any arrival here. And keep your men warned: they must stay together and behave well. I have forty men with me – the six you see will light your way. The rest you will not see. You may keep your weapons, but the first sword to clear its scabbard, axe to be unstrapped, or arrow to touch bowstring, will earn its owner a new life as an archery target.

'I am sorry to have to say this to someone I have known since he was a cub, but times have changed recently, and it is what I must do. I know you well, Einarr, but I do not know, and so cannot trust, everyone with you.'

The Captain slapped him on the back. 'If Ulfar shirked his duty, I would fear a changeling had taken your form and was trying to deceive me. Have no fear, my men will not object to your restrictions.'

He gestured to Cannick to come over to the side of the ship and instructed him to bring everyone onto the jetty, emphasising the need to keep all weapons sheathed and untouched. The ship's warriors rose to their feet and half of them moved to the jetty. The rowers were unchained and, in small groups, were herded down a broad board that had been set up to ease their passage to the jetty where they were met by the waiting warriors. The remaining warriors then came ashore, two of them helping the seeress who had made her way from below deck.

The company formed into a rough column, mostly four abreast, with the warriors down the sides and the slaves in the centre. There was no need for the warriors to draw their weapons to deter any attempts to escape – the thought of thirty-four bowmen shadowing their progress was sitting large in the minds of the slaves.

They left the jetty and, all on foot but for the old lady who had been helped into a small cart hurriedly filled with blankets and cushions from the ship, started up a gently winding, but steeply inclined, path, lined with bushes, trees and plenty of shadows. Brann was glad of the slow pace; his legs had become strong from his method of rowing, but they were taking a while to remember the motion of walking.

When he glanced back at the boys who had started alongside him on the rowing benches, he realised for the first time how much they had changed physically. The six others had filled out across the chest and shoulders and down their arms and legs and, while not able to examine himself in the same way, he assumed that the effect on his body had been the same. It certainly felt that way. While they were still well short of the physiques of the other rowers, they had, nonetheless, grown far more powerful than they had been when they were brought aboard.

The slope levelled out in front of them before rising to the peak of a hill. Dawn was breaking, and the mist was leaving, allowing Brann to see that a town lay before them, its stone walls powerful and well-kept. Beyond the walls, he could see a few stone-built buildings, but the fog had not lifted enough for him to see any further or any great detail.

The area approaching the town was level and clear of vegetation and the accompanying bowmen came into sight. Rather than merely walking alongside the column, Brann noticed that they worked in three groups on each side.

One group would be lined alongside them, standing and watching with bows half-drawn and ready. Another group would be in position ahead, waiting for them to reach them, while the third group, who they had already passed, would be looping behind their companions to take up position further on. Once they had passed the group watching them, they would in turn run ahead, as part of the continuous exercise. It ensured that there were always bowmen beside them watching and ready, steady and alert. These were no novices, Brann thought. Nor were they treating the visitors with any complacency.

Heavy gates swung open at their approach and they were herded into an open area. The bowmen surrounded them, watching carefully but not objecting as Cannick walked down the column to Brann.

Without a word, he unlocked the boy from the chain and led him to the front, rearranging his father's black cloak around his shoulders more neatly. When they were halfway to the front, he murmured in Brann's ear while pretending to adjust the cloak once more. 'The Captain needs a page. He is a man of position here, and must look the part. Our profession does not tend to include a need for a page, but

179

right now our circumstances are different. Among those of the right age, you are the only one that he knows in any way, so it's you, whether you like it or not.'

Brann was not only bewildered at the turn of events, but was feeling a growing panic at his lack of knowledge of how to perform his duties or, indeed, of what those duties might be. Those thoughts were evident on his face. Cannick smiled. It was a grim smile, but a smile all the same.

'Don't worry, lad. Say nothing and do nothing except stand behind and to the left of the Captain, unless you are given an order otherwise. In that case you, well, obey the order, of course. And try to look innocent. I know it's hard after sitting beside that tattooed reprobate, but try hard. Here we are now.'

Cannick positioned Brann behind the Captain who glanced round without expression, then returned his gaze to the front. They stood in silence; the only noise in the still, clear, early-morning air was a gentle murmuring from curious townsfolk who had gathered around them.

Bored, Brann glanced about him. They were a tall people, mostly fair-haired although the occasional shock of dark hair could be seen beneath a woollen cap or wisping from a hood, as both men and women wore their hair long. Their clothes were those of any folk you might find in any town, but they all, Brann noticed as he glanced from one to another, carried a weapon of some sort – even the women.

They were quiet, but not cowed. Rather, they bore the calm assurance of people who regularly fought nature and man for the right to live on – and live off – their land, and were at ease with both battles.

Movement at the edge of his vision caught his attention, and he glanced around further. A lean figure, his cloak pulled tightly around him and his hood pulled far forward so that his face was concealed in shadow, kept back against the surrounding buildings as he edged around, seeking a better view of those at the head of the column.

Even among a people of such height, he was inches above those around him and, as he passed under a protruding beam, the end of a nail caught in the cloth and pulled his hood back, revealing a shock of white-blond hair that framed the face of a boy in his late teens. His gaze locked with Brann's eyes and, for an instant, he glared furiously as if his unmasking were Brann's fault, then grabbed the hood and flung it back over his head. Rather than be relieved at mostly retaining his anonymity, the youth's furious look conveyed a venomous resentment at Brann noticing him. *And I thought I had issues*, Brann mused. *What in all the hells has he been through? Or maybe he's just an arse.* The boy wheeled, and slipped away among the buildings.

Cannick had not noticed the momentary exchange, but he did see Brann's examination of his surroundings. Kicking the boy's ankle from behind, he growled, 'Eyes front, you fool. Remember you are supposed to have the sense of duty and importance of a page. Try to remember that or we may all be in trouble.'

Unnerved, Brann snapped his eyes forward and stood stock-still until the large figure of Ulfar strode down the road towards them.

'Sorry about the wait, Einarr,' he rumbled. 'Rules and all that. Anyway, Lord Ragnarr will see you now.' He glanced at Brann, who was standing impassively (the boy hoped) behind the Captain, despite the nerves that threatened to drain the strength from his knees. 'You may, of course, bring your page. The others will be taken to a barn close to here.

It is simple, but dry and warm, and there is food waiting for them.'

The Captain thanked him and fell in beside the man-mountain as he started to lead the way through the town. Brann, prompted by a less-than-gentle nudge from Cannick, forced his legs to move and followed close behind, and the rest of their party moved off in turn as they were directed. He had noticed that there had been no mention of food for either him or the Captain, and felt hunger and resentment stab through him. The injustice of having to attend some formal welcome or boring meeting while the others sated themselves lowered his brows and he cursed, silently, the Captain for plucking him from the crowd.

They wound their way along what seemed to be the main street of the town, forcing a path through the merchants who had risen early to prepare for the bustle that would soon follow. Unlike those living near the main gate who had been roused by the clamour of their arrival and prompted by curiosity to emerge to examine the visitors, the majority of the residents were soundly unaware of the small party passing their windows. Their route rose as they went, their footing secure on rough-surfaced rocks that had been embedded into the ground to offer grip in almost any weather.

It was remarkably different from Millhaven, the only other town he had seen in his fifteen years and a gentle market town that opened itself gratefully to visitors (and potential customers) rather than closing itself to intruders. Where the wide, straight streets of Millhaven were lined with bright and open shops, with broad windows and deep sills to display goods and invite curiosity, the shops here comprised heavy trestle tables that sat alongside the road, in front of the shopkeepers' houses that appeared – from the current activity that they were forging through – to double as storerooms. Shops and houses alike had, curiously, only narrow, deep-set windows on the two or three upper storeys and no windows at all at ground level.

The roofs were gently pitched, with the front wall extended higher than the edge of the roof, and the buildings ran on each side in a continuous terrace, broken only by occasional alleys, each of which could be closed off at ground level by a tall, stout, wooden gate, banded and studded with heavy iron.

The Captain caught Brann's curious gaze. 'A killing zone,' he said. Brann jumped, startled by his voice. With Ulfar deep in conversation with another local warrior, there was a chance to talk, although doing so had been the last thing Brann had expected. The tall, stern man nodded at the buildings. 'The street is a killing zone,' he reiterated. 'The whole town is, in fact, as every street is the same as this one. No road is straight for any greater length than a bow shot, hampering cavalry charges, and allowing blockades and obstructions to be set up at every bend. There are no windows low down, reducing access to the buildings. Upper windows are suited to archers and behind those parapets at the roof run walkways from which defenders can drop anything that takes their fancy on top of those below. And any intruders who try to use the alleys to move to another street would be slaughtered in such a confined space either from above or from archers at the far end who could hardly miss – or from both.

'This place is built for defence. Anyone trying to storm the town would find that breaching the walls is the easy part; their troubles and casualties would only be starting once they reached the streets. In fact, very often when a town like this is attacked, they will leave the gates open if the aggressors have siege engines, preferring to save the walls and instead massacre them in the streets. Sometimes they will even close the gates behind them to ensure no one escapes.'

Brann looked with increased apprehension at the townsfolk in the street around him. At first, they had appeared much like those he would have imagined inhabiting any town – early risers were already buying, browsing, chatting and laughing, some moving with some purpose in mind, others meandering from stall to stall. Beneath that veneer, however, he now saw them as a sinister collection of murderous fiends, ready to butcher strangers without a moment's hesitation.

Noticing the boy's dramatic change in expression and demeanour, the Captain chuckled quietly, the sound strange from one normally so stern. Guessing at the gist of Brann's thoughts, he said, 'Don't be too harsh in condemning them. Any friendly visitor will find them warmly welcoming, even over-hospitable, if a little boisterous. But this is a dangerous land and, judging by the attitude of Ulfar, these are even more perilous times than normal, so if they want to live to be good hosts to visitors with peaceful intentions, then they must be ready and able to defend themselves against those with the other sort of motives.

'Generally, however, you will find that the fact that the town is built so formidably will prove to be enough of a deterrent – most leaders are not willing to accept the huge losses they will suffer if they mount an attack.' He looked down at the boy. 'Just remember, if it seems foreboding and dangerous, that is good: while we are guests here, we are protected by those qualities.'

Brann nodded and continued in silence. His temporary apprehension about the local people had left him, allowing his terror to return about the masquerade he was being forced to perform. His stomach churning with nerves, he trotted behind the Captain's long strides.

They were reaching the town's centre, and abruptly left the buildings to enter an open area that led to the foot of a huge mound, encircled at its foot by a fence of narrow metal spikes, rather than a solid wall. The Captain gestured to it and was about to explain, but realisation struck Brann and he blurted, 'It is so they can shoot through it. It will slow attackers down, and it will afford no protection to them from defending archers, who can stay in the safety of the main building.'

The Captain nodded and Ulfar growled over his shoulder, 'What your page lacks in etiquette, he regains in analysis. You are training him well, Einarr.'

The Captain's amusement at the irony was safely hidden behind Ulfar's back, and Brann's step bore more of a spring for a few paces until his nerves overwhelmed him once more.

The gates in the fence lay open, but Brann noticed that the pair of guards on duty were alert and watchful. Ulfar nodded to the guards and took the Captain and his 'page' up steep stone steps set into the smooth-sided mound. They reached the wide, flat, circular top, where a low stone wall, patrolled by more grim-faced guards, rimmed the plateau. The residence of the lord, three storeys of foreboding granite, sat in the centre. No watchtower was necessary: the whole mound served as a lookout post, offering a clear view for miles around.

Ulfar stopped in an area that was paved in the same fashion as the streets below to afford defending soldiers as firm a grip as possible in most conditions. 'Welcome back to Ragnarr's Hall,' he said expansively. 'I assume it looks familiar.'

The Captain nodded. 'When you have been away for a while, you expect it to have changed. I don't know why – it has looked like this for five generations.' He smiled. 'Funnily enough, it is good to see it. Considering the fact that I may be about to receive a hot reception inside, I should feel as if I'd prefer to be anywhere but here, but it does, actually, feel good.'

'Well, enjoy it while you can, because I know exactly the reception that awaits you,' Ulfar growled ominously. He let the Captain move past him before he turned to Brann and winked outrageously, his face a picture of glee at the discomfort he was trying to instil in Einarr. His expression was so infectious that Brann could not help but grin back.

The massive, wooden, iron-bound outer doors to the hall lay open but, as with the gates below, a pair of sentries flanked the opening. These two men were huge, even by local standards. They wore the full pelt of a bear as a cloak, with the head resting on their own skulls, and were resting before them massive war axes, a single heavy blade on a haft almost as tall as the men who bore them. Brann had no doubt that they could swing the fearsome weapons as if they were swatting flies and, at the sight of them, his stomach churned twice as fast. If he were exposed as a fraud, would those razor-sharp edges be aimed at his neck with more skill than the late, unlamented Boar could muster in several life-times? He kept his gaze fixed firmly on the Captain's back, reminded himself to breathe, concentrated on not tripping and followed the other two through the portal.

A further set of sturdy doors, smaller but no less imposing due to the ornate carvings of hunting scenes and battles of yore, faced them at the other end of a short hallway that was otherwise broken only by arrowslits set high in the wall, ready to rain death upon anyone who breached the outer doors and then found themselves trapped in this confined space.

As they approached, these doors were pulled open by two further warriors, who had presumably been instructed to do so by someone watching unseen by the trio. Brann had expected the doors to move with great creaking and groaning and much effort from those pulling them, but instead they swung effortlessly and silently, as if crafted and maintained with great care and balanced to perfection. They entered an antechamber, with corridors leading off right and left, but Brann's eyes were drawn by Ulfar's direct and huge strides towards another set of double doors. These were less solid than those they had just passed through, being designed for privacy rather than defence. Strangely, they were less ornate than the large heavy doors that had just opened for them, and bore merely a representation of a bear's head carved with simple but clean lines into the dark wood. Without any undue ceremony – in fact, with no ceremony at all – Ulfar slammed the heels of his hands on the double doors and, with his considerable weight behind them, swung the doors wide open.

A man sat in a high-backed, ornately carved, wooden chair. He was turned away from them while he conversed with an elderly man to his right but, as they entered, he turned to face them. Brann caught his breath at the sight. The man before them was an older, broader version of the Captain. His clothing, in hues of brown, was rougher, although of no less quality, than the Captain's, and his long, grey hair hung loose and was kept in place by a leather band around his brow that bore what appeared to be a circular gold emblem at the front. But the similarity in the features was unmistakable.

'Ah, Ulfar,' he said, his tone deep and measured. 'You should have the guards announce you, lest your subtle entrance goes unnoticed.'

Brann was so nervous, he almost giggled. Ulfar merely dismissed the remark with a grunt, and said, 'Our guest, Lord Ragnarr: Einarr, master of the *Blue Dragon*.'

Ragnarr turned his cool gaze to them. 'Greetings, Captain,' he said. 'Yours was one face I had not expected to see in my hall, nor to come sailing so brazenly up my fjord.' He smiled, a warm sight. 'But you are welcome nevertheless, nephew, and it will never be otherwise. Our Lady left with you, and she would not have done so with a man with evil in his heart. And you have returned her in safety, although I'd wager the power to bring harm to her lies not on many mortal men. In short, it is good to see you, my boy.'

Einarr inclined his head, with a slight glance towards Ulfar, as if to say that he should never have believed his predictions of a dire welcome. 'My thanks, Ragnarr. It always did and, I hope, always will, give me great pleasure to come here. But I would bring no ill to you or your people: I will tarry here no longer than a night, if I may, before departing for my father's hall.'

Ragnarr launched himself to his feet and came to grip Einarr's shoulders. 'That you will not, nephew. A traveller in need will always find a place here for as long as he needs and as long as I decide – others outside our borders will never dictate the level of hospitality in my hall. Only one man commands such authority over me, and I do not think my brother would disagree with me on this occasion. My honour, my hospitality and my family count more in this hall than any exile imposed elsewhere.

'And you cannot travel just now, anyway. There is bandit trouble between here and your father. I have men already helping him to pin them between us, and not enough remain here to give you an adequate escort.'

'That is not a problem,' Einarr said. 'I have good men with me, if I could prevail upon you to keep the slaves while I am gone and provide quarters for Our Lady.'

The lord shook his head. 'You misunderstand me. I know you would fight your way through, but you would arrive with only half of your men, and I am sure you would be loath to suffer such losses. My escort's value would not be in combat, but rather in being of such size that it would deter any attack in the first place.'

The Captain nodded, although he was clearly not happy. Ragnarr slapped him heartily on the back. 'Do not worry, boy. It will only last a few days, a week at the most, until sufficient men return from patrol, and then you can be rid of the uncle you obviously cannot bear to stay with.'

Einarr smiled. 'Apologies, uncle. I forget myself, and the allure of your famed hospitality. We would be delighted to stay. After all, you always were my favourite uncle.'

Ragnarr guffawed. 'I am your only uncle, you cheeky brat,' he roared, enveloping the younger man in a powerful embrace. Stepping back, he regarded Brann. 'Your page looks a little off-colour, Einarr. Is he all right?'

The Captain glanced fleetingly at him, as panic stabbed through the boy. 'He is just nervous, that's all. He is new, and terrified to step out of line and incur the wrath of a foul-tempered old warrior like yourself.'

Ragnarr's keen eyes narrowed. He stepped over to Brann, his menacing bulk dwarfing the boy. Without looking directly at him, he leant forward and, in a conspiratorial manner, growled in his ear, 'I expect you are also cold, tired and very, very hungry.'

Brann was unsure if he was allowed to answer, or even nod. Gambling that he could get away with nodding, he did so. Ragnarr bellowed with laughter, almost rendering the boy deaf.

'I'll bet you are,' he roared. 'You islanders are all the same – no stamina.' Brann was feeling more confident that this was what passed for good-natured banter in these parts, and risked a weak smile. 'That's the spirit, lad,' Ragnarr encouraged him. 'My son will see that you receive food and heat. Sleep, I'm afraid, may be longer in coming.' He turned to one of the guards. 'Fetch Konall,' he ordered.

'No need, father, I am here,' said a voice from behind. Brann's heart sank as the tall, blond boy who had glared at him from the shadows in the town walked through the doors. Trust him to make a poor start with none less than the lord's son.

If Konall recognised him, he hid it well as he acknowledged his father and led Brann from the room. As soon as they were through the door, however, his demeanour changed. Without turning, his voice dripping with disdain, he snarled, 'Don't think you are getting any special treatment, islander. You'll eat in the kitchen with the servants. Your prying eyes can look all they like there, but there's nothing there for you to see that you shouldn't.'

Still racked with nerves, Brann's voice faltered as he said, 'I am so hungry, I am just grateful to be getting fed at all.'

'Of course you are. A sheep from the islands of sheep is grateful for the slightest thing. A sheep can do nothing for itself, but be *grateful*.'

'I should be grateful. Your father was kind to think of me.'

'My father is soft,' Konall spat. 'He bothered with you because he is fond of your lord, though why he is bothered with an exile who has lost his honour is beyond me.'

'I don't know anything about that,' Brann mumbled.

Konall wheeled round without warning. 'You don't? I suppose you wouldn't. A sheep knows only how to go where he is herded. And bleat.' He smiled, coldly, malice in his narrowing eyes. 'Well, perhaps there are some things you should know about your precious lord. But why would a wolf educate a sheep? The sheep would still be a sheep.' His lip curled in disgust. 'A nation of farmers and merchants are not true men. They are the providers for stronger men.'

'So who grows your food? Do you not have farmers? How do you eat?'

'Our farmers are warriors first and farmers second. They grow their crops and rear their animals, but they can fight themselves to keep their land. Our women can fight. Your people serve.'

Hot anger surged through Brann. 'When the raiders came, my village fought. My family fought. If they had run, they might still be alive, but they fought. *My family fought.*'

Konall looked at him with disdain. 'Not very well, if they are all dead.'

He turned and stalked down the short corridor. Brann fought now. He fought to push down the desire to batter the haughty prick to the ground and smash his sour face against the stone floor until his arms grew numb. But he couldn't escape his precarious situation. He had probably already overstepped the mark. Forcing his breathing slower, he pushed down the emotion in a process that was becoming familiar and automatic and eased his clenched fists.

The pair wound down a spiral staircase and emerged into the kitchens, where a thin, harsh-looking woman and two young servants cleaned pots and utensils at a large stone sink.

The three women straightened as Konall entered. He flicked his head at Brann. 'Give him some food. If you only have scraps, that will do.' Without waiting for a reply, he turned and swept out.

The older woman looked Brann up and down. 'We have more than scraps, boy. There is fresh meat, bread and cheese there... but only if you help fetch more water. It has been a long day and the bucket is large. Valdis will show you where.'

One of the girls beckoned to him and led him through a door at the far end of the room, handing him a large wooden bucket as they went.

'Don't mind Dagrun,' she said, her accent lilting. 'She sounds harsh, but she is fair. And she is skilled with food – which is useful, because she is the castle cook.' She giggled and walked ahead. Mesmerised by the swing of her skirt, Brann followed, the bucket banging unnoticed against his leg.

They reached a small chamber close to the kitchen with a well in the centre. Brann lowered the well's own bucket and heaved it up, brimming with ice-cold water, with the aid of a pulley. He filled the kitchen bucket and lifted it off the floor. It was heavy, but he hefted it more easily than he had expected. His time on the rowing bench must have indeed made a difference to his strength.

'Oh, it is so good to have a big, strong man around the place!' Valdis exclaimed in mock delight, standing up and blithely ignoring the fact that she was slightly taller than he. 'Normally we girls only half fill it and make two journeys.'

Brann blushed and stammered something about returning to the kitchen, but the girl was already off. He followed as fast as he could, gripping the handle with both hands. Within half-a-dozen paces, he was revising his assessment on the ease of carrying the bucket.

Back in the kitchen, Valdis told him to put the bucket down beside a cauldron that was hanging over an open fire within a large hearth. Dagrun had drained the water from the sink and was replacing a stone plug. Valdis saw him looking curiously, and said, 'Never seen a sink before? You must be from a village like my aunt and uncle, where, when we visit, we only ever have basins that we take outside and empty by hand. These sinks, however, lead into sluices that take the water outside – and considering the amount of work that is done within the sinks, we could not manage any other way.'

Brann nodded, but was still confused. 'But how does the water drain to the surface if we are in the basement, underground?'

Valdis giggled. 'Oh, so you do have a voice after all.' Brann blushed. She continued, 'We are inside a hill, remember, silly boy. The sluices lead out and down to the side of the hill. Channels then lead to the river behind us.' Brann blushed an even deeper shade at his stupidity and moved closer to the fire, hoping that they would think that it was the heat that was flushing his cheeks.

'Come on, you two, enough chatter,' Dagrun snapped. 'Idle talk does not refill the sink.'

Following Valdis's lead, Brann filled large bowls with hot water from the cauldron, and poured them into the sink. After several trips back and forth, the sink was full again, and the young maid helped him to tip the bucket's contents into the cauldron.

The job done, Dagrun was true to her word, and piled steaming venison, large slices of fresh bread and a huge chunk of cheese in front of him, along with a sharp knife. Brann wondered how they would feel if they knew they were handing such a weapon to a slave, rather than to a page, but hunger dismissed the thought as he wolfed into the food while the three servants returned to the dish-washing.

Before long, the water was drained and the gleaming kitchenware was stacked and racked with organised precision. The three kitchen servants had been engrossed in the routine of the operation, and Dagrun had forgotten about their guest. She turned to ask if he needed anything else, but found the boy snoring gently, his head resting on his arms on the tabletop.

'Will you look at that,' she said to the girls. 'A typical man, lying around sleeping while the women are hard at work.'

Valdis bent over him and stroked his hair away from his forehead. 'Oh, leave him be, the poor thing,' she said softly. 'He must have been exhausted.'

Dagrun grunted. 'And hungry, too, looking at the little that is left from the food he was given.' She scowled. 'And don't you be getting sweet on him, my girl. You have enough to do around here, and you know he will be gone soon enough.'

The other maid giggled, but Valdis just smiled gently. 'I am not getting sweet on anyone. I just think he looks so peaceful. It would be a shame to wake him, that's all.'

The older woman turned away and took off her apron. 'You've got that right, at least. They seem to be getting younger all the time, these pages. Let him rest while he can, or at least until we need the table.'

She beckoned to the other girl. 'Come, Eona. Time for us to get some rest. Since Valdis is not getting sweet on the boy, there is no risk of her falling head over heels in love if we leave her with him, so she can wait here in case anyone calls down for food – or for a page.' She looked pointedly at Valdis. 'I will be back later to shut up the kitchen for the night. Behave yourself, girl.'

Valdis assumed her most innocent expression as the pair left the room, then pulled a chair into position, facing Brann. Clasping her hands in her lap, she sat back and watched him breathe. Some time later, he grew restless, starting to moan and twitch. She moved around the table, and, stroking his cheek, she whispered soothingly into his ear until he settled again.

She returned to her seat, smiling to herself. 'Sometimes,' she said softly, 'this job is not so bad.'

A little over an hour later, a bell clanged in the corner of the kitchen, its sound harsh in the calm that had enveloped the room. Brann, and Valdis – who had also started to doze – jerked awake as one.

For a moment, Brann's confusion as to his surroundings and company was evident. Walking past him, the servant girl patted him reassuringly on the shoulder.

'Take your time to come to,' she said, impish amusement back in her eyes. 'It is my job to go and see what they want.'

Smoothing out her simple dress, and with a mischievous glance back over her shoulder, she skipped from the room and disappeared up the stairs. Almost before Brann had managed to regain a sense of his surroundings, she reappeared. 'Your master has need of your services, whatever they may be,' she told him, the glint in her eyes dancing hypnotically.

Brann desperately wanted to impress her with a mature reply – or, at the very least, not to sound like a mumbling idiot. The best he could manage, however, was, 'I suppose I'd better go up then.' He silently cursed himself.

Still smiling, the girl said, 'Don't worry, I'll show you the way.'

She turned and started up the stairs. Blushing, Brann followed her. They continued past the ground floor and exited the stairwell into a corridor that led across the tower. Einarr was waiting at the far corner, in front of a door that would open into a room overlooking the town and its approaches. With a lurch in his stomach, Brann realised that these would probably the lord's rooms.

Valdis halted in front of the waiting man. Bowing her head in deference, she said, 'Your page, my lord.'

'So I see,' Einarr murmured.

'Will there be anything else, my lord?' the girl asked demurely.

'No. Thank you,' the tall warrior said. 'That will be all.'

The serving girl turned, winked at Brann, and returned down the corridor. Brann could not help noticing the sway of her skirts as she went. Talking to the Captain in his cabin on the ship seemed so distant, now, but one thing he had said, about his heart starting to open up in time, in small steps, seemed actually to be correct. For the first time in a long while, he felt good. He smiled.

'Confident girl,' Einarr observed, bringing Brann back from his reverie with a jolt. He looked up at the tall man to see amusement playing on his face.

'Yes, Captain,' he stammered.

'Well, now that she has settled your nerves – or, perhaps, added to them – you need to forget about her and concentrate on the task in hand. Which is, in case you have forgotten, the small matter of being my page.

'When we go in, stand at the back of the room, by the door, as if you are ready to run any errand I may ask. I won't, but you should look as if you are expecting it. If things get particularly private, you will be told to leave the room, in which case you wait here until summoned back in or sent elsewhere. But that may not happen. You will be surprised how much pages are trusted here. Mainly through necessity, because nobles need someone at hand at a moment's notice and it is inconvenient to keep kicking the pages out and having to bring them back in all the time. But also because of the fact that the penalty for a page passing on information to anyone in these circumstances is death. Which is something you should probably remember.'

Brann gulped and nodded. It was not a lot to understand, but it was a great deal to take in for a boy whose life had been transformed so much in such a short time. In many ways, he still felt in the midst of a dream – or, to be more accurate, a nightmare.

Einarr raised his hand to knock at the door, but paused and turned back to the boy. 'And one other thing: take your lead from your serving girl and address any noble as "my lord", myself included. I am many things to you: when you row, I am the Captain; as a slave, I am your master; but as my page, I am your lord and, to a page, that transcends all else. And noblewomen are addressed as "my lady", but you probably guessed that already.'

Brann smiled weakly and nodded again as Einarr turned back to the door, and with no hesitation this time, rapped the thick wood twice. A voice called from the other side and Einarr strode in, surprising a page on the other side who had been about to open the door for them.

A log fire roared in a massive stone fireplace, tall enough for a man to walk into. Dramatically silhouetted in front of it, with his back to the flames, stood Ragnarr. As they entered, he moved to one of a pair of high-backed, carved wooden chairs, gesturing to Einarr to take the other.

As they sat, Brann turned to stand at the door. Finding the other page there already, he stumbled in trying to avoid walking into him. The boy, a good couple of years older than him, helped to steady him with a sympathetic smile and directed him to the other side of the doorway. Thankful that neither of the men by the fire had seen the incident, Brann took up his station and, with a surreptitious glance, copied the other boy's stance, with his hands clasped behind him. He did not know if such a position was mandatory, but he was taking no chances.

Ragnarr picked up a large flagon from a table beside him and gestured to a similar one at Einarr's side. 'I trust you have eaten and drunk well already,' he rumbled, 'but I always think this helps to settle the stomach after a meal.'

Einarr smiled. 'I must admit, I have missed your ale these past ten years, Ragnarr.'

The large lord's eyes widened in mock shock. 'Just my ale? Is that all you miss from your second childhood home?'

Einarr laughed this time. 'Of course not, uncle,' he said. 'And there is much we have to catch up on in each other's lives.'

Ragnarr sighed. 'That there is, boy, that there is. But I am afraid that is for another time. The hour is late and I will contain myself to our current situation.'

Einarr's eyes narrowed, but he made no reply, letting Ragnarr continue.

'I know nothing of your reasons for returning, though I know they must be of importance or you would not risk the upheaval that could follow, not least to your own future good health.' He held up his hand to deter any response. 'I will hear of them later, I know. Anyway, if ever there was a time when you might be able to slip in unnoticed, this is it. We have bandit trouble.'

Einarr nodded. 'So you said when I arrived. But that is nothing new. There have always been bandits.'

'Not like this,' Ragnarr growled. 'There are more of them, and they are bolder. And they raid further into our lands than before, rather than just keeping to the hills. They will not venture within range of the townships, so the farms close to us are mostly undisturbed, but any travelling is affected. There are large pockets of the land where a sizeable escort, as I said in the hall, is needed to discourage them, and lone travellers do not survive. Which is why there are no lone travellers any more.'

The large warrior swigged from his flagon, droplets of ale glistening in his beard as they caught the firelight, and he stared into the flames for a moment. He took a deep breath, as if steeling himself to utter something he was unwilling to say aloud.

He spat savagely into the fire, producing a loud sizzle. 'But there is more, and worse. Most of the bandits are what we are used to: scum who have been run out of town or village for thieving, murder, or whatever. But not only are they more organised and co-ordinated – not the random, opportunistic bands you will remember – there is also an element among them that are savage, almost inhuman. Where they strike, none is left alive, and there is almost a joy in the killing itself.'

Einarr leant forward, his dark eyes intent. 'The bodies: mutilated?' he asked tensely. Ragnarr glared at him and nodded, and Brann felt nausea sweeping through him as he remembered, like Einarr, the reports from the south island that had sent them in shock across the sea.

'Not just mutilated – they were unrecognisable. Hacked to pieces, and left like butcher meat. Whole villages: men, women and children. It has only happened in three places, so far, but already the rumours have started. These scumbags have never been seen – not, at least, by any who have lived to tell – so there is much talk in the villages, and even the towns, of the monsters of the myths: men who are half-bear, or half-wolf, or even both. You know, the sort of things the older boys used to frighten you with when you were a child. Of course it is not that, but try telling that to the people out there.' He sighed. 'Maybe I am getting old, but I just cannot imagine any man acting like these do. The gods know I have seen many things in my years: as a warrior, I have seen men killed in battle with terrible injuries, and as a lord, I have cleaned up after murders and examined the corpses. None of it has been pretty, as you will know yourself. But I do not have the stomach for this.'

He ran his hand through his hair and wiped the back of it across his eyes; a weary gesture. 'I know I have not seen you for a decade, nephew, and I am sorry to burden you with such gloom, but it is of too much import to be left unsaid for any length of time.' He took a long draught of his ale.

'I have seen such things already,' Einarr said slowly. 'That is why I am here.'

'What?' Ragnarr slammed down his flagon. 'Where?'

Einarr rose to his feet and stood in front of the fire, staring into the dancing flames. 'On the islands, where I was… working.'

Ragnarr grunted. 'Do not be embarrassed. I know what you do. I have ears and eyes beyond the boundaries of my town and even beyond our land, you know, and I am well aware that the cargoes that you carry are not always inanimate objects. A man in your position must make a living somehow. And who am I to judge, having stood by while my brother's son was exiled rather than defend my family?'

Einarr turned. His face was an impassive mask. 'We talked through this a decade ago, my father, you and I. There was no real alternative: one man leaving, still with his life in his own hands, rather than many men dying and lands being lost to defend the folly and shame of that one man's action.'

'I know, I know.' Pain was still etched into Ragnarr's face. 'But it has not been an easy ten years to bear, for us as well as for you.' He stood and took Einarr's ale to him. 'So, you saw the work of these monsters, too?'

Einarr nodded. 'Yes. Well, not personally. But some of my men did. They were more shaken than I have ever seen. And these are men who do not have the most genteel of pasts.'

Ragnarr stood and burped with a ferocity that widened Brann's eyes. Despite the tension in the room (or perhaps because of it) he had to fight to stifle a giggle.

'Then it is vital we speak with your father as a matter of urgency,' the chieftain declared.

Einarr looked up, puzzled. 'But I thought there were not enough men here for an escort.'

Ragnarr smiled coyly, an odd expression on one so large and fearsome. 'I thought about that after you left the hall earlier, and took the liberty of sending a messenger.' Einarr started to speak again, but was halted by the raised hand of his uncle. 'Yes, yes, I know what you are thinking, that I have just told you of the futility of a lone traveller attempting to make any journey at the moment. But one man *can* get through... by boat. The bandits are an inconvenience on land, but they have not taken to the sea yet. Weather permitting, he should take only one day longer than he would travelling on horseback.'

Einarr grunted. 'If I set sail in the morning, I could be there before him. I could be travelling, after all.'

'Don't let your heart rule your head, boy,' Ragnarr growled. 'You know as well as I do that the sight of your ship arriving at your father's harbour unannounced would cause more than a minor stir. It is easier to turn up here out of the blue, where the town is inland from the anchorage, and be welcomed, but to sail right into the city that is the warlord's seat of power with no prior warning would not be fair to your father and would cause problems you would have to be stupid not to predict.' He sighed, his tone softening.

'Don't worry, you'll see him soon enough. I reckon he will be here in a week at the most.' He looked directly at his nephew. 'How do you feel about that?'

Einarr smiled gently. Brann was startled – he had never expected to see a look so tender on the face of the Captain. 'It will be a long week,' he said quietly. 'I have missed my parents terribly these past ten years. Being away in itself has not been the problem; knowing that I had no choice to return has been the intolerable part.'

Ragnarr slapped him heartily on the back. Another man could have been knocked headlong, but a warrior's instinctive reactions, honed muscles and the experience of regular childhood visits to his uncle combined subconsciously to see Einarr step forward slightly to ride the blow initially and then brace himself to prevent any further movement. The corners of his mouth creased slightly in what Brann guessed was the closest he would come to a wince.

'Oh, get to bed, you girl!' Ragnarr roared. 'You will have me in tears soon with all this heart-rending claptrap.'

Einarr nodded and, smiling, turned to go. He paused. 'Thank you, uncle,' he said softly.

Ragnarr grinned, an expanse of white teeth breaking out in the midst of his midnight-black beard. 'It is nothing, boy. I am your favourite uncle, after all, am I not?' Stepping past his page, he opened the door himself. 'And welcome back, Einarr. I hope you will not take so long before the next time.'

Einarr's eyes smiled back at him. He gestured to Brann to follow, and left the room. Neither spoke as they walked along the corridor, stopping only when they chanced upon a servant boy. Einarr asked the lad to show his page to the chamber that had been set aside for him, and turned to Brann.

'Sleep well, boy,' he said simply. 'You have much missed rest to catch up on.'

'Shall I show you to your quarters first, my lord?' the servant asked.

Einarr shook his head. 'I was playing in these corridors before I could walk, lad. I will be able to find my own way.'

He strode back up the corridor. With fatigue striking him for the second time that night, Brann followed the boy to the most eagerly anticipated bed he had ever known.

Chapter 7

He had visited the oracle once.

He had never been one for superstition. A man's fate lay in the hands of his guile and endeavour, nothing more. To abdicate responsibility to the utterings of another was the action of those too weak and lazy to take a decision themselves or formulate an approach to any given situation. And it gave the author of those utterings the opportunity to guide your actions, should they so wish. He preferred to direct his fate himself. Those weak and lazy in his position had a short lifespan.

Curiosity, however, directed his feet to the oracle, once. To form a true opinion on something, it must be an informed opinion. She had offered him guidance or prediction. He had, of course, dismissed guidance.

He had never visited her again. There was no need. His opinion, now informed, remained the same. He had not disregarded her, though. From time to time, she had proved useful, when he wanted those more gullible than he to be guided along a certain path. He had always had a feeling for the form of persuasion suitable for each individual. For so many, it was gold or fear. For others, it was the temptations

*of the flesh, or the threat of those temptations becoming
known. For some, it was the word of the oracle. For those
who filled the position of oracle in his time, it varied. But
he always found it.*

*Her words to him, he had dismissed at the time. Vague
claptrap, as he had expected. But he had never forgotten
the words.*

*And now, plotting once more, those words, for reasons
unknown, came unbidden into his mind. His plans needed an
instrument. If the words were indeed claptrap, he would find
an instrument elsewhere. But if they did, against expectation,
come to pass, he would be handed one.*

*Inexplicably and utterly against character, the feeling
nagged at the corner of his mind that they would come to pass.*

****

Crisp snow crunched softly underfoot and breath hung heavily
in the still, sharp air. The small party moved through the
sparse fir trees as the foothills steepened into the mountains
that rose to the landward side of Ravensrest, on the far edge
of a small plain dotted only with the occasional farmstead.

Brann caught his breath and absently shifted one twig
at his feet in line with another as Konall signalled a halt.
Shortly before dawn, a servant boy had wakened him with
the news that Lord Konall was mounting a hunting trip into
the mountains that day, and needed two pages and a couple
of servants to accompany him. The outbreaks of banditry
had been exclusively confined to areas out of immediate
range of the forces from the larger settlements, and even
then were largely targeted at the roads where travellers were
easily spotted and ambushes simply laid. As they were headed

across rough land and into the mountain areas that were unpopulated but for the occasional shepherd, they were not expected to encounter anything other than the local wildlife, although four battle-hardened veterans had been sent with them as a token gesture towards caution.

Lord Ragnarr had suggested that, in addition to Lord Konall's own page, Lord Einarr's page should also go, as it would save him from being cooped up in the hall all day, and Lord Einarr had agreed.

Lord Einarr had also suggested that, instead of two servants, they take two slaves, as all of the servants in the hall were busy dealing with the extra work caused by the arrival of Lord Einarr's party and the imminent visit of Lord Sigurr. Lord Einarr, the boy faithfully continued, had said that his page should choose the two slaves. He said that, in selecting them, his page should have trust as his main consideration, and that his page would understand.

His page did. Accordingly, he had ordered – as Einarr had expected him to – Grakk and Gerens to be brought to join the party. The pair had been roughly shaken from their sleep and, as they met up, a frantic, but concealed, signal from Brann had kept their mouths shut despite their puzzlement at finding him in the hall – although he knew that an explanation would be demanded at the first opportunity. Glancing at the pair as they rested in the shade of a tree – Grakk squatting quietly, breathing easily despite the heavy load of provisions on his back, and Gerens pacing up and down, finding it difficult to contain his frustration at having to waste time resting – Brann knew why Einarr had meant for him to choose them. Grakk's experience and simple practicality would be an obvious asset and he was intelligent enough, despite his savage appearance, to know that any attempt at an escape in a strange land while in the company of experienced warriors and skilled trackers would be folly. Gerens was, like Brann, new enough to slavery to be wary of attempting escape, and he also added his own brand of deep, dark consideration and unscrupulous logic to every situation. And, most of all – as the Captain had hinted – there was a mutual trust between the trio, formed rapidly but strongly in the short time that they had shared a rowing bench. Even if the boys felt that they knew the bare minimum about Grakk, they had been encouraged by his seeming acceptance of them, and they had come to rely on the tattooed barbarian, and his contrasting suggestion of a civilised education, as if he were a guide in this new world they had been thrust into. Likewise, the boys' eager acceptance of his advice had appeared to please Grakk, and he had taken them under his wing. Such a relationship had become silently accepted by all three, and Brann felt better for having him with them on the hunting trip.

Konall's voice snapping through the sharp air jerked Brann from his musings. His legs had stiffened during the short break, and he groaned as he forced himself upright, the weight of his pack trying to pull him backwards as he rose. He had insisted on carrying an equal load to that of the two slaves – much to the bewilderment of the other page, an otherwise cheerful boy who then had to follow suit to avoid losing face in front of the foreigners – because he felt that, despite the need to maintain the pretence, there was only so much that his conscience would allow. Now, however, as he shrugged his pack higher on his shoulders, he was beginning to wonder if his principled stance had been so wise. Ironically the other page, with his bear-like physique more suited to the toil, was dealing far more easily with the effort that they had both been subjected to by Brann's decision.

Berating himself, he smiled slightly and trudged after the long-striding Konall, who was leaving the trees for a gentle slope broken only by occasional rocky outcrops that looked even blacker against the bright, sunlit snow. Brann had been worried initially about the less than pleasant prospect of having to endure conversation with the lord's carnaptious son, but at least the fact that they were hunting had ruled that out – silence was essential so they could hear, rather than be heard, as much as the noise of their passage allowed. In any case, Konall seemed to prefer to keep his own counsel.

After more than two hours' walking that seemed, through boredom and fatigue, to have lasted several days, they cleared a rise to descend into a broad, wooded, ravine-strewn valley that lay between two towering, harsh rock faces.

Konall pointed. 'There is better hunting here,' he said curtly. 'This valley has more sun and more shelter, so less snow lies and more grows. So there is more wildlife. We will camp down there and hunt properly in the morning.'

They found a sheltered clearing with a small, clear stream running rapidly through it and set up camp. Dry wood that had been carried with them was used to start a fire that gave off as little smoke as possible, while newly gathered firewood was ranged around the fire to dry. These were men, Brann observed, used to surviving without being noticed. Maybe in this land, surviving and remaining private amounted to the same thing.

Darkness had fallen and the fire, prepared in a small pit to reduce the chance of being noticed by unwelcome eyes, had died to a deep glow by the time they had finished a meal prepared – expertly, as it transpired – by Grakk. Hunger and fatigue had kept conversation to a minimum as they ate and, immediately the food was gone, they settled down, wrapped in blankets and close to the heat, which was fed occasionally by the sentry. Brann noticed that he shielded his eyes as he did so to preserve his night vision.

Despite his weariness, however, Brann found he was unable to sleep: too much was whirling through his mind. He stood, taking care not to wake those lying close to him, and gathered his father's black cloak around him, as glad of the familiarity it brought as he was of the protection against the chill. He took a leather water flask from the supplies and, conscious that the guard was watching him with suspicion, he made sure that he kept himself in sight as he moved to sit on a boulder at the edge of the small clearing, sipping at the water.

'Any room for a nine-and-a-half-fingered man?' a voice whispered in his ear. Brann jumped violently and he dropped the bottle. Gerens, ignoring his reaction and catching the spinning flask, sat down beside him.

Brann smiled as the other boy took a long, slow swallow. 'How is the finger? What's left of it, that is?'

Gerens held up his hand and flexed the fingers into a fist and back out again, the white bandage on the foreshortened digit catching the dim firelight. 'It moves, it needs only water now rather than that foul-smelling ointment they were using and what remains won't fall off as long as I keep it clean. Can't complain, chief.'

Brann's smile grew broader, and the pair looked at the stars until Gerens broke the silence. 'So are you going to tell us what is going on?' He handed back the water container and fixed his solemn gaze on Brann. 'So…' he prompted again.

Brann sighed, and shrugged. 'Nothing much to say,' he whispered. 'Apparently, the Captain needed a page to look

209

the part, and I was the nearest appropriate person. Oh, and remember the reports of the villagers getting slaughtered?' Gerens nodded. Even those who had not been close enough to hear the warrior's harrowing report to the Captain had soon learned of the horror as word spread through the benches. 'Well, it seems it has been happening here, too.'

Gerens's eyebrows raised. 'Is that your idea of "nothing much", chief?'

Brann paled as the memory of the penalty for repeating anything discussed by the lords, over-ridden by his enthusiasm at talking to a friend once more, returned. 'I should have not told you even that. Please do not repeat any of this, Gerens.'

The boy snorted. 'Out here? To who?'

'Not even when we get back,' Brann insisted. He changed the subject. 'The servants are certainly very friendly at the castle, or stronghold, or whatever they call it round here.'

'The servants,' Gerens queried. 'Have you met many of them, then?'

'One or two,' Brann said. 'Well, one, really, to any great extent,' he admitted.

Gerens's eyes narrowed. 'And *she* was very friendly, was she, chief?' He was clearly enjoying Brann's discomfort. 'Exactly how friendly are we talking about?'

The smaller boy bridled. 'Not that friendly. She was just helpful when I did not know anything or anyone. Don't get the wrong idea.'

Gerens's laughter came in a snort, startling Brann as he had never even seen him smile before. 'You've fallen for her!'

A small stone ricocheted off his back. The pair jerked around in alarm, and saw the sentry glaring at them. 'Quiet,' he hissed. 'Sound carries for miles at night up here. Whisper or nothing.'

'Grumpy sod,' Brann grumbled. But he did so in a whisper. The warrior was large, with more scars on his face than he could count. Even the snarling bear tattooed on one arm had a less fearsome demeanour.

Gerens took the water container and sipped from it, before offering it back to Brann. 'Take care. He is one to be wary of. The word among the slaves is that those tattoos are awarded, not chosen. A reward for an act of bravery. Looking at these people, I'm guessing the bravery involves chopping enemies into small pieces, not retrieving puppies that have fallen down wells.'

'What has it been like for you?' the smaller boy said, accepting the water.

Gerens shrugged. 'They do not seem to have slaves around here, same as at home, so they don't know how to treat us. They just make sure we have enough food and drink, and leave us alone.' He indicated the sleeping figures. 'I think we should get back. It would not be a good idea to draw attention to ourselves, especially for a bad reason.'

Brann nodded his agreement, and they returned to the fireside. The conversation had settled his swirling thoughts and, within moments, sleep had claimed him.

A rough shake on his shoulder and a hand over his mouth wakened him what seemed like only a few minutes later. As his eyes cleared, however, he saw that dawn was breaking. The guard took his hand from Brann's mouth.

'A large animal has been heard,' he said. 'From the level of noise, it can only be a boar, bear or man. Lord Konall is anxious to move in case it is a bear. It is not yet quite time for hibernation, and many will still be roaming these hills, eager for food.'

Not relishing the thought of becoming a bear's breakfast, Brann quickly made ready to set off. The utensils from the previous night's meal had been washed and packed as soon as they had been used in the event that a sudden departure proved necessary.

Grakk squatted beside him and helped him to fasten the straps on his pack. 'I can understand Konall's anxiety,' the boy said. 'I don't particularly want to meet a hungry bear, either.'

Grakk's eyes narrowed in amusement. 'You misunderstand, little one. We are the hunters. He seeks the bear. He would wear the skin it wears and, should he kill it, he will do this. Then he will be a man among his people.'

Brann looked sceptical. 'Where I come from, it takes four, maybe six, men to tackle a bear. Even then, men have died.'

Grakk shrugged. 'This is not where you come from.'

Konall called the group together. He was trying to appear calm and authoritative, but his eyes were shining with excitement.

'Whatever the creature, it is close,' he said in a low voice. 'We may be lucky. I had expected to have to descend below the snowline, but it seems that my bear may be coming to us. Perhaps that is an omen, perhaps it is merely good fortune. Either way, it matters not: I want my bear.

'So we will move to a larger clearing a short distance from here. We have snared a rabbit – we will use it to attract the beast. And we will wait.' He looked at the foreigners. 'Silently.' His words came quicker as his excitement grew. 'If it is any creature other than a bear, we kill it as quickly as possible and move below the snowline as we originally intended. But if it is a bear, no one will come near it but me. Only the guards will be permitted to become involved, and even then only if it is necessary to encourage the bear in my direction. They know what to do.

'Anyone else who interferes, will do so knowing he faces execution as a result. But, most of all, remain silent. If this is my bear and you cause me to lose him, I will wear your skin instead of his.'

They were dispersed to make their final preparations for leaving. As they strapped on their packs, the guards produced strips of cloth and used them to muffle anything that may make even the slightest noise. As a warrior attended to his load, Brann murmured to him. 'What if the bear is about to kill him, and we could distract it, or scare it away? Lord Ragnarr would have our heads if we stood by and let his son die.'

The huge man grunted. 'Lord Ragnarr would do worse than that – but only if you stopped the bear,' he growled. 'It is a straight fight, boy and bear. If the bear wins, Konall was never meant to be a man. If the boy wins, he walks away a man. It is no more complicated than that. It is the way of our people.'

Brann was stunned at the cheapness of life. It showed on his face. With a hint of a smile, the warrior said, 'Do not worry. We are not monsters. Our boys are trained all their lives for this. It is a necessity. If any of us finds ourselves alone in wild country, and we know we can kill a bear single-handedly, then there is nothing really to fear.

'This ritual proves as much to the boy himself as it does to others. Some die, yes, but some people die slipping on the ice in a town street.' He finished his work and slapped Brann's pack to signify the fact. 'I believe he will be fine, do not worry.' He moved on to help Grakk.

Brann nudged Gerens, and gestured at the young nobleman standing separate from the rest, aloof and arrogant. 'I am not worried. If it is a one-on-one fight, bear against brat, and we are just spectators, I know who is getting my support.'

Gerens nodded, his face as serious as ever. 'Agreed. After all, it has probably got better breath than he has.'

Remembering their admonishment from the guard during the night, Brann stifled his laughter.

They left in single file, moving slowly and quietly through the trees. They had been told it was only a short distance to the clearing, but the need for silence was paramount, forcing them to creep forward, watching the ground as they placed each step. After around three hundred yards, they encountered a difficulty. The snow in this area was more a result of drifts from higher ground as it was of fresh snowfall. As such, its depth was unpredictable. The section they were about to cross presented more of a problem. Protruding occasionally were black, slick rocks, a sign of what lay under the snow. With the depth of the crisp, white covering impossible to gauge, they did not know if they would step into several inches of snow, giving them a fairly secure grip, compacting around their feet, or if a rock was concealed by only a thin veil of snow. In such cases, feet would stop unexpectedly soon, and the rock underneath was as slippery as ice.

The party's nerves were already on edge, making their movements tight and their balance less likely to be caught quickly on any occasion that it was lost.

And so it happened. Konall's page, burdened by a heavy pack with a large, round shield strapped to it, stepped on a barely concealed rock. His foot shot to the side, striking his other leg, and he flipped, with the iron-embossed shield foremost, towards a large rock.

With scarcely believable reflexes, Grakk, who was next in line, was already diving to divert the boy into soft snow. He succeeded but, in doing so, a small shovel strapped to his pack glanced off the rock with a resounding clang.

The party froze. Konall, at the front, wheeled around, his eyes wild with fury. 'You careless fool!' he spat at Grakk.

'You will pay for that. You had better pray to whatever gods you follow that you have not scared off my bear.'

The two warriors at the rear had been scanning the way they had come to guard against them being surprised from behind and had missed the incident, and the group moved on – even more carefully. Impassive as ever, Grakk fell back into line.

They reached the clearing without further mishap. The freshly killed rabbit was placed in the centre of the open area, and Konall smeared its blood across his face, giving him a macabre look as he stood just inside the treeline. He had cast off his heavy cloak to ease his movement but, despite the sharp cold, he stood unmoving, his gaze fixed across the glade with almost fanatical eagerness and a spear with a thick haft and a broad, flat blade, designed to slip between an animal's ribs, cradled in both hands.

Three of the warriors positioned themselves strategically around the clearing, hidden within the trees but ready to step forward to direct the bear back towards Konall if necessary, while the remaining guard shepherded the pages and slaves into the cover of the undergrowth – but not so far in as to obstruct their view.

They did not have long to wait. The sound of heavy movement through low-hanging branches grew closer as a soft breeze carried the scent of the dead rabbit and its fresh blood away from the clearing. Then, sooner than the noises had suggested, the animal appeared from the trees.

The guard beside Brann sucked in his breath sharply. It was indeed a bear, and bigger than any that Brann had ever imagined, never mind seen. It moved slowly towards the rabbit, its snout lifted and its head swaying from side to side as it followed the scent. Satisfied that there was no danger

– or its caution overpowered by hunger and the proximity of food – it speeded up, its rolling gait covering the ground surprisingly quickly and sure-footedly.

When it reached the centre of the clearing, Konall stepped forward, roaring his defiance. The bear, almost upon the rabbit, bellowed in anger and warning to whoever may challenge it for the food, and cast about for the source of the sound.

Brann felt sick. He glanced at Gerens. The boy's face was impassive. Although they had joked about the outcome of the encounter, in reality he had no desire to watch anyone being savaged by such a beast. And he was unable to bring himself to believe that Lord Ragnarr's reaction to news of his son's death would be anything less than fury and retribution aimed at those who were with him at the time.

Horrified and nauseated at the thought of the carnage that was about to ensue, Brann nevertheless found himself unable to prevent his eyes being drawn to the scene at the centre of the clearing.

Finding its enemy, the bear launched itself at Konall. Brann urged the boy to turn and run, but he knew it was already too late. The bear would have been on his unprotected back within a few paces.

Instead, with a calmness that stunned Brann, the tall boy stepped one pace forward to meet the attack, levelled his spear and braced himself for the impact. Rather than running straight onto the spearpoint and obligingly impaling himself, however, the huge animal reared up in front of Konall, teeth bared and dripping with saliva and eyes glaring. Blasting the boy with another baleful roar, it swiped a massive, clawed foreleg at him. For an animal so large, its movements were astonishingly – and terrifyingly – fast but Konall, his gaze cold and calculating, merely swayed back, allowing the paw to miss him by the merest distance.

Again it swiped and again, with either paw. Each time, Konall moved out of reach, either leaning or stepping back as necessary, his spear held ready as he waited for an opening to attack. Enraged, but mystified at its lack of success, the animal pulled itself fully upright to assess its prey, never considering that such a puny creature could possibly be a danger to it – only a victim.

Seizing on the moment, Konall sprang forward, thrusting his spear at the bear's chest. In the instant that the tip pierced its hide, however, the bear's paw moved in a blur, snapping the shaft neatly in half like a twig.

The force of the blow knocked two segments of spear through the air. The butt end fell from Konall's hands into the snow beside him, while the other half, its spearhead flashing as it caught the sun, spun end over end to embed itself a little more than twelve feet away.

Automatically reaching for any sort of weapon, Konall started to crouch, his right hand stretching for the broken shaft. Fortunately, he had been trained well. He never moved his gaze from the beast so, when the bear resumed its enraged momentum with a rapid series of swipes, he was able to stumble back, leaving the piece of spear, until he was out of the creature's reach and he could regain his balance.

The previous pattern re-emerged: the bear, now relentlessly pressing forward in fury at the pain the spearpoint had inflicted, swinging its massive paws at its now apparently harmless foe.

Over and over, Konall swayed and stepped barely out of the bear's reach, his face a blank mask – surprisingly, filled not so much with intense concentration as a serene calm.

217

After a few long seconds, Brann realised that, this time, there was direction to his movements. Where, before, his focus had been on avoiding the bear's flailing forelegs to seek an opening for a strike of his own, now he was moving the encounter towards the half-spear that had landed point-first in the snow.

As Konall neared the broken weapon, Brann admired his efforts, but wondered what use they would be. Even if Konall reached the spear – as he appeared to be achieving, slowly but surely – he would be left with a spear roughly the length of a longsword. To inflict any wound of consequence, he would have to be well within the grasp of the bear: an unsurvivable action. Perhaps, faced with such dire danger, Konall was merely grasping for any weapon as a comfort, as perhaps a means to retreat without being run down. With Konall's only option to move back to the others to allow the warriors to give him another spear, Brann guessed that the weapon, in its reduced state, would merely be used as a deterrent to allow him to reach help.

Whether through rage and frustration, or emboldened by his obviously harmless opponent, the bear's swipes were becoming wilder and larger; Brann felt that a single blow could decapitate Konall like a child flicking a stick at a flower. Surely it was only a matter of time before a misjudgement from the boy would be his last living action.

But Konall had reached the upright section of spear. He stretched his hand out but, still staring at the bear, he missed the wooden shaft and had to step back from yet another wild swipe of a paw.

The weapon was now within the edge of his vision, and this time he made no mistake. His hand closed around the shaft and, in one smooth movement, he was upright and armed.

The bear swung wildly again, not realising yet that its foe was no longer harmless. Before it could adjust to the change, Konall acted.

A flailing foreleg swung again. Konall slipped under the strike, so close to the bear's body that its fur must have been almost brushing his face. In a single flowing movement so graceful that it appeared to be in slow motion, although in reality it was over in a blink, he ducked and spun away from the beast to a safe distance once more.

The bear bellowed, and Brann looked anxiously at Konall. The boy, however, stood stock-still, impassively watching the bear. His hands were empty.

Brann jerked his gaze back to the bear. The spearshaft was protruding from its chest, a clean strike directly into its heart.

The huge animal tried to roar once more, but this time it was a hoarse, rasping sound. It fell at Konall's feet, and lay still.

The watchers ran from the trees to gather round the two protagonists. Konall swayed, and one of the warriors stepped forward to steady him. A withering glance from the boy stopped him abruptly.

Konall steadied himself. He knelt beside the bear and drew a long hunting knife from his belt. A few expert cuts, both into the hide and inside the carcass, and he was able to breach in and underneath the ribcage and pull the heart from the beast that, only moments before, had come close to tearing him apart. He cut a chunk from the still-warm heart, and lifted it to his mouth.

As he chewed it, he slowly wiped his blood-smeared hands across his brow and down his cheeks. In silence, he opened his tunic, and cupping more blood from the heart in the palm of his hand, he smeared it on his chest over his own heart in a design alien to Brann.

He stood, breathing heavily, and tossed the remainder of the heart into the trees.

The warriors bowed their heads. The most senior, who had quietened Brann and Gerens the previous night, said simply, 'Your father will be proud that his son is now a man.'

Konall nodded to two of the warriors. 'You two, skin it and take the meat.' He led the rest of the group to an area of the clearing where they would make camp. 'Pages and servants, unpack and gather firewood.'

As they moved to start, Konall pointed to Grakk. 'Not you,' he snapped. He gestured to the two remaining warriors. 'One of you has first sentry duty. Organise the shifts between you. The other, take him,' he glared at Grakk, 'and secure him in the trees. The gods only know how he did not alert my bear. He does not deserve our fire, our food or our company tonight.

'Give him bread and water, and a blanket. And he's lucky to get that.'

Stunned, Brann looked aghast at Grakk, standing with no show of emotion, waiting to be led away. Why did no one tell Konall that Grakk was innocent, that he deserved the punishment less than anyone? He had tried to catch the falling page, after all.

Brann looked across at the page, who was a picture of misery. Wracked with guilt, but with fifteen years of upbringing preventing him from questioning a noble's judgement at a time when it would have been humiliating for Konall to back down, he looked as if he would scream with the dilemma. His conscience appeared to win. He started to blurt an explanation, but one of the warriors who, like Brann, had noticed the internal torture he was suffering, was ready. He 'accidentally' bumped into the boy, knocking him headlong into the snow, and silencing him.

'Apologies, youngster,' he said, picking up the boy and brushing the show from him. 'A slippy bit of ground, that.'

Konall returned to the bear to retrieve his half-spear from the ground beside the carcass, where it had been carefully placed by the men working on the animal. They knew it would be as much a prized memento as the skin they were working so hard to strip from the dead creature.

The warrior beside Brann fetched a length of rope and a blanket and walked over to Grakk. The wiry slave stood calmly and nodded, following the larger man into the trees.

Brann grabbed Gerens's arm. 'What is going on here?' he hissed. 'Why are they all going along with something so wrong?'

Gerens shrugged. 'I do not know the people, I do not know the country, but I do know that you do not question a nobleman. Especially one who has just stuck a blade between a bear's ribs from a range of about one inch.'

Brann was getting more agitated, however. 'It does not matter, it is not right that Grakk is punished when he is not to blame. Most people could not even have reacted quickly enough to do what he did.'

The final warrior was stowing his pack with the other supplies before heading for his sentry duty. 'The servant is right,' he said, without looking up from the ties he was tightening in case the weather worsened. 'In this land, especially up here in the mountains, your life can be easily snatched away by man or beast – more easily than you can realise. We must have discipline, within ourselves and as a group. It is the only way to have everyone working in such a way that each is used for the good and safety of the party.

'To question any decision throws all of that in doubt. We cannot afford doubt – it leads to hesitation, hesitation leads to death. Sometimes that is hard on individuals, like now.

But it is the way that life is, and the way that my people have survived.' He nodded towards the trees. 'He knows that, and he knows it could have been worse. He could have been put to death at a nobleman's whim, but he was not. He will have a hard night, but he will be brought back in the morning and it will be over. We are a hard people, but mostly we do not bear grudges.'

He stood up, towering over Brann, and looked directly at him for the first time. 'It would be wise to remember that you are not in your own country now. You will learn more, and survive better, if you listen, watch and do not argue. We have got it right for many hundreds of years. Maybe it is different in your land, but you are not there now. This is what works here.

'Oh, and one more thing: I do not know how things are in your home, but here it would be seen as strange to ask advice from a slave. It is not the sort of attention you want to attract.' He started towards his sentry post.

Brann coloured. 'I would not know about that,' he blurted. 'We do not have slaves where I come from.'

The warrior wheeled round, his face hard. 'Listen, boy,' he snapped. 'I am only giving you this advice because, at your age, I was sent away from the only village I had known to learn my craft at Ravensrest. I found it hard, so the gods only know what you are going through, so far from your home.

'But do not ever answer me, or any other man here, like that again. That is the only warning you will get on that score, and you are lucky to get it.'

Brann paled, and the warrior started away again. 'And we do not have slaves here either. I just know rank and position, and I know how your actions appeared to others. You are a fool if you do not realise that.'

Brann sank down onto a pack, his situation crashing down upon him. He felt faint, and close to tears. Talk of his own land had brought back the pain of images of his family and the helpless loneliness of being so far from home in such unfamiliar surroundings. And the talk of slavery, while he was pretending to be a page, reminded him of his own demeaning and terrifying reality. These were all thoughts that he thought he had buried by concentrating on each task that came before him, large or small, second by second and minute by minute, but now it threatened to sweep up and overwhelm him once more.

Gerens started to attend to a pack that was conveniently behind the visibly trembling Brann. He nudged his friend in the back with his shoulder. 'He is right,' he murmured. 'It is hard, but we have just got to get on with it. And do not worry, there will be plenty of time to mix with the likes of me when we take our boat out for a bit of a row again.'

Brann found himself smiling, and took a deep breath. He reached behind him and squeezed Gerens's shoulder in thanks. In spite of all that had been said, he did not care if anyone saw – he knew how much he owed to Gerens and his constantly practical spirit. But no one saw, and he stood and got back to work.

Camp was set up quickly, and they ate well, thanks to Konall's triumph. Even without Grakk's newly discovered culinary expertise, the dinner was superb – it did not require much skill, after all, to roast a steak of bear meat over a fire. Despite feeling guilty at the thought of Grakk tethered to a tree while they feasted, Brann was overpowered by the smell of the cooking meat. He assuaged his conscience by secreting a large chunk of roasted meat for Grakk, and tucked into his own portion.

After feeding so well on top of the day's exertions and motions, sleep came quickly and deeply to those clustered around the fire, the silence broken only by the soft crackling of the burning wood and the occasional snore or grunt from the slumbering figures.

They were wakened by the roaring of the sentry. 'Defend yourselves! Defend yourselves!' he cried between bellows of rage and the ringing of weapon on weapon. Disorientated, Brann staggered to his feet, still groggy from sleep and unsure if he was dreaming, and frantically rubbed his eyes to clear them.

This was no dream. The three warriors who had been sleeping by the fire were already on their feet, weapons to hand, staring into the darkness to spot any attackers. They were moving away from the glowing fire, into the relative safety of the darkness, where their eyes would adjust to the gloom and they would not be such easy targets. They were not quick enough. An arrow whirred from the trees, hammering into the chest of one of them, knocking him from his feet. A guttural cry rasped harshly from the darkness. Presumably it was an order to stop shooting, although Brann was not sure why that would be so. Maybe their foes surrounded the site, and they were worried that an arrow may miss its target and fly through to hit them in the trees in the far side of the clearing.

Brann did not pause to ponder the point. Terrified, he grabbed a hunting spear and whirled round and back again, not knowing which way to face. The trees offered the obvious cover and the few opportunities they had to hide – but that was where the danger was coming from. And it was coming closer, rapidly. With the chance of surprise now gone, the attackers were making no attempt to remain silent, and were crashing through the undergrowth, howling and bawling their eagerness.

What must have been the scouts for the attacking party were still battling with the sentry as the main force rampaged closer from all sides. The sentry roared more in rage or frustration than pain or fear, and then the noise of his fight fell silent. Those who had fought him did not appear immediately, preferring to wait the few moments before the rest arrived.

Brann sensed movement to his left. His heart lurching, he jerked around to face it. It was Konall, who had been sleeping close to him.

'Easy, easy,' the tall boy said, a nightmarish figure in the glow of the fire with the bear's blood still smeared across his face. His sword was in his hand, held ready and easily. 'Stand back-to-back with me, and stick that thing in anyone who appears. Just make sure you pull it out again quickly, or the next one will get you. And try not to soil yourself: it makes the footing a bit tricky.'

Brann guessed that the last comment was the closest Konall got to humour, and that it was an attempt to calm his nerves. It did not. But, strangely, the feel of Konall's back against his – even if his shoulders did reach only halfway up the other's torso – was reassuring, although hearing the attackers approach was still filling him with so much fear that tears were streaming down his face. It had only been a few seconds since they had been awakened, but the time seemed to pass so slowly.

The three warriors were on the other side of the fire with Gerens and Konall's page. They had spotted Konall, and were moving around to protect the noble boy. Before they could reach him, however, figures burst from the trees and hurled themselves at the little band. The three warriors formed a

225

loose triangle around the two boys who were with them, and Brann and Konall pushed back against each other as if bracing themselves against the onslaught.

Most of the howling mob descended upon the group on the other side of the fire, not noticing Brann and Konall, but five or six – it was all too much for Brann to count properly – emerged from the trees beside them and fell upon the pair.

Konall's blade flicked out, slicing into one man's arm, and their attackers fell back slightly, surrounding them and snarling as they sized up their opponents – especially the one with the blood-smeared face. Brann gripped the spearshaft tightly, trying to look as if he knew what he was doing – he knew that any sign of weakness would be seized upon in an instant.

And, in an instant, it started. Brann realised that his tears had stopped and he was filled with an unexpected calm, taking note of all around and his options and opportunities. It was exactly at that moment that their attackers leapt at them, and his surprise at his demeanour almost allowed them to catch him with his attention slightly distracted. Without a word, but as if some silent command had passed between them, the snickering men around them sprang forwards as one.

Brann had barely enough time to swat a sword away with a desperate swipe of his spear and stab forward with the point at a screaming man with an axe. It caught him just below his shoulder, not deep enough to seriously incapacitate him, but enough to provoke a bestial squeal of pain.

The third man facing him had been too cramped by his two companions to attack with his broad, rusty, ragged-edged sword – more like an oversized cleaver than a military weapon, but all the more fearsome for it – and took a step back with the other two. Noticing the space clear in front of him, however, he seized his chance and, blade held high above his head, ready for a swing that he knew would be unstoppable by a mere spear, he charged forward.

Brann pressed against the strong back of Konall as the other boy twisted and turned in his own battle and pushed back against his larger companion to let him take a sudden step forward himself. His attacker, expecting Brann to fold in terror before his fearsome onslaught, came upon the spear-point a full yard before he had expected. He ran onto it without a chance to pause and before he even realised it was there. It pierced his rags and pressed on into his chest with such force that Brann was knocked backwards. Before he could lose his balance, he struck Konall's back.

'Glad to be of service,' the white-haired boy said dryly over his shoulder as the clanging of metal-on-metal and the occasional cry of pain attested to his own efforts. Brann marvelled at Konall's calm, but realised as he did so that, from the onset of the action, his nerves had left him. He felt cold and automatic, assured of movement and logical of thought, acting and reacting as if every move were simple and obvious – which they were. At this most basic level of combat, there was no subtlety involved: it was just a matter of knocking away weapons as they came at him and trying to stick the point of his spear into any part of a body that presented itself.

His victim had grunted once – more in surprise than pain – and fell backwards, freeing the spear just as the other two re-launched themselves at him. Brann steadied himself, expecting them to be more cautious after seeing their companion's death, but that had only seemed to have enraged them further. Weapons swinging, spittle flying and guttural curses filling the air, they vented their fury at the boy with the spear standing before them.

The next few moments became a whirl of axe, sword and spear. Unable to duck or dodge in case the blow passed him and hit Konall, Brann fended and struck out with a cold precision, knowing that to let his concentration waver for even an instant from what was in front of him would be fatal. It seemed like an eternity of effort, but it was over in a matter of seconds. By chance, as he tried to deflect an axe swing (if he had met it full on, his spear, even with its thick shaft designed for hunting, would have been shattered) the speartip slipped under the ribs of the axe-wielding bandit. His face contorted in pain and, dropping the axe, he reached with both hands for the spear. The other man glanced across, saw the spear embedded in his companion, and, with a howl of glee, smashed his heavy sword down on the shaft. The wood cracked in two, snapping the point upwards into the chest of his companion, making his already impending death instantaneous.

In a scene eerily reminiscent of Konall's duel with the bear, Brann was left with half a spear, although in his case it was the heavy butt end, grasped tightly in his right hand. The force of the blow had knocked the half-spear down and to Brann's right, and he continued the turn to spin in a complete circle, making sure to stay away from Konall, and using the momentum to add force to his swing as he smashed the wood against the side of the larger man's head. The force of the blow almost knocked the shaft from Brann's hand, but he managed to maintain his grip and, as the dazed man started to raise his sword, he drew back the shaft and thrust the sharp, splintered end two-handed through his attacker's unkempt beard and deep into his throat. The man sank to his knees, and the life had drained from him before he came to rest on the ground.

Brann grabbed the sword from the grubby, lifeless hand and turned to see how Konall was faring. The taller boy had despatched two of his opponents and was facing the remaining one, a wiry snarling man who looked as if he had more guile – even if it was in the form of animal cunning – than the others. He was watching Konall's blade carefully as it moved rapidly (not so much flickering; it was too heavy a weapon for that, but Brann was nonetheless impressed with the speed and ease with which the boy handled the weapon). Brann moved to join Konall. He had no training in using a sword but, then again, he had never been taught how to use a spear in combat, so he reckoned he should at least be able to distract the man long enough to allow Konall an opening. It looked as if the ragged wretch would be lucky to measure his life in more than a few seconds. Their foe realised this, too, and his eyes and movements became more desperate.

Without warning, there was a dull thud and Konall dropped to one knee, blood starting to stream from his temple. A fist-sized rock that had been hurled at him rolled to one side as he fought, one hand on the ground before him, to steady himself against unconsciousness. It was not a life-threatening wound in itself, but it was in its consequences: the boy was stunned enough to be unable to offer any defence. Brann stepped in front of him, holding the sword two-handed but – even without the three gibbering bandits who had broken from the other fight (one of whom had thrown the rock) – he knew that the initiative had swung lethally away from the two boys.

In the blink of an eye, the single foe before them became four. As they fell upon them, Brann knew his time was short. He had taken on, and beaten, almost as many men just seconds beforehand, but now he was exhausted, wielding a

229

sword that was too heavy for him, and without anyone to cover his back. He flailed wildly, knowing that he had no finesse to make use of and hoping that the wide scything movements may keep the others at bay for a few moments longer. It was only delaying the inevitable, and he felt what little strength remained in his limbs draining from him with each swing. The men laughed contemptuously and, within moments, Brann had been easily separated from Konall. The wiry man who had originally faced Konall stepped back to the boy. Standing over the noble as he groggily and desperately tried to regain his feet, he spat on him and swung back his sword in both hands for what would clearly be a decapitating swing. A blur from the nearby trees caught his attention and he stopped at the top of his movement. A figure flashed from the woods and passed in front of the man. Grakk's momentum took him into the heart of the three men facing Brann as, behind him, blood – bright, shining crimson in the clear morning air – started to spurt from the throat of Konall's would-be executioner. The sword dropped from his fingers and Grakk was already spinning and whirling high and low as his lifeless body crumpled to the ground, a large rusty knife a blur in his hands. Before they could comprehend that their comrade was dead so suddenly, one of the men had been hamstrung, another had had his throat cut and the third was twitching his last movements after a knife-thrust up under his ribs and into his heart. The crippled man groped desperately for his sword but, before he even came close to grasping it, Grakk had despatched him also.

He turned to Brann, who was frozen in astonishment, and roughly shook the boy. 'Help him,' he said urgently, nodding at Konall. 'We must get him back to his father.'

'Yes,' Brann gasped. 'Yes, of course.'

He ran to Konall, who was supporting himself with his sword, using it as a crutch as his legs buckled beneath him. They grabbed an arm each and half-dragged him towards the trees. An embankment sloped steeply down for around twice the height of a man just after the undergrowth started and Grakk grunted, 'Here', as he placed Konall down and started him sliding, feet first, down the snow. Brann started down after him but scrambled to a halt as Grakk turned back to the clearing.

'What are you doing?' he gasped. 'Let's go!'

Grakk shook his head. 'You take him. They must think I did that,' he said, jerking his thumb towards the bodies behind them. 'They will not follow you if they think I did it. If they find no one to blame, they will come looking. If this is not done, all three of us will die. Had not your fight with Boar ended when you did, all three on our bench would have died from his indiscriminate axe. You played your part then, and now I must play mine. When they leave, so do you.'

Without a further word, he scrambled back into the open ground. Tears welled up in Brann's eyes as he watched a man he had become close to in such a short time go to his death, even though he knew that Grakk was right. If Brann was the one to stay, the bandits would know that he could never have killed seven men single-handedly, and a hunt for the others would ensue. Grakk, however, appeared far more plausible as one who could have acted upon his own, so the bandits were more likely to end their work with him and assume that they had dealt with the entire party.

Brann pulled himself back up to the top of the slope, and peered over the edge and through the bushes. If his friend was going to die for him, he would at least watch his passing so his heroics could be recounted in full when they returned to safety. The combination of the undergrowth and the relative gloom of the trees compared with the snow-enhanced glare of the clearing, now that dawn had broken during their fight, would make him invisible to their enemies. Or so he hoped.

Scrabbling noises behind him made him jump, until he remembered that Konall was with him.

'Help me up,' the older boy hissed. 'This man saved my life. If he is to die a hero to save me another time, I would do him the honour of witnessing his glory so his valour will not be lost in anonymity, but remembered in tales for generations to come.'

My thoughts exactly. But put a little more grandiosely.

Any tinge of humour, however, vanished as he dragged Konall up beside him and they peered into a scene of horror. Grakk had been spotted as he reached the scene of their fight, and almost the entire group had turned to confront him. The three remaining warriors who had been their escort lay dead, their multiple and dreadful injuries attesting to the fight they had put up. Two ragged bandits held Gerens and Konall's page, still apparently alive, face down in trampled snow while the rest, fanning out, ran howling towards the solitary figure of Grakk. Brann was able, for the first time, to look more closely at their enemy. Their appearance was as uncared for, dirty and dishevelled as he had imagined lawless bandits to be, from their matted tangled hair, ragged clothes and their skin darkened and toughened by weather and grime, to their haphazard collection of weapons, some with military origins, some once farm implements, some self-made and all rusty, pitted and ragged-edged.

The lack of quality in their clothes and weapons was compensated by – and, in some ways, added to – the fear induced by their behaviour. More akin to wild beasts than men, they howled, snarled, roared and laughed as they marauded towards Grakk.

Grakk glanced around, but his only line of possible escape was back towards the boys hiding in the woods. He had no option but to stand and fight for as long as he could and hope to find, or create, a gap in the crowd to make a break for another side of the clearing. Brann knew the likelihood of that chance materialising, and choked back a sob. Konall's sword was lying across in front of him, and the noble boy's grip tightened on the hilt. Brann grabbed his shoulder, and held him down.

'Stop,' he hissed. 'I know what you are thinking. Stay down.

Konall grabbed his wrist. 'Get your hand off me, boy,' he growled. 'My head has cleared. I cannot lie here and watch this happen.'

Brann's eyes blazed. 'How do you think I feel? That man is my friend. He is going to give up his life purely to let you get back to your father. If you decide to die beside him, you will waste his sacrifice. We may as well all have run and taken our chances while being hunted. And do not call me boy. If I was good enough to fight back-to-back with you out there, I am good enough to be treated with more respect than that.'

Konall stared at him for a long second, then turned back to the scene as the bandits closed with Grakk. The tattooed barbarian had stripped to the waist despite the cold, and had grabbed the lightest sword he could find from the corpses around him, transferring the knife to his left hand.

Again he fought, arms and legs whirling, but this time the emphasis was less on speed and more on tactics, dealing with the closest threat in the most effective fashion. The sheer numbers facing him indicated only one result, however.

A burly bandit, indistinguishable from the rest other but for the fact that they listened when he spoke, strode up behind the mêlée and barked out an order, which he emphasised with hefty slaps with the flat of his sword on the backs of those nearest to him. Brann glanced at Konall. With the clamour from the fighting, his words were unintelligible.

Konall did not turn around, but sensed his questioning glance. 'I cannot make it out either. Suffice to say that I would guess they were ordered to take him alive from his manner of speaking.'

'Oh, gods, I hope you are right,' Brann sighed, the despair lifting from him as his hope soared.

Konall grunted. 'That depends on what they intend to do with him.'

With the objective clear, the result of the fight was no less certain: it merely involved more casualties among the bandits. Life seemed cheap among the attackers, however, adding to the numerical advantage they already held.

Grakk was inevitably overwhelmed, a club blow to the back of his bald head rendering him unconscious. The speed with which they bound him and the thoroughness of the binding attested to their view of Grakk's fighting ability.

As Grakk was being secured, the remainder had unfinished business – or pleasure, as it turned out. Roaring with glee, they capered back towards the bodies of the three warriors. Brann's stomach heaved as the corpses were torn apart, not only by knives or axes, but mainly by fingers and teeth. Two of the fiends impaled one of the warriors on a short spear and raised his lifeless form aloft, cavorting around the group and jerking him so that his limbs flailed in a macabre dance of death as the other bandits howled with laughter and danced about the grotesque trio. The corpse eventually fell from the spear and was torn asunder like the others, body parts being waved triumphantly and organs held aloft as if they were the spoils of war. In the basest of senses, Brann supposed that was exactly what they were.

Horrified and stunned, yet unable to tear his eyes from the grotesque scene, Brann felt fear grip him at the thought that such people could exist. The revolting actions were bad enough, but the pervasive primeval terror that swamped him was born from the sounds they were making – not the howls or cackles of the mad, but the laughter and cries of triumph and excitement that could be heard from groups of men engaged in any number of normal pursuits, from sporting contests to sharing a flagon of ale around a roaring hearth. These were not insane mountain barbarians; they were men who knew exactly what they were doing, and were revelling, even exulting in it. He was witnessing unadulterated evil.

The snow around the carnage had been churned into a crimson slush as the hideous revels continued, and Brann felt his gorge rise, starting to cough and retch at the same time. Konall's hand clamped across his mouth.

'Cough, and they could hear you,' he hissed. 'Puke and they could smell it. Either way, it is not good for us.'

Brann nodded and swallowed. 'They are worse than animals. How are men capable of this?'

Konall's face was a cold mask. 'My people will make them pay. I will see to that.' Brann often found Konall's form of speech to be blustering but, this time, he believed him.

The bandit who seemed to be in charge called over to a group of the men who were standing slightly back from the butchery, not taking part but enjoying the spectacle with hearty laughter and shouts of encouragement and praise, apparently more senior members of the party. The men moved further away and towards the two boys. Brann's breathing caught in his throat and he made ready to fly, but Konall's hand steadied him, the older boy having discerned that the men were merely seeking to move to a spot where their leader could address them above the noise of the others.

The commander started to shout, his voice having to be raised despite them moving to this spot, and his words carrying easily to the boys hidden in the trees.

Brann found the accent too strong to understand, but Konall's eyes narrowed. 'The more he speaks, the more I can pick up,' he breathed, cupping his hands around Brann's ear to mask even his soft whisper. 'They are taking the prisoners to their base, or home. Your tattooed slave seems to be the subject of some curiosity, and they think their leader would find him of interest. In what way, I do not know. And I do not think I want to know.

'The two boys, they are unsure about. No, wait: they think one of them is me. This was no random attack. They knew I was hunting here, and they wanted me. He is congratulating them on dealing with the entire hunting party – so at least they believe they have got us all – and he is extolling their skills in battle.' He snorted in derision. 'Now he is saying something along the lines of one of the boys being me, but they just don't know which one. He is saying that, until they determine which one is me, neither boy should be harmed.'

They watched as the leader drew his long knife and, without warning, sliced it across the throat of the man beside him.

'He is saying,' Konall continued, 'that death, as they see before them, will instantly visit any who harm the prisoners, and I think he has made his point quite effectively. Now he is saying that, once they have discovered the identity of, well, me, then they are free to have their sport with the other.' He shook his head, his long hair trailing in the snow. 'Hell awaits them both before death. I hope the gods are kind to them after it. He is stressing again that they are not to be harmed, and that they need not be impatient for their fun because the right boy will be identified when...'

He stiffened, his fingers tightening so hard on his sword hilt that the blade shook.

'What is it?' Brann hissed. 'What did he say?'

'It is of no import to you, but there is no reason for you not to know,' Konall said, his voice, although still a whisper, clearly suffused with suppressed rage. 'He mentioned a name. He said the right boy would be identified when Loku arrives.' He paused, as if saying the name had almost caused him to lose control of his fury. He took a breath, and steadied himself. 'Loku is the ambassador from the court of Lord Bekan, a neighbouring warlord to our lands. He is a powerful and, at the moment, peaceful lord as far as we are concerned. Loku, as his representative, has been welcomed as an honoured guest at my uncle's court, where he spends most of his time, but also during his frequent visits to our hall – where he is right now. It turns my stomach to think that a man who has shared my father's table is in league with these vermin.'

He slid down the slope. 'Come. We must return with haste.'

Brann joined him. 'Of course. We must prevent him from leaving, so he cannot reveal that neither of the boys is you. Then there will be more of a chance of your father rescuing them and Grakk.'

Konall started into a loping run that Brann struggled to match. 'The lives of a page and two slaves are now of secondary importance. It is the future of my people that must be addressed. We must see that Loku is captured to enable him to be interrogated. If he returns to them and discovers that I have slipped their net, he will know that it is too much of a risk for him to return in case I have discovered the truth about him, and we will have lost our chance.

'Now save your breath and run.'

Chapter 8

He cursed.

Plotting schemes, crafting intrigues, had been second nature to him; now it was toil. The fatigue in his mind was a reminder of the years that had been and gone.

Still, it was toil he relished, an escape from the endless monotony of existing. Now he lived again.

Nevertheless, while it invigorated his mind's interest, still it drained his mind's energy. He found his attention wandering to images of times past, of times so very different.

They had knelt to him once.

He saw himself on a seat, high-backed, carved from gleaming ivory to depict victories won, key battles that had built an empire; images that reminded all who gazed upon them of the crushing force that had created harmonious union, and the crushing force that would maintain it. Carved from gleaming ivory and set with the most precious of gems, five stones of the deepest hues of blood, leaf, sky, sun and, most entrancing all, of water; five stones, each the size of a fist, set around the top of the arching back of the seat; five stones to display to all who gazed upon them the visible trappings of all that power brings. Power over wealth. Power over the five elements. Power over man.

Power.

Power is all. Power: ever born of knowledge and influence. The right knowledge, and the right influence, and seldom the brand of each that was visible to the many. Knowledge and influence – when combined by one with the ken to use them, in the right way, at the right time – bred power.

They had knelt to him once.

They would again.

****

Dusk was draining the light from the day when, after what seemed like a lifetime of running, the citadel came into sight. Brann stumbled up to the landward gate and stood unsteadily as Konall spoke in low tones to the warrior in charge of the guard. A runner had already been sent to alert Lord Ragnarr, and Konall was issuing further instructions that Loku should not be allowed to leave.

The warrior was in an uncomfortable quandary. 'He is the ambassador of a warlord, sir. I do not have the authority to detain him without Lord Ragnarr's express order.'

'Then do not detain him,' Konall snapped. 'Delay him. Be inventive: tell him the gates have been closed because bandits are raiding nearby, tell him that my father has an urgent message for him before he sets off; I don't care, just stop him.' He glanced over at the swaying, white-faced Brann. 'And see to the boy.'

As if that had been a signal, Brann's eyes rolled upwards and he slumped into the arms of an approaching, and surprised, guard.

He woke – or, rather, was wakened – at dawn for the second time in two days. He had a vague recollection of having

240

been roused from his exhausted slumber at some point the previous evening to have soup of a forgotten flavour administered by that nice girl from the kitchens. He wondered if it had been a dream rather than a memory, but the discovery of dried remnants of the food staining one corner of his mouth confirmed not only that it had been real, but also the flavour: vegetable. The information seemed trivial as memories of the previous day's horrors surged back over him, but Konall interrupted his thoughts with another rough shake of his shoulder.

'Hurry,' he said, his tone as urgent as the command. 'We do not have much time.'

Brann swung his legs around to sit up. 'Time for what? What are you talking about?'

Konall tossed over a light undershirt, tunic, breeches and a thick pair of socks. All seemed hardy, and of good quality, and all were of a pale grey hue.

'It is the best colour for concealment when you hunt among snow and rocks in these mountains,' Konall said, noticing Brann's quizzical look, although his tone exposed his irritation at having to explain such a basic fact. 'Clothe yourself quickly – they will serve you better than those you had.' He pointed to the foot of the bed. 'There are boots, also.' Brann looked and, predictably, found them to be the same shade of grey. 'I took your own ones to the store as a guide, so these should be a good fit.'

Brann began to suspect that there was intrigue as well as haste involved here – even in his sleep-befuddled state, he had noticed that Konall had taken the boots to the store himself rather than have a servant do so, and the only reason he could envisage for this was that the boy had not wanted anyone else to know what he was up to... whatever that was. His urge to stop and ask what was happening was over-ridden by the natural authority in the young noble's voice, and he was almost dressed before his curiosity became too much to resist.

Konall merely handed him the boots and said, 'We do not have time to waste chatting in this room, and I cannot tell you in the corridors in case we draw attention to ourselves. I will explain once we are on our way.'

The instant that Brann finished pulling on his boots, Konall opened the door and peered up and down the corridor.

'There will be only the occasional servant about at this time,' he murmured. 'But if we meet anyone of consequence, I am taking you to the market at setting-up time so we can be undisturbed as you get yourself new clothes to replace these that I have lent you.'

Brann grinned. 'Which also explains why we are dressed identically,' he suggested.

'Exactly,' Konall agreed solemnly. Brann groaned inwardly. When was he going to encounter someone cheerful? Between Konall and Gerens, he had barely been treated to a ghost of a smile, let alone anything more open. But, at the memory of Gerens's predicament, his own spirits darkened also, and his grin faded.

As it was, they encountered no one who would have started a conversation with the lord's son, either in the corridors or on the streets of the town. They reached the gate by which they had entered the previous night where a guard nodded to Konall at their approach and fetched a pair of bundles from the gatehouse, handing one to each of them.

Following Konall's lead, Brann unwrapped his to find a pack and a belt bearing a sword, a long knife and two shorter knives. The short knives were ideal for throwing if one had the skill to do so rather than, as in Brann's case, if one had only watched such activity as a side-show at the travelling fairs that occasionally visited Millhaven.

He hefted the sword, feeling its weight, and looked questioningly at Konall. 'Considering I have never used one of these before, would a light one not have been more suitable?'

Without pausing as he strapped on his accoutrements, the tall boy shook his head. 'If you have not used one before, a slightly heavier one is easier for you to do some damage with, especially against those with the minimal abilities that we witnessed yesterday. You need a degree of skill to be dangerous with a light blade. Having seen you with the spear, I thought a heavier one would be better for you.'

Brann ignored the barb; it wasn't meant as an insult, merely a considered statement of fact. He weighed the sword in his hand again. '*Slightly* heavier?'

Konall shrugged. 'Among my people, yes.'

Brann grunted. 'If I swing it at someone, I will have to make sure I hit them to get it to stop moving.'

He buckled on the belt and, lifting the pack onto his back, he adjusted the straps to let it sit comfortably. An upbringing helping his father lift sacks in the mill had given him strong shoulders and legs, a foundation that had been built upon by his recent intensive rowing, so the weight of the burden presented him with no real problems. He looked up to find Konall holding a bow and a broad quiver with a flap tied down over the top to protect the arrows as they travelled.

'Do you know how to use one of these?' Konall asked. 'There's no point in taking one if you do not.'

Brann smiled broadly. 'This, I can use. Where I come from, we hunt smaller, faster prey than boar and bears: more rabbits, deer and suchlike. They may not do you as much harm, but they do not let you get close enough to stick a spear in them, so this,' he took the bow, 'is the best option. I am no expert, but I can hit a few.'

'If you can hit a rabbit, you can hit a man.' Konall looped the quiver over Brann's head, ensuring it sat neatly alongside the pack, and used straps on the side of the pack itself to secure the unstrung bow. 'There are three strings in a pouch on the quiver.' He slapped Brann on his laden back with enough force to make him take a step forward. 'Let's go.'

He slung on his own quiver – he had strapped on his bow before donning his pack – nodded to the guard to open the gate and, without further comment, started towards the foothills.

In the stronghold above, Ragnarr burst, unannounced and cheerful, into Einarr's room. 'Good morning, nephew! Come, breakfast awaits. We have much to do in the wake of Loku's departure and Konall's news. I feel much better when we have action to take and would value discussing our next move with you.'

Einarr was standing at the window, surveying the snow-gilded plain stretching away from the town. 'It seems that your son and my page have already decided their next move.'

The hulking lord moved to the window with a speed that belied his size. He saw the two figures, indistinct in their grey garb, heading steadily for the hills. 'The fools! Thanks be to the gods that you noticed them. There is still time enough for riders to bring them back.' He wheeled around and headed for the door.

'Uncle.' Einarr's voice stopped him. 'You may wish to consider letting them go.'

'Are you mad, boy?' Ragnarr thundered. 'Why in this or any other world would I do that?'

Einarr shrugged. 'Because they are the only ones to have faced those madmen, so they are not heading off under any illusions – they have made their decision despite the truth. Because they feel guilt, and they have a debt to repay. Because we all eventually reach an age where we have to, and are able to, respond to our sense of duty. Your son killed his bear yesterday and became a man, and just because he was not able to enjoy the celebrations that there should have been, it does not mean that he cannot start making a man's decisions.'

He turned to face his uncle and stared straight into his eyes. 'And, most of all, because you, now or at Konall's age, would have done exactly the same thing.'

Ragnarr stared at the distant figures. 'That's what I am scared of. The boy is smarter than me – takes after his mother that way. He should know better than to blunder off on a fool's mission that will more likely than not end in his death.'

Einarr smiled. 'He also takes after you, uncle,' he said softly. 'He knows the right thing to do, and he must do it, or he could not hold his head high as a man. And we both know that if we want a life where death does not ever confront us, we would have to move to a land I have not discovered yet. And, if he has half of your ability to deal with unsavoury characters, I would not bet against seeing him again before long. If he is to lead your people when you are gone, he must be the sort of man who would do exactly what he is now doing – and the sort of man who would survive it.'

'If he doesn't survive it, I'll kill him!' Ragnarr snorted in laughter thick with nerves. 'Don't mind me, Einarr. When you are a parent, you'll understand.'

Einarr became very still. For a long moment, he seemed not to breathe. Only a hand moved – up to his face to briefly trail his fingertips along the line of his scar. Before his uncle turned round, he sucked in air abruptly as if to drag in strength along with it. 'Regardless, politics may make this decision for us. Where Bekan's ambassador is concerned, it may have awkward consequences if the warlord's brother becomes involved. However, two young boys…'

Again Ragnarr grunted. 'Damn you, you make sense, I suppose. At least he has a friend with him.'

His nephew looked at him, his eyes wide with surprise. 'Brann? His friend?'

'Believe me. This is the closest Konall has got to anyone. He has always had a strong sense of duty towards the position he will one day inherit. He is diligent to the point of obsession with every aspect, from weapons training and fitness, to languages and letters. He is better educated than I would be if I lived twice, but I am not so blind as to ignore his character. I believe the kind expression is "aloof". He does not suffer others of his age easily; he finds them frivolous. The good of Ravensrest is his only consideration. That does not leave much room for friends. And his bluntness of speech – his rudeness, if you will – does not exactly invite friends, either.'

He grinned mischievously. 'Mind you, it reminds me of another noble youth, and you did not turn out too badly.'

Einarr's expression darkened. 'Pray he does not turn out like me.'

'Well, he has one advantage over you.' Ragnarr's grin grew more malicious in its glee. 'Better a friend, than a girl. Far less trouble.' He nudged Einarr roughly. 'What do you think about that, nephew?' he bellowed with laughter.

Einarr's expression turned even darker for a few moments before his uncle's infectious good humour overwhelmed him.

Enveloping the younger man in an inescapable bear hug, the huge lord led him from the room. 'Come. Let us leave the heroic quests to idealistic youngsters. We will plan like grown men: over a hearty breakfast.' Still with his arm around his nephew, he growled, 'But I will still be increasing the patrols in that general area.'

He glanced down at Einarr. 'Do not worry, not close enough to alert the people they are after. It is a small gesture, but I am a father. I have to do something, after all. Their fate may be their fate, but there is nothing to stop me trying to weight it slightly in his favour.'

Einarr smiled. In a country where life was harsh and men – and, for that matter, women – were routinely expected to make decisions and follow the consequences to their conclusion without presuming upon others, it was more than a small gesture. Nonetheless, he was glad of it – for both boys' sake.

Below them, and now approaching the foothills, the boys' thoughts were also turning to food. Brann had settled into a comfortable stride: with the need for speed not so frantic this time, Konall had set a more manageable pace. At his suggestion, Konall consented to produce a small amount of bread and cheese.

'We will eat while we walk,' the tall boy said flatly. 'There is no point in wasting time just because we are not going at the pace we descended.'

Brann looked dubiously at his meagre portion. 'I know we have to ration ourselves, but...'

Konall did not even turn around. 'Eat more if you want to be sick and find yourself dragging along a heavy stomach. If you want to keep your strength up and be able to handle the pace, eat a little, often. We have enough to last us, trust me.'

Brann glared at his laden back, but he understood the logic of Konall's words. In these circumstances, he would have to trust to the boy's greater knowledge.

As the terrain steepened, Konall refused to slacken the pace, but Brann found that, by settling into a steady rhythm, the initial weariness left his legs and he was able to stay with Konall's now familiar long lope. The sky was clear, however, and, as the sun reached higher, the heat grew and their exertions negated the slight chill in the air in the foothills. They stopped for lunch in the shade of a large rock, mostly silent as they caught their breath apart from Konall's urging to start moving again to avoid any stiffening in the muscles of their tired legs.

It was not until they stopped to make camp for the evening that any sort of conservation was possible. Konall had chosen a spot at the foot of an outcrop of rocks, where the small cliff-face formed a corner, allowing them to shelter. The angle it formed afforded cover from the wind that periodically blew and meant that the ground, with the snow cover sparse there, was bare and dry. And, Brann thought, remembering the previous day, it was far more desirable than an open clearing.

He started to collect firewood, but Konall stopped him. 'No fire tonight. The cloaks are warm enough, and none of the food needs cooking. It is a different game hunting men than bears, and we will not be giving them any help at all this time.'

Brann shrugged and dropped the sticks in a pile. He paused as he started to walk back to the rockface, then picked up the wood once more and scattered it back among the trees. Konall watched silently, a flicker of a smile twitching the corner of his mouth. When Brann returned, the noble boy made sure that he was busy unpacking food from his pack, ostensibly having noticed nothing.

Konall handed him bread and dried meat, and sat a water flask between them.

'I thought a good warrior would tend to his weapons first, and then eat,' Brann said, more with curiosity than criticism or sarcasm.

Konall chewed on the meat. 'Only in stories. My weapons were fine this morning, and have never been used since. I will check them tonight but, more importantly, there is no use having sparkling weapons if you are too weak from hunger to use them.' He reached for the water. 'Anyway, for your information, a good warrior is more than just his weapons: he must take care of himself as well – diet, cleanliness, fitness, strength, ability. These are more important than the tools you use. You can break a sword and pick up another. Swapping your paunch for someone else's flat belly is not so possible.'

Brann took the flask from him and bowed his head in mock humility. 'I stand corrected. Or, at least, I slump corrected.'

A slight narrowing of Konall's eyes indicated that, on some level, the humour appealed to him. Brann counted that as a major advance.

They ate in silence for a while before Brann broached the obvious subject, one that had bothered him from the start, but which breathlessness as they travelled had prevented him from bringing up until now.

'So, it is clear where we are going, but why? When we left the scene of the attack, you were quite happy to leave the others to their fate. Especially when two of them, as slaves, were of little consequence to you. What is so different now?'

Konall stared hard at the ground between his feet, as if struggling to find the words to explain his thoughts and feelings. It struck Brann as he watched him that there was no 'as if' about it: it was an unusual – or unknown – experience for Konall to have to do so, even to himself.

Brann had resigned himself so much to receiving no explanation that he jumped when Konall did speak. 'I was not happy about leaving them. But in my position, my happiness is not a luxury I have when considering my options. And if I had the choice again, of course I would do the same thing.' He sighed, and picked absently at a stone caught in the sole of his boot. 'But several things formed my decision for this. The first was hearing that Loku had left before we arrived.'

Brann started. 'But the guard at the gate thought he was still there.'

Konall nodded. 'As far as he knew, that was correct. But the snake had left by boat that afternoon. Which gives us one advantage – on foot, going directly, we have a chance of beating him to their lair, if we can find it in time. He will travel along the coast a distance under the pretence of his stated mission to my uncle's court, then he will put ashore secretly to visit his vermin comrades.' He spat and rubbed the small damp patch on the ground with the toe of his boot.

Brann started to take off his own boots to ease his aching feet, but Konall stopped him. 'Keep them on. On this sort of journey, you must always be ready to leave at a moment's notice. So boots stay on, weapons are always within reach, and if you open your pack to take anything out, you fasten it back up immediately. And, if what you took out was not for eating, you replace it as soon as you have used it.'

Brann pulled his boots back on. 'Anyway,' Konall continued, 'even given all that, I would still not have come. There is no advantage to Ravensrest for those three to be saved: none of them knows enough to be a risk to our security, and none would probably survive long enough to tell much anyway. There was no reason strong enough, if I was being purely logical, for the heir to the title to risk himself.'

'So,' Brann persisted, 'what was the reason for the heir to the title to risk himself after all?'

Konall threw the stone that he had retrieved at last from his boot into the trees. 'It is you, damn your soul. I could not stand the thought of your little accusing face looking at me wherever I went for the interminable period until you leave. If this is what I have to do to escape that, then so be it.'

'So you thought you would bring me for my invaluable assistance,' Brann grinned.

'So I thought I would bring you in case I needed to shield myself with someone, so do not push your luck,' Konall grunted, wrapping his heavy cloak around him and curling up against the rock wall. 'And,' he added quietly, 'a slave who I had tied up in the woods and left to his fate saved my life and, as if that were not enough, he was willing to sacrifice himself to let me escape – though I, my town and even my land mean nothing to him.

'Unlike your precious Captain, I have done my duty to my father and my people. Now I must do my duty to him.'

Brann looked curiously at him. 'Why do you hate Einarr so much? He must have been gone for much of your life, if not all of it. How can you know him enough to feel so strongly?'

Konall stared into the trees. 'One does not have to be in another's presence to know someone if the other's actions speak for themselves.

'You have kings in your country. Therefore you have corruption at the highest level and rulers who know nothing of most of their territory or people.' Brann thought this a bit of an assumption, but nerves – and curiosity – kept him silent. 'We have warlords. Their territory is smaller than a kingdom, but they know their lords beneath them and their people beneath them. The warlords may fight one another over disputes of various origin, but that keeps us ready for invaders and means that each man must rule well or lose his position. Not like your complacent kings.

'Einarr's father, Sigurr, is our warlord. My father is his brother, fifteen years his junior. He adores and looks up to Sigurr, though he would never admit it, and though the gods only know why. Sigurr has not extended his borders by one hand's width in forty years of rule. Neither my father nor two other minor lords have gained through his rule. We have kept what we have, and no more.' He spat on the stone floor, his opinion of this state of affairs evident.

'Einarr had it all,' he continued, his voice still bitter. 'He would have taken over from his father and was born to rule some of the richest fishing shores in the land. But he wasted it over a woman. The daughter of Lord Styrr, of Blackcliffe, the next town along the coast, she was promised to the son of another warlord. But Einarr fell for her charms, and she for his. As if they wanted to demonstrate to the world the feeble extent of their weak natures, they surrendered to their feelings. The night before she was to leave with her suitor to travel to his father's hall for their wedding, the young lovebirds tried to flee. The fools did not get far – how did they ever think they would? When they were stopped, her husband-to-be had the warriors accompanying him relieve Einarr of his sword and, justifiably and honourably, drew his own sword to dispense justice to the dog who had tried to steal his bride. Einarr had a knife in his boot, though. He threw off those gripping him and killed the lord's son, and taking his sword, slew the two warriors, also.

'In the confusion, the girl took a fatal blow as one of the warriors fought against the bride-stealing dog. Distraught, Einarr returned to his father, having destroyed a marriage, killed a bride and groom, and brought two warlords to the brink of all-out war. Amazingly, his father spared him. He exiled him, and somehow war was averted.

'But now he comes sweeping in as if he has a right to be here. He will bring war to us, at a time when our warriors are stretched by bandit trouble, rather than at a time when we are strong and could seek to gain advantage from it – and all because of his stupidity and vanity. The warlord he wronged is three times more powerful than we are and surely must seek vengeance. Our only chance against him, if we were at full strength, would be to use our knowledge of our land and terrain, and hope that our cunning was greater than his might.

'But we are not at full strength and Einarr has destroyed us. Yet my father welcomes him back with an embrace. He is a fool. If our dominion were a bear, Einarr would be the poisoned thorn in its paw. Unless the thorn is removed, the bear will die.

'Now get some sleep, you will need it.' Brann started to answer, but was met with a wave of the hand. 'We have talked enough. I will wake you at dawn.'

Curling into a ball beside Konall, he felt fatigue sweep over him as quick as his blanket.

True to his word, Konall woke him with a rough shake just as the sun was rising. With scarcely time to stretch, they set off once more, eating as they walked. They kept their cloaks round them at first but, as the exercise worked up their body temperature, they took them off and, rolling them up, strapped them to their packs.

253

They came to a stretch of land where cover was sparse and, with the sun high in the sky again, the glare from the snow was painful. Konall halted.

'Your tunic has a hood on it. Pull it up,' he said.

Brann frowned. 'I'm not cold. I have a cloak with me if I want to be warmer, although the colour doesn't exactly match the rest of my outfit. But in any case, I'm actually too warm walking in this sunshine.'

'It is because of the sun that you need it. Rolled up at the front of the hood is some light gauze. Untie it and let it fall over your face. If the wind gets up, you can tie it to the neck of your tunic to stop it flapping. You will be able to see through it. Without it, the glare will have you blind shortly, and will burn your face.'

Pulling the cover over his face, Brann felt ridiculous. After a moment's reflection, however, he snorted in derision at his own vanity as he reminded himself of the number of people around him who could judge his appearance.

Konall had started to walk once more, and he hurried to catch up.

Brann looked around them. 'I do not recognise this way from before. I thought we would be heading for the clearing where we last saw them so we could follow their trail from there.'

Konall shrugged. 'You feel free to go along two sides of a triangle if you want. I know the direction they went, so I would rather head straight for that area and look for them from there.'

'I think I'll stick with you,' Brann decided. 'So, now that we are agreed on that, what are we going to do when we find them?'

'It is pointless to try to plan for a situation when we have yet to see what we have to deal with, in terms of enemy numbers, terrain or defences. In the meantime, we shut up. In this situation, ears are just as useful as eyes in discovering danger.'

His advice was proved correct later that morning. Konall's hearing, keener than Brann's (it would be, Brann thought, less than charitably), picked up the murmur of voices ahead. The two boys were moving through sparse trees and had their hoods down, but even when he stopped and concentrated, Brann was unable to hear anything. He was, however, happy to follow Konall's signals when he realised what the boy was communicating to him.

They drew swords slowly and quietly. Brann's blade had felt heavy when he picked it up that morning; now, with the possibility looming of having to use it, it felt twice as heavy and ten times more awkward. Konall gestured that the voices lay ahead and slightly to the right, where the ground rose sharply and rockily. The easiest, and most obvious, way forward lay straight ahead, veering slightly to the left to pass in front of the steep ground; it was almost certain that those who lay ahead of them were watching that path, either in ambush or as sentries. Konall led Brann slightly back on their tracks and to the right, creeping through the widely spaced trees in a broad loop to take them well behind the source of the noises. The ground rose, not as sharply as the hillock they had originally faced, and they soon found themselves on the higher level.

They crept forward, trying not to dislodge any rocks underfoot or to let their packs or, even more importantly, their swords knock against any of the hard surfaces they passed. Konall peered carefully and painstakingly around the edge of every gap they passed until, as they were about to clear a large boulder, he froze. He lowered himself flat, and used his fingers and toes to lift and edge himself forward until there was enough room for Brann to follow. When he did so, moving alongside the older boy, he copied Konall's example and raised his head just enough to see over the crest of a small rise, his heart pounding so hard that he could hear it in his head. The ground dropped sharply before them and, in a small hollow around twenty feet below them and thirty feet ahead, sat two men, similar in appearance to those they had faced the day before. The sight, although expected, made him jump so hard that he ducked back down out of sight. It was one thing to see the enemy in his mind's eye, but a different prospect altogether to see them in the flesh.

He peered down once more. The pair were definitely sentries, anyway. That much was apparent from the fact that, although their position was well chosen for reasons of attack – with good vision of, and cover from, the area below and easy exit behind them – they were paying scant attention to the possibility that anyone may pass below them and were, instead, intent upon some simplistic game involving what Brann, at first, thought were animal bones but then realised with a surge of nausea were human fingers – some still bearing fragments of skin. These were obviously two men who were passing their time as they performed a chore, and were not expecting to see, never mind ambush, anyone.

Brann sensed movement beside him and turned to see that Konall had silently laid out two arrows beside himself. He gestured to Brann to do likewise, and started to inch his bow from its fastenings.

Eyes wide in alarm, Brann grabbed Konall's hand, stopping the movement. Unaccustomed to anyone ever restraining him, or even touching him, never mind at a moment such as this, Konall glared round, eyes blazing in fury.

He mouthed, 'What?'

Brann pointed at the bandits, drew his hand across his throat, and shook his head violently. Konall's expression was eloquent enough; he did not have to utter the word 'lunacy' to tell what was going through his mind, and he reached again for his bow.

Brann leant over and breathed into his ear, 'If we kill them, we leave a sign we were here.'

Konall twisted so that his mouth was over Brann's ear. 'You do not leave enemies behind you. It is suicide.'

Brann, exasperated, whispered back, 'If they do not know we were here, they will stay far behind us. If they are relieved and corpses – or no one at all – are found, we will be hunted. We will be caught between those behind us and the others that we seek in front. And we lose any surprise we may have.'

Konall stared hard at him, weighing what Brann had said against any alternatives he could imagine. After a long moment, his face tightened but he nodded once and began to slip his arrows back into the quiver. Brann breathed a silent sigh of relief, and they eased themselves back from the position. Once they had retired a reasonable distance and, now knowing that they would not chance upon the sentries around any more corners of this rocky outcrop, they were able to move at a reasonable pace once more.

Still, though, they did not dare to speak until they were well clear of the area.

Konall said, in his usual emotionless tone, 'That was good thinking.'

Brann smiled. 'It just seemed obvious.'

Konall grunted. 'Not to everyone. Sometimes it is good to have a mind uncluttered by military doctrine.' It was a few more paces before he added, 'And now that we know where they are, we can get them on the way back.'

Brann had been thinking more of avoiding them on the way back, but knew that his chances of dissuading Konall on that occasion were less than nil.

Konall continued, 'Anyway, it has told us one thing.'

Brann was already out of breath from the combination of the current exertion and the nerves of their recent near-encounter, and was finding speech less easy with each passing step. Only the thought of Gerens and Grakk drove his fatigued legs forward. Instead, he made a strangulated grunt that he hoped sounded both as if he were interested and he wished Konall to continue. It worked, to his relief.

'We are closer than we thought. Their base must be in the general area I had thought, but at the side of it that is nearest to our lands. It is good for us, right now, because we have less distance to travel and, more importantly, less distance to travel back when we may be pursued. But it is also extremely worrying that these scum live only maybe one full day's forced march from Ravensrest.'

He stopped. 'At any rate, if we are this close, we should be more careful – and ready.' He pulled out his bow and strung it, before unbuckling the protective flap from the top of the quiver and tucking it in to reveal the arrows. This time Brann had no thoughts of stopping him, and did likewise. 'And we had better drop the pace. It would be wise to be more alert.' Brann agreed.

Their bows strung and held in their left hands, they headed on, more cautiously than before. Brann became particularly jumpy, wheeling around frequently and jerking his head towards one side and then the other. Aiming to be as ready as he could, he drew an arrow from his quiver and held it with his bow. He stopped short of nocking it to the string, but held it along the length of the bow, ready to grab it if the occasion arose.

'I know what you are thinking,' Konall said. 'But you would be better keeping it in the quiver. It will only be a further encumbrance in your hand, and we have enough open country around us to see anyone coming, so any time you would save by holding the arrow there would be unimportant. In any case, if you do not have enough time to get it from the quiver, you will not have enough time to use the bow. You would be better with your sword.'

Brann could see the sense of Konall's words and replaced the arrow.

'And while we are on the subject,' Konall continued.

Oh, gods, Brann thought. *There is no stopping him. He stays silent for days, but when he speaks, he can't shut up.*

'Try not to be so nervous.'

The colour rose in Brann's cheeks. 'I'm not nervous!' He was, but he was not about to admit it to Konall.

'Well try not to be so "cautious", if you prefer,' Konall shrugged. 'I am nervous. It is not a bad thing. It keeps your senses on edge and your reactions sharp. It is just that if you are overly so, it works against your reactions and you lose any smoothness of movement you might have had. And you start finding enemies in every shadow and every noise of the wind. So, when they appear for real, it still catches you by surprise after so many false alarms.'

Konall glanced over and saw Brann's irritation. 'I am only trying to help you stay alive. You are no use to me dead. If you would rather narrow your chances, I will keep quiet.' Brann smiled. More at the thought that this was possibly the first time that Konall had voluntarily explained himself to anyone than an attempt to show that all was well, but it had the same effect. Konall, apparently satisfied, returned his attention to the terrain around him.

Brann, also, returned to his watchfulness but, acknowledging the sense of Konall's advice, irritating though it was, he tried to calm himself down. It was not easy. He was nervous. Very nervous.

In watching around him, Brann was able to observe the terrain more closely than he had been able to – or had the energy to – do before. As someone who had been brought up in rolling countryside, where the highest peak was a comparatively gently sloping hill, he had always envisaged mountainous countryside to comprise nothing but near-vertical slopes clad in sheets of lethally smooth ice. He had become amazed, however, at the variety around him. True, there were treacherous slopes – but they merely avoided those. Elsewhere there were wide plateaux, some with shrubs and trees, some bare; there were wooded slopes of various gradients, complete with streams and glades; there were dells and small lakes, waterfalls and rocky outcrops complete with caves. They walked along narrow paths halfway up deep ravines and slid down snowy slopes. As they did so, they were drifting above and below the snowline, so they were negotiating everything from crisp whiteness to the bare black, grey and brown of rocks and earth, and every patchy combination in between. Their surroundings changed in every conceivable way – sight, sound, smell, conditions underfoot, dark shade or a complete lack of shelter – every few minutes and, under a cloudless sky and majestic sun, Brann could not help musing that it was the most beautiful and captivating journey he had ever taken… if it were not for the savage madmen who could be waiting around the next corner.

And it was only Konall's sharp senses (again) that prevented them from walking headlong into such a group of bandits. They were on a natural path that wound its way along the sheer wall of a frighteningly deep ravine: a sharp V-shaped chasm that, Brann thought, looked as if an axe the size of a mountain had, with a single chop, taken a massive notch out of the world's surface. The path itself was not particularly dangerous or worrying – it would easily have accommodated at least five or six men walking abreast – and there was not a trace of snow or ice to give its flat surface a hint of treachery. It seemed well used, possibly indicating their growing proximity to the enemy stronghold, but also indicating its safety – providing, that the unwary traveller did not look down, an action that produced fear and dizziness. On looking upwards, a distance that appeared to be as far to the top of the cliff as it was downwards to the bottom, Brann found to his surprise that it caused just as much disorientation and light-headedness.

As they were about to discover, the sharp corners of the trail also appeared to mask sound, even from a close stretch of path. Perhaps it was the scuff of footsteps echoing softly from the opposite wall; perhaps it was some sort of sixth sense for danger: even Konall did not know or, at that moment, care. His arm shot out to halt Brann as they were about to round a right-hand corner, and the pair froze, arrows nocked to bowstrings, straining every sense for an indication of others present.

Hearing nothing more, they had to resort to eyesight. Konall crept to the corner and eased his head around. Brann heard his companion's breathing quicken and watched as he, equally slowly, moved his head back. Brann's initial thought was that he would have darted his head around the corner and back to minimise the time he would be visible to anyone on the other side but, watching Konall's method, he realised that a sudden movement like that would be more likely to attract attention.

If I live long enough, I could learn quite a lot about not dying, he thought with half a smile.

Konall's hand signals brought him back to serious reality, and he chided himself for losing concentration. The older boy indicated that there were seven bandits, and gestured to Brann to move his head closer. 'They are on a long stretch with only one boulder on it, which they are about to pass, and there is no other cover,' he whispered urgently. They both, simultaneously, glanced back down the path. There was no cover for them either; nowhere to go.

'I know,' whispered Brann. 'We have to take them on.'

Konall nodded but, to Brann's surprise, there was no glee about him, just business-like efficiency. 'We will take as many as we can with the bows. We will step out and let fly – with luck, the surprise should let us get most of them. If the survivors come at us, or go to ground, we finish it with swords. If they run, we go after them, and if we could use the bows, it would involve the least running and greater chance of success.

'Whatever happens, none must survive. If even one gets away, we are dead.'

They finished their preparations, which were not many – mainly ridding themselves of cumbersome packs and cloaks, and settling quivers and swordbelts securely on themselves.

Konall glanced down at Brann. 'Ready?' Brann nodded, trying to hide – from himself as well as from Konall – his almost paralysing nerves. 'In a few moments, they will be in range. We will give it a few moments more; we do not want them too close, but we do not want them on the edge of where we can reach in case any of them make a break away from us. When I nod, step around the corner. I will go first, so you will not have so far to go. Aim for the chest – they have no armour, and it is the biggest target. And start at the right and work your way towards the centre. I will do the same, from the left, which will reduce the chances of us going for the same target.'

He fell silent. Brann grew even more nervous – something he had not thought possible – and wished he could just turn and run away from it all. Then, all too soon, Konall nodded and, without a pause to draw breath, stepped calmly around the corner and several paces across the path.

Brann followed, less assuredly but there all the same. He had drawn three arrows from his quiver: one was already being drawn back to his cheek while the other two were held in his left hand, along the length of the bow in the manner Konall had told him not to adopt earlier. This time, however, he knew what he was about.

He loosed his first arrow at almost the same instant as Konall did but, as the taller boy reached in a smooth practised movement for another from his quiver, a flick of Brann's fingers swivelled one of the two arrows into position and he let fly just before his first arrow struck home. He barely registered that it had, like Konall's first shaft, struck resoundingly into the centre of a bandit's chest, flipping him backwards before he had even registered that danger was present. Brann's second arrow speared into a bandit's stomach just after he had loosed his third and, as he reached to his quiver for another shaft, he had a fraction of a moment to glance across to see how they were faring. His third target was struck also, the arrow slicing through the man's arm and into the side of his chest as he turned to draw his weapon.

Konall was working with fluid rapidity, but was aiming more deliberately and had been slower than Brann to obtain arrows for each shot. His accuracy was astounding and devastating, however. He would stare down the long shaft, eyes narrowed, breathe out softly and let fly – and in each case, his target was down with a shaft protruding from the exact centre of his chest. His third victim was put down in the same way, just as Brann struck home with his fourth arrow at the final man, at the back of the group.

He knew, however, that this shot was not as true. He had taken more time over his aim and was annoyed at himself, for he knew that whenever he had time to think about a shot, he was never as accurate. So it proved on this occasion.

The bandit had started running backwards and to the side, aiming for the cover of the boulder Konall had mentioned, unslinging a heavy crossbow as he moved. By chance, Brann's slightly skewed shot hit him as he lurched in that direction, but it was anything but a successful kill, striking him in the calf, and, by a strange chance, passing by half its length through that leg and embedding itself in his other. With a savage roar, he fell sideways as his legs were flipped out from beneath him, and he crashed to the ground and lay writhing, trying in vain to separate his legs.

'Don't worry, he's going nowhere,' Konall said evenly, dropping his bow and racing forward, his sword appearing in his right hand and his knife in his left. Brann followed suit, but drawing only the knife – the sword seemed too cumbersome under the circumstances.

Konall reached the bodies, and started cutting their throats methodically and coldly with his knife, whether they appeared dead or, in the case of the man hit in the stomach by Brann, heading there.

As he did so, the man that Brann had hit in the legs roared in a mixture of pain and fury and slammed his hand down on the shaft restraining him, snapping the wood. He leapt to his feet and, a bizarre apparition with lengths of arrow protruding from both calves, he moved with scarcely believable speed back up the path.

Konall reached for an arrow but realised at the same time as Brann that they had left their bows back at their original position. Brann grabbed one of the short knives from his belt and, trying to remember the style used by the showmen in the fairs that had visited his village, gripped it by the blade and hurled it spinning after the fleeing man. Never a natural thrower, he was amazed to see it strike the man on the back of his head... with the hilt. The man fell to his knees, dazed, and Konall was on him in an instant to finish the job with his knife.

The older boy handed Brann's knife back to him. 'Novel approach, opting to stun him,' he observed, his face a deadpan mask.

Brann took the blade and slotted it back into its sheath with brisk efficiency. 'I thought I had caused enough mess,' he said haughtily, and turned back to the corpse-strewn path. He knew that they would have to retrieve any arrows that were still serviceable because of their limited supply. But knowledge of the fact did not make it any less distasteful. Konall saw his expression.

'It is never easy the first few times. Just pretend that they are animals and you are just out hunting,' he said. 'I brought arrows with no barbs – they do not cause as much harm, but at least you do not have to push them all the way through to get them back out. We may have to retrieve them in a hurry at some point.'

Brann felt the same and, taking a deep breath to keep down the nausea, he managed to pull out two of his arrows intact. The man he had hit in the stomach had fallen forward, breaking the shaft, and his final arrow had, of course, been snapped by the bandit whose legs it had pierced.

He followed Konall's example of wiping the gore from the arrows, and returned them to his quiver. All three of Konall's arrows were fine for re-use: his pinpoint accuracy had knocked each man flat onto his back, killing him outright, so the shafts were standing, indicating their presence like small flagpoles, waiting to be retrieved.

Grunting with the effort, Konall started rolling corpses to the lip of the ravine and tipping them over the edge. Brann did likewise, and was surprised at how heavy a dead body could be.

As he reached the edge, Konall – breathless also from the effort – said, 'Make sure you are not caught on any part of his clothing or equipment. If the body starts dragging you over the edge, you will be gone before you realise it.' Brann did not need to peer into the ravine to remind himself of the danger. He checked three full times that nothing on the dead bandit was snagging on his clothes. And then a fourth time, just to make sure. Still, when he rolled the man over the edge, his stomach lurched with nerves until the man disappeared without taking him on the journey as well.

The second man was easier to manage – mentally, if not physically – but the third swept away his self-control in an instant. The man – the one that Brann had hit in the stomach – was slumped forward, almost on all fours. When Brann started to roll him onto his back, his head lolled back and the wound that Konall had sliced across his throat gaped wide. Brann vomited violently. Twice.

Konall leapt across and dragged him upright. 'Take deep breaths and get yourself under control,' he commanded sharply, holding Brann steady.

Brann gulped and forced himself not to retch again. He gasped, 'Apologies for the mess. The vomit will be a tell-tale sign.'

Konall made sure that he could stand without swaying and started heaving at the corpse that was the problem. 'I am not concerned about the mess you have made. We have enough blood to clear up anyway – a touch of puke on top of that is nothing. I just do not want you weakening yourself. If you throw up any more, you will not have enough strength to walk far, never mind fight if need be.' He started rolling the corpse towards the precipice. 'Walk around to clear your head. I will see to this one, and the only other one left is the one I was about to push over the edge when you interrupted us.'

Brann did as he was told, happy to let Konall finish the gruesome task. The tall noble boy walked over to him carrying a typically grubby tunic. 'You do not want to know what the body underneath it was like,' he said in disgust. 'Hygiene does not seem to be a great factor among them if this one was anything to go by. Perhaps we should just leave them all alone and let them die of one disease or another.'

He started to sweep as much of the mess – including Brann's lunch – over the edge. He then used a dry portion of the tunic to brush what little dirt and dust was available over the bloodstains, and scuffed the patches with his boots so that they did not look too unnaturally tidy. Brann was impressed by his attention to detail, but one thing was still nagging at him.

'Should we not have gone through their clothes to see if there would be anything of use to us?'

Konall shook his head. 'Their weapons could hardly be described as quality in any way, and as for their food, I would not eat any of it if you held a knife to my throat. Would you?'

'Point taken.'

Konall surveyed his work. 'It will have to suffice. It is still visible, but we have to hope that the low level of intelligence these scumbags seem to possess and a few days of weathering will mean that, if any more of them pass this way, they will not notice. In any case, we do not have time to do any more.'

They returned to the corner to collect their packs, cloaks and bows. Konall replaced the string on his bow with the spare one.

Brann said, 'Is that good military practice, or have you damaged the one you were using?'

Konall had finished the task already. 'Neither. Just personal preference. I feel that, if I alternate the strings every time I use the bow, they will last longer as a result.'

It made sense to Brann. He nodded, and replaced his string also. It took only a few seconds and they were soon on their way again. This time, however, they each kept an arrow nocked to their bowstrings, ready to draw in an instant. Before rounding any corner, in particular, they were much more cautious than they had been. Aware, however, that the longer they were on this trail, the more likely they were to come across other groups of bandits, they increased the pace between corners or on stretches where they could see well ahead.

It was on one of these stretches, as they scuttled along, that Brann asked, 'Do you think that was a patrol that we came across?'

'Why?'

'Well, if it was, then we have a chance of getting past this area before another patrol is due to come along. If, on the other hand, this is in general just a route used by random, ordinary bands of lunatic bandits, we are much more likely to come across more of them.'

Konall glanced over, approval in his expression. 'A good point. Also, if they were a patrol, they may be expected to be out for a while, and will not be missed for several days at least – which would be good.'

He thought for a moment. 'I think they *were* a patrol. They were all male, and – to judge from the one that tried to get away – fanatical, and they carried very little apart from weapons and food, so I can think of little else that they would be doing other than patrolling. Unless they were a raiding party, which would give us even more time before they were due back.'

'In any case,' Brann suggested, 'I think we should keep moving as fast as we can.'

Konall nodded his agreement, realising that they had slowed as they talked, and they resumed their stop–start progress.

As they rounded a right-hand corner in their usual fashion – with Konall easing his head around to check the safety of the next stretch, and Brann waiting with bow half-drawn in case anyone appeared unexpectedly as he did so – Konall stopped.

'Look,' he said. 'I have never been so glad to see the end of a path in my life.'

Both sides of the ravine came together around half-a-mile ahead, where a towering but slender waterfall fell gracefully, sparkling in the sunshine like a glistening silver pillar. Unnoticed by the pair, the top of the cliff above them had been gradually dropping lower, and in the last stretch it took a steeper dip to meet the lower level of the land beyond the ravine. The path was visible for the rest of its length, curving lazily in a long sweep from right to left, and rising in its last third to exit the ravine to the right of the waterfall. It was empty. For the time being.

The two boys looked at each other as if to check the other's thoughts, returned their arrows that they had been holding ready to their quivers, and broke into a run. Brann grinned with exhilaration, and Konall's eyes narrowed and one corner of his mouth turned slightly – which equated to much the same thing.

Brann stared at the end of the path, willing it closer and expecting, at any moment, to see figures appear from the area beyond. Much to his relief, they made it unaccosted. The thundering of the falling water as it landed too far below to ponder, was too loud to allow conversation, and they continued their run into the edge of a wooded area, where they slid, feet first, and lay breathing heavily as they recovered in the shade of the trees. The tension of the last few hours flowed from Brann with each breath, and he suspected Konall felt the same – although he expected that his companion would never admit it.

He rolled onto his stomach to look out over the country-side they had entered. It was the most beautiful area they had come across in their journey so far.

A river flowed gently through a shallow green valley that undulated further than he could see. Where the river was funnelled to slip over the edge into the waterfall, it broad-ened into what was almost a small lake, its glassy surface providing a near-perfect mirror for the bold green and blue of the hillsides and sky beyond it. On their side of the river, woodland covered the valley floor and stretched up and over the hillsides bounding it whereas, on the far side – whether by accident or human design – trees were sparse, being dotted here and there, singly or in groups of no more than three

or four. Also on that side, a wide dirt track, more a road of
sorts, had been worn into the grass by frequent use. Shortly
before the river widened, it split: one fork heading beyond that
side of the ravine and the other leading over the most basic
bridge that Brann had ever seen – uneven planks fastened
together and resting on thick posts driven into the riverbed.

'It is so beautiful. How can it be, such green life so high
in the mountains?'

Konall had raised himself onto his elbows 'You're right,
it is,' he said softly. 'I have heard of areas like this. Inside
these mountains, there once was heat. Maybe still is, but it
doesn't spill out now the way the legends say it did. But some
remains, in the form of hot springs, like rivers and streams and
pools under the ground. Sometimes they reach the surface,
and sometimes, like here, they must run close enough under
the surface that they fool the ground into thinking it is not
high on a mountain.' He grunted. 'But we did not come up
here to admire the view like a couple of lovers. Unless you
are trying to tell me something, that is.'

'Well, now that you mention it,' Brann grinned, 'you do
have lovely hair.'

The look Konall gave was not one of adoration.

However, as they rose to leave, Konall turned to Brann.
'You did well with the bow back there.'

Brann shrugged off the compliment, but was quietly as
pleased as he was surprised at hearing it. 'You mean the thing
with holding the arrows?' Konall nodded. 'It is just a trick
I developed with someone at home.' He paused, catching
his breath as he remembered the trips with Callan into the
woods, an image from another, idyllic life that seemed so far
away it was almost as if it had been experienced by someone
else. He forced himself to carry on, using a comparatively

271

mundane explanation to stave off the emotion that threatened to swamp him. 'It is handy when hunting small, fast animals that it may take several shots to hit, or if you want to try to hit a few targets before they bolt.'

Konall regarded him evenly. 'It was more than just a trick. It is one thing shooting fast – it is another hitting the target. The only time you were wayward was when you took time over aiming.'

Brann smiled. 'I have always been the same. When I react, I seem to do things right; when I have time to think about it, it all goes a bit awry. It was a running joke, whether I was hunting or playing games like...' He had been about to refer to the cairn game, but the memory of Callan and thoughts of his family racing out to meet him after the victory were so overwhelming that he was unable to check them this time. A lump in his throat blocked his words and he turned away and busied himself with his pack to mask the tears that had sprung to his eyes.

Konall had, however, noticed. Picking up his own load, he ended the conversation by saying simply, 'Come, we have wasted enough time. Let's go.'

Gratefully, Brann followed him. A bleakness started to settle over him, though, as thoughts of Callan refused to leave his head. He looked at Konall's back, so close ahead even he couldn't miss with an arrow. It would be so easy.

Glancing warily about, Konall ran swiftly to the river and stopped at the water's edge under the cover of the bridge. He unslung a leather water pouch from his shoulder to top it up.

The sight of it snapped Brann from his melancholy thoughts. He slid down beside Konall, catching his arm before he could dip the container into the water.

'What are you doing?' Konall snapped, his recent relative good humour gone.

'Do not use that water,' Brann gasped, out of breath from the sudden burst of speed that had been needed to reach the older boy in time. 'We cannot trust it.'

Konall regarded him as if he were mad. 'It is water from a mountain river. It is fast-moving and clear. Even if you have not learnt on military patrols that these are exactly what you look for if you want fresh water, a country boy like you should know that anyway. What do you do when you are out hunting? Or did you never stray far enough from your mother's apron strings that you could not return home if you were thirsty?'

He moved to lower his water pouch to the river's surface, but again Brann grabbed him. Konall rounded on him, but the look of fury in the smaller boy's eyes stunned him – he had no idea of the effect of his reference to Brann's mother, and had no time to wonder about the reason for the anger before Brann growled, 'If you were not my only guide out of these stinking mountains, I would let you risk drinking it, and enjoy any effects it may have as I remembered your ill-mannered arrogance. If you bothered to think about it instead of worrying about your precious authority, you might realise that their settlement looks as if it is upriver and, from the look of the bandits we have come across so far, hygiene and sanitation will not be top of their priorities.

'So we have no idea what they might be putting the water further up the river. That's the logical part of it. The more immediate reason is a bit more obvious.' He pointed a short way up the course of the river where the corpse of a sheep lay rotting. 'If you still want to drink it, go ahead.'

Konall slowly removed Brann's hand from his arm and, his face a stony mask, nodded once. He slung the pouch back over his shoulder and, scanning the surrounding area, he rose in silence and skimmed across the grass to the cover of the woods.

Struggling, as usual, to keep up, it took around a dozen paces of Brann's shorter legs before his anger began to fade and he wondered to what extent his choice of words had made his time with Konall more difficult.

They wove their way between the trees, heading up through the valley. Almost immediately, they came upon the road as it cut through the end of the woods and, as Brann had surmised, a way had been cut or, rather, hacked through the vegetation. Like everything else the bandits had a hand in, there seemed to be an ugliness about their work.

Checking back and forth to make sure the way was clear, they bolted across into the relative safety of the woodland on the other side.

Hesitantly – the anger was no longer there to give his words any assurance and he was nervous of the reaction he might provoke – Brann asked, 'Do you think we should keep going through the trees in case we cannot cross the river further up? You would think the road over there leads to their camp, which would mean the camp is on the other side of the water.'

'I think we have no choice,' Konall said simply, with no trace in his tone that the previous conversation had ever taken place. 'If we are close to their lair, we are more likely to come across them, in greater numbers and with untold support nearby. I do not see many places to hide over there.'

'I think we should stay with the trees,' Brann declared, the relief at Konall's apparent dismissal – for now – of his impertinence to a noble leaving him almost giddy. He strode off purposefully, nearly catching a low-hanging branch with his forehead. Konall almost smiled.

With the trees reducing visible distance – and therefore the notice they would have of any enemy presence – they both had an arrow nocked to their bowstrings. Although Brann's method of holding several spare arrows along with his bow had served him well during the fight with the bandits, he knew that Konall's advice – that the extra shafts would be an encumbrance when moving – was right, and he took only one arrow from his quiver. Konall noticed but, as was his way, said nothing.

Brann's hunting experience and Konall's military upbringing served them well in moving through the trees. The techniques from each background were surprisingly similar in this environment – surprising until they realised that the objectives (to move quickly and silently while remaining able to spot and react to their prey in an instant) were the same. They fell naturally into a pattern of move and cover, with one slipping a short distance ahead and then waiting, bow half-drawn and scanning for any sound or movement, while the other passed and took up an identical station further ahead.

It was a manoeuvre that rapidly ate up the distance and time, and Brann was startled when Konall called a halt. Memories of the way that Gerens had seemed compelled to protect him on the ship had filled his mind more and more as they drew closer to their goal. 'Dusk will soon start to fall,' he objected. 'Should we not press on if we are to try to find their camp tonight? If we have to start looking again tomorrow, anything could happen to them overnight.'

Konall looked up from where he was crouching, taking food from his pack. 'Can you not hear them?' he said in a low voice. 'From the sound of it, I think we can afford to stop to get some food inside us and still make it there very soon.'

Brann stood motionless, straining his ears until they became attuned to the same sounds that Konall had perceived. At first, he heard nothing but the noises of the forest but, gradually, a low murmur of the voices of many people going about their daily business grew in his consciousness. The more he listened, the more he heard: the clank of metal on metal, the creak of wood, the cry of fowl. So different were they from the sounds he had become accustomed to in the woods that he wondered how he could not have noticed them as quickly as Konall. But they were faint – so faint that a slight change in the breeze obscured them briefly – and he was forced to admit that Konall was simply better at noticing such things than he.

They ate quickly, forcing down food despite their nerves and moved in the direction of the river, where the clear ground would let them see further. The edge of the trees came so quickly that they almost stumbled into the open and had to throw themselves backwards to halt their momentum and ensure that they stayed within the relative gloom of the woods. They remained still until they were certain that their movement had not been noticed, before each moved to a tree close to the riverbank. Standing flat against the trunk to disguise their human shapes, they peered across, then up, the river.

Brann caught his breath. It was one thing fighting groups of the bandits, or even hearing the sounds of their encampment; it was another, totally, to see them as large as life in their lair.

The bandits' home was a sizeable settlement but, in comparison to Brann's village, it was as if a part of hell's domain had been lifted to the realm of men. The encampment lay within a hollow; with no walls or fortifications of any kind, its location had been chosen for concealment rather than defence, and would have been invisible if the boys had been two hundred yards further back down the shallow slope that approached it. If a large force came upon it, the inhabitants would, Brann guessed, flee by the nearest available route rather than stand and fight for their homes. If the buildings could be referred to as homes, he corrected himself. Ramshackle huts had been thrown together in a layout of no particular order, and had been constructed with the same lack of expertise and care as had been afforded to the bridge at the other end of the valley. To say they were basic dwellings would be understating the case – it was as if building them was an onerous chore that had been completed with the minimum of effort, with the result being accepted by the inhabitants on the basis that, in doing so, they would have to undertake no more work.

Some were lying derelict, although there was little to distinguish them from those in use but for the fact that there were no people coming or going from them. Around the site, the refuse of life lay where it was dropped, with no regard for personal pride or hygiene. Whether broken tools or excess raw materials of the construction process, or the daily detritus of the feeding process (in varying proportions of the original animal), there was scarcely an area uncluttered by piles that attracted children and rats in equal measures and with an equal lack of interest shown by any of the adults towards either offspring or rodents.

The settlement spilled up against the far bank of the river from the boys' vantage point, with the filthy debris travelling one stage further and spilling into the water, causing a film of scum to spread outwards until it was broken up by the flow of the current. Konall caught Brann's attention as he stared

277

at the contamination of the river, and nodded meaningfully. Brann guessed that this was the closest to an apology for the incident at the bridge that he was likely to receive.

The inhabitants of the settlement teemed over it or slumped in any space that took their fancy, often forcing those moving around to step over them or, in some cases on top of them; arguments that spilled into violence – which more often than not involved a short flurry followed by a retreat, with exaggerated defiance, by one of the participants – were frequent as a result even in the short period they had been watching.

The people seemed, in appearance as much as actions, to have more in common with their rat cohabitants than with normal villagers. Their appearance was much as those Brann and Konall had already encountered: unkempt and aggressive, as if their demeanour was the first barrier to any challenge, verbal or physical. The domestic setting now added women and children to their experience of these people and, although distinguishable in appearance, the women shared their attitude with the men... when dealing with those of their own gender; when around the men, however, they varied between fawning and fearful, and the occasional, violent and casual cuff that was administered explained why. Communication was sparse and brief, and covered a narrow spectrum from what seemed boastful or mocking statements to aggressive and bullying exchanges, if the tone used was any indication. Leaving the greatest impression, however, was – when the wind swirled their direction – the stench from both moving and unmoving, living and rotting creatures that inhabited the site, an overpowering smell that caused Brann's head to swim.

As his eye cast about the settlement, however, his disgust changed to horror. In an open area at roughly the centre of the village, there were a number of posts bearing impaled bodies in various stages of decomposition and attention from carrion. Although tattered, the remnants of their clothes were still clearly of superior quality to those worn by the living who passed them by, suggesting that they had been captives rather than inhabitants. Although it was too distant to distinguish any features on what the birds had left of their faces, the state of the corpses showed that they had been there for several weeks, and so none could have been the remains of the three who had been taken so recently. The sight did, however, make a strong case for urgency on the boys' part.

Konall grunted. 'I see from the state of the river that you offered good advice at the bridge.' Despite the unexpected addition to his previous nodded admission of Brann's correctness, he received no reply. He glanced at Brann and noticed his whitening complexion and quickening breathing. 'Keep your stomach under control, farm boy. If you are like this now, what will you be like when we get closer?'

The colour returned to Brann's face in a rush. 'I am no farm boy,' he blurted hotly, 'although most of my friends were and there is no insult, as you intend, in being compared to them. And, although I am nothing more than a mere *mill* boy, I have been through more recently than any of the boy heroes you mix with manage to experience in years.' The initial rush of anger subsided and he remembered to whom he was talking and the secrets he must hide. 'We cannot all be great warriors, you know,' he mumbled, turning away.

Konall looked appraisingly at him. 'Maybe not, but you seem to learn quickly – or you would be dead by now. But it changes nothing of what I said: you must control yourself and find a way to stand apart from your emotions when you see such things. If we creep around there tonight, you will see many things that will turn your stomach. Never mind managing to keep down your last meal – if you even stop to stare you will not notice the scumbag who creeps up behind you.'

He paused, and stared back at the settlement. 'I meant no insult,' he added quietly. 'You have undertaken much to be here.' He paused again. 'Apologies.'

Bran was glad that he had the support of the tree at the final comment. He guessed there had been few, if any, occasions in the past when Konall had uttered that word or anything similar. He had certainly never expected to hear it directed at him.

He shrugged casually. 'I probably over-reacted. It is of no importance.'

Konall stared intently at him. 'But do you accept my apology?' he asked urgently. It seemed vital to him, now that he had crossed such a difficult barrier, that the matter was concluded properly.

Brann was tempted to offer a flippant reply to try to defuse the situation, but realised that it was more likely to have the opposite effect. Adopting Konall's serious tone, he said, 'Of course I accept it.'

Konall nodded. They stared at the village in awkward silence until Brann decided that there was a more pressing question to be addressed. 'So, what's the plan?'

Konall snorted, a derisive sound that Brann was beginning to realise was not always to be taken personally. 'Normally, when planning an attack, whether it is an all-out attack or a low-key infiltration such as awaits us, one would study the defences and the patterns of those within them. But here, there are no defences, and the vermin we are watching do not seem to be able to walk in a straight line, even if they were interested in doing so in the first place, never mind conform to any sort of routine behaviour.'

'So...' Brann prompted.

Konall shrugged. 'So, I suppose it makes our plan simpler. We wait until darkness, slip in – avoiding, or attending to, any sentries – find and release the prisoners, and move away at whatever speed seems most appropriate at the time.'

Brann took a deep breath. He felt anything but qualified to criticise but, with his life depending on their actions that night, he had to overcome his nerves.

Konall noticed his expression. 'You disagree?'

He had no option but to speak now. 'Not as such,' he said slowly, choosing his words with care. 'I just think there is more to it than that.'

'Like what?'

'Well, what you described was accurate, but it seems to be more of a description of what we have to do, not how we will do it.'

'But that is all there is to it,' Konall snapped. 'It is so simple, that the objectives and the method of execution are one and the same. This conversation is a waste of time.'

Now that Brann had managed to start to speak, he found it easier to continue. 'Actually, I think there is much more to it although, as you say, the objectives are simple. And, anyway, what time are we wasting when we have to wait until darkness before we can move?'

There was a long silence. Brann began to wonder if Konall had heard him. Then, with an exaggerated sigh, the white-haired boy turned to him. 'All right, *mill* boy,' he said with an emphasis that was less insult and more an indication that he was trying to lighten the tone with his unique brand of humour. 'Enlighten me.'

Brann grinned. 'I would be delighted to, oh mighty warrior,' he said grandly, with a sweeping bow.

'Do not test the limits of your fortune,' Konall growled.

'Well,' Brann began hastily, 'first of all, as we have time, I think we should move further up in the woods, to see the village from a different angle. Maybe we could spot somewhere that looks as if captives are being kept there – one of the huts might be more solid, or might have guards outside.'

Konall nodded, taking interest. 'Go on,' he invited.

Brann was warming to his subject. 'Then we have to consider where we cross the river.'

'Does it matter?' Konall asked dismissively. 'It seems to be the same width and speed in this stretch as far as we can see. All that we know for sure is that we will get wet.'

'True, but there is more to consider than just the river itself. Do we cross as far away as this, where we are less likely to be seen by chance by anyone in the settlement, or do we do so closer to the development where there are more background sounds to mask any noise we may make?'

Konall shrugged, and pondered the question. 'I think here, and we try to be as quiet as we can. We can listen ourselves for any movement on the other side before we cross to judge if there will be any ears to hear us. In any case, I think that if there are any guards at all, they will be close to their creature comforts, such as they are, and not beyond the village borders. From what we have seen of the people here, they do not expect to be disturbed. This valley, and the settlement within it, is secluded enough, and they have their sentries watching the trails in the unlikely event that any force may venture up this direction. Every day must be the same repetitious squalor, so why would they expect today to be any different?'

'Agreed,' said Brann. 'But, once over the river, where do we go? On the basis of what you have just said, they are most likely to watch only the approach directly up the valley, if they watch at all. If we circle round to the side, we will probably find it quieter.'

Konall nodded. 'Even if they do guard the side, which I doubt, their numbers would be light there. If they are anywhere, they will concentrate on the front.'

Brann paused as a thought struck him. 'Actually, it might be good to come across the occasional sentry that we could, well, dispose of.'

Konall's eyebrows shot up. 'Your attitude is improving.'

Brann smiled. 'Far from it. Let me keep talking and I can forget how close to throwing up every part of this brings me.'

'I never thought I would say it,' Konall said dryly, 'but please keep talking.'

'What I mean is,' Brann continued, 'that if we kill a sentry, not only do we clear a path that we can retreat down in a hurry if we have to, but we can take his weapons.' Continuing over Konall's snort, he said, 'I know they will be poor quality, but we may have to force a lock or a door, and it would be better not to have to use our own blades.'

Konall nodded, approvingly. 'And it would help to be able to arm the prisoners when we release them.'

'Of course,' Brann said. 'But then, I think, we come to the most important part: how do we get back out?'

'That is no problem,' Konall said. 'The settlement has no walls, so we leave any way we choose.'

'Exactly,' agreed Brann. 'So I think we choose the best way now, rather than when it is more difficult to remember the layout of the village or the terrain around it. And we might have other pressing matters to deal with at the time. What's more, we might be able to gain an advantage.'

Konall's interest grew. 'In what way?'

'Well, we do not know where the captives will be, or whether we will be able to remain undiscovered or will be fighting our way out. Or where the majority of the enemy will be at the time. But we do know where we want to go.'

'Do we?' Konall asked. 'Apart from home, fast, that is.'

'Yes we do, actually,' Brann said, reflecting on the strange change of attitudes that saw him being the serious one and Konall offering flippant answers. 'Back across the river as soon as possible.' Konall raised a questioning eyebrow once more. 'Well, if we are being chased, it will also slow down anyone following us, assuming we can get across without being shot.'

'And without swallowing the water, which might be worse,' Konall pointed out helpfully. Brann was not sure if he preferred the old Konall or the new one.

He continued, choosing to ignore the comment. 'If, on the other hand, we manage to slip away unnoticed, we can cross the river and choose between using the trees for concealment or the flat riverbank for speed. If we are being pursued, we can, again, use the riverbank for speed or the trees for cover from missiles. We can judge it best at the time.' He stopped to reconsider. 'Actually, if we are being chased, I think we should opt for speed: they will be racing down the other side to get to the bridge at the end of the valley – or any other bridge or ford we do not know about, to get ahead of us. Then we would have a big problem.'

Konall shrugged. 'We would have to go up and over the side of the valley and find another way home. But, if we do, we will enter unfamiliar country and there may be other patrols of these vermin, or even others of their nests, out there. Our best chance is to return the way we came, so it would be best to stay ahead of them.' He frowned. 'We should have destroyed the bridge.'

It was Brann's turn to shrug. 'We were not to know. In any case, there may be other bridges, or fords, that we passed without noticing because we were among the trees, so it may have just been a waste of time or a sign to any returning patrols that someone unfriendly was in the area. And, anyway, we may not be allowed a chance to cross back over the river up here, so we may need the bridge ourselves.'

'Pray that we can regain this bank,' Konall said darkly. 'I do not think much of our chances if it develops into a straight race down the open country of that side of the river, especially since the captives will have been weakened by their experience.'

'I feel a great deal of prayer is needed to help us to return alive,' Brann said, equally grimly.

Staring at the encampment, Konall digested Brann's suggestions. It did not take him long. 'Not bad for a mill boy,' he accepted. 'You are full of surprises. I must say, I have never come across a stranger page.' He paused, and his eyes almost twinkled. 'I do not suppose Einarr would like to do a swap?'

Brann grinned. 'I will take that as a compliment and ignore the fact that the highest I can reach in your estimation is to be regarded as your servant.'

His expression as serious as his tone, Konall replied, 'Do not presume my good mood allows you to be impertinent. I can always withdraw such an attractive offer.'

Brann laughed, but quickly checked himself as he remembered their situation. Still it was reassuring to know that Konall did, after all, possess a sense of humour. Albeit a unique one.

Moving back into the cover of the trees, they moved upriver in the same cautious manner as before, but now with a definite purpose about them. And, once again, Brann felt sick.

Chapter 9

There was one among them who should not be there.

In truth, none of them deserved to be there. In generations past, this calibre of man would not have risen to such lofty perches. They would know the ruling court only by tales from the lips of others, yet now they formed it. In generations past, the court would be ruled by those born to it, educated since birth to be equally adept in the skills of ruling and the machinations of courtly intrigue, alongside those few who had proved to have had those qualities bestowed upon them by fate and nature; now it was ruled by those who had bought their way to power, who ruled for self-aggrandisement and personal wealth.

But generations past had passed, and a man can only ride the horse beneath him, no matter how much he wishes to better it. The court is what it is; his life is what it is.

But rule for the gathering of power, such as had built the Empire, forces the ruler's eyes outward, to watch each small part of his demesne, to maintain and grow the source of that power, and so the Empire prospers; rule for the garnering of riches and personal pleasure turns the ruler's eyes inward, to his chambers, his treasury, his harem, and so the Empire's many parts begin to rule themselves. The Empire must be run by one court, and one Emperor, for the greater good; if the court is run in its own interest, then the serving demesnes will run themselves in their own interest, and so an Empire is no more.

But while they were undeserving of ruling the Empire, still they were from the race of lions. Weak, self-serving lions they may be, but lions they were nonetheless. But among them sat one who should not be there. Among them sat a jackal. A pale jackal from other lands, an envoy from distant shores who, with promises dipped in honey of wealth and luxury untapped, had been accepted, nay welcomed, by lions. A jackal, whose promises dipped in honey curried such favour that his whispered advice fell into receptive ears, ears that questioned not how the Empire would fare, but how their coffers would fill.

A jackal who was a threat. But a threat need not be stamped upon. A threat can be used; a snake could be stamped upon, but equally could be lifted and set among the den of leopards harrying your goats. A coward would run. A swift man could crush the danger. But a wise man could use the danger to his advantage, if he could but find the way.

The court was as it was. But it need not ever be so.

It would not be so.

* * * *

Less than an hour later, Brann and Konall were working their way back through the now-familiar woods opposite the village. Their study of the settlement from further upriver had proved fruitful: not only had they spotted a building that was more substantial than the rest, with two guards at the entrance – surely a prison of some sort – but an unexpected bonus had also presented itself. Bobbing gently at the water's edge, beside a rough wooden platform that was probably meant to serve as a jetty but which was as much under the water as above it, were five or six long, low boats. Even if they were not sufficient to offer a means of travel – and escape – down the river, they would at least give them a quicker, and drier, means of re-crossing the river, assuming that that avenue proved to be open to them. The condition of the boats was impossible to tell in the increasing gloom of dusk, but discovering them had boosted the boys' confidence.

They returned downriver in silence to the point from which they had originally watched the village, and hid their packs under the cover of a large and thick bush. The spot was marked by a leafy branch that Konall had rammed upright close to the river's edge. 'Anyone seeing it will know it is a marker,' he said, 'but they will not know what it is signalling. In any case, it will not be visible from the village, especially at night, and if we are still here when they are up and wandering about tomorrow, then we will have more to worry us than finding our packs.'

Following Konall's lead, Brann stripped and bundled his clothes together, wrapping them tightly in his cloak. The pair waded slowly into the water, the chill around Brann's ankles feeling like ice, and he hesitated, his natural reaction being to do anything other than move into deeper water. Taking a deep breath of resolution and gritting his teeth, he forced himself forward, but his determination caused him to move more quickly than he had meant and, as the water reached his thighs, he splashed slightly.

Konall twisted round, hissing, 'If you wish to attract arrows, do it away from me.'

'Sorry,' Brann whispered. 'It is just so cold that I wanted to get it over with as quickly as possible.'

'You will certainly feel no pain once an arrow or six have been in you for a while.'

Brann nodded. 'I admit, that consequence is rather less appealing. It will not happen again.'

Konall softened. 'Ensure that is so. For both of our sakes. Anyhow, once you have been in the water for a few moments, your body will become accustomed to it.' He felt ahead with his foot. 'It gets deeper sharply here, so swim on your back. You can do that, can you not?'

'Yes. Why?'

'It is easier to hold your clothes out of the water that way. No point in taking them all off and then getting them wet after all, is there?'

Brann did not feel an answer was needed.

They reached the far bank without any further noise. The pain from the cold, if anything, had increased as they progressed and made breathing more difficult with every passing second. Although the river was not wide enough for them to be long enough submerged for numbness to set in, Brann still felt, as he climbed onto the grassy bank, that his limbs were stiffening up.

'Well, I did not get used to the cold at all,' he whispered crossly.

Konall shrugged. 'If it is any consolation, neither did I.'

Brann's eyes widened. 'But I thought you said...'

'It got you moving into deeper water,' Konall cut in. 'Anyway, what temperature did you expect? This is a mountain river. You will not get many hot springs up here.'

Brann began to unwrap his clothes. 'All I can say is: we had better make it to those boats.'

'Get dried quickly,' Konall advised. 'Once we are moving again, your arms and legs will ease and you will heat up. Wipe yourself with your cloak, but shake off as much as you can like a dog does, first. That way, your cloak will dry quicker as we walk, and you do not want it to be soaking – drips make noise.'

Shortly afterwards – Brann had never dried himself more quickly, as much from a desire not to be discovered undressed and unready by any locals as from the cold – they were on their way. Konall had turned his clothes and cloak inside-out, and told Brann to do the same. The garments were a darker shade of grey on the reverse, making them less visible in the dark. They crept through the gloom, part way up a hillside to the left of the village. It never seemed to get completely dark in this country but, when Brann had mentioned this to Konall the previous night, the older boy had merely shrugged and suggested that Brann extend his visit until the winter, when it never seemed to get totally light. 'We appreciate the sunlight when we have it,' he had said simply.

The shadows, however, were deep and although the hillside was empty of all vegetation, taller than grass, fires in the village made the unlit surroundings seem darker by comparison.

Both had arrows nocked to their bowstrings, as they had done in the forest. This time, however, Brann had reverted to holding a couple of spare shafts along his bow – if they had to use their bows, it was likely that they would have to do so rapidly and repeatedly to try to ensure that no alarm was raised and, in such circumstances, every second would be vital.

Konall froze. Brann automatically half-drew his bow and strained his eyes for a target. Konall, noticing his reaction, shook his head and beckoned Brann forward beside him. He pointed down, behind the buildings. As Brann stared hard in the direction of the boy's finger, he began to make out dim, but regular, shapes, and some movement among them. He looked questioningly at Konall.

'Tents,' the older boy breathed into his ear.

Brann nodded in understanding. 'The more senior bandits live separately,' he whispered in reply.

Konall shook his head in exasperation. 'These, ordered; village chaos,' he said, his voice barely loud enough to be called a whisper, and keeping his words to a minimum. 'So must be "others" present. In force: tents for around forty, set out in military style. Probably bandits in normal sense, with warrior training, not like rest of vermin down there. Or maybe mercenaries. Either way...'

Brann swallowed. 'Not good news.'

Konall pulled his head close and cupped his hands around Brann's ear as he went into greater detail. 'Think not all are there. A party arrived, on horses – that's what caught my attention. If it is Loku, others from tents would have come out to greet, but no movement there. Also, picket lines for horses and supplies for the beasts, but no horses other than those that have just come in. Think they use this as base. Others maybe patrolling or raiding. If Loku, better move fast or captives are dead.'

Brann started forward immediately. Konall's hand on his shoulder stayed him.

'Easy,' he whispered. 'Know my page from birth. I care, too. Me first – better eyes.'

Brann nodded his acknowledgement. He dropped behind Konall once more, but was glad to see the tall figure moving at a faster pace. They would take their chances with sentries – finding the prisoners urgently had become a far greater consideration – although the change was comparative: they still moved with care, just to a lesser degree. They would free no one if they ran into an ambush.

They reached the outskirts of the village, however, without encountering anyone. Whether the lack of sentries was due to the slovenly, dim-witted nature of the inhabitants they had observed already, or the lack of expectation that any outsiders would approach, the pair did not care. Their thoughts were confined to heading for their target, and being ready to react instantly if necessary.

When they started between the first of the buildings, Konall swapped his bow for his sword. Brann realised that any person they came across unexpectedly would be more likely to be within the range of the blade, and did likewise. His heart pounding and sweat threatening to drip into his eyes despite the night chill, he followed Konall's example and stayed close to the buildings, keeping as much as he could to the shadows cast by the spectacularly bright moon. It was late enough for the inhabitants to be under cover, and a selection of snores and grunts attested to the fact that they were asleep within the shacks that the pair crept past.

They had to remember to look down as well as forwards, however – not infrequently, they had been forced to step terrifyingly over the slumped bodies of those who had not managed indoors before falling asleep. The first such bandit they had encountered had not been afforded such cautious treatment: Konall had, while starting from the shadow of one hut to another, stumbled over what he thought was a heap of rags. The bandit wearing the rags had begun to rouse and, in an instant, Konall had pressed the keen edge of his sword, one hand at either end of the weapon to force it down, against the man's throat. With his full weight upon the blade, it had sliced almost all the way through the bandit's neck. The man's eyes had widened in shock at the first pressure, and Brann had grabbed a handful of rags and held them hard against his victim's mouth to stifle any noise he may manage.

There had been no need. The eyes had turned blank as the life flowed from the bandit's neck in moments.

Brann had stared at the tableau, gripped by the horror of the silent, swift and coldly deliberate end of a man's life. Konall had looked up at him briefly, wiped his sword on the man's rags and moved on. This was not the occasion for counselling, and he knew that Brann had no option but to follow. He was right, but Brann was hugely relieved when he saw Konall notice, and step over, the subsequent sleeping forms.

They were making their way, as accurately as they could manage, towards the prison – if it could be given so grand a title – that they had spotted from across the river.

Following Konall closely, Brann realised that he was merely staring at the boy's back. He was unable to help in spotting any potential trouble and, if they were accosted, he would have to move around Konall to assist him. Yet, if he moved alongside him, he would have to leave the shadows and would be more likely to be seen. Moving, as they had done in the woodlands, in the overlapping manoeuvre that allowed one to always cover the other would be too slow and would, in any case, involve the use of bows to provide cover – and they had already decided that swords were the most appropriate weapons in these surroundings.

Instead, Brann moved to use other huts as cover. The buildings were, as they had seen, haphazardly placed, so he was able to plot a course roughly parallel to Konall's while still remaining close enough to reach him within a few strides if necessary. Konall noticed his move, understood, and carried on.

They saw the prison hut simultaneously, and stopped to consider their next move. They had come upon it from the side and could just make out the sentries at the front. One had fallen asleep, while the other sat in a crouch, idly picking at a straggly beard. Konall signalled towards the rear of the building and they crept, placing each foot agonisingly slowly, to meet there. Brann had further to travel, and arrived slightly after Konall.

The tall boy stooped to bring his mouth hard against Brann's ear. 'Awake. Voices.'

Brann nodded, having heard them also. He was puzzled. They could not make out the words, but the tone was more animated than he would have expected from prisoners captured in such horrific circumstances. Perhaps they were trying to keep up their spirits.

Konall's head pressed against him again, his breath hot on his skin. 'You go one side, I the other. Take one sentry each.'

Brann shook his head. 'Prise apart wood here. Bring them out unknown to all.'

'Too noisy,' Konall objected.

Brann pressed the tip of his sword against a plank. It crumbled slightly. 'Rotten,' he whispered. 'Could come away quietly. Dead or missing sentries could raise alarm. Bigger start on them: better.'

Konall stared at him for a moment in an interplay between the two that was becoming familiar, and nodded. He lifted his sword to work on the flimsy wall.

The voices came closer. The boys froze, realising together that, with walls as rotten as these, prisoners would have to be bound in some way to prevent escape. Restrained people do not move about.

Konall's eyes narrowed, and his hand gripped his sword so tightly that the weapon quivered. 'Loku,' he mouthed.

Brann felt panic rising. They had not found the captives, and Loku was in the heart of the village, meaning that if it had not been discovered yet that Konall was not among the captives, it would happen too soon for them to discover the prisoners' location and free them.

Konall read his face and, with a single abrupt gesture, eloquently ordered him to control himself. He brushed a stray lock of white-gold hair from over his ear – he had bound it behind his head when they had entered the mountains in the same manner as prior to fighting the bear – and pressed the side of his head against the wall. Brann was not sure whether he should keep watch or listen also. Curiosity took over, and he quickly chose the latter.

Although the hut was larger and more substantial than the others, it had been built by the same shoddy workmen and the planks that formed the walls were ill-fitting. Gaps were abundant, and there was no difficulty in picking up the words as those inside came closer.

Brann was surprised to discover that he could understand the speech: similarly to Konall, those inside were using the same language as he did, but with the lilting local accent. Expecting to hear an interrogation taking place or, at least, anger being expressed at not finding Konall among the prisoners, Brann was confused instead to hear a deep voice, warm and almost friendly, discussing the merits of resting after a long, hard-paced ride.

Brann had expected the scheming and treacherous ambassador to sound oily and manipulative – instead, the voice was resonant and exuded power. He glanced at Konall and mouthed Loku's name. Konall nodded confirmation.

The ambassador continued, 'It is a strange day indeed when one finds himself referring to a hovel such as this as one of his homes, but it is shelter, it is mine, the views – beyond the village boundaries, of course – are spectacular, and I am exhausted. So, even if it is merely for a few nights here and there, on occasions such as this, it is indeed my home.'

Understanding and despair hit Brann simultaneously. This was not the prison, and they had no idea where the prisoners were being kept.

Another voice spoke, more rough and commonplace, interrupting his thoughts. 'Should we not visit the captives now, my lord?' Brann guessed it was a warrior, perhaps a personal guard. He caught his breath, waiting for the answer.

'No, they are going noplace,' Loku laughed, and Brann breathed again. They had a chance once more, slim though it may be. 'We will visit them when we are ready. We rest and eat first, at our leisure. Ragnarr's arrogant whelp,' Brann saw Konall's knuckles whiten, 'cannot partake of the pleasures of a latrine pit for long enough, as far as I am concerned.'

Brann's spirits soared almost to exultation in comparison to the despair he had felt until now. In a single sentence, Loku had narrowed their search dramatically. Such a pit would be on the outskirts of the settlement. What was more, it was unlikely to be alongside the river – there was little room between the buildings and the river and, also, water would be liable to seep into it and raise the contents towards ground level, which would defeat the purpose of digging it in the first place. No, it would be on the landward side.

He made to rise to begin their search, but Konall's hand stopped him as the soldier spoke again. 'What's to become of them, my lord? The captives?'

'The boy can form the locals' evening sport,' Loku's rich tones continued, incongruous with the subject matter of his words, 'as can the barbarian. The raiding party thought I might find him of interest; it was indeed a thoughtful gesture but, frankly, once you have seen one monkey, they are all much the same. No, they will keep our friends happy. It is amazing how they never fail to find sport in an impalement, with their little races using the different weights on the ankles. Remember the last time, when one of them got over-excited and leapt onto the legs of one of the victims. He was not so excited when those who lost their bets as a result used him to replace the dead man, but it was extra entertainment for the rest, especially when they let the children swing on his feet.' The warrior laughed, and Loku chuckled with him. 'Yes, they are almost sweet when they are at play like that.' His tone darkened. 'The young lordling, however, will be mine. Much as I would love to look into his eyes as he sinks onto a spike, his death must be precise and to plan – although the fact that torture is involved will let me indulge myself after all.' Konall was quivering with rage, and clearly finding difficulty in not bursting through the wall. 'Sometimes fate rewards one well. I have long enough endured the sight of him stalking the corridors of his father's hall, snootily looking down his nose at me and dismissing my importance just as quickly.'

Brann nudged Konall and, with an expressive look, suggested that this may be a fair assessment of his companion. Konall scowled at him, but the tension was broken, and colour started to return to Konall's face.

'If you don't mind me asking, my lord,' the soldier began again, 'how will this work? Wars have been started this way since history began. Surely they will see through it.'

'That is precisely why it will work,' Loku purred. 'This ruse has been used so often because it works so well. Yes, it is obvious. But when an only son – or, in the case of the opposing side, an only remaining daughter – becomes a mutilated corpse, the raging grief of a father blinds him to reason, blinds him to all but retribution. And the timing is perfect: when I pass on the news of Einarr's return, old wounds will be opened and their blood will feed the flames of fury.'

'I understand, my lord,' the soldier said. 'I just wonder what all this – the raids, the trick, especially the war – is for. What is the point?'

'The point is, my dear man, that you are a common bandit who, along with your fellows, I have elevated to the position of mercenary. You do not question either my decisions or the orders of my master. And, by my master, I do not refer to Bekan, you understand, but a man who will be far more powerful than he, or any of the other lordlings and petty kings. I let you speak, this evening, because I wished to talk, and you were convenient. If you question me again, you will wish that I had given you over to these savages. And do not imagine that any of your men will support you. They will be clambering over what is left of your body to receive the few extra coins for filling your place. Do you understand?' His voice bore the same silky tone as before, but the words carried all the more menace for that, and the warrior could not convey his understanding quickly enough.

Loku yawned, loudly and casually. 'Now, leave me. I would eat and rest in peace. Wake me just after dawn, and we will visit the prisoners when they are disorientated by fatigue. It will be more enjoyable informing them of their fate at that time, when they will have all day to contemplate their part in the evening's entertainment. Do not disturb me until then.'

Clearly disturbed, the man muttered his obedience. The noise of his leaving was easily followed, especially the kick aimed at the sleeping guard and the sound of the man's reactions – startled, furious, and then fearful as he realised the source of the blow.

Brann prepared to leave, but realised that Konall was moving to head around the other side of the hut. He grabbed the tall boy before he could think about his response to such restraint. Surprisingly, Konall seemed to be becoming accustomed to Brann's unconventional and disrespectful methods of attracting attention, and merely turned, exasperation clear on his face.

'This way,' Brann hissed, desperate for Konall to listen to him but conscious that his voice could carry through the wall as easily as Loku's had in the opposite direction.

Konall shook his head. He pointed into the hut and drew his finger across his throat. Already familiar with Konall's simple and straightforward solutions to any sort of injustice, Brann had already guessed that the opportunity to rid themselves of Loku's influence and manipulations would be too much for the boy to pass up, and he was ready for Konall's decision. Before the tall boy could realise or resist, he pulled him to the relative cover of a large pile of putrid refuse where they could raise their voices to a faint whisper.

'I know what you are thinking,' Brann breathed. 'I understand, but it is not the best course.'

Konall told him what he could do with his 'best course' and turned to go. Brann grabbed his sleeve barely in time to stop him. 'I mean it is the best course for all, including your people.'

Konall's eyes narrowed. 'I know what is best for my people. Loku dies, and many lives are spared.'

'If you kill him, you, I and the prisoners will probably die as a result.'

Konall shrugged. 'If the lives of many of our people are saved as a result, it will be a favourable trade for us.'

Not for the first time, Brann cursed Konall's relentless sense of duty. He shook his head. 'You heard him: he has a master pulling the strings. If Loku dies, another will be sent to orchestrate this other man's plans. Then we will have died in vain and your people will have lost the heir to your father's position at a time of great crisis.'

Konall was in a quandary, and his agony was evident. He could see the truth in Brann's words, but the thought of Loku, and the treachery he represented, being separated from him by nothing more than a flimsy wall was consuming him.

Brann gripped Konall's shoulders and stared into his eyes. He felt awkward with such a dramatic gesture, but felt it would be effective with one so formal as Konall. He tried to speak with as much conviction as he could muster. 'Loku will not go away, we can be sure of that. You, or someone fighting your cause, will face him at some point. Remember, if we spirit the prisoners away before he sees them, he will never know that you escaped from the original raid with news of his treachery. If he thinks you were a captive here and escaped before encountering him, he will consider that the location of the village will be revealed, but nothing more. As far as his knowledge will extend, his involvement will remain undiscovered. So he will carry on with his charade, oblivious to our knowledge, which will give you and your father a great advantage that can be exploited in many ways. And he is likely, then, to meet his end, but in a way that will best serve the interests of your people.' His grip tightened on Konall's shoulders. 'Please think about it.'

The immediate temptation was powerful, but Konall had to admit the sense in Brann's reasoning. The fact that his people would gain a comparatively greater benefit by this alternative was the crucial factor, and he did not take long to come to a decision. He sighed abruptly. 'You are right. Again. If he lives, as you say, my father and uncle will be able to plan a strategy that may reveal the grander plan behind the horrors brought by this child of scum.' Brann had, in the intensity of the moment, forgotten that he still gripped Konall's shoulders, and the young noble reached up and removed them. 'You are proving more than merely an extra pair of hands, even if you do have a remarkable lack of etiquette about you.' His expression darkened once more. 'But be certain that, whatever transpires, Loku will die.'

Brann did not doubt it.

They began to move away, but Konall stopped. 'One thing, miller's boy,' he murmured. 'Be careful. Stay alive. I am beginning to think I will have you as my special advisor when I take the title.'

Brann grinned. 'I will consider it, if you make it worth my while.'

They crept back through the village in the same manner in which they had reached Loku's hut. As they flitted from shadow to shadow, it dawned on Brann, to his surprise, that his fear had left him. The more they moved about in the heart of the village, surrounded by people who viewed an impalement as an evening's entertainment, the more a surreal feeling of invincibility settled over him. And the longer they went without being discovered, the more he felt that they never would be, that they could move with impunity. It was such a powerful and ridiculous sensation that he had to suppress an urge to giggle. He forced himself to calm down, wondering if he were developing madness, and repeated an instruction to himself to concentrate as if it were a religious mantra. He was annoyed at himself for his lapse but, at the same time, curious that the situation could have affected him that way.

They reached the edge of the settlement, and stopped.

'What now?' Brann whispered.

Konall grunted. 'We look for a latrine pit. I suggest you use your nose as much as your eyes. Hard though it may be to imagine, I suspect it will smell even worse than the rest of this lair of scum.'

'Right,' agreed Brann. 'But which way do we go? Or do we split up so we can cover more ground?'

'We do not split up,' Konall said immediately. 'When one of us found it, he would have to retrace his steps, find the other, then work back to where he had already been. We will be quicker moving together, then we can act as soon as we find it. And it will mean that, if we run into trouble, we will not do so alone.' He paused. 'Which way first, though?'

'If I were digging such a pit, I would not want it near to the entrance of my village,' Brann said slowly, thinking as he spoke. 'And it will not be too far from the perimeter – from the look of this lot, they will have had to be forced by the mercenaries to use a latrine, so they will not site it any further than they can get away with.'

Konall was already moving before Brann had finished, his departure as clear a signal as any of his agreement. He paused, however, in the shadow of a rickety structure to replace his sword with his bow once more.

'If there is a sentry, we will need to dispose of him before he sees us,' he explained. 'You may as well stick to your sword. I have seen your accuracy when you have time to aim.' Before Brann had time to retort, he was moving again.

They found the pit almost exactly where they had expected, but entirely by accident. No sentry stood guard over the captives – a stroke of luck, but also the reason that they had not, in the dim light, noticed the large hole. Brann inadvertently kicked a small stone and the pair froze in apprehension as it rattled across the rough surface for several yards, the sound magnified by their nerves, before disappearing abruptly from sight. Its progress halted audibly as it cracked against something solid.

Gerens's voice rang out. 'Can you flea-ridden, incontinent, degenerate bags of pus not control yourselves until morning?' He added a highly imaginative and disgusting suggestion as to what the bandit he assumed was approaching could do as an alternative to using the latrine. Brann was astonished, not so much at the content of the outburst as at the animated tone from one normally so controlled as Gerens.

Konall looked at Brann. 'That slave has a most encouraging attitude. I can see why you enjoy spending time with him.'

Brann was still stunned. 'I have never heard him like this before.'

Konall shrugged. 'You try sitting at the bottom of an active latrine and discover if you maintain your normal demeanour. Personally, I would say that, revolting and humiliating as his situation may be, a benefit of it is that it does seem to have well-informed his view of these people.'

Anxious to avoid silhouetting themselves, they crawled across the short expanse of open ground to the edge of the pit, where a grille of thick wooden bars lay across the opening. The smell was overpowering and Brann fought to prevent adding his vomit to all else that had been already sent down upon the captives.

He swallowed hard and whispered, 'Gerens, it is us!'

'Brann?' the boy said, as loudly as before. 'By the gods, how can that be you?'

'It is too long an explanation for just now,' Brann hissed. 'Just accept it and keep your voice down before you bring down the whole lot of these maniacs upon us.'

'Do not be concerned,' Grakk's calm tones reassured them. 'He has scarcely desisted from the insults and complaints since we were brought here. It would attract more attention if he were to be silent for any length of time.'

'I like him even more,' Konall observed, struggling at the same time to conceal his surprise at the contrast between Grakk's speech and his memory of the man's appearance.

'Who is down there?' Brann asked, his voice wavering with the elation and relief of finding his friends alive and in surprisingly good spirits.

'Just the three of us,' Gerens said, returning to his normal considered delivery as the vestiges of his tirade at the supposed bandit wore off. 'Grakk, Hakon and myself. The guards died at the clearing but for some reason they took us alive. I could not see if Lord High and Mighty survived, however.'

'I am here,' Konall said implacably, looking over the edge of the pit.

Gerens was unperturbed. 'Very good,' was all he said, although his tone hinted that he was not sure if Konall was a welcome member of any rescue party.

The noble boy dismissed the subject. Working at a bolt that secured the wooded grille, he said, 'My page, how is he?'

'I am fine, Lord Konall,' the boy said from the shadows. 'I am uninjured, although I have smelt better.'

'If that is the worst that you are, then you are lucky,' Konall reassured him. He stood and flipped open the grille. 'And, Hakon...'

304

'Yes, my lord?'

'I am pleased that you are well.'

If the page was astonished at this unprecedented show of feeling, Gerens was more pragmatic. 'If I could interrupt, I feel we should move from here with some urgency. These savages occasionally manage to make it as far as this pit to relieve themselves, and several times already tonight, we have been visited.'

As if to prove his words, there was movement from among the buildings and a figure emerged from the gloom, already pulling apart his clothing in anticipation of reaching the pit. Brann and Konall dropped flat and lay still, hoping that, by some miracle, they would not be noticed. They could not even reach for their weapons for fear of the movement attracting attention.

The bandit stumbled drowsily to the edge of the pit, rubbing sleep from his eyes. Looking down, he at last noticed the open grille and the two bodies lying at his feet, returning his gaze. Before his surprise could register enough to allow any sort of reaction, vocal or physical, Konall had hammered his straight arm into the back of the man's calves. He was close to the edge, and the blow was enough to send him dropping into the darkness. He landed with a squelch and, almost immediately, there was a sharp crack as his neck was broken.

The episode sparked them into hurried action. The rag clothes were stripped from the corpse and knotted together to form a rough rope that was tossed to the boys above. Brann and Konall held it together and braced their feet against the open grille as they pulled up the three captives.

The smell from them was overpowering. 'Pardon me if I do not embrace you,' Brann said to Gerens.

The larger boy smiled. Looking around, he said, 'Where are the others?'

Brann shrugged. 'This is it.'

Gerens nodded. 'That makes sense. Two of you slipped in to avoid detection and the rest are waiting out of sight.'

'No,' Brann said. 'This is it. We came on our own.'

Gerens was a picture of confusion. 'Only two of you, right to the heart of their camp?' He looked at Konall. 'Including him?'

'There were debts that required repayment,' Konall said simply, and led them away from the hole. Brann ran to catch him.

'I presume you are heading for the boats,' he said.

'You presume correctly. It was our preferred option, was it not?'

'Yes,' Brann agreed. 'But that was before we knew that we would have to pass through the village for a third time to reach them. Our luck in remaining undetected can only last so long.'

Konall stopped to allow him to speak before they came too close to the buildings. 'Managing it twice already merely proves twice over that it can be done. And the boats are still the quickest means of escape. Especially as the legs of these three will probably have cramped up slightly in that confined hole for so long.'

'Good idea,' Brann acknowledged benignly. 'I believe you are learning from me.'

Konall ignored him. 'As I am more experienced in such matters, and as I am the noble here – a fact that you appear to conveniently forget all too often – I will lead the party to the boats. You protect the rear.'

'Behind the smell,' Brann observed.

'Precisely,' Konall said, and headed into the village.

Gerens looked questioningly at him as he passed, as much puzzled by Konall's change in demeanour as by the fact that Konall had come to rescue them. 'I will explain later,' Brann whispered, and took up his place at the back of the line.

The three captives soon managed to each collect a weapon – poorly made, as expected, but better than bare hands – among the detritus through which they had to pick their way. Brann noticed that Gerens winced slightly as he bent down, and resolved to ask him at a more appropriate time about the cause of the problem. Their main objective, however, was not to use their weapons, but to avoid any confrontation – something that, much to their surprise, they achieved, though not without their nerves being severely tested on several occasions. Movement was heard within huts; on two occasions, figures – presumably prompted by their bladders – moved from the doorways (though, thankfully, not in the direction of the latrine pit that now contained one corpse rather than three live captives); and Konall had visibly struggled with his self-control as they passed within sight of Loku's residence.

They heard the river before they saw it, but they still came upon it sooner than they expected, having fallen into a rhythm of moving silently, with every nerve on edge, from one shadow to the next. As they slipped around the corner of a hovel, they found it, an expanse of darker gloom, before them. The surprise caused them to bunch as they avoided spilling into the open, and Brann found himself beside Konall.

'What are we waiting for?' he hissed nervously. 'We need to get out of here.'

Konall whispered evenly, 'Not so easy to work out the advantages and disadvantages when you are in the midst of a frightening situation, is it? Have patience: we need to check that the way is clear of obstacles, whether there is anything that may have to bear our weight, or if there are any guards. Small matters like that.' As he spoke, his eyes had been scanning the ground ahead of them. 'That is why.'

Brann followed his pointing finger and stared into the dim light. It took a few moments – irritatingly long – for him to start to see what Konall had spotted amid the broken barrels, rotting food and miscellaneous debris. A pile of rags had initially looked to be just that but, the more Brann looked at it, the more he realised that it was a man's slumped body under a voluminous cloak. And it seemed alive – a fact that was confirmed almost immediately by a loud snore.

Whatever the reason for the bandit's presence, whether he had fallen asleep in sentry duty or succumbed to drunkenness, they were left with the same decision to make.

'We cannot creep past him,' Konall breathed into Brann's ear. 'He is directly in front of the jetty and we do not know how much noise it will make walking on that structure.'

Having witnessed the bandits' construction expertise at close quarters, Brann was inclined to agree – they would be lucky if they managed to pass over the jetty without it collapsing, never mind having to rely on it being built soundly enough to bear their weight without a single creak. 'So how do we dispose of him?' he whispered.

'How do you think?' Konall replied, taking his bow from his back.

Brann put out a restraining hand. 'What if you do not kill him outright? It is dark, and you cannot make out his shape clearly under that cloak. If he screams…'

Konall sighed. 'Well, what do you suggest? I think I preferred it when you just wanted to run blindly from here.'

'I do not know,' Brann whispered. 'Maybe we could both shoot him at the same time. Then there is more chance of hitting something vital.'

Konall grunted. 'Not with your accuracy. You would probably hit a bucket and wake up the whole village.'

As they debated, a shadow slipped past them. Grakk drifted silently through the strewn refuse. His blade poised, he moved right up to the slumped figure. With no undue fuss, there was a sharp downwards movement, and he turned to wave them forward.

Konall turned to Brann. 'Slaves or not, your companions do have a certain appeal,' he muttered.

They crept to the jetty, apprehensive about knocking against anything that might raise the alarm. The structure, when they reached it, met their expectations exactly. To describe it as ramshackle would have been kind. To a man, they looked at it dubiously. The boats were tethered to it, so they would be forced to cross it, yet it looked as if it would collapse under the weight of even one of them.

Gerens shrugged. 'There is only one course available to us. One of us swims around, brings a couple of the boats as close to the bank as possible, and the rest wade out to them.' He started towards the water's edge. 'I am more desperate for a wash than you will ever know, so it may as well be me that swims.'

Konall's hand shot out and dragged him back. 'Not a good idea,' he said. Gerens angrily shook off his hand, and Brann stepped between them.

He said quickly, 'Konall and I saw the state of the river in daylight. I don't think hygiene is of great importance to these people. From the look of the scum on the surface, you would be lucky to reach the boats without being poisoned.'

Gerens, who had fixed Konall with a hostile glare, shrugged and turned away. Brann stepped onto the jetty. 'I suppose, as the smallest one here, I should try it out.'

This time, nobody objected. Stepping gingerly, Brann moved onto the jetty. To his surprise it seemed more solid than it looked to the naked eye. He stood, waiting for movement beneath his feet. The others watched intensely, holding their breath as much as Brann was doing. Other than the creaking that would be expected from any such structure, there was little noise and even less movement. He bent his knees and, without letting his feet leave the surface, he bounced several times. Still, nothing untoward transpired.

'Well, boy,' he said quietly to himself, 'it is all or nothing now. We have got to know, one way or another, and quickly.'

He bent his knees once again, but this time he jumped slightly off the surface. As quietly as he could manage, he landed… with no undue effects. He jumped again. And again.

'All right,' Konall said. 'Do not get carried away. I think it is safe to say you have tested it for us. Let us go.'

Grakk spoke softly. 'Speed is important, yes, but one at a time. Best not to risk too much, yes?'

Konall paused, then nodded. 'Yes.' Gerens and Hakon's eyes widened in surprise. If Grakk felt the same, as usual, he did not show it. Konall continued, 'We must move at once, however. You three take one boat. I will take Hakon in another.'

Brann stepped into what looked like a sturdily built boat – then stepped back quickly onto the jetty as water began to rise around his feet. More tentatively, he tried another that was big enough to take the three of them. This time, he had more success, and he turned his attention to the knot on the rope holding it to the jetty. The water had swollen the rope, and he started working at it so that he would be ready by the time the others were aboard. Quickly, the others joined him, and Konall and Hakon started across the jetty. Hakon tried a narrow boat, little wider than a canoe, and found it, as far as cursory testing could show, to be watertight.

Checking behind him, Konall ran back and hoisted the dead bandit over his shoulder. He headed back over the jetty and dumped the corpse in a third boat.

'No sense in there being any tell-tale signs of our departure,' he grunted. As he moved towards his own boat, however, the jetty shifted sideways violently. With a look of alarm, Konall made an ungainly lurch for his boat, succeeding in boarding it as, with a creaking groan, the jetty tilted, then fell sideways into the water, leaving only the posts at its outer edge, which the boats were tethered to, standing starkly along in the water.

They froze, but the sound must have seemed greater to their ears than it had been in reality, or the locals have been much sounder sleepers than they had feared. There was no apparent reaction from the nearby huts, and the relief prompted Brann to giggle at Konall's discomfort. He managed to stifle the sound, but Gerens was less successful at hiding his amusement.

'Did you say something about tell-tale signs?' Gerens asked with fake innocence. 'Did that include noise, or was it only referring to dead arseholes?' Sitting behind him, Brann dug him in the ribs, then returned to his attempt to untie the rope. The impulse to laugh at Konall passed quickly as his desperation grew, and he ignored the raw pain in his fingers as he frantically tugged at the knot. Grakk turned calmly and, with a swipe of his blade, severed the taut rope. The boat immediately started to drift, and Brann leant out and grabbed at the ropes tethering the remaining boats to the posts. He fumbled for his sword, but it was jammed at an angle underneath him, and he could not draw it and hold the ropes with his other hand at the same time.

Breathing heavily with the effort, he gasped at Grakk to pass him his machete-like sword. The tattooed tribesman did so without question, although Gerens was looking anxious at the delay. Konall had followed Grakk's example and sliced the rope tethering his boat with his sword, and they were already heading downriver. The effort in hanging onto the ropes took too much of his strength to allow talk, much as he dearly wanted to explain himself. The other two, however, noticed his struggles. On climbing into the boat, they had found rough-hewn paddles, and they now used these to help Brann, moving the boat against the current. He was able to turn properly and hack at the remaining three boats. To his surprise, the ropes were severed fairly easily – Grakk's blade must have been sharper than it looked. He grabbed the severed ropes and they pushed away from the moorings, with Brann towing the three boats behind them.

'Removing one method of pursuit, are we?' Gerens grunted.

'That we are,' Brann replied, managing a smile through his exhaustion.

One of the boats soon began to fill with water and Brann let go of the rope to allow it to founder. The other two, he towed until they stopped for Konall to leap ashore and retrieve their packs from the undergrowth. As he did so, Brann pulled the other two boats alongside and, with the help of his two companions, they used their weapons to ease the wood apart as quietly as they could, allowing the water to rush in and flood the boats. The body of the bandit in one of them floated as the boat that had borne him sank beneath him.

'Leave him,' Konall said shortly, returning with the packs. 'It matters not if they find him. By that time, they will already know that we are gone.'

Grakk said, 'They check us when they wake in the morning. We should have several hours' start by then.'

Brann shook his head. 'Not today. Loku is intending to pay his respects just before dawn.'

Hakon's head snapped round in surprise. 'Loku?'

'You heard correctly,' Konall said darkly, settling back into the boat. 'I will explain as we travel.' He glanced eastwards. 'The sky is beginning to lighten. We should move.'

Brann looked at the relevant part of the sky, but could see no difference in the half-light that had served as night. He was inclined to take Konall's word for it, however, and picking up his paddle, he pushed the floating corpse – which had drifted against their boat as if loath to leave them – out into the river. He thrust the paddle into the water and started to drive the boat forward. The others were doing the same and soon they had picked up speed, although Brann found himself breathing more heavily from the effort that he had expected.

'You are out of practice, my friend,' Gerens called back to him. 'Either that, or you are not used to facing the way you are going in a boat.'

Brann kicked him sharply in the back, alarmed that Konall had picked up on the truth revealed by Gerens' words. Fortunately, however, Konall appeared not to have heard; he was lost in concentration as he worked with Hakon to forge their boat through the water, his long, white-gold hair blowing in the slight wind that was following them.

Realising his mistake, Gerens slapped himself on the side of the head in a self-chiding manner. Brann hoped that it was a sign that his friend's new-found devil-may-care attitude towards what he said and to whom was wearing off. Apart from the danger of revealing any secrets, it was beginning to irritate him.

Gerens spoke up again, but in a more restrained manner, Brann was relieved to note. 'So what lies ahead of us?'

As he grew more used to the rhythm, Brann found his breathing easing, although speech was still more laboured than his pride would have liked. 'There is a waterfall ahead.' He sensed Gerens's alarm at the words. 'Do not worry: even if we do not hear it, there is a bridge before it to warn us that we are getting close. We can ditch the boats there and the rest, I am afraid, is on foot.'

Gerens shrugged. 'At least we seem to be making good speed. We should be well clear of them before they head after us. We'll have built up a good lead upon those bandit scum before we have to take to foot.'

'True,' Brann agreed. He remembered the picket lines and ordered tents back at the settlement. 'But it could be touch and go with the horsemen. I am sure they will be trying to get to the bridge before us to head us off.'

'Horsemen?' Gerens shouted. 'Do you hear that, Grakk? It seems to have slipped his mind to tell us that there are horsemen involved.'

Konall, who had heard this particular exchange, observed, 'Your friend seems to have a problem with gratitude. Maybe we should have left him where he was.' Brann grunted. 'Maybe we should leave him here,' he suggested darkly.

'Say what you will,' Gerens said. 'But it still would have helped to have known that there were horsemen involved. What do you think, Grakk?'

Without turning round, Grakk said, 'I think that chatter is a waste of energy. And that the noise of chatter would be a good help to any bandit patrols that may be ahead of us returning to their home.'

Both points had a sobering effect, and the party fell silent as they redoubled their efforts. The current was strong and helped them to bring the bridge into sight before they heard the ominous thunder of galloping hooves. Konall looked back and quickly gauged the speed and distance of the horses behind them.

'We should make it to the pass before them, but they will quickly catch us after that,' he called across to their boat.

Brann felt the now-familiar lurch in his stomach. *If only there was a way to collapse the bridge*, he thought as they steered slightly towards the centre of the river to avoid low overhanging branches that lay ahead. His eyes widened as a thought struck him.

'Steer towards the branches!' he yelled. 'Stop the boats there.'

'What?' Gerens shouted. 'Are you mad?' Even Grakk cast a dubious glance in his direction. Konall, however, was becoming accustomed to Brann's ideas.

'Do as he says,' he snapped.

In seconds, they had reached the trees. Brann grabbed a slender, leafy branch and, using it to steady him, stood in the rocking boat and hacked at it with his sword. As he had hoped, the recent sunshine had left the bark and, especially, the leaves, dry. Tinder dry.

The branch quickly came loose and he tossed it to Konall, before cutting a similar one for himself. Forcing himself not to look back at the horsemen, he shouted at the others to start forward again – something they needed no encouragement to do – and told them to stay close to the bank.

'Grakk, throw my pack ashore, then you and Gerens follow. Konall, throw yours and let Hakon ashore as well.'

As Grakk steadied himself to throw, Gerens said, 'Why not move right into the side? We could jump instead of swimming.'

'We cannot afford the time. You will understand,' gasped Brann, tossing his weapons and cloak onto the bank.

'Just do it!' Konall roared, following Brann's example, and the three former captives plunged into the water and made for the bank.

Brann grabbed his paddle. 'Out towards the middle and point it directly at the bridge.' Konall nodded, and did so.

In position first, Brann took out his flint and quickly sparked the dry leaves into the beginnings of a flame. Comprehension dawned on Konall's face – quickly replaced by alarm.

'My flint was in a pouch on my swordbelt,' he shouted. 'Throw yours to me.' Brann did so, cursing himself for not giving Konall better instructions beforehand, and dropped out of the back of the boat into the water. The exertions had left him drenched in hot sweat, and although the icy mountain water at first took away his breath, it soon had an invigorating effect and his head cleared. He moved behind the boat and helped it on its way with a shove, although the current was already doing the job for him. Splashing noises to his right told him that Konall was doing the same. Tendrils of smoke were wisping from the boats and, as he started to swim, Brann hoped with a slight panic that the fire would take hold. When he glanced again after a few strokes, however, the flames were already leaping up into view thanks to the dust-dry leaves; now his hope was that the fire would not spread so quickly that the boats would sink before they reached the bridge.

His main consideration now was just to get onto dry land. He rued the fact that he had not time to throw his boots onto the riverbank; they were now dragging down his feet and making every movement of his legs a draining effort.

He managed to make it to within a few yards of the bank before the first arrow zipped and plopped into the water behind him. The sound, so innocuous compared with the lethal connotations of its source, gave him a sudden sense of déjà vu – a feeling that was heightened when Konall's hand grasped him by the back of the tunic and hauled him forwards, landing him this time on the grassy riverbank rather than the slavers' ship.

He was given no time to recover. Hands grabbed his wrists and he was dragged out of range of the horsemen's cavalry-type short bows.

Having failed to hit any of the fugitives, the mercenaries realised too late the plan for the bridge. They spurred their horses in desperation at the crossing but, with blazing boats lodged underneath it, the upper structure that was as sun-dried as the branches Brann had cut had quickly succumbed to the flames. Fire was crackling from one end to the other already, and the horses reared and shied away as they were ridden up to it. Two riders managed to drag round the heads of their mounts and, savagely beating the beasts with the flats of their swords, they unbelievably managed to force the wide-eyed and flared-nostriled animals onto the bridge.

Their combined weight was too much for wood that was shabbily built and further weakened by the fire. With a creaking groan reminiscent of the collapsing jetty at the village, but with a volume resoundingly greater, the bridge disintegrated, taking the rearmost horse and rider with it into the fast-flowing river and to an inescapable drop over the waterfall. Spurred on by instinct rather than its rider, the leading horse had leapt forwards an instant before the collapse, and had managed to scramble onto the track beyond, dried earth sent flying by its flailing hoofs.

Surprised with the unlikely appearance of the horse from the flames, the party watched, stunned, as the rider roared and raised his sword, kicking his mount towards them. Snapping out of the daze, Konall dived headlong for his weapons, rolling over and rising to his feet with his bow and an arrow in his hands. In one fluid motion, he stood upright, drew and, without seeming to aim, let fly. The arrow streaked past the horse's head and took the rider square in the chest. At that short range, the force of impact was awesome, lifting the man clear of his saddle and, with a violent thud, into the dirt behind him.

The mercenary surprised them for a second time in as many moments. Despite both the effect of the arrow and the crashing impact on the hard ground, he tried to rise. As he reached a sitting position, however, Grakk's blade cartwheeled, flashing in the early morning sunlight, through the air and into his chest beside the arrow shaft. This time, he did not get up. As Grakk moved to collect his sword and ensure that the man had finally died – a trifle over-cautious, Brann thought, considering the punishment his body had taken – Konall retrieved his quiver and selected another arrow. The riders on the other bank had paused, milling in a group as they watched to see if their erstwhile companion would have any success; they had forgotten that, although the fugitives were outwith the short range of their bows, they were themselves very much within the range of Konall's weapon.

The tall boy gave them a sharp reminder of the fact. His arrow flashed across the water towards one of the riders. An instant before impact, the man's horse bucked slightly and the arrow drove into the rider's stomach. He lurched forward with a hoarse scream, clutching with one hand at the arrow and with the other grabbing at the horse's mane to keep himself in the saddle.

The rest of the group moved back out of range as Konall grumbled, 'Damn that horse. That should have taken him in the chest like the last one.'

Grakk squinted across the river, his hand shielding his eyes from the morning sun. 'No matter. He will not last the night. And now he will slow them down.'

As he spoke, one of the riders, a large man with flaming red hair, moved his mount alongside the stricken man, who was now roaring, the rage, anguish and agony clear in his cries. With a swift motion, the redhead cut his throat, and the cries stopped.

'No, he will not,' Gerens grunted.

The dead man thudded to the ground and, ignoring his corpse, the red-headed warrior grabbed the reins of the now riderless horse and led it away. Casting cries and glares of fury and abuse behind them, they wheeled their mounts back upriver and thundered off.

'They will be looking for the nearest ford,' Konall shouted. 'And they have just shown us how much they want to catch us. We do not know how near, or far, they will be able to cross, so let us move now.'

Grakk had abandoned his rusty blade in the chest of the dead mercenary, swapping it for the man's sword. As he took the belt and scabbarded the weapon, he removed the sheathed long knife and tossed it to Gerens and offered the short bow and quiver to Hakon.

'You know how to use this?' he asked the tall boy, who had spoken few, if any words, since the rescue had begun.

Hakon looked insulted at the question, but nodded his thanks and took the weapon.

Agitated, Konall urged them on, but Brann, still coughing and spluttering, staggered to his feet and waved at them to wait. He walked with studied calm to the dead man's horse, murmuring reassuringly to it. He stroked its nose and scratched its ears, and the beast, clearly well-tended and strong, rewarded him with a whinny and a nuzzle.

Brann looked at the others with a quiet smile. 'Tempted as I am just to jump on, I have another suggestion: why not use it as a pack animal?'

Understanding quickly, Konall took the two packs and deftly used their straps to fasten them together, before slinging them over the horse's back and lashing them to the saddle.

Brann ensured they were secure. 'That should let us move faster,' he observed, pleased with his idea.

'Then let us do so,' Konall said and, with no more delay, they started at a fast jog for the head of the ravine. As they neared it, Konall faltered, unsure whether to take the familiar path they had come along or to opt for the route along the top of the cliff.

'I know what you are thinking...' Brann started.

'Just tell me which way,' Konall snapped. 'You can explain why as we run. We have wasted too much time already.'

'The way we came,' Brann said immediately, and they broke into a sprint in that direction.

Grakk's voice rang out. 'Slow down. We will tire more quickly at this pace. We need to last a long time.'

No answer was needed. Their youthful impatience duly curbed by his experience, they settled into a more sensible lope with Brann, leading the horse, at the rear.

Konall dropped back beside him. 'So, why?'

Brann glanced up at the other route. 'It was tempting to try the other path in the hope that it might be quicker,

320

but that would have been no more than a gamble. And, although we would be able to spot danger from a distance because it is more open up there, that would be more of a disadvantage than an advantage – we would be more easily seen, also. Down here, any bandits coming towards us will not be expecting us at all and, if we run into them, we will be less surprised. And we will still have advance warning of the horsemen catching us as we will easily hear the hooves as they push the pace on this hard surface.

'And we at least know the lie of the land ahead of us, and what route to take.' Another thought occurred to him. 'And where the sentries are at the other end.'

Konall's eyes narrowed as he digested the theory. 'And,' Brann continued, 'from a military point of view, we would be cut to pieces in seconds if caught in the open by horsemen. Here, however, on this narrow curving path, they cannot manoeuvre and could not attack more than two abreast – or less in places. We will have more of a chance.'

Konall was silent for a few paces. He grunted, a decisive sound. 'I agree. Your logic is sound. Now, all we can do is make the best of what chance strews in our path.'

He moved back to the head of the group, and they continued at the same pace. As they rounded a corner, Brann noticed that Gerens – who was next in line in front of him – stumbled slightly.

'Are you struggling?' he asked, moving alongside the boy. 'If we need to take a rest, we will just have to do so.'

Gerens shook his head. 'I am fine,' he said through heavy breathing. 'I just have not had much sleep recently. I will manage.'

'Are you sure?' Brann was still concerned.

'Of course I am,' Gerens snapped, his anger rising sharply. 'I would rather be tired than dead. And the thought of

321

horsemen coming up hard behind us is helping me to keep going, believe it or not.'

Brann dropped back in the face of the rare show of anger from his friend, but resolved to watch him more closely. In doing so, however, he found himself observing not only Gerens, but each of the members of their little group. They had settled into a steady pace, the horse was obediently following Brann's direction, there was – for the moment at least – no sign of the enemy, the sun was warm on their shoulders and the air was cool and fresh: he was astounded to find that, despite the situation they were in, he was growing bored with running. Studying the others at least occupied his mind, and his position at the rear afforded him a perfect opportunity to do so.

Gerens had lost the reckless cynicism that had characterised his speech in reaction to the harrowing experience, and had reverted to his normal self, if a little tetchy. The slight falter in his gait, no matter how much he tried to disguise it or fight it, was continuing, as was Brann's concern. Grakk, as always, was simply Grakk: experienced, unruffled by any eventuality, simplistically logical and watching everything with the wry outlook of a man who knows that fate, the gods and other men's mistakes and decisions control the lives of everyone, from kings to beggars, and it was up to each to cope as he could with whatever situation faced him at the time. Hakon, Brann did not know, but the boy seemed capable physically: he was a good couple of inches shorter than Konall – although he would still tower over most men in Brann's homeland – but his shoulders were broader and hinted at the strength he would possess once his body matured to match them. His straight black hair bounced jauntily between his shoulder-blades as he ran, in contrast to his demeanour, which was even quieter than that of Konall, although, in his case, he was more withdrawn than aloof. Brann wondered how much of that reticence was a result of his recent experience – an opposite reaction to that of Gerens, but for the same reason. He seemed in a state of shock and, watching him, Brann felt empathy rising strongly within him as he remembered feeling so similarly, so recently. In fact, who knew how strongly it might return to him once the current situation, which was so dominant in his consideration at the moment, was over.

He switched his attention to Konall, who now seemed so familiar despite the short time since their circumstances had flung them together. The change in him had been astonishing – not simply the transformation that had bemused Gerens from sneering, unapproachable self-centred noble who barked orders with unquestioned and ruthless authority to a more open – by his standards – young man who was not only willing to listen to alternative views, but was inclined to ask for advice. It was more than that, for it was possible, even likely, that the old Konall would return once they returned to Ravensrest and, although he had changed, he had not lost – and probably would never lose – his air of superiority and the need to lead or, at least, to be seen to do so. In itself, Brann mused, that was probably no bad thing in someone who would one day, and possibly at a moment's notice, have to assume the responsibilities that awaited Konall.

No, it was something else: it was his attitude towards Grakk. While the southern tribesman, true to his accepting, impassive style, bore in his manner no apparent enmity towards Konall over the treatment he had received after Hakon's slip in the snow when they hunted the bear, and seemed to have entirely dismissed the matter, Konall, by contrast, appeared to be aware of it with increasing discomfort.

He seemed awkward around Grakk, and the more the wiry slave seemed unconcerned by the whole affair, the more it troubled Konall. The young noble appeared to have discovered a conscience, and was finding the experience bewildering.

Brann's reverie was abruptly disturbed as Konall skidded to a halt, his arm raised in warning. The others bunched up behind him and Brann, slower to react than the surprisingly well-trained horse, was jerked to a standstill by the reins – a curious reversal of roles, he thought. He frantically scanned the path ahead for an enemy, reaching for both his bow and his sword in his confusion.

Grakk's calming hand on his arm stopped his fevered movements and he followed the pointing of a slender finger to raise his gaze above the trail. A small landslide had started at some point but had, it seemed, stopped almost immediately. Whether it had been initiated by a rock disturbed by the weather or the foot of a passing creature was impossible to tell – and immaterial. What mattered was that a small, but potentially lethal, number of rocks and small boulders were poised precariously, waiting for the slightest reason to crash down upon the path. Konall and Brann, with their attention fixed continuously on rounding the next corner they faced, must have passed under the danger unaware when they had travelled in the opposite direction.

'Very slowly, and very quietly, we move past, one at a time,' Konall whispered. 'The horse first.'

Brann looked at him questioningly. He knew he would have to be the one to lead the horse, as he had earned the trust that would be vital to keep it calm over the next few moments. And he could understand why they were moving singly – if the rocks came down, casualties would be minimised. But why first? Surely, as the one most likely to bring down the rockfall, the horse should go last and allow the others to pass before they risked blocking the path.

Konall guessed his thoughts, and looked almost gleeful. 'I cannot believe I have reasoned this ahead of you,' he whispered. The others looked at each other in surprise at the admission of Brann's superiority in any way. 'I assume you think the horse should go last. But if one of the others brings the rocks down, the horse will be trapped on the wrong side. If it comes down and any of us are on this side, all we have to do is scramble over. Humans climb better than horses.'

Brann smiled. 'You are right. Absolutely right.' He paused as a thought struck him. 'But, if humans can climb it, why risk them walking under it? Once the horse has got through, why not bring it all down? You can all then climb over in safety. And,' his eyes widened in excited realisation, 'it will delay the horses pursuing us!'

Konall nodded. 'I agree. But you would never have thought of it without my idea in the first place. Admit it.'

Brann held up his hands in submission. 'I admit it, I admit it. Now can we begin? I am having enough trouble with my bowels at the thought of creeping under those rocks without delaying any longer.'

Konall indicated his agreement, and Brann started to lead the horse forwards. As they passed him, Konall pulled a long cavalry spear – almost a lance, as Brann would recognise one, but not as long as those few he had seen in his homeland – from the fastenings on the saddle.

'We need something to dislodge the rocks,' he said quietly. 'Assuming, that is, you do not do it for me.'

'Thank you for your reassuring words,' Brann grunted, then moved on. He felt sweat coat his brow, then run down his temple, as he carefully and painstakingly placed each foot in turn. He found he was more tense even than he had been when creeping through the village of sleeping savages or edging onto the pier: in those cases, the consequences would not have been instantaneously lethal. And, in those cases, he had not been leading a laden horse.

To his relief, the horse seemed to notice his careful movements and moved calmly and with a sureness that, Brann felt, was even more quiet than his passage. He wiped his sleeve across eyes that were beginning to sting with seeping sweat. He could feel the rocks waiting on the steep slope above his left shoulder, and he was constantly ready to explode into a lunging sprint at an instant's notice. His breathing became ragged and heavy, leaving him light-headed, and his concentration was such that he almost did not hear Gerens' voice. 'All right, all right, you can stop now,' he was calling. Brann looked up in surprise to find that he had passed the danger area by several yards. Blowing out a huge sigh, he turned to watch the others, patting the horse's neck in gratitude for its compliance – and in relief that the beast had, like him, come to no harm.

Ironically, after so much whispering – there was, of course, no further need for such quiet – Gerens's shout had failed to encourage any movement from a single stone. Even more strangely, Konall, after scrambling along a slope until he was level with the lowermost of the waiting rocks, was similarly unable to dislodge any more than a few fist-sized stones that skittered mockingly down onto the path. Cursing, he prodded the point of the spear, several times, hard against a rock the size of his head that had several smaller stones backed up against it. The rock slid, then rolled amid the other stones and much dust, onto the middle of the path. Emboldened, Konall crept forward for an assault on another rock but, as he did so, the entire collection of waiting rocks and boulders crashed abruptly onto the trail.

Konall launched himself backwards in reaction, landing on his back and rolling down the slope in a few bounces. His life had been saved, however, not by his reflexes – such was the speed of the rockfall that it had been completed by the time he had started to jump – but by the precise manner that the rocks had fallen straight down the slope. Had they spread as they dropped, he would have been taken with them, and buried beneath them, before he even knew it was happening. As if to emphasise his luck, or to mock him, depending on the watcher's perspective, a pebble careened across the slope and, as he sat up, precisely and comically bounced off his head.

Gerens and Hakon, their nerves enhanced by relief at his safety, laughed unfettered, while Grakk smiled. Konall, relieved even more than they, fell back theatrically with his arms outstretched as if knocked unconscious by the small stone.

Brann, his view obliterated by the thick cloud of dust that was obscuring even the rocks, and calling to the horse that had become skittish at the sudden landslide – although not as alarmed as he would have expected, giving another indication that it had been trained to battle-readiness – heard the hilarity and guessed that all was well on the far side of the obstruction. As the dust started to clear, he saw that they had met with even more success that he expected: the rocks had formed a barricade slightly greater than the height of a man, and composed of sufficiently large boulders to make it impassable to a horse – had it been mainly scree, it would have been effectively a mound that a horse could simply have walked over, but here the boulders were large enough to offer gaps that would be lethal to any horse that attempted to negotiate them, but not large enough to offer safe footing for the beasts.

Four heads popped up at the top of the barricade, and Brann was soon joined by his companions.

'Easy, really,' said Konall casually.

Gerens snorted. 'I do believe that the young lord is developing a sense of humour.'

'Oh, he has one, all right,' Brann said. 'It is just different from everyone else's.'

'You are just jealous of my barricade-building skills,' Konall said haughtily.

'Well, give me your barricade-building tool,' Brann said, grabbing the spear. He lifted a helmet that was hanging by its chinstrap from the pommel of the saddle, and started up the slope.

'What are you doing?' Konall called, serious again. 'We need to press on, and that spear would be handy if the riders catch us.'

Brann reached the top. 'It seems to me that anything that could buy us more time before they catch us would be more valuable than one extra spear.' He positioned the helmet so that the top of it could just be seen from the other side of the rocks, and placed the spear upright beside it so that it was protruding a third of its length above the rocks.

'There,' he said, scrambling back down. 'Now there is an ambush to slow them down even further.'

Konall snorted, holding the reins out to him. 'They will not fall for that. That is the oldest trick there is.'

'We know that, and they know that,' Brann said. 'But they do not have the same disregard to their own lives as the savages we have come across – these are mercenaries who will fight, but would not really want to die if they don't have to. So they cannot afford to take a chance, in case it really is an ambush. Which will give us more time.'

'Which we are now wasting, talking about it,' Grakk pointed out.

'True,' Brann said. 'So give me my horse and let us go.'

Konall's eyebrows raised. '*My* horse?'

Brann set off at a run. 'After leading him under those rocks, I would say he is most definitely mine.'

Jogging past him, Grakk grinned mischievously. 'You went under the rocks together, yes. But who led who, might be a question.'

'I think this conversation has gone on long enough,' Brann complained, sparking laughter before the effort of picking up the pace once more ended the conversation in any case.

They emerged from the pass with no further incident, much to Brann's surprise. He had been consumed with watching Gerens's condition – which, he was relieved to see, was still causing him to be unsteady but no more so than before – and had not realised how far they had come when Konall called a halt.

'Recognise this place?' he asked Brann.

The smaller boy stared for a moment before comprehension struck. 'Of course. The sentry post.' He turned to the other three. 'We passed two sentries in a rocky perch above the path just ahead when we were coming this way before. We left them alive so we would not alert anyone to our presence. It was not too hard to sneak past them last time as they were not too alert, but I do not think we have time for too much sneaking now, and, anyway, we cannot assume it is the same two. They may been relieved by more alert bandits, if such exist, or there may be even more of them up there.' He glanced at Konall. 'So I think we need to work this one out.'

Hakon spoke up, and several of them jumped in surprise at the unfamiliar sound. 'We seem to spend a great deal of time talking about things when we have horsemen chasing us. Why do we not just go ahead and deal with it? They are only ill-equipped, deranged savages.'

'Ill-equipped, deranged savages that destroyed our hunting party, butchered four fine warriors and captured you three,' Konall pointed out.

Hakon blushed. 'My lord, I apologise,' he stammered. 'I spoke out of turn.'

Konall's tone softened. 'Calm down, Hakon,' he said, reassuringly. 'I understand – until a few days ago, I thought the same. But it appears that sometimes we can profit more by considering alternatives. As a leader, I will be honoured to have men who would be prepared to die for me. But I would prefer to have them alive to serve me longer, if I can find another way to achieve what must be done. Much as it pains me to say it, therefore, it is of value occasionally to at least listen to the diminutive mill boy.'

Hakon smiled, and Konall nodded at Brann to continue. 'Right,' he started. 'I am still getting used to trying to work these things out, but this is what seems sensible to me. First of all, we do not have too much time to waste – we do not know how long it will have taken the riders to realise that there was no ambush and that they would have to double back if they want to keep their horses with them. As the horses are their biggest advantage in trying to catch us, they will certainly have retraced their steps. But we do not know how long it will take them to find a new route. I also think that they will have started cautiously in the first place on the trail along the gorge, wary of an ambush at every corner but, as they encountered no danger each time, they will have become more confident and impatient and will have started to force a faster pace. As we do not know how much, or how little, time we have, I do not think that we can count on adopting too stealthy an approach.'

'Agreed,' said Konall and Hakon simultaneously.

'But,' said Brann, looking pointedly at the pair, 'neither can we charge straight at them – they are too well placed for us to reach them without having whatever they have available to them thrown or launched at us, and we will need to be right upon them to do them any damage, so there would be too much risk of injury to us in that approach. For the same reason, we cannot run past them and trust to catching them by surprise: the lookout spot is well chosen and there is too much open ground for us to cover without being spotted and attacked. As this is the only trail that we know of that goes in our direction, and the undergrowth is too thick to go any other way, we can really only go in front of them or behind them, creeping as we did on the way here.'

Gerens shook his head. 'But you have already said that one of those involves us in getting attacked and the other is too slow. So we have no option open to us.'

'We do, if we take both approaches at the same time.' Brann looked around at the quizzical faces. As before, he was finding that he was warming to his subject. 'We need to get quickly up behind them without alerting them, so we need a distraction in front of them.'

Gerens did not like the sound of this. 'So some of us get shot at as a diversion? That does not sound much better.'

'Quiet,' Konall snapped. 'Listen to him.'

'Of course that is not the idea,' Brann continued. 'But they certainly will attack you if you merely appear in front of them. We need to confuse them. If they see people who are apparently quite happy to be seen by them, they will wonder why this is so long enough for others of us to get behind them. So we need the dirtiest, smelliest ones among us to pose as bandits.'

Gerens grunted. 'That narrows it down to three people.'

'Two, actually. They will be distracted just as easily by two as by three, so it makes sense to have as many bowmen behind them as we can.'

Gerens looked at Grakk and nodded, accepting his fate. The tattooed tribesman turned to Brann. 'What should we do?'

Brann smiled his thanks at their simple acceptance. 'Start up the path, as noisily as you can. Remember, you do not need to be perfect, just carefree enough to make them wonder.'

'We do not speak their language,' Gerens pointed out, looking nervous. 'So what do we say to each other?'

'That is true,' Brann admitted. He glanced around at the group. 'Any ideas?'

Konall shrugged. 'The bandits do not seem to do much talking, anyway. Not anything you would class as a conversation. As long as the tone of the noises you make is right, it probably doesn't even need to be real words considering the distance you will be away from them.'

Gerens sighed. 'It is not the best plan I have ever heard, but I do not see any alternative.'

Brann turned to Grakk. 'Are you happy with it too? Is there anything you would like to add?'

Grakk had been squatting, head bowed, as he listened intently. He looked up. 'Just make sure you kill them quickly, if you don't mind.'

Brann smiled. 'I do not think you have to worry about there being a lack of eagerness to slaughter bandits where these two are concerned,' he said, gesturing to Konall and Hakon.

The pair nodded confirmation, clearly quite contented with their role.

'If there is nothing else, I think we should start immediately,' Brann said. Grakk and Gerens were already making themselves suitably dishevelled.

'You head off,' Gerens said. 'We will check each other's appearance, and then start up the path.'

Brann gripped his arm. 'Take care. You too, Grakk. And remember, make as much noise as you can – it will make them think you are happy to be seen, even wave at them to let them know you are aware of them. When we hear your noise, we will know that we can move faster.'

Konall pulled at Brann's tunic with urgency, and they left the pair to their last few preparations. They had reached a point just off the trail, climbing to higher ground, when they heard the raucous bellowing begin.

Brann said quietly, 'That would be our cue,' and they picked up the pace. They still moved cautiously, swords drawn in case of coming face-to-face with a bandit, but now they scuttled from the cover of one rock to another rather than keeping their movements painstakingly slow. They were soon on the ridge along the top of the rocky outcrop, and their progress became more urgent as the noise from the two pseudo-bandits grew closer. They sounded impressively authentic, ostensibly arguing in a series of unintelligible shouts and roars. Brann was impressed – until Gerens could be heard breaking into a wild, wordless song.

'Oh, gods,' Brann muttered. 'He is overdoing it.'

Konall turned. 'I think it would be wise to hurry,' he said dryly.

'I do not know,' Hakon observed. 'If that is how he sings, perhaps it would be a kindness to let him be shot.'

He stopped speaking abruptly as Konall halted and gestured the other two alongside him. As they moved forward, Brann found himself in the same spot from which he had observed the lookout post previously. The scene was so similar – the bandits appeared to be the same two that they had seen the previous time – that he felt that he had left his vantage point only moments before. The only difference now was that, where the sentries had previously been engrossed in their game, now they were on their feet, leaning forward against the rocks at the front of their eyrie and watching Gerens and Grakk approach below. They seemed excited, perhaps believing that their relief had arrived early, and the three behind them used the chance to quietly sheath their swords and swing their bows into position. They drew their arrows back and sighted down the shafts at the centre of the rag-covered backs before them.

Konall breathed, 'Wait for my word. I will take the left, Hakon take the right. If Brann hits either, it will be a bonus.'

'Cheeky pig,' Brann said under his breath, although he knew that it was true.

One of the bandits exclaimed suddenly, and whacked his companion's arm to emphasise his point. Whether he had seen through the ruse or not, they would never know. Konall hissed, 'Now!' and they loosed simultaneously.

Konall's arrow thumped into the centre of his target's back, passing straight through him with the force of such a powerful bow at such close range and striking the rock he had been leaning on. A blink of an eye later, Hakon's arrow, shot from the less powerful short bow, struck the other bandit identically, hammering him forward against the rock. Brann's arrow – much to his disappointment as he had been sure he was aiming at exactly the same spot as Hakon – smashed against the angled face of the rock, a full arm's length to the right of the bandit, and shot towards the sky.

The two bandits slid to the ground, and Konall was already on his way, long knife in hand to ensure that they would not get up, although they already looked lifeless to Brann. Without waiting for Konall's confirmation, he shouted to the pair below, who were still blissfully roaring and singing, unaware that the danger was past.

Gerens yelled, 'Thank you', and waved up cheerfully. Brann waved back, just as, with a whirr, and a thud, Brann's errant arrow landed point-first in the hard earth between the two decoys.

Even at that distance, Brann could see the colour drain from Gerens's face. Without a blink, Grakk stepped forward and pulled the arrow from the ground. He held it up, displaying it to Brann.

'Is this yours?' he asked helpfully. 'Would you like it back?'

Konall appeared at Brann's shoulder and peered down. 'As I said, it would have been a bonus...' he observed.

'Not everyone is as accurate as you. It was only a little off-target,' Brann objected ruefully.

Gerens had heard his comment, and Brann thought it prudent to move away before he could bear the full force of the string of expletives that formed the boy's reply from below.

Konall, however, was impressed. 'He would fit in well at our barracks,' he observed. 'I wonder if he can fight.'

'You may find out if you let him reach me in the next few moments,' Brann said. 'I think I will go and collect the horse.'

By the time he had returned, Gerens had calmed down. Slightly. Brann thought it wise to keep the horse between them.

With thoughts of the possibility of pursuing horsemen large in their minds, the party moved off quickly, conscious that any advantage they may have gained with the landslide on the gorge trail may have been negated by their own negotiation of the landslide and this latest incident. After only a few hundred yards, movement on the other side of the horse caught Brann's eye. Still tense after the stalking of the bandit sentries, he jumped and reached for his sword.

'Relax,' said Gerens, his face appearing behind the arrow that he had waved to catch Brann's attention. 'If you feel nervous, think how I feel after a close brush with this thing.'

'Sorry,' Brann said sheepishly. 'I am not much good when I have time to think about it.'

Gerens regarded him solemnly. 'You seem to have a talent for understatement.'

Brann held his hand up in defeat, forgetting that he was holding the reins. The horse's head jerked around, almost smacking him in the face, and he lurched back in fright. Gerens looked amused, and Brann considered that the last ten minutes or so had not been his most auspicious in this company.

'I admit it,' he conceded. 'If I am ever in an archery contest, I would advise you to bet on the other man.'

'If you are ever in an archery contest,' Gerens said, 'I have the feeling that the safest place to stand would be in front of your target.' He held up the arrow once more. 'Do you want this back?'

Before Brann could speak, Konall, at the head of the tight group, turned and hissed, 'Stop the chatter. Have you forgotten that we are fleeing an enemy, in his own domain? Our ears are useless if all we can hear is our own inane prattling, and you are warning every enemy within a hundred yards of our approach.'

Grakk, beside Konall, nodded his agreement. Shamefaced, the pair mumbled an apology. The group settled back into a steady jog and, in the quiet that was filled only by the noise of their feet, the horses' hooves and the occasional sound of wildlife, Brann's thoughts turned to the horsemen behind them. Over the next two hours, he had little else to occupy his mind, and brooding on the subject caused him to become increasingly edgy, looking back more and more frequently, and seeing the signs of pursuit in every rising flock of birds or each wind-blown swaying tree.

Gerens, who had taken to resting his hand on the horse's shoulder, noticed. 'You will waste energy turning around all the time,' he gasped between breaths. 'Do not worry, if they are catching us, we will know about it.'

Brann looked across to nod his agreement, but was taken aback by his friend's appearance. Gerens was drenched in sweat – they were all running hard and, although Konall and Grakk showed no outward signs of feeling the strain, Brann expected that the other two would, at least, have broken sweat, but not to this extent. Gerens's hair was plastered flat and dripping, rivulets were streaming down his face and his clothes looked as wet as when he had emerged from the river.

His pallor was no better. Rather than being florid from the effort, he was as pale as a corpse, the only colour in his face being red rings around his eyes.

Alarmed, Brann called on Konall to stop. Irritated, the tall boy was ready to vent his feelings as he turned. Brann cut him off. 'I think we should rest for a minute. Gerens...'

The others noticed the boy. Grakk, concern flitting across his normally impassive features, moved quickly to the boy's side.

'He has a fever,' he said, as the others grouped around them.

Gerens swayed, his eyes unfocused and his knees starting to buckle slightly. Konall caught him by the arm to steady him but, in doing so, he brushed against Gerens's hand.

The sick boy recoiled with a hiss of pain, but the feeling seemed to clear his senses momentarily. 'I am fine,' he protested, but his voice was weak. 'Come on, we cannot afford to waste time.'

He tried to shake them off, but his efforts were feeble. Konall lifted the hand that had been the source of pain. The bandage that had been applied to Gerens's finger when he was expertly treated on the ship following Boar's attack was now grubby and ragged and, like the rest of Gerens and the other two former captives, was caked with dirt and the gods only knew what else. The finger, shortened by Boar's axe at the final knuckle, was scarlet and swollen, and the hand was showing signs of following suit.

'What happened here?' Konall asked.

'A madman with an axe on the ship,' Brann said dismissively, as if it had been a perfectly normal occurrence.

Konall was confused. 'A madman with an axe attacked a slave, and the slave lost only a finger?'

Brann shrugged. 'He was attacking me, and I had to dodge a lot because I only had a knife to defend myself. Gerens just could not get out of the way at one point.'

Konall stared with curiosity at Brann. 'He was attacking you? I have many questions for you, mill boy, when we reach my home once more,' he grunted. 'You were lucky that Einarr's men reached him before he could slice off some of you as well.'

Grakk gently took Gerens's hand from Konall. 'They didn't. The boy made his own luck.'

Konall's eyes narrowed as he digested the thought, but Grakk continued before he could ask anything else. 'This hand is the cause, indeed. There is infection in him. Skilled herbmasters can help this, so there is now even more need for haste.'

Hakon stepped forward. 'Put him on the horse, then. He will never last at this speed, never mind if we go faster.'

They quickly rearranged the horse's load to position Gerens on its back.

'Tie him on,' Konall instructed, and Grakk efficiently complied. Konall continued, 'We will not maintain much of a pace if he keeps falling off.'

'Not the most caring of attitudes,' Brann observed.

'But true,' Grakk added simply.

They started again and increased speed immediately.

'A miller's son who kills an axe-wielding maniac with only a knife?' Konall muttered as they settled into a run. 'Many questions, indeed.'

Not if I can help it, Brann thought. *I think I will make sure that I will be spending all of my time with the Captain. Maybe we will sail soon anyway. I never thought I would be glad to be back at sea – unless it was to go home, of course.*

Thoughts of what he had left behind – what he had been snatched from – caused the misery to well up in him once more, and the thought of their exhausted little band being chased by brutal, and angry, riders filled him with an overwhelming hopelessness.

He concentrated on the effort of keeping up with the pace that Konall was setting and, glad that he was the one to lead the horse, watched Gerens to ensure that he remained stable on the beast's back. Gradually, he forced the misery from his mind and buried it deep within him. *Saved for future reference*, he thought sardonically.

They were well across an open plain when, for the first time, the signs of pursuit were visible and definite. Through his exhaustion, Brann felt his stomach lurch with the nausea of fear. While the horsemen had been out of sight, it had become easier with every passing minute to pretend that they did not exist. Now, reality was thrust back upon them, suddenly and harshly.

The riders were still distant, and although the openness of the plain afforded no cover for the fleeing boys, it at least afforded them warning of their pursuers' approach well in advance of them being caught. A small cloud of dust indicated that they were galloping, and within it several tiny figures were evident. Konall's eyes narrowed as he stared over his shoulder, without missing a stride. 'I cannot see exactly how many, but I would say between a dozen and fifteen, unless there are more behind them that are hidden from view.'

Brann gasped, 'They must have picked up the others when they doubled back.'

'It is no matter,' Grakk said. 'They were too many for us before, anyway. Too many is too many.'

Konall, who had clearly harboured intentions of defeating the original group of riders, shot the tattooed tribesman a withering look, but Brann knew that what he said was true. Their only real hope had been to out-run the riders.

'Can we reach cover in time?' he called.

'If we really go flat out, we may reach the end of this plain before them,' Konall shouted. 'But it will be close. After that, there may be rocks, or even trees, that may help us. Anything that breaks their momentum. Or there might be nothing.'

'And if there is nothing, what then?' Brann yelled, panic rising in his voice as he thumped his feet onwards, not aware that he was still holding onto the unconscious Gerens. 'If there is no cover, all we can do is wait to die.'

Konall turned in his stride to move alongside Brann. He grabbed a handful of the back of his tunic and thrust him

340

forward. 'You never, ever, wait to die,' he snarled. 'While you live, you fight, and while you fight, you always have a chance.'

Spurred on by Konall's words, and the thought of the riders behind, weight seemed to evaporate from their limbs and they launched from the exhausted stumbling run they had managed until then into a headlong dash; a race with only the faintest hope of survival as the prize. The plain was on a plateau, so its end left them with no indication of what lay beyond – and what they could expect from the terrain. Staring at their target, they forced themselves on, running still harder as the irregular drumming of the hooves started to intrude on the, until then, overwhelming sound of their frantic breathing as they dragged the cold mountain air roughly down raw and gasping throats. Soon they could also hear the riders' excited cries, urging on their mounts as the proximity of their quarry fired their bloodlust.

Konall flung a look back over his shoulder, then looked ahead once more, calculating the distance to the tantalisingly close edge of the plateau.

'Stop!' he cried, anguish evident amid his natural ring of authority in his command. 'We are not going to make it.'

'We might,' Brann cried in dismay. 'We are so close.'

Konall skidded to a halt, and the rest automatically followed suit, unwilling to run on and leave him. 'They will catch us,' he said, his voice grim. 'We cannot fight with our backs turned.'

He dragged out his sword and rammed it point-first into the ground, then swung up his bow, an arrow at the string. Brann fumbled for his own bow, too scared to risk wasting his time on drawing his sword. He pulled out several arrows, ready for rapid use.

'Wait until I say,' Konall shouted. 'We have three bows and four swords – we cannot afford to waste arrows or energy. They will be on us soon enough.'

Brann felt a tear run down his grimy cheek, knowing that he was counting the rest of his life in seconds, on a lonely mountain so far from everything and everyone he had ever loved. He clenched his teeth and gripped the bow so tightly that the weapon shook, and raised it to try to sight along the arrow.

'Now!' Konall roared. 'Kill the bastards!'

Almost caught off-guard, Brann let fly and reached for another arrow. A hail of arrows flew into the charging mercenaries who had not even readied their own short bows, desperate to close in and use swords and axes.

A hail of arrows? Brann watched, dumbfounded, as several of the riders were knocked from their saddles. More arrows whirred past them into the horsemen, closely followed by a rush of bodies as roaring men, some as tall as Konall but all broader and hairier, charged forward. The riders, as astonished at the change in the situation as their intended victims were, milled in confusion. They lost the momentum of their attack and the two dozen of Konall's father's warriors – as Brann now realised they were – crashed into them with devastating impact.

Konall howled with glee and, dropping his bow, grabbed his sword to join the fight. A huge hand caught his tunic from behind and hauled him back as easily as if he were a small child.

'No, you don't, youngster,' Ulfar's voice growled. 'I promised your father I would bring you back alive, and one chance sword-stroke or flailing hoof and I may as well not have bothered coming up to this abnormally high place.'

The fight was brief, in any case. While Ulfar's twenty-four men outnumbered the twenty riders, in reality half their number would have coped just as easily. With brutal efficiency, they went about their business: a sweeping chop to the fore-legs of the horse brought the animal crashing, flailing and screaming, to the ground and, almost in the same movement, a second swing of sword or axe finished the rider. Most of the mercenaries were dead before their horse had finished falling.

Ulfar unceremoniously thrust Konall to one side and stepped into the midst of the fray. 'Remember we want one alive,' he bellowed above the horrific cacophony of the carnage.

His intervention came just in time. A warrior wielding a huge axe was in the process of despatching the final merce-nary. In mid-swing, he twisted his weapon so that the flat of the gleaming axe-head smashed against the side of the man's head. Brann thought he would be lucky to survive the blow, although it seemed as if the warrior had, with an amazing show of strength, managed to pull up the blow slightly as it impacted.

The warriors checked that the remainder of the mercenaries were dead before dealing mercifully with the stricken horses.

'Considering the disgust you have shown for these people,' Brann observed, 'I would have thought your men would have put the horses out of their misery before the riders.'

Konall never took his eyes from the scene. 'A wounded horse never got up and came at you with a sword or produced a hidden knife. Compassion for the animals is fine, but it takes second place to safety.'

'A fair point,' Brann admitted, and turned to see how Gerens was faring. The boy was slumped unconscious against the horse's neck, and even the clamour of battle had not roused him in any way.

'Oh, gods, do not let him have died,' Brann said in shock at the sight. Rushing to the horse's side, relief swept over him as he noticed signs of breathing, although it was faint and irregular enough to indicate that only urgent treatment would prevent his soul leaving for the Halls of the Dead. Ulfar appeared beside him. His experienced eye quickly assessed the situation, and he called over two of his men.

'Take the boy back as fast as you can. He needs immediate treatment. Leave at once.' Without hesitation, the pair took the reins and set off at a run.

'They are my fastest two,' Ulfar rumbled. 'They will keep to that pace without faltering. If anyone can get the boy back quickly enough to save his life, they will.'

He turned to attend to the aftermath of the fight, but was stopped by Brann's voice. 'Should I not have told them what I know of his injury, so they can pass it on?'

Ulfar's brows drew together, and Brann suddenly felt very small and very scared. 'I know nothing of the customs of your folk, boy, but in this land it is not healthy for a page to question a warrior's orders.'

Konall moved quickly to join the interchange. 'He means no disrespect, Ulfar,' he said quickly. 'There is a bond between him and the two slaves, for whatever reason. And he has been through much for a mill boy in recent days.'

Any surprise that Ulfar may have felt in discovering that Einarr had chosen a miller's son for a page – the gods only knew how he would react if he found out that the page was really a slave – was eclipsed by the fact that aloof, single-minded, duty-obsessed Konall had intervened on the boy's behalf. Such was the huge man's astonishment that his reaction was to explain his actions – something Brann guessed he seldom did to anyone other than Ragnarr.

'If the boy is to live, we need to use profitably every second available to us. Any healer worth his position would find the wound immediately and diagnose the problem as quickly. Consequently, any useful information you could add, he would know himself. It matters not how long the boy has already been in that state, only how long the doctor still has to work on him before his life slips from him.'

Scratching his beard absently, he wandered off to attend to more familiar matters than a couple of youngsters who were full of surprises.

Brann grinned. 'It seems your character has improved sufficiently to flummox your compatriots.'

'Watch your step, mill boy,' Konall growled. 'Men have been hanged for less impudent comments to nobles.' He moved off to retrieve his bow, muttering, '"Flummox"? Who uses such a word these days? The gods preserve us from these quaint foreigners.'

Brann's grin widened, then slipped away as exhaustion began to catch up with him. At least now they would be able to rest.

Ulfar's voice rang out. 'Right, you have had enough time to get organised after all that fun. Let's move.'

Brann groaned. Hakon came over and helped him to unstring his bow and strap it to his back. 'Do not worry. We will rest soon,' he said quietly. 'It is just that they do not know how many others there are in this area, and it is too exposed here to remain for long.'

Brann started to reply but Hakon had already moved away.

Moving in a loose bunch, the group started to descend the steep slope beyond the edge of the plateau. Overwhelmed by weariness, Brann felt his head swim and tried to concentrate merely on moving his legs as they wound down through rough ground between rocks and the occasional growth of hardy vegetation or took advantage where they could of random, animal-created trails. Such was his fatigue that just the one task of controlling his legs took all of his attention – *if they were attacked, I probably would not even notice and would run right into the enemy's midst*, he thought self-mockingly.

He realised a voice was trying to penetrate the fog in his brain. Shaking his head to try to clear it, he found that Grakk had fallen in beside him.

'Sorry, Grakk, I did not hear you,' he said. His words, annoyingly, were thick and slurred.

'I was suggesting that you keep your mind active. Try to think about something,' the wiry man said patiently. 'It will help to keep you awake.'

Brann grunted. 'I am more worried that I will not keep going as well as everyone else. Any advice?'

'Do not fall over.'

He caught Grakk's toothy grin at the edge of his vision. 'Why, thank you. That is most helpful. I will try to bear it in mind,' he puffed as they half scrambled down a stretch of scree.

Sooner than he expected – probably because he had lost all concept of the passage of time – the slope began to level out and they veered towards the edge of a small wood. As they neared the trees, half-a-dozen warriors stepped from the undergrowth, each one leading several horses.

Horses! Seldom had Brann felt his heart lift so dramatically. He stumbled, the strength draining suddenly from his legs at the sight of a respite from running. Remembering Grakk's advice, he caught his balance and, as the group slowed, he moved beside Konall.

'Not that I am disappointed to see the horses,' he said, 'but I thought your people fought on foot.'

'We prefer to, yes,' the tall boy said. 'But we do not believe that we should therefore have to run around between fights when there are perfectly good animals for the job.'

Brann smiled. 'The gods bless that attitude.'

The warriors mounted up, leaving five horses for the four members of the rescued group. Brann counted the animals, frowning for a second before his fatigue-befuddled mind began to work. 'Of course,' he said. 'They had not anticipated that we would bring a horse with us. That extra horse was to be for Gerens.'

Konall grunted disinterestedly. Brann was undaunted by his lack of enthusiasm. 'It is flattering, though, that they expected us to be successful in rescuing all three of them and managing to return alive, and they brought enough for all of us.'

Konall leant towards him conspiratorially. 'Do not get carried away. They were prepared for all eventualities, rather than expecting just one of them. I would not speak in such a way too loudly if you do not wish to become the subject of ridicule.' He paused. 'If truth be known, they probably expected to use more of those five horses for bodies than riders.'

Brann realised that his high spirits, now curbed by Konall, had raised his energy momentarily. With his tiredness flooding back yet again, he grabbed at the nearest available horse and hauled himself into the saddle. Grakk caught the horse beside him and swung himself with practised ease onto its back.

Brann's eyes widened. 'Somehow, I never thought of you as a horseman, Grakk,' he said as the wiry tribesman casually wheeled his mount around to face the same direction as the rest of the party.

Grakk shrugged. 'We prefer nimble ponies to these over-sized, clumsier beasts, but any one of my people who cannot ride by their fourth summer is considered a slow starter.'

'All right, I misjudge you again,' Brann conceded. 'Any more advice for me?'

Grakk grinned. 'Do not fall off. It is easier to fall asleep sitting down than when running.'

He dug his heels into the horse's flanks and it sprang after the rest of the party. Brann hurried to follow suit and, heading down gentler slopes to the mountains' foot and the plain beyond, he glanced back at the peaks behind them where, all of a sudden, such recent horrors seemed so far away.

Chapter 10

He had but once consulted her.

The speaker of sooth, the reader of the many paths yet to be. Or the useful fraud, depending on your stance. And, oft times, he had found her of use. Once, however, he had consulted her. Once he had tested, to seek if any value lay in what was revered by other men. But he had dismissed her as merely an instrument of use.

Her words, he had never tried to memorise. Nonetheless, they had remained engraved in his mind more clearly than if they had been carved into stone tablets and placed by his bedside for him to recite every morning for the half-century since he had heard them uttered. Whenever his mind touched upon the matter, the words were there. Unbidden, they were there.

One will come
Thought nothing by all,
A seed there will be
In a breast thought so small,
From one who is nothing,
Greatness will spring,

Of the deeds of that one
Great songs will they sing,
But the seed must be nurtured
And the shoot must be fed,
For the flower to blossom,
For the man to be bred,
And nations will stand
Or nations will fall,
When heroes and kings
On the One come to call
On one they once thought
So small.

In recent weeks, her words were entering his mind so frequently that they seemed to be a backdrop to all of his other thoughts. The oracle, she had been an instrument of use. Now he felt, another instrument was coming his way. Every instrument needed a hand to wield it.

His right fist clenched. He smiled.

* * * *

For the second time in an astonishingly short few days, Brann woke stiff and aching in his small room at Ravensrest without any memory of having arrived there. This time, however, rather than being wakened as dawn was about to break, he had been allowed to sleep and strong sunlight was streaming from a high sun through the narrow window.

He jumped from the bed in alarm. 'Oh, gods,' he moaned aloud. 'It must be almost mid-day.' He was hours late and the Captain would be furious at being let down in front of his uncle.

He paused at the realisation that he was thinking of himself as a real page. Maintaining the pretence during the stressful and harrowing times in the mountains had made it difficult to accept that he was still a slave.

Even so, he thought grimly, *I still have to act as a page, and arriving half a day late for my duties is not the most convincing way to do so.*

He had fallen asleep – he had no idea whether he had made it to his bed by himself or with the help of another – in the same clothes that he had been wearing during the past few days; only his boots had been removed. Glancing around, he noticed the boots placed neatly at the foot of the bed, confirming that he had received assistance in reaching his bed: if he had been so exhausted that he was unable to remember reaching his room, then tidiness would have been his least consideration. He only hoped that he had not embarrassed himself in any way.

He grunted as the combined smell from himself and his clothes assaulted his senses. 'Whoever was my assistant, they possessed bravery and strength of character to withstand that.' He glanced around the small room in case a victim of the stench was lying unconscious as a result.

His mood turned serious once more as the sight of a towel and a filled basin reminded him of the pressing need to clean himself and find Einarr. He peeled off the offending garments and hurriedly washed himself. Fresh clothing had also been left for him, and he pulled it on frantically, grabbing his boots and hoping that his feet would block the smell that remained within after their overnight airing. He found, however, that not only had the leather been cleaned externally, but that herbs had been sprinkled within, eradicating the expected smell.

Without pausing to wonder about the effort that had been made in assisting him, he burst from the room, almost knocking Valdis and the tray she was carrying into the opposite wall of the corridor. With a squeal and an impressive display of reactions and dexterity, she managed to recover without spilling any of the food and drink that she was carrying.

'Now, now, master page,' she scolded with amusement. 'I believe you need to calm yourself. I did not tuck you in and look out fresh clothes for you only for you to try to hurl me through a stone wall.'

Brann blushed. 'Oh, it was you,' he stammered. It was not his most erudite of answers, and he was not sure whether his inept performance was a result of the thought of her putting him to bed, the fact that he had almost flattened her or her usual effect on him. He guessed it was all three, which left him little chance of making anything but a pathetic impression. 'I should... I mean... well, thank you,' he continued lamely, confirming his prediction.

Valdis unleashed the devastating effect on his knees of her smile, and curtsied elaborately. 'I accept your gratitude with pleasure, kind sir,' she said, 'and I am delighted to note that you smell so much better than you did last night.'

Brann's blush grew even deeper. He started to stutter a reply but, before he could say anything of sense, Valdis blithely continued.

'In any case, where are you off to in such a hurry? I do hope that you are not setting off on another jaunt into the mountains so soon.'

The encounter with the girl had driven from his mind all thoughts of his panic over being late, but he was sharply reminded by her question.

'I must find the Cap... Lord Einarr at once. I have over-slept terribly and must attend him at once.'

'What a strangely sudden passion for your duty,' she teased him. 'Disappearing for days with no warning or explanation was fine, but missing a morning is a calamity.'

It was difficult to argue against such simple logic, but Brann felt he had to try. 'When I left that morning, it was under Konall's orders. I mean, *Lord* Konall's orders. My apologies, but I really must find Lord Einarr at once.' He stared around wildly, trying to remember the direction of the Captain's quarters.

Balancing the tray expertly on one arm, Valdis laid her hand gently on his sleeve to calm him. It had the opposite effect, her touch causing his arm to jump abruptly.

She smiled, amused. 'Do not worry: I am having fun with you. Lord Einarr left word that he did not wish to see you until you had rested and eaten.' She paused and stared distantly as if straining to remember a detail. 'I believe it was along the lines of: "He has left me to manage on my own for days, so another morning will not matter."'

Noticing his alarm, she added quickly, 'Calm your panic. He was joking also.' She tapped his arm reassuringly again, but this time without eliciting the same reaction. Brann found himself beginning to enjoy the feeling, and the removal of his need for a terrified rush to attend the Captain had allowed his hunger to awaken.

He looked hopefully at the tray. 'I don't suppose that is for me, then?'

Valdis laughed, an entrancing sound. 'You are getting carried away with yourself now, young adventurer. Lords Ragnarr and Einarr will be having their *lunch* while they discuss the information you and Lord Konall brought back with the captives; your *breakfast* is waiting for you in the kitchen. You may be one of everybody's little heroes, but you are still a long way off having your meals delivered to you.'

With a swirl of her skirts that captured Brann's gaze and refused to release it, she swept up the corridor. Watching her retreating form, Brann decided that he cared not about 'everybody's' opinion – there was only one person whose 'little hero' he wanted to be. With a sigh, he headed for the kitchen, where he found Hakon enthusiastically demolishing a mouth-watering array of fresh bread, cheese and fruit that had been laid upon the large wooden table.

Hakon looked up. 'Good afternoon,' he said pointedly. 'Do you realise how long the rest of us have been up and about?'

Brann grinned. 'In your case, not much longer than me, considering the enthusiasm you are showing for your breakfast.'

Hakon slapped the table in mock annoyance. 'I am found out,' he said between mouthfuls. He noticed Brann's dishevelled clothing. 'Did you panic about sleeping in, by any chance?' Brann nodded. Hakon cut a hunk of bread and tossed it to him. 'Me too. They seem to be taking it well, though.'

Brann sat opposite him and started to gather food. 'What: the sleeping in or the antics in the mountains?'

Hakon shrugged. 'Both.'

'It is all right for you,' Brann objected. 'You had no choice in the matter. They cannot criticise you. But Konall and I ran off without permission. And I can imagine it is a great deal easier for their anger to be directed at a page than a noble – at least Konall has some authority to make his own decisions.' He looked morosely at his food. 'I should probably make the most of this. It may be the last meal of a condemned man.'

354

'I would not worry overmuch,' the tall boy said, reaching for the cheese. 'They are too excited about the news you brought back about Loku, the bandits, the location of their settlement, the involvement of the mercenaries and the level of organisation behind the bandits' activities. It is a fair bit for them to take in, and they have to work out the best course of action. Add to that the fact that you helped to give Konall a chance to enhance his reputation, and that he seems to have returned marginally more human than he left, and it seems that it may have turned out to be an all-round success. So, as I said, I would not worry if I were you.'

Encouraged by the emergence of a much brighter character in Hakon than the experience in the mountains had previously allowed to be revealed, Brann fell on his food with gusto.

In mid-swallow, he stopped and looked up, his eyes wide in alarm. Avoiding the possibility that the food was a problem, Hakon guessed correctly the cause of his reaction. 'Your injured friend?'

Brann nodded. 'My, er… yes, the slave.'

'Your *friend*.' Hakon shrugged. 'Relax, we aren't too fussed in this part of the world. A man is either a good man or a bad man. You either like him or you don't. He is your friend, or not.'

Brann started to get up. 'Whatever, I must see how he is.'

Hakon waved him back down. 'Do not panic,' he said in what was already beginning to be a familiar instruction that day. 'He made it here in one piece, and in time. The infection has been caught and he is sleeping off the effects of whatever was poured down his throat to achieve that. They have cleaned his wounded finger and dressed it again and they are waiting as long as they can before removing any more of his finger in case it will recover first. Do not worry, he is in good hands with Old Leeches, our resident doctor. He has treated far more gory wounds than this one in his time.'

Brann was startled. 'Old Leeches? Do not tell me you still...'

Hakon laughed. 'No, we do not still treat people with leeches around here. As with everywhere else, that went out long ago. We use herbs and potions and the gods know what, the same as your people probably do. No, we only call him that because he is so old we joke that he must remember using leeches himself.' Brann smiled in relief and returned to his food. That was the trouble with sleeping so long: everybody else seemed to know so much more about what was going on. His eyes narrowed.

'How *do* you know so much? Have you been up longer than you said?'

Hakon smiled. 'No, just long enough to catch Valdis in here before she took the lords' lunch upstairs. Take it from me: if you want to know what is happening in a place like this, ask the servants – they know more than the lords.'

Brann helped himself to a corner of cheese. 'That is certainly true. They seem to get everywhere. I suppose if Valdis is doing everything from serving food to chamber duties, then she will hear things all over the place.'

'You are half right,' Hakon said, pouring water for each of them. 'As one of the kitchen maids, she delivers food to all parts – the nobles, the main hall, the infirmary, the barracks, wherever it may be needed at any given time – and between that and talking to the other servants, the news gets passed around. But as for tending to the chambers: believe it or not, we do have separate staff for that. We are not such uncivilised monsters that we work the same few girls to death with every job in the building.'

Brann was confused. 'But she said she left out fresh clothes and washing water for me, and that last night she...' Hakon lifted an eyebrow in interest and insinuation. Brann coughed embarrassedly at the thought. 'And that last night she took my boots off,' he said, hoping that this minimal version of the assistance given to him would suffice.

'Oh, she did, did she? That is not quite the treatment the rest of us received. Personally, I woke halfway up the stairs over the shoulder of a large hairy warrior. I assured him I could make it the rest of the way to my room by myself, and I,' he grinned, 'took my own boots off. I also, by the way, found my own fresh clothes and fetched my own water for washing.'

He pushed across more food towards Brann. 'I would eat plenty. It looks like our Valdis has got her eye on you. You will need to keep your strength up.'

As Brann blushed violently (again), they heard the sound of footsteps on the stone stairs and Valdis returned with a bundle of blankets and clothes in her arms.

'Ah, we were just talking about you,' Hakon said mischievously.

Valdis smiled and fluttered her eyelashes extravagantly. 'Oh yes? And what would you two boys be saying about me, then?'

'Oh, Brann was just...' Hakon cried in pain as he was cut short by Brann's kick under the table. 'I seem to have banged my shin on the table leg,' he exclaimed, with a look of exaggerated innocence.

'Which is around four feet away from your foot,' Valdis pointed out, her hands on her hips.

'I have long legs,' Hakon said simply, before continuing, 'anyway, as I was saying before I banged my leg on that

distant part of the table, Brann was merely expressing his...'
(he ignored the mix of horror and outrage that Brann was
managing to convey in a single glance) '...his amazement
at how much information you manage to amass because of
your duties.'

Brann slumped back in relief that Hakon had not revealed
any more – then remembered at the last moment that he was
sitting on a bench that had no back to it. Frantically grabbing at the table-edge, he just managed to stop overbalancing
backwards in a fall that would probably have constituted
the most humiliating experience of his life. Hakon grinned.
'Oh yes, and that he thinks you are astoundingly gorgeous.'

Valdis giggled and, with a groan, Brann fell forward and
let his forehead thump off the heavy wooden tabletop. Valdis
patted him on the shoulder as she passed. 'As my mother
would say: "At least you have got good taste."' She paused
in the doorway. 'And you are going to love me even more
when you realise what I have got here is your bedding and
clothes for washing.'

'Now that is definitely not fair!' Hakon objected. 'I notice
you did not bring mine down.'

'You, Hakon, son of Ulfar, know perfectly well where to
take yours. Brann, on the other hand, is a guest who does not.'
She tossed her head haughtily. 'And a nice polite guest at that.'
She disappeared through the doorway, but her voice called
back from the passageway. 'With excellent taste in women!'

'You are going to die!' Brann cried at Hakon, throwing
an apple and missing the boy's head by the span of at least
a couple of hands.

His target watched with interest at the fruit bounced
against the far wall. 'Konall was right about your aim,' he
mused. 'Anyway, you should not be filling your head with

such thoughts of violence. Your heart should be singing with thoughts of love and you should be dancing with joy at the thought of having Ulfar as a father-in-law.'

Brann stared at him, comprehension slowly dawning. 'But she said that Ulfar is *your* father.' He shook his head in despair. 'Oh, gods. She is your sister.'

'That she is, my boy, and she has got it bad for you,' Hakon said, beaming. 'Lord Ragnarr likes to staff this place with as many families as possible for reasons of trust and loyalty and suchlike, but she is risking even his good nature and my mother's – I believe she made you some dinner when you first arrived.' Brann groaned and nodded weakly. It just got worse and worse. He was surrounded by this family. There was no escape in sight from sources of teasing, torment and nagging. But Hakon was continuing blithely. 'You see, she is not meant to bring dirty laundry through here. It is all to do with dirt and food and things like that. So that is why I say that she must have it bad for you: she is risking a dressing-down just to let you know that she is doing your washing for you. Rest assured: she would not risk that for just anyone.' He thought for a second. 'In fact, she would not even do the washing in the first place for just anyone.'

Brann's eyes narrowed. 'Why are you so relaxed about it? I thought brothers were meant to be over-protective about their sisters? Shouldn't you be telling me right now that you'll beat me to death with my severed arm if I even go near her again?'

Hakon's grin had barely faded through the whole conversation. 'Oh, it's you who is far more likely to need protection in that relationship. My sister is absolutely capable of lethal severed-arm beatings all by herself. And, besides, it is much more fun making you squirm than any alternative.'

'Stop it, please, Hakon,' Brann objected. 'A man can only take so much before he breaks.' Secretly, however, he hoped that the boy would continue. He found that he was enjoying being linked in the conversation with Valdis. Hakon did not let him down.

'My father always fancied having a second son. I am sure he will like you, even though you are probably around half the size that he had imagined. We could maybe fix you up with some stilts, though. Or stretch your legs with some weights.'

'Considering the size of your father, I think anyone would seem small to him,' Brann pointed out.

'There, you see,' Hakon said triumphantly, 'you are coming round to the idea already.'

'I am not,' Brann objected. 'Yes I think she is the most gorgeous girl that ever walked this world. There, I have admitted it. But I hardly know her. And I am unlikely to ever know her when I get so nervous every time I see her that I can barely speak a word of sense.'

'No change from normal there, then,' Hakon pointed out helpfully.

'And I am terrified of your father,' Brann said, ignoring him. 'He is huge, he is loud, and when he rescued us, he did not even, well...' He tailed off, realising that what he was about to say would be hurtful.

'He did not even acknowledge me?' Hakon finished for him. 'Or look relieved that I was alive? Or ask about me? It is all right, do not look so shocked. It is all an act – everyone knows it is, but he is scared witless at the thought that anyone would think that he is showing me any sort of favouritism, and this is the way that he decided that he would handle things.' He leant forward conspiratorially. 'He is actually quite a softy really. In fact, Valdis said he cried twice at home this week: once when news came through of my capture, and again when he brought me home again safely.' He grinned. 'But do not dare tell anyone that, or I will have to kill you and the person you spoke to in order to protect the family name.'

'Seems fair to me,' Brann observed, and they laughed, falling into easy banter as they ate. While they did so, Brann mused over the speed at which Hakon's personality had changed from the withdrawn boy badly affected by the experience of his capture – and who would not be? – to this easy-going, light-hearted boy before him, with a nature that put Brann instantly at ease. Perhaps his rapid recovery was due to a harder day-to-day life here than the one Brann had left behind; the ache deep within him from all he had endured – particularly the deaths of his family and the brutal murder of his brother in front of him – never abated: he had merely become used to the pain being there as a constant companion that, unheralded, violently erupts then recedes to its simmering constancy. Although Hakon's experience had been only a few days compared with the weeks – with no end in prospect – that Brann was enduring, and while the alien experiences he had faced were fewer in number than those that Brann had encountered and continued to do so, what he had gone through had been horrifying almost beyond belief. And it had been at the hands of the most terrifying form of humankind that surely existed; whereas, Brann admitted, he had – with the exception of the Boar episode – been treated unexpectedly well considering his new status as a slave. He wondered at the resilience of the boy facing him, who could return to normality after only one night's – and a morning's – sleep. But, then again, he had returned home, to his normal life... and to his family. Again, the ache swelled up.

361

Valdis breezed back into the room, and Brann's attention, split between Hakon's chatter and his reverie, instantly found a new object.

'Sorry, boys,' she chimed, sweeping across the kitchen with a pail brimming with water. 'But your time of sloth is over. Your respective lords require your presence.'

Brann groaned and Hakon spoke for both of them. 'Is there no respite? Duty is a merciless beast of hell.'

'A touch over the top,' Valdis observed, assembling vegetables before her. 'But you would have had to leave in any case: the real workers around here are needing the kitchen now.' She paused and fixed Hakon with a twinkling gaze. 'Mother will be here any moment.'

Hakon leapt to his feet with vigour. 'Come, Brann, our wonderful duty calls,' he proclaimed enthusiastically.

Brann gathered the remnants of their meal into a neat pile. 'It seems the wrath of our respective lords is nothing compared with the prospect of a certain lady,' he observed.

Hakon fixed him with a baleful eye. 'Do make light of it. If you would rather learn the hard way whether to fear the men or the women in our family, feel free to linger here.'

Brann got hurriedly to his feet. 'I think I will decline that lesson,' he acceded, brushing crumbs from his tunic. He paused in the doorway. 'Thank you,' he said to the girl.

'For the meal?' she asked coquettishly.

'For everything since last night,' he said, awkwardly and shyly.

'But you do not know if I told you all that I did for you last night,' she smiled innocently, then laughed at the colour and horror that exploded in Brann's face as he fled the scene.

By the time Hakon had directed him to Einarr's quarters, the flush had faded from his face. In fact, colour had fled his cheeks altogether as he remembered that there was a good chance that he was about to face a lord who was furious about the events of the past few days.

Einarr's barked response to his timid knock did not bode well; neither did the stern expression that met him when he entered.

The tall man, clad as ever in black, noted the boy's pale complexion.

'Feeling nervous?' he said. Brann saw no advantage in denying it, and nodded. 'Well you might be. As a page, to leave your lord's service for days, without permission, is about as serious an offence as you could commit. As a slave, you were risking even more dire sanctions.'

He paused. 'Fortunately for you, Konall has claimed that you only left with him under protest after he ordered you to do so, although I have my doubts. In any case, as a noble and the heir to the title, he has the authority to do so, irrespective as to whether he was right or wrong in using that authority.

'The end result is that you are off the hook. As for my cousin, it is for his father to decide. However, the information you brought back is invaluable, and the possible blow to the morale of these people, both through the fact that we now know the location of one of their settlements and the ignominy of captives being rescued from under their noses, not the mention the wiping out of a fairly substantial band of mercenaries, is also an immense boon. Best of all, we are on to Loku and, even better, it is almost certain that he does not know that. Which will make things interesting. So, all that considered, the advantages are such that I would expect Lord Ragnarr to be more pleased than displeased with his son.'

He stood and moved to the window, gazing across the rooftops to the harbour beyond. 'The boy has certainly enhanced his reputation among the warriors he will one day lead. And,' he brought his dark eyes to bear on Brann, 'I must say he speaks highly of your abilities. Which is no faint praise from one such as Konall.'

'I have noticed,' Brann agreed. 'Though I think he has improved over the last few days.'

Einarr was unable to totally hide his amusement. 'That depends on how you define "better". Anyway, if half of what Konall relates is true, you have a talent. Where did you learn to fight?'

'Nowhere. It is not something we ever did in our village.' He noticed something, quickly masked, flit across Einarr's eyes. Guilt? Regret? Sympathy? He had no way of knowing. He shrugged. 'I just did what seemed right at the time. Most times I did not even know what I was doing until after I had done it.'

'You have a talent,' Einarr confirmed, 'whether you like it or not. But do not be disparaging about it – it may save your life.' He reflected for a moment. 'It already has, several times on your little trip, so I hear. And do not forget the incident with Boar.'

Brann shifted uncomfortably. 'That was not necessarily me.'

Einarr barked a laugh. 'Do not put on that act. You are not in trouble. And it is fairly pointless anyway, since I saw the whole episode as I ran to try to stop what everyone thought would be your certain death.'

Brann was stunned. 'You saw it all? Then why was I not executed? Why have I not been punished?'

The Captain returned to his vigil at the window. 'We are a different people to yours. Among us, such incidents are not uncommon. Those who are smart learn from the mistakes of others. Those who are not so smart are usually not around long enough to pass on that characteristic to

364

future generations.' He sighed. 'It may seem brutal to you, but that is the way here. So it did not seem harsh to me – it was just the way of things. It is a hard life here, and it needs hard men. And, from the news you brought back, it looks like it will get harder still. So, go now. I have sent the ship out for a couple of days of rowing practice – the men were getting soft, and needed the exercise. I have no real need of you at the moment, so take the opportunity to recuperate. I presume you may find some diversion or other in the kitchen.'

Brann blushed, and Einarr laughed. There seemed to be a recurring theme developing, Brann thought ruefully. He decided, wisely, against replying – embarrassment was freezing his thoughts, in any case – and, as Einarr held the door open for him, he left the room in silence, much to the Captain's increasing amusement.

He walked slowly along the passage, wondering where he should go. He knew where he *wanted* to go, and eventually his desire overwhelmed his nerves and he tentatively made his way down the stairs towards the kitchen. The hubbub as he approached, however, raised doubts as to whether he would be welcome there, and the maelstrom of activity that greeted his eyes when he peeked around the corner into the room confirmed his suspicions. He waited long enough to catch a glimpse of Valdis before, breath catching in his throat, he retreated unseen back to his room. He felt alone. The fact that he did not belong in this place made him feel nervous about venturing abroad in the town and, more than at any other time since he had been snatched from his home, he had a deep aching sense of the vast distance between him and all that he had previously known.

One of the shutters that opened inwards to the room had swung partially closed, and he moved to push it flat against the wall, retaining it with a small hook. He leant on the sill, fiddling absently with a small, loose fragment of stone before flicking it idly over the edge. As he watched it fall, his gaze fell upon the afternoon bustle of the town.

'If I am going to be bored and lonely,' he thought, 'I might as well be down there with something to look at rather than up here brooding.'

He made his way downstairs and, after fewer attempts than he had anticipated, found the main doors leading to the outside world. Once in among the townsfolk he felt as lonely as ever – even lonelier, if truth be told, as he seemed to be the only one who did not know everybody else. He meandered awkwardly through the crowds of traders offering goods, potential buyers examining everything from farm produce and clothing to weapons and utensils, and warriors moving purposefully but with the relaxed look of those comfortable in their hometown. Here and there, people had stopped to chat and, as he waited for a chance to pass one such group, he felt a rough shove on his shoulder.

'Out of my way, peasant,' a cold voice snapped. He looked around in time to see Konall brusquely pushing past him. 'How dare you sully my path with your inferior existence,' the young noble added for good measure.

Such was Brann's feeling of uneasiness, it took him a moment for him to realise that it had been one of Konall's attempts at humour.

'Just laugh and encourage him,' Hakon said, moving beside him.

Feeling relief flood over him at encountering familiar faces, Brann fell into step with Hakon as far as the crowds would allow. 'I expect he is finding it a little awkward to be funny after so many humourless years,' he suggested.

Hakon grinned. 'That is not all he is feeling awkward about. Look at him. Do you know what is different?'

Brann shrugged. 'Well, he is not exactly skipping along, humming a jaunty tune. How would I know what has changed?'

'Of course, of course,' Hakon accepted. 'I keep forgetting you only arrived so recently. Well, previously when Konall ventured forth among the people of the town, his desire for privacy meant that he dressed in a long cloak with a deep hood to hide his face. Everyone knew it was him, of course, but they all went along with it to keep him happy – or at least,' he corrected himself, 'so as not to upset him. Now, since his little jaunt with you,' Brann noted yet again the local penchant for trivialising danger, 'he is a changed boy. He is not exactly a court jester, but this is Konall we are talking about. Other than issuing commands, he spoke to me twice today, which – believe me – is unheard of, and now this: venturing forth among the little people with his identity in full view!'

Brann laughed. 'Do not talk about "little people". I am less than average height in my homeland, but here I feel like a small child. I have had nothing but strange and curious looks about my lack of inches since I came down here.'

'Worry not, Stumpy,' Hakon grinned. 'It is not strange and curious looks that my sister gives you – at least not in this sense.' Brann treated him to a hefty dig of his elbow. 'Anyway, you are not liable to be attracting any attention now that the great unhooded one has appeared. The trouble is, he wants to do it, but feels awkward about it. And the people around him do not know how to react. Should they approach him, or is it not etiquette to do so unsolicited? Or should they act as if it is all perfectly normal, although would

367

that be considered just as rude, as if they were ignoring the heir to the title? It is all incredibly entertaining.'

They had reached a market square, and a ripple of excitement was spreading through the throng. Surely, Brann wondered, Konall's appearance was not as startling as that. They caught up with the tall boy, who had stopped a merchant to ask the cause of the excitement. The startled man was being dismissed by Konall as they reached him.

'There is a boat docking,' the noble boy said. 'They do not know yet what sort of goods it is bearing, but new wares always lift spirits.'

Brann shrugged. 'I suppose we will just have to wait and see.'

'Not me,' Konall said. He turned abruptly towards the house nearest to them and strode up to the man standing in the doorway. 'Do you mind if I use your roof?' he asked the astonished householder.

Eyes wide, the man stammered, 'Of course not, Lord Konall.'

The tall boy disappeared into the building, only to reappear in a rush not long afterwards. His expression purposeful, he said, 'It is no trader. That ship bears Sigurr's crest. I would say that our leisure time is over, boys.'

They walked fast back to Ragnarr's hall but, before they had travelled far, a messenger raced past. Quickening the pace, forcing Brann to break into a trot, Konall said, 'I presume we will all be needed in our various capacities, so it would be wise to be there as soon after the messenger delivers the news as possible.'

They reached the hall at speed, Brann breathing more heavily than the other two, he noticed with irritation – he knew they were extremely fit and he was not; he just didn't like being reminded of it – and went their separate ways:

Konall, followed by Hakon, to find his father and Brann to Einarr's quarters.

He knocked on the Captain's door and was immediately called inside. Stripped to the waist, showing the lean, tautly muscled torso of a seasoned warrior, Einarr was splashing water over himself.

Without looking round, he said, 'Get yourself freshened up. Make sure you look tidy and be back here in five minutes.'

Brann left the room without a word, hurrying to make sure he did so in the allotted time. From Einarr's tone, he was sure that lateness would not meet with the same relaxed reaction he had enjoyed earlier in the day.

He reached his room just as Valdis emerged from the doorway. Startled, they both jumped. Just for a moment, the girl's composure deserted her and she flushed, eyes wide and slightly biting her lower lip. It was, however, just for a moment. She brushed her hands down the front of her dress to make sure it was sitting properly and, by the time she looked back up, she was as assured as ever. Brann was impressed. He knew that he was still blushing furiously – and the knowledge made him blush even more.

Valdis curtsied flamboyantly. 'I took the liberty of leaving fresh water and a clean tunic for you, young sir,' she said demurely. 'We have to ensure that you are looking your most handsome for the warlord's arrival.'

Brann was torn between the consequences of being late for Einarr and snatching a few extra moments with Valdis. She smiled, and he forgot Einarr. 'Well, what are you waiting for? Are you wanting me to wash you as well?' she asked wickedly.

Before he could stop himself, Brann said, 'That would be nice,' with more hope in his tone than he had meant.

She laughed, and it was the most appealing sound that he had ever heard. 'I am sure it would, you cheeky boy,' she admonished him, turning him to face the doorway and propelling him forwards with a gentle slap on the seat of his breeches, 'but you will just have to manage yourself. And you had better hurry: I do not suppose that Lord Einarr will be too happy to have to wait for you this time.'

The thought snapped Brann from his stupor and he hurried to get ready, as Valdis turned pertly and tripped down the corridor. Her voice echoed behind her, 'That would be nice!' She laughed again.

Brann forced himself to concentrate and washed hurriedly. He pulled the tunic, a smart cream-coloured garment, over his head and buckled his belt around him as he ran from the room. Composing himself outside Einarr's door, he checked his appearance, knocked and entered on the Captain's summons. Einarr, now fully clothed in his customary black but with every garment freshly laundered, looked up from pulling on his boots. He nodded in approval. 'Very smart,' he smiled. 'I can see that it helps to have influential friends looking after you.'

Brann flushed. Again. He seemed to be doing little else these days. 'I am sure any other guest would be treated with the same level of hospitality,' he suggested.

'Oh, I am sure of that, too,' Einarr replied, sounding anything but. 'Right,' he said decisively, standing up. 'A-courting we will go – but in the sense of attending the lord's court, not the way you would interpret it, I hear.'

Brann groaned. He could see that there was going to be no respite over this, wherever he turned. Einarr smiled. 'Get used to it, boy. Households like this thrive on gossip. And I am sure it is one of the more pleasant things you will have to become accustomed to at this point in your life.'

Brann had to admit that it was a fair point. And he was starting to get used to it. And, if truth be told, he was even beginning to enjoy it. But he still could not prevent himself from blushing again.

Starting from his chambers, Einarr grabbed his sword-belt on the way and strapped it on in an action that was almost identical to Brann's exit from his own room – except that Brann's belt had been devoid of weapons, those that he had used on the mission to rescue the captives having disappeared overnight.

'This is what you will do,' Einarr said with efficient urgency as Brann trailed behind the fast-striding warrior. 'Nothing. As before, absolutely nothing. Unless you are spoken to, of course, but then that is obvious.' His words, though not his movement, paused as a thought struck him. 'Actually, they may want to talk to you. You and Konall are the only two people to have survived so much contact with these savages. Konall told us as much as he knows this morning,' (*Trust him to be up early as normal*, Brann thought to himself) 'but my father and uncle may want to determine if there is anything additional that you may be able to supply.' They had reached a stairway at the rear of the building and began to wind their way downward. 'If you happen to be asked about anything, keep your answers concise, and do not embellish them – these are men who have weighty matters to consider and little time to do so. The lives of many depend on their decisions and they do not suffer fools or time-wasters gladly.'

They had reached a small room. It appeared to be some sort of antechamber, but Einarr was talking so rapidly (and engendering such a state of nervousness in him) that Brann found it hard to examine his surroundings as well as concentrate on the words.

The Captain paused before a closed door that almost contained the rumble of deep voices within the room beyond. 'Mostly, however,' Einarr continued, 'you will stand, unmoving and unspeaking. Pages are, by and large, a decoration. Their function as a page is more to learn than to be of any great use to the noble during their service – the lord will reap the benefit in later years when he has men around him who understand the working and the complexities of ruling the land about him.' He smiled. 'Although it is also handy to have someone around to handle some of the tasks considered too menial for those fortunate enough to have been higher-born. But, as I said, you are mainly cosmetic. Remember that: this is a serious business and, over the last week, it has quickly become far more serious than even it was before.'

He opened the door towards him to reveal a heavy crimson curtain. 'Now,' he murmured, 'if I have timed this just right...'

He slipped through a gap in the material and Brann followed him, emerging at the rear of Ragnarr's hall to one side of the lord's seat of office – currently occupied by the man in question. Einarr slipped into position to Ragnarr's left; Konall was already there and was, as the heir to the title, on his father's right. Brann noticed Hakon standing discreetly behind Konall and moved quickly to the equivalent position behind Einarr – just as the giant doors were slammed open. Einarr had indeed timed it perfectly. Brann was not surprised.

Ulfar burst in, in what was, presumably, the only way he knew how. He began to announce the new arrival but was cut off by a tall man who strode past him with purpose and calm assurance. Even had he not already been expecting him, Brann would have needed no explanation of his identity. If Einarr bore a striking resemblance to his uncle, the similarity to his father was stronger still: the man who entered *was* Einarr, but an older version, his dark hair and beard flecked with grey and his face lined by passing years and hard decisions. His eyes were different – piercing blue where Einarr's were dark and unfathomable brown – but otherwise he had the same lean features, broad shoulders and narrow waist, the same fluidity and grace of movement and the same impression of contained and controlled strength: a born and trained warrior or athlete or, more probably, both.

'Apologies, Ulfar,' he said, his tone resonant and with an easy undercurrent of authority. 'I do not mean to be rude, but we have little time and so ceremony is not a luxury we can afford at the moment, especially among family.' Ulfar bowed his huge head in silent, but eloquent, agreement. 'Is that not so, little brother?'

Ragnarr stepped forward from his seat, a massive grin gleaming from the midst of his shaggy beard. 'It is ever so, dark times or not, *big* brother,' he boomed, enveloping the warlord in a sweeping embrace. He stood a full head taller and was half again as broad as Sigurr but clearly still looked up to his older brother. When Sigurr was released amid much back-slapping and laughter on both their parts, his gaze turned to Einarr. No words passed between but, as father's and son's eyes locked, Brann witnessed a softening, just for a moment, of the authoritative eyes and an almost imperceptible nod from Einarr, and felt the emotion of the moment sweep over him. Then Sigurr's expression resumed its veneer of control and he barked, 'We must talk at once. Shall we retire to your quarters, Ragnarr, or have you somewhere else in mind?'

Ragnarr, his arm draped around his brother's shoulders as if reluctant to let him go, led him from the room, saying,

'I have already taken the liberty of having a light snack laid out in my chambers, and it would be a travesty to waste such good food – and risk the wrath of Ulfar's good lady wife – by meeting elsewhere.'

Sigurr laughed. 'You do not change, do you, brother? And thank the gods for that. It has been far too long since I visited you last: the effects on your family are the parts of the job that they never mention to you when you are growing up.' He laughed again. 'And if you still have the same opinion of what constitutes a "light snack", then we may as well invite the whole town to help with the leftovers.'

'Oh, I would not worry about there being any leftovers,' Ragnarr assured him sincerely.

Einarr and Konall followed them. Brann was unsure whether he was invited also, but an eloquent jerk of Hakon's head was instruction enough and they fell in at the rear along with Ragnarr's page, a surly-looking brown-haired boy, shorter (by local standards) and stockier than Hakon, and Sigurr's page, who appeared around two years younger than the rest of them and who seemed overwhelmed by the whole experience.

They reached Ragnarr's rooms and Sigurr turned at the door. 'You pages will remain initially on this side of the door. Do not wander off.' None of them would have dared contemplate otherwise.

The door closed solidly. 'Well,' Hakon said lightly. 'Serious business, then.'

Ragnarr's page, his brows seemingly permanently set in a glower, sneered at him. 'Why, you are a clever boy today,' he snarled sarcastically.

Hakon pointedly ignored his presence while responding to his comment. 'Please excuse Olvir,' he said to the two other boys. 'Manners and good cheer are not among his strengths.'

Olvir bridled, his colour and voice rising together. 'Whatever my strengths and weaknesses, at least I would not surrender like a timid puppy to a rag-tag band of savages.'

Hakon turned slowly, his eyes cold and hard. 'If you had even half a brain,' he said quietly and slowly, clearly barely keeping his fury in check, 'you would know better than to pass judgement when you have few, if any, of the facts. You would do well to remember that four fine and respected warriors lost their lives at the hands of that "rag-tag band of savages". Their memories deserve to be treated with honour, not associated with the ill-judged insults of an ignorant boy.'

Brann felt on edge. The argument had, very quickly, started down a steep track with no room to manoeuvre – neither of the boys could turn back now, and their words were careering ever more out of control.

Olvir flushed, and snorted disdainfully. Brann groaned inwardly. The sound was so replete with derision that he knew that the boy was about to say something that would push Hakon's already straining self-control beyond its limits. He knew it, but he was powerless to stop it, aware that an interfering foreigner would only make the situation even worse.

'Honour?' Olvir spat. 'They were bested by gutter scum. The only recognition they deserve is to be ridiculed as a lesson to children who would learn their craft properly.'

Brann's assessment had been accurate. Hakon's punch lifted Olvir clear off the ground. He landed in an untidy and unconscious heap in the middle of the corridor, just as Konall opened the door behind them.

The pages froze. Without any show of surprise, the young noble took in the scene before him.

'Guard!' he called, and a large, heavily armed warrior strode from his post at the end of the passage. Konall nodded at Olvir. 'Lord Ragnarr's page would seem to have suffered a nasty fall.'

Impassively, the guard nodded. 'That was my understanding of the incident, my lord. I am only surprised it took so long for him to suffer it.'

'Good,' Konall said, broadly indicating that he had heard enough of the argument to understand the truth of the matter. 'Take him away and acquaint him with a bucket of water. When he comes to, bring him back here. He will not have time to dry off. And advise him that I would rather he refrained from conversation for the remainder of his time outside this door.'

Without a word, the warrior hoisted Olvir unceremoniously over his shoulder and ambled down the corridor. Konall glanced at Hakon's swelling knuckles. 'You seem to have banged your hand trying to break his fall. Ask your sister for some ice and come straight back here. You are less use to me if your right hand stiffens up.' The incident was now officially closed. He looked at Brann. 'It is fortunate that *you* managed not to incur any injuries in the short time you were out here, as you are required by their lords.'

He stepped back into the room and Brann, after shooting a look of surprise towards Hakon – one that was mirrored by the other boy – followed him. The scene that greeted him was similar to the last time he had been in this room; this time, however, he would not be a silent onlooker, but would be involved in the proceedings. Konall stood to one side and Brann faltered as he felt the full force of becoming the focus of the attention of three such powerful men.

'Come along, boy,' Ragnarr barked. 'No need to dawdle: we will not eat you.' The reassurance did nothing to calm his nerves. If anything, the huge man's thunderous tones compounded them. Fortunately, he gained a moment's respite as Ragnarr turned his attention to his son. 'What took you so long to bring him in? Was there a problem?'

'Nothing of note, father. Merely an unfortunate slip that requires no more medical attention than some cold water.'

'Really?' Sigurr's measured tone cut in. 'I could have sworn that I heard the sound of knuckle on bone. And a rather hefty sound at that.'

Konall shrugged again, an eloquent gesture of inconsequence. 'It is amazing how sometimes things can sound just like a punch.'

Sigurr's gaze swept round to Brann, filling him with even more nerves, something he had not hitherto thought possible. 'And what would you say, young foreigner? Is that true?'

Brann felt the world closing in around him and wished he could just vanish from the room. 'I would say...' he stammered. What would he say? Konall could maybe get away with lying to the lords because of his position but, if they already knew the truth, how would they view anything but the truth from a page who meant nothing to them, no matter how well-intentioned he may be? He coughed, clearing his throat to buy time. 'I would say... that it is true.' He took a deep breath to try to stop the shaking in his voice. 'It is true that sometimes things can sound just like a punch.'

All three lords around the fire erupted into laughter. Konall shot an approving glance in his direction, and nodded almost imperceptibly.

'Well said, youngster. Well said!' Ragnarr boomed, guffawing still.

Sigurr, however, had already recovered himself. 'Very good,' he agreed. 'But I am afraid we are not here to test your skills of diplomacy, however amusing the experience may be. We would hear your account of the events of the past few days, from the moment the bandits first struck the hunting party. Konall has already described it to us, but we want you to talk as if yours is the first account we have heard. Leave nothing out.'

Brann cleared his throat once more, and started. As he continued, the attention that the three paid to his words encouraged him, and the nerves began to recede as he found himself falling into the flow of the story. The men listened in silence, Sigurr moving only once to stand at the fire – surprisingly closely – and stare at the flames as he concentrated on Brann's words.

He came to the end, when Ulfar had saved them from the mercenaries, more suddenly than he had expected and stopped abruptly. His audience were less surprised, however, and immediately started firing questions at him, covering everything from the layout of the settlement to the route they took to get there, and his estimate of the number of mercenaries for whom the village had provided residence, to his assessment of the type of people that the bandits were. They spent considerable time on Loku's overheard conversation, asking question after question, urging him to try to remember every word precisely.

At one point, Brann looked across to Konall for confirmation. Einarr stopped him. 'Just answer from your own memories. In fraught situations such as you experienced, it is easy to become confused about the details around you as you concentrate on the matter in hand, which is usually dominated by deciding what you have to do just to survive. Konall has already been asked much the same questions as you. We are looking for as many parts as possible that tally between both accounts: these, we will know, are most probably accurate.'

They continued for over an hour and, by the time Sigurr called a halt to the proceedings, Brann was pale again, but this time from exhaustion rather than nerves.

Without standing on ceremony, Einarr poured some water and brought it to him. 'I would give you mead, but I am afraid that, in your condition, it may not have the desired effect.'

Brann took two sips, then enjoying it too much – and not wanting to delay his departure from the room any more than necessary – he downed the rest.

As he finished, Sigurr, who had resumed his seat some time ago, raised his chin from the knuckles that had supported it as he had considered each reply that Brann had given.

'Thank you,' he said. He had the same considered deliberation behind each word as his son but, where Einarr seemed to lighten up on occasion, or show emotion unexpectedly, the warlord seemed constantly in control and constantly serious. The effect of responsibility in such a land, Brann surmised. And, anyway, why would he be in any way otherwise with a lowly page?

'You have been extremely helpful.' Brann thought that he would hardly have dared to be any other way. 'We will now consider Konall's page's impression of his experience, so send him in as you leave. You are free to go now. Be thankful that you are not of the nobility: Konall is not only a source of information here; for him, it is also a part of his training, so he will be here as long as we are. Make the most of your chance to eat and rest.'

Brann smiled a tired smile. 'I am often thankful I am not a noble, my lord. It seems a far more simple life to take orders than to give them.'

'That depends on who is giving them to you,' Sigurr warned him. 'But, in most ways, you are right. Go now, and take my page with you. We will have no need of him and he has endured a hurried journey.' Brann started to leave, but the warlord stopped him. 'One more thing, boy. You skimmed over the finer detail of the incidents of fighting. Konall, however, was more forthcoming. It seems you acquitted yourself well, both before and during these incidents, especially for a foreigner who has no need to care about our affairs here, and an untried miller's son, inexperienced in combat, at that. That counts for much around here – the attitude even more than the ability. I suspect that we will have to keep an eye on you. And that Einarr should nurture you carefully.' Brann glanced at Einarr, but the Captain's expression was a study of neutrality despite the irony of a slave being described in such terms. 'Well done,' Sigurr concluded in a tone that left him in no doubt that the conversation was over.

Dismissed, Brann headed for the door for a second time. Under other circumstances, he would have more of a spring in his step after such praise, but he felt as if he had been mentally drained as much in the past hour or so as he had been during the events he had been describing. That was a nonsense, of course, but he was surprised at how much it had taken out of him.

He opened the door and beckoned Hakon inside. As the boy passed him, Brann absently plucked the sodden cloth, which had previously held the bundle of roughly hacked ice, from his hand. 'You probably do not want to draw attention to that,' he murmured.

Hakon smiled, nodded and wiped his hand dry on the back of his tunic as he continued walking. Brann offered the still-cold cloth to Olvir – after all, his jaw was swelling rapidly

– but the glare he received in reply indicated that Ragnarr's page was treating the gesture as an attempt at mockery. Brann decided against pushing the matter, and turned to Sigurr's page, informing him of his release from duties.

'What about me?' Olvir asked shortly.

'They never said,' Brann answered, equally curtly, turning his back on the boy and leading the young page down the passageway. He was not rude by nature – on the contrary, he usually went out of his way to avoid any unpleasantness – and he knew that, especially in a foreign land and in unfamiliar surroundings, it was unwise to develop enemies. But he was finding it extremely hard to be pleasant to Olvir, thanks to the boy's manner and compounded by his fatigue and the after-effects of the week's activities, along with his constant resentment at being separated from his home and losing his family. In short, after all that he had endured, he just could not be bothered being nice to such an unpleasant oaf.

And, he smiled to himself, he was glad that Olvir had refused the wet cloth – he would much prefer the chance to return it to the girl who had supplied it to Hakon in the first place.

At the thought, his step did lighten at last and he began to chat to Sigurr's page as he took him to the kitchen. The boy was still over-awed by his experience, however – not least Hakon's response to Olvir's provocation – and all that he could extract from the boy by the time they approached the kitchen was that his name was Erlandr.

He enjoyed even less success in returning the cloth to his intended recipient. Valdis was conspicuously absent. It transpired that she had been sent on an errand before being allowed to head home for the day, following the late hours she had been needed to work the previous night, but Brann was uninterested in the details: the simple fact of her absence was all that mattered. In no mood for conversation – the thought of Valdis's company had been all that had provided him with any momentum – he left Erlandr to the tender mercies of the kitchen staff, who had already declared the small boy with the dark hair, darker eyes and heart-shaped face to be unbearably cute. They seemed to find his shyness an added attraction and were fussing around him with delight, so Brann felt he was leaving him in good company as he took a selection of food and his leave, and headed for his room.

Feeling ridiculous that he was so tired despite such a late rise – in his village and on the ship alike, he had been accustomed to rising at dawn – he ate his food more out of a sense of necessity than desire. With such a lack of enthusiasm, it was hardly surprising that he became bored with eating fairly quickly and settled back to doze and reflect on recent events. There was not much of a chance for reflection, however, as within minutes he had slipped into a deep sleep. He did waken at dawn the next day, however. Or, at least, was wakened. With no attempt at courtesy – in fact, without even a knock – Hakon burst into his room with all the enthusiastic excitement of a dog let out for its exercise.

'Get up, get up, get up,' he cried. 'The sun is out, the sea is calm – and we are off to Yngvarrsharn.'

Chapter 11

He stared at it, as ever transfixed.

He had to force himself to reach out, to touch it. Not that it held a mystical magic. Rather its difference held the attention. The way that it broke the rules for its kind. Its otherworldliness.

Where others had a blade that curved as the crescent moon, this was straight, double-edged, tapering at its tip to a needle-point; raised in a slight bevel along its length to stop flesh and sinew clinging to it as it was withdrawn for use again; the hilt, unadorned by jewel or wire of gold or silver, but merely wrapped in soft leather, tooled to afford a grip that would not slip, rather than wrought with ornamentation to draw admiration; a crosspiece, if it could be described as such, with no ostentatious turns or flourishes, but merely enough of a block to prevent the hand from inadvertently sliding onto the blade.

And that was a blade you would not wish to slide your hand along. He pulled a stray hair from his gown, a hair whiter than he cared to contemplate. Holding the hair's end, he drifted it down against the edge of the blade held across in front of his tired eyes; the weapon was held just as easily as the hair, its bewildering lightness and perfect

*balance allowing one finger and thumb to perform the task;
eyes that had seen so many wonders watched in awe as the
hair parted, its unheld half drifting floorward in the firelight.
Firelight that should have been reflected by the blade with
brilliance; would have done on any other blade, the shining
silver dazzling. But this was no shining silver. Obsidian black,
with a dull gleam that seemed to absorb light, that seemed to
hold the eye with fascination: this was the otherworldliness.
Never had he seen its like. Never had anyone seen the like.*

*Nor would anyone, for now. With reverence, he laid it in
its box, the black velvet fitting snugly around it, the wooden
lid snapping shut. The box slid perfectly back into the alcove
created for it in the side of the fireplace, and the brick fitted
perfectly once again into the gap, showing no sign that it
had ever been moved.*

*It was no ornament; it was a weapon. A weapon with
purpose. And its purpose would come.*

****

Brann lifted his right hand away from the oar to wipe the
smattering of spray from his face; strangely, he found it
refreshing rather than irritating. Perhaps even more strangely,
he had felt a sense of relief at returning to his position at
the oar. What had seemed agonisingly unfamiliar not so long
ago was, in comparison to the events of the past week, now
a haven of normality.

'Keep that hand on the oar,' Gerens snapped in mock anger.
'You are not a pampered page now, you know.'

'Do not worry,' Brann grinned, 'I will pull my weight.'

His companion grunted, squatting beside him just out of
the way of the oar's movement as he massaged his bandaged

hand. 'Considering your lack of size, that is not the most encouraging offer of help we could have had.'

'It is all right for you,' Brann countered. 'Poor Gerens is excused rowing duties because he has a sore finger. I am still trying to work the stiffness out of my muscles.'

'He will not get away with that excuse, will he Grakk? You have all your fingers but managed to swan about with the nobility when you could have been reacquainting yourself with decent hard work. Although if they had seen you row, perhaps they would have realised that it would not have made much difference whether you were here or not.'

Cannick had wandered down the aisle, as he had a habit of doing on a regular basis. 'If you can talk, you are not working hard enough,' he growled. 'Cut the chat.'

Accustomed by now to the grizzled warrior's ways, they waited until he had moved back out of earshot before resuming their conversation.

'There is one thing I do not understand, though,' Gerens mused. 'The folk around here do not seem to have slaves. In fact, you must have seen the reaction to the Captain being involved in that trade, and we have certainly found them to be awkward around us, as if they do not know how to react to slaves.' He flicked his head towards Sigurr's ship, which was leading the way, an arrowshot ahead of them. 'So if that is the case, who is rowing that ship, then?'

Brann let out a mock-triumphant laugh. 'At last!' he said joyously. 'There is something I can explain to you!' He paused and leant towards Gerens conspiratorially, speaking in a low voice from the corner of his mouth. 'Actually, Hakon explained it to me before we left, but please do not spoil my knowledgeable image in front of the others – it does not happen very often.'

The large rower in front of them glanced over his shoulder, and growled, 'Oh, for the sake of the gods, just tell him. Everyone else knows the answer anyway. Just tell him and shut up before your chatter becomes so irritating that you find yourself swimming home.' He grunted. 'A shrimp like you would not make a noticeable splash, anyway,' he added pointedly.

Brann smiled weakly. 'The men around here are always warriors first and foremost, but they seem to see themselves as being able to adapt to anything related to the sea – warriors, traders, raiders, fishermen and sailors. They would take it as an insult if you suggested that they needed someone to row for them, and anyway it would mean extra mouths to feed on any voyage. This ship we are on is from a different land, with different traditions, and the Captain "acquired it", and the galley slaves with it, at some point during his exile.'

He paused, catching his breath, realising that he may have revealed information that he should have kept to himself. Gerens's expression, and his nod for him to continue, let him know that some amount of information about Einarr's background seemed to have reached the slaves as well. 'It is much bigger,' he continued, 'a sort of cross between a warship and a merchant ship, with bigger oars and more to carry, so it needs rowers like us to handle certain situations. We need to be able to fight at sea (as we did against the pirates) but their ships, even Lord Sigurr's over there, are purely designed to transport warriors from one point to another as quickly and effectively as possible.'

Gerens nodded. 'I can see that. They have a shallow draught,' he noticed Brann's puzzled expression, 'which means they do not extend too far under the water. They can be run into quite shallow water, close to a beach and, more importantly, back out again fairly quickly and easily. And, being small and light, they would be able to out-run and out-manoeuvre any larger ships enough to stay out of their range.'

'From what I have seen of this lot,' Brann said, 'I am not sure that they would run. They have probably got a trick or two that they could use if someone was mad enough to take them on.'

'I would not be surprised,' Gerens said, nodding solemnly. 'Thank you for your explanation. Now I think we should cease our conversation before anyone objects.' Without further ado, he stood and wandered to the stern.

Brann agreed and was glad that he was unable to see the expression on the large rower's face in front. They spent the rest of the day in silence, alone with their thoughts, and – as his muscles became accustomed once more to the rhythm of the oars – Brann found his musings turning repeatedly to Valdis. He sighed. Nothing, he was sure, would come of it, but at least thoughts of the girl left him in a better humour than the morose brooding about home that usually occupied him at such times.

The wind picked up later, allowing the sails to be used and the rowers to be rested. When night fell, however, the wind did, too, and the slaves were called into action once more, as were the warriors in the ship in front, rowing through the hours of darkness as the ships pressed urgently forwards. The cool feel of the wind as it picked up again – and perfectly behind the vessels – shortly after dawn was as welcome to them as food to a starving man and within minutes of the sails billowing once more and the oars being stowed, the rowers were, to a man, sound asleep.

They were wakened as much by the rattle and clicking of the sails being put away as by Cannick's bellowed orders to make the oars ready once more. Brann rubbed the focus back into his eyes. 'How long have we slept?' he mumbled, adding a stretch to his repertoire.

Grakk pointed to the towering, shining walls of a fjord that they were turning towards. 'What matters more is where we are – it looks as if we are nearing our destination. And it looks like your services are required elsewhere, young page.' Cannick had approached with a replacement rower and Brann knew what was intended. The man had taken his place on the rowing bench as they had left Ravensrest while the pretence that Brann was Einarr's page continued. Cannick nodded to Brann and, as he was expecting the move, the switch was made quickly and without the need for words. Brann felt self-conscious as he was led, between the other rowers, to the rear of the ship, but these men had seen many things that were far more unusual in their time at sea and scarcely even glanced in his direction.

He was deposited in the Captain's cabin, where Einarr, busy with documents and maps that were spread across his desk, indicated a basin and a towel. As Brann approached him, he noticed the clothes he had worn in Ravensrest – and which he had swapped for coarser and harder-wearing garments on resuming his place among the rowers – laid out on one side.

He washed quickly and pulled on the clothes. As he was tugging his feet into his boots, Einarr swept the pages into a rough pile and pushed his chair back. 'My apologies for messing you about, boy,' he said, running his hands wearily through his hair, 'but image is important to some who may be watching us. The requirements of the situation dictate our actions, whether we like it or not.'

Brann shrugged. 'It may be a little confusing at times, but even a page has a better life than a galley slave, even if it is only for a short while.'

Einarr smiled, but it was more in sympathy than amusement or reassurance. 'Unfortunately, this situation we find ourselves in means you are involved more than you, or I, would like. Not only have you had experiences that make you useful, but you will, as a page, be entering a world of politics and intrigue that you have been given no preparation for.' He stood and, crossing the room, gripped Brann's shoulder and looked into his eyes. 'I do not mean to alarm you, but you need to be prepared. When I first made you my page, I expected to be paying a brief visit. Unfortunately, as you know, events have taken a dramatic turn that leaves us in a pretence that places more obligations on you than one in your position, with your background, should be expected to bear. But we cannot change that, so we must deal with it as best we can.'

He indicated a chair. 'Sit down and listen carefully.' He waited while Brann did so, then crossed to an open window at the rear of the cabin and stared out over the water as he continued. 'When I say that you will face intrigue, I do not mean that you will have to deal with it incessantly, dawn to dusk. But any politics you come across, no matter how seldom, will be more than you are used to. The trick is to find out who you can trust, and there will be few that fall into that category: Loku has taught us that. You probably could trust most people – it's just that you do not know which ones, so stay with the ones you know from Ravensrest – Konall and his page, basically – and, as far as the rest are concerned, just smile and be polite, and no more.'

He turned. 'What I am about to tell you, one in your position would not normally be privy to but, on this occasion, it is important that you have an idea of what we are doing so you do not react in the wrong way at an inopportune time. If Loku appears, we will not take any action against him.' The strength of the surprise on Brann's face caused him to smile slightly. 'Do not worry, we know what we are doing... we hope. As far as we know, Loku does not know that we have uncovered him: he has no idea that you overheard him at the settlement, and when he went to the pit, the slaves were gone and so did not see him. What is more, no member of the party pursuing you survived to say that you, and more importantly, Konall, were ever there. As far as he knows, the captives – including one that they thought was Konall – were confined to the pit before escaping and were fortunate enough to run into a patrol of our warriors. He will expect that we will destroy the settlement, so we have duly sent warriors to oblige – not that that was a hard decision to make, although I am sure that our men will have found it deserted when they got there. Loku will now have to play a dangerous game, for it is in the interests of whatever plans these fiends are laying that he continues his work among us.'

Brann blurted, 'But surely then, his work should be stopped.'

Einarr gave a single nod. 'That is one possibility. But we think that if we watch him and feed him the information that we want him to receive, then we can both discover more about him and subtly apply pressure in the hope that he will make a mistake. Ultimately, we want the person controlling him, and Loku is the only way we have of finding him.'

Brann nodded his understanding, and the Captain walked to the door. 'That is all you need to know just now. It is enough for you to deal with, anyway.' He opened the door. 'Now let us go and enjoy some fresh air and the view. We must be nearly there, now, anyway.'

They climbed to stand beside the helmsman. At first, Brann was transfixed by the sight of the rowers, facing him, smoothly going about their work. There was an almost hypnotic beauty in the synchronised rise and fall of the oars. It was an image that was lost on those actually carrying out the action, yet, having seen it from this aspect, Brann found himself feeling pride at having been – and, presumably, soon returning to being – a part of it. He was also feeling uneasy, and guilty, at standing apart from it while his fellow rowers sweated before him, and he tried not to meet the gaze of any of them, until he realised that not one of them had even been interested enough to cast a glance in his direction. Apart from one: Grakk, predictably, had caught his eye; totally unpredictably, he had stuck out his tongue. The gesture broke the spell and Brann looked around him – and was astonished at the breathtaking beauty he had been missing while he watched the rowers.

The fjord was narrower than the one that had led to Ravensrest – it had been more of a wide bay, whereas here, the sides of the cliff were sheer, shining almost blindingly in the sun. Their size, when added to the glassy flatness of the water and the deep blue of the cloudless sky, created a profound stillness that was almost overpowering. Another feeling began to overwhelm him. The size of the cliffs on either side, their proximity and their almost vertical gradient gave a sense of height and – more uncomfortably – of depth, a sensation increased by the dark stillness of the water. He had, he reminded himself, travelled over much greater depths of water when he crossed the sea than there was beneath him here, but that logic made no difference. His stomach churned and his legs felt weak. He moved to the side to grip the rail tightly – it felt better (slightly) to do something physical.

The Captain moved beside him. 'You feel the depth of the water? Do not worry: you are not the first, and you will not be the last. It cannot be explained, it just happens to some people.' He paused. 'I usually find it helps to look ahead, not up or down, much as you would do on a narrow mountain pass.'

Brann looked up in surprise. 'You feel it, too?'

Einarr nodded. 'Not as much now as when I was a child, but I have had many years since to become used to it. And I had to hide it more as it was around here that I learned to sail in a small boat. It would not have been the done thing for the warlord's son to show fear on the water in a nation of sailors.' He glanced up. 'If looking ahead does not work, try taking your mind off it with other things: look up, but not at the face of the cliffs. Look instead at their top, at the shapes they make against the sky – anything to make your mind wander. It is unlikely that you will ever be a helmsman or a lookout, so you have the advantage that you can do such things.'

Brann tried to take his advice, and soon found that something did catch his attention: small figures dotted here and there along the line where the rock walls met the sky. He was about to alert the Captain, when he noticed some of them waving down, with some of those on Sigurr's boat returning the greeting. His panic eased: if he had not felt so tense, he would have realised sooner that they were only sentries, rather than seeing danger at every turn.

The warriors on the cliffs were too distant to make out any details, but he was able to discern, on two occasions where the path became narrower, large catapults with what appeared to be – what must be – piles of boulders alongside them, ready for use. Any enemy vessel trying to reach Sigurr's stronghold would have a hard – if not impossible – task.

He had been so engrossed in looking up that he had failed to notice that, on rounding the last bend, they had brought their goal in sight.

He was surprised. He had expected the capital of the warlord's domain to be a spectacle of sprawling grandeur – a carpet of buildings of imposing design littered with cloud-touching towers and proud banners. Instead, it was merely a larger version of Ravensrest, except that, where Ragnarr's town had a docking area for ships and boats, with a steep path leading through itself, the fact that here the land rose in a shallower gradient and over a broader area meant that the buildings could extend right to the water's edge. The cliffs that had towered over them so imposingly during their passage up the fjord had, unnoticed by Brann, decreased slightly in height so that it was not too far inland before the ground rising from the dock area reached the level of the cliff tops. The town – for, disappointingly, Brann could not bring himself to describe it as a city, no matter how much he exercised his imagination – seemed to extend beyond this point, but how far into what he could only guess was a more level plateau was invisible from sea level. What he could make out, however, was that the town and, more importantly, the fortifications, extended back for a distance along the top of the cliffs on either side, like a dragon's armoured wings folded back alongside its body for protection. Obviously, Brann thought, it was imperative that no enemy should gain control of the cliff tops overlooking the town, from which they could, unthreatened, rain missiles upon the buildings below. Otherwise, it was built to the same design as Ravensrest, with the architecture and street plan making it a murderous place for any enemy to enter – and therefore making control of the cliff tops an even more significant factor.

Sigurr's boat had already come to rest against its allotted jetty, and Einarr made sure the helmsman had seen the signal from a warrior on the shore to indicate a berth for them. The ship glided towards the shore and the order was given for a single backstroke to slow their advance to perfection; it was an extremely difficult operation for so many rowers to co-ordinate, but they made it look calmly efficient. He had not even realised it existed as an order, and smiled slightly as he imagined Grakk and his experienced counterparts in the front benches having to school their young companions in an instant as to what was expected of them.

His amusement was interrupted by the Captain. 'There it is, boy,' he murmured, his voice a mixture of pride and excitement – or, at least, as much excitement as Brann had ever heard in him. 'Yngvarrsharn. In the old tongue of our people, it means "the Anchorage of Yngvarr", who was my ancestor who discovered this place, and who became the first warlord of this area. It is also known to some as "the Lair of the Wolf", after my family's emblem.' He shrugged. 'I suppose it sounds a bit silly to foreigners but my people always did enjoy their tendency towards the dramatic. Anyway, it is the oldest settlement in this part of the coast, although it has changed greatly since its early days as little more than a harbour, an inn and a hall, as you can see.' He glanced up at the cliffs. 'Whoever holds the advantage of the cliff tops, controls the harbour.' He smiled. 'There is a story that Yngvarr hurled a boulder from the edge of that cliff, just there,' he pointed to a part of the cliff top that jutted out just slightly, 'and crashed it clean through an approaching ship, from deck to hull. The boulder came to rest far down on the seabed – as did the ship and all aboard her, very soon afterwards. It is said that no unwelcome ship has ever tried to enter this harbour since.'

Brann was not sure what impressed him more: the ability to hurl a boulder at all, or the accuracy to hit a ship, no matter how big, from such a height. 'Is it true, the story?' he said in wonder.

Einarr smiled. 'Who knows? I would certainly like it to be. In any case, this is still a particularly dangerous place to invade from the sea, although these days we do not throw the rocks ourselves.'

Remembering the catapults that he had noticed earlier, Brann nodded and turned his attention back to the town ahead of them – or, rather, to the side of them as, with a soft bump that was testament to the skill of those the Captain had entrusted with the approach, the boat came to rest alongside a stone jetty. Einarr leapt ashore with barely concealed eagerness, and Brann scrambled to keep up, moving far less confidently in negotiating the small, but varying, gap between the boat and shore. He landed in an ungainly heap and picked himself up quickly, hoping – without much expectation – that it had passed unnoticed. Muted chuckles from within the ship told him that his lack of expectation had been well founded.

Feeling the blush burning his cheeks, he hurried after Einarr. He risked a quick glance at the ship as he ran alongside its length, and was greeted by a selection of grinning faces from the rowing bench. He smiled back sheepishly. At least they were amused, rather than mocking. They seemed, in general, to bear him no ill will for his double identity; it was almost as if they were willing on one of their own to succeed. This seemed to calm his nerves, which surprised him, considering he knew only a few of their number – perhaps he was beginning to feel as if he was representing them, which meant in turn that he was, after a matter of weeks, coming to think of himself as belonging among them. He was not sure that was a good thing but, if it helped him get through whatever lay ahead of him in as near to a sane state as he could manage, then he would seize upon it for now.

His ship having arrived ahead of the *Blue Dragon*, Sigurr was already, with his party, well ahead of them and Einarr was striding out in a walk that was only a fraction slower than an ignoble run, in an attempt to gain some ground on them before they reached the warlord's hall. The shorter-legged Brann was relieved that the lesser standing of a page allowed him to break into a trot, as he would have been unable to keep up otherwise.

They reached Sigurr's home and climbed to the main doors. The building had been constructed to exactly the same design as Ragnarr's, but bigger, to accommodate the greater number of people who would visit, work and live in the place. *Or, rather*, Brann mused as he climbed the steps up the front of the mound, *considering the age of this settlement, it was more likely that Ravensrest's hall had been built to the same design as this one, but on a smaller scale.*

It is amazing the pointless things you think about when you are tired, he thought. Einarr glanced at him and, perceptive as ever, said, 'You look exhausted. Just make one last effort to keep going for the short time that you will be needed before this day is over. It will not be long until dinner, which will probably be formal, worse luck.'

Brann glanced up in alarm. 'I do not know what to do at dinner. Do I stand behind you and serve you? How will I know the etiquette?'

Einarr slowed slightly, to allow himself to speak before they reached the guards at the top of the steps. 'Do not panic, boy,' he said quickly. 'We are not as grand as that here. On the odd occasion that we require our pages to be functional and actually get some use out of them, it is only where practicality necessitates it, nothing more. We are perfectly capable of feeding ourselves – too capable sometimes, if you look at my uncle's belly. You will be dismissed for dinner and, while we have the "pleasure",' his tone indicated that he anticipated it being anything but, 'of dining formally, you will retire to the kitchen as you did at Ragnarr's hall.' A slight smile played at one corner of his mouth. 'You never know, you may even find another nice kitchen maid to run after you.'

Even if Brann could have overcome his embarrassment enough to reply, he would have had no chance – Einarr had timed his teasing to coincide with their arrival at the doors. Deliberately, Brann was sure.

The guards at the entrance, each as huge as Brann had come to expect, astonishingly managed to show no sign of surprise at the sight of their lord's son striding purposefully towards them, despite his ten-year absence. Instead, they merely nodded respectfully and opened the doors for them, showing no sign of any opinion on whether his return boded well or ill for their lord and his people. Einarr nodded his thanks and, without slackening his pace, strode into the building. Brann noticed his face – it was set determinedly firm, betraying none of the myriad of emotions that must be churning within.

The layout inside appeared, from what little he could see, to follow the pattern set by the exterior: similar to the stronghold at Ravensrest, but bigger, with more corridors leading away from them and a greater sense of space around them. Either the designers of these buildings had little imagination or, more probably, Brann thought, they had evolved a practical and effective format.

Before he had any further opportunity to ponder the matter, they entered Sigurr's great hall. Its layout, as expected, was much the same as that of Ragnarr, but there was more evidence of history: ancient banners hung high on the walls, some so faded that their designs were virtually indiscernible. Those that were evident were mostly emblems relating to the wolf, a symbol that had endured through what seemed to be centuries of rule here, though its appearance varied from era to era. Other banners were emblazoned with a range of creatures, some real and some mythical, and were invariably spattered with, presumably, the long-dried blood of those from whose hands they had been prised. They could only be spoils of war, Brann guessed – and some looked uncomfortably fresh and bright. On the other hand, he mused, perhaps it was actually comforting: they were evidence that he was among people accustomed to winning. Scattered around the walls, between or below the banners, were a variety of weapons. None of these looked remotely recent, all had seen some intense and hefty use, and most were either in more than one piece or were missing part of themselves. It was difficult to tell if these were more trophies from vanquished enemies, but he had the feeling – and he did not know why – that they were instead relics of great heroes who had once graced these halls, each of whom had spawned fantastic sagas passed with reverence from each generation to the next. Whatever the true reason for the display, Brann decided that he liked the latter one best and, till proved otherwise, that was what he would stick with. He wondered if any of the men in this room would ever be remembered by their sword or axe in all its battered glory, hanging upon these walls.

He returned his attention to those men in question – and caught his breath. A broadly built, but not fat, man with oiled, midnight-black hair slicked back to hang to his thick neck, and wearing heavy, ornate clothes, stood talking to Sigurr. He was partially turned away from Brann but he glanced around constantly as he talked, never looking in any direction for more than a moment and seldom at the object of his words, and something about the inestimable craft and calculating guile in those eyes told Brann that he was looking at Loku. His breathing quickened and he felt his senses heighten at finding himself in the presence of the man, and he quickly glanced at Konall, half expecting to see him launch himself, sword and teeth bared, at the object of such intense hatred.

His expectation seemed to be not far from the truth. Konall's face was an impassive mask of neutrality, and he stood with a perfect air of nonchalant calm – but it was too perfect a pose to be natural, as confirmed by the fire in his eyes, the exaggerated line of his jaw caused by his tightly clenched teeth, and the white knuckles gripping his sword hilt as he strove, almost successfully, to stop his hand from shaking. It was not immediately obvious to a casual onlooker, but to those who knew him well – including one who had spent several days in his company in the mountains – the signals were clear: Konall, through force of character and a lifetime of training, was managing to control his fury for the sake of duty, but he was only a breath away from crossing a disastrous line.

Einarr had noticed, too, and from behind Loku managed to catch his father's eye. Sigurr recognised the danger and, taking Loku's elbow, steered him around to face Einarr – and away from Konall. 'You will not have met my son, will you, Loku?' he said smoothly. 'I will introduce you but, first, I suggest we allow the pages to retire. It is many hours since they last slept or, indeed, ate and I expect they could do with both. My nephew, also, has had a busy few days recently and deserves some respite from the boring matters to which we must attend, so I will excuse him also until the morrow. Thank you, Konall,' he said pointedly to the youth.

Loku inclined his head in their general direction and Brann once again felt the impression of danger from the man. Fortunately, Konall's stiff bow towards his uncle coincided with Loku's cursory glance in their direction, masking the boy's expression from what Brann assumed would be extremely perceptive eyes. The ambassador would have been unable to miss the change in the demeanour of the haughty, emotionally reserved boy that he knew from his visits to Ravensrest.

Konall stalked from the room and Brann rushed to follow the pages who were slipping away rather more discreetly than the noble boy ahead of them. He stormed up a flight of stairs, presumably towards his quarters, while Erlandr led the way to the kitchens. The boy was still nervous in the presence of the older pages but, being back on home territory, he had gained a little more confidence and was able to use the fact that none of the others had visited Yngvarrsharn before to allow manners to give him a reason to talk – something he had not, as far as Brann knew, managed in the few days prior to this. He politely directed the little party to the kitchen area, which was around three times the size of the facility at Ravensrest. The familiar look made Brann think of Valdis with a sharp pang, a feeling that was reinforced when her brother clapped a large hand on his shoulder.

'I will pop up and see if the young lord needs anything,' he murmured. 'Keep some food for me,' he added with a grin, pointing to the table that was laden in anticipation of their arrival. 'I know how you foreigners enjoy your feasting.' He looked over at the large, foreboding cook waiting at the far side of the table and, undeterred, told her, 'Do not be put off by his size, madam. I have seen him put away the best part of a cow.' He excused himself and left the cook staring at Brann with a mixture of curiosity and suspicion that Hakon may not have been entirely serious. Brann contented himself with mumbling awkwardly that one should not believe all that one hears, but that the fare before him looked wonderful nonetheless, and sat quietly beside the others.

They were, indeed, both tired and hungry as Sigurr had indicated, and the result was that they concentrated on eating rather than talking. With his dining companions being the quiet Erlandr and the surly Olvir, Brann had not expected sparkling conversation, but the silence was heavy nonetheless and made Brann, normally fairly shy himself with strangers until he got to know them, even more self-conscious about saying anything. He concentrated instead on tackling the food before him, and soon found himself attacking it with such gusto the cook was in danger of believing Hakon's frivolous assertions. He became so absorbed in eating – partly through hunger and partly to take his mind off the overbearing lack of speech – that the time passed quickly and he was surprised enough to visibly jump (as did the others, he was glad to see) when Hakon came bounding back into the room.

'Well, that was fun,' he greeted them. 'Now, where is my dinner?'

Brann moved slightly along the bench to give him room to sit down. 'How was he?' he asked.

'Not a happy boy,' Hakon grunted. 'Put it this way: I have seen drunks in a less aggressive mood after being sent home early from the inn for being too full of mead and fighting talk, and then arriving home to find their wife with another man.'

Brann smiled slightly, noticing that over-verbose speech was not just the preserve of Konall. Olvir sniggered, but his amusement was directed at the fact that Konall should be in such black humour. Irritated, Hakon flicked a chicken leg across the table to catch Olvir square on his swollen jaw. Even in country where table manners seemed perfunctory at best, the move caught Olvir by surprise and gave him no time to flinch out of the way. Admirably, Brann had to concede, he made no sound of pain despite the accuracy of the flying drumstick, although his eyes did start to water slightly.

'Something in your eye, Olvir?' Hakon asked innocently. 'Or are you, the gods forbid, coming over all emotional all of a sudden?' He smiled gently, a picture of concern.

Brann smiled again, and Erlandr could not resist a giggle. Olvir glared at him but, Brann noticed curiously, did not direct any anger towards the boy, despite his lack of size, lesser years and – most importantly – his laughter. As the warlord's page, Brann thought, the boy must hold a position of sufficient magnitude to make Olvir, even in his current state of ire, think twice about directing any unpleasantries his way.

Instead, he started to say something extremely rude to Hakon, then remembered that there was a woman present and halted his words. Unsure of how to react, he slammed to his feet and stormed up the stairs.

Hakon noticed the cook's disapproving stare. 'My apologies,' he said. 'But there is a fairly unpleasant history to our relationship.'

'And he is not a very nice boy,' Erlandr piped up helpfully. The two other pages burst into laughter at the unexpected interjection, and the older woman turned away and busied herself with the sink to hide the smile that may just have crept across her austere features.

Brann tore off a piece of bread. 'So, Konall took it well, then?'

Hakon grinned. 'If I say that there a few dents in the furniture in his room that I am sure were not there when we arrived, and that it took both of us to extract his sword from a chest that it had inexplicably become embedded in, would you get an idea of the sort of reaction we are talking about?'

Brann made a show of pondering the image. 'I do believe I would,' he confirmed.

'What is the matter with him?' Erlandr asked, and the older pages remembered that the explanation was not one that should be aired at that time.

Brann stood. 'It is a long story, young man. We will tell you, but not tonight. I would, however, be obliged if you would show me where my room is. If I am lucky enough to have a room to myself, that is. Knowing my luck, I will have to share with Olvir.'

Erlandr jumped up, eager to please. 'No, you get your own room, although it is not very big.'

'That is not a problem,' Hakon assured him. 'Brann is not very big either.'

The boy led the way and Brann followed, giving Hakon a friendly slap on the back as he passed. The large page raised his hand in acknowledgement without turning from his food. They climbed the stairs to the level they had entered upon, and travelled a short way to the side of the building before finding a further stairway. Erlandr showed him to a corridor a flight up, and then let him past into the passageway.

'Go to the end, there, and your room is the first one once you are around the corner.'

Brann thanked him and resisted the temptation to ruffle his hair. Weariness started to hit him hard and, as he turned the corner, he at first failed to see the figure loitering in the shadows.

'Quite a hero, are you not, just because Konall took you into the mountains to carry his load?' Olvir's malice-ridden voice said. Brann looked at him, startled and annoyed at himself for not noticing the other boy.

He shrugged. 'I am no hero,' he said, wanting merely to end the conversation and go to bed. He turned to his door and reached for the latch. Olvir's hand swung him round, and he found the boy's face uncomfortably close to his own.

'I know that,' he growled at him. 'But, then, I can see through you. You are not one of us; you could not have survived for two minutes up there without someone to hold your hand. You do not belong here, and I am sick of seeing you around.'

Brann felt strongly that to show any fear would be a grave mistake – despite the churning in his stomach. Forcing his voice to remain even, he replied, 'If you do not want to see me, do not look at me. I certainly will not be seeking your company, if that is what you want.'

A malicious leer came over Olvir's face. 'Quite the opposite. I will be looking for you. Because sooner or later, you are going to be somewhere, alone, where an accident can happen to you. And, little boy,' he grabbed Brann's chin roughly between his fingers, 'I will make sure that it happens.'

Brann slapped the hand away, his anger rising suddenly and overwhelmingly and blazing from his face.

'Why not try it now?' he snapped. His rage, fierce but strangely cold, rose with every word, giving him an unaccustomed confidence. He started shoving Olvir's chest with both hands to punctuate his words. 'I am alone now, am I not? You have your chance. Why not take it? What are you going to do?'

The larger boy, stumbling back with every push, was startled by the aggression from Brann. He had expected to be met by a fearful boy who would cower before his boorish threats; instead he found not only a complete lack of fear, but almost an eagerness for a fight. Unsettled by the unexpected, he had no idea how to react and merely stared, the bullying hostile expression still flushing his cheeks, down at Brann.

'Are you going to do anything?' Brann demanded, his voice thick with contempt. He turned his back. He wanted to show that he contemplated absolutely no threat from the other boy, but he knew he was taking a risk and tensed with every step, expecting to feel a thunderous blow from behind. Forcing his walk to be casual, he added, 'Didn't think so.'

As he opened his door, Olvir at last found his voice. 'I will get you when it suits me, and not when you tell me to,' he snarled, the statement as much for his own self-belief as for Brann's information.

Without turning, Brann replied, 'Of course. Whatever you say,' and flicked the door shut behind him. He rested his back against the wood and took several long breaths to try to calm himself as Olvir audibly retreated up the corridor with much cursing and stamping. During the exchange, he had felt strangely calm and assured, his senses heightened and his urge to respond eager. Now that it was over, however, he had started to shake and was nervously restless. Eyes staring and cheeks burning, he felt an urge to run and yell to relieve the tension, but had to content himself with pacing furiously around the small room, stopping frequently to pummel his bed.

Feeling a little foolish, he forced himself to lie on the thin mattress rather than assault it. In the absence of physical movement, his mind raced, deceiving him into thinking he felt wide awake. Sleep was able to creep up on him unnoticed, and took him by surprise.

He woke the next morning feeling as if he had not rested at all. Despite besting Olvir the previous evening, he felt nervous at the thought of coming face-to-face with the abrasive boy and was relieved to meet Hakon as he hurried down the stairs to the kitchen.

'What is the matter with you?' the tall boy asked cheerfully. 'You look as tense as a pig in a butcher's shop. Anything wrong?'

Where do I start? Brann thought ironically, but he shook his head and merely said, 'I just slept badly last night.' He knew that, if he told Hakon of the encounter with Olvir, Konall's page would immediately accost the other boy, making it appear that Brann preferred him to fight his battles for him and destroying any impression Brann had made the night before.

Olvir was already at the table as the pair entered the kitchen and fixed them with a malevolent glower that managed to darken still further when Hakon tossed a cheery greeting his way. Brann was thankful for his friend's presence, which ensured that he was not the sole target of Olvir's attention as he breakfasted.

There was more bustle about the kitchen at this time of day than there had been on Brann's previous visit and plenty of young kitchen maids to cast, in equal measure, appraising glances and giggles towards the visiting pages, albeit restricted by the intimidating glare of the cook. They had barely begun to eat, however, before Erlandr shot in, excited to be bearing news. The lords expected to be locked in discussions for at least all of the day, he informed them with the importance of one in the know, and what was to be said was for their ears only. The result, he said delightedly, was that the pages were relieved of any duties.

Brann raised his eyebrows and looked at Hakon. 'Not that I am complaining, but do pages in this land have much to do at all?'

'Have no fear, newcomer,' Hakon reassured him. 'We are not involved as much when they are discussing things, only when they are putting their decisions into practice. And, believe me, there will be plenty of errands and tasks for you then.' He grinned. 'You will not be bored.'

Brann's foreign accent had caused no end of interest among the young maids – a fact that had not gone unnoticed by the cook. 'You pages will certainly not be hanging around this kitchen, bored or otherwise,' she proclaimed. 'We have enough to do without tripping over redundant pages while we are at it.'

'Then we shall trouble you no more, kind mistress of all things cookery,' Hakon declared grandly, performing an exaggerated and sweeping bow. 'You have treated us royally and we will take our leave, taking with us, if we may, a small reminder of your culinary magnificence.' Scooping up a handful of bread and cheese, he flashed his most winning smile her way. As startled by the unexpected response as Olvir had been by Brann's the night before, the buxom cook was struck by the same reaction: speechlessness. Hakon bowed again and strode from the room. Brann, nodding his thanks to the kitchen in general, grabbed a random selection of berries and hurried after him, closely tailed by Erlandr.

The trio headed into the town and began exploring the streets. Brann, already feeling unsettled as his morning's malaise persisted, grew more withdrawn and morose as the time passed. Erlandr, conversely, revelled in his role as local expert and, excited at mixing with older boys whom he was clearly beginning to hero-worship, became more garrulous as he scampered around them. Shortly before mid-day, his exuberance grew too much for Brann's darkening mood and he made an excuse and left Hakon with the young guide. With no money to spend – Einarr had either felt that supplying his 'page' with finances was a step too far in the deception or had merely forgotten about such matters – he was glad that he had followed Hakon's example in bringing food from the breakfast spread. He sat on the edge of a stone water trough and took out the berries, absently gazing on the passers-by as he picked at them.

At first, watching the local people going about their business served to slightly alleviate the boredom; shortly, however, it began to feed his sense of belonging to another, very distant, culture. His melancholy grew and, his appetite diminishing, he wrapped up the remainder of his lunch in the small cloth he had brought with it. His restlessness growing as his despair deepened, he began to wander the streets, noticing little about him and furiously fighting an overwhelming urge to weep.

Hours later, the gloom of dusk having fallen, the small figure, lit only by the lamp outside a dockside tavern, was found by Hakon sitting on a broken crate alongside a creaking rope that led out towards the darker shape of Einarr's ship. Indeed, Hakon would have missed the silent boy, unaware of his presence among the clutter left by sailors and dockers, had it not been for the small, flickering brand that Brann was nursing intently. So intently that he jumped violently when Hakon said, 'There you are, trouble-maker. You have caused quite a stir with your disappearing act.' Brann looked up sharply. 'Calm down – only among the pages. Their lordships are still locked in their mighty discussions.'

Brann shrugged. His voice flat, he said. 'I felt like some time on my own. And were we not told that the day was ours to do with as we wished?'

If Hakon was shocked by his tone, so different from the Brann he was accustomed to, he showed no sign other than a concerned narrowing of his eyes. He offered no comment on it, merely pulling over a crate to seat himself beside the boy.

He sighed, and said, 'Well, we all need time to ourselves now and again, do we not? But you will understand that we were a little concerned: a young boy, on his first day in a new place, goes missing. And, most worryingly in your case, he misses dinner.'

The burning brand being twisted slowly in Brann's hand revealed that his comment had not drawn even a flicker of a smile. There was no reaction at all, as Brann stared at the flame before him, his eyes flitting occasionally to the rope securing the boat while his free hand played with a repaired tear near the hem of his heavy black cloak.

Choosing his words carefully, Hakon said slowly and evenly, 'That torch gives off a welcome heat. Fairly takes the edge off the evening chill, does it not?'

There was still no answer, but he at least had Brann's attention as the smaller boy's gaze turned briefly towards him.

'You would need to be careful, though,' Hakon continued, his tone casual. 'A stray spark, or even a slip of the hand, and that tarred rope could be alight before you know it.'

This time Brann did not look up, but he did speak, in the same, low, bleak voice as before. 'It might.'

'Which would be a grave danger for all on board,' Hakon said, as if it were nothing more than an idle observation.

Brann stared at the dark shape of the ship. 'There is only one person on board, on watch, and if he could not get off in time in the event of a fire, he would not be paying proper attention to his duty.'

Hakon shrugged. 'Still, it would be a shame to see a ship such as this destroyed.'

Brann slowly turned a cold stare upon him. 'Would it? Would it be a shame?'

Hakon gazed at the boat, as if oblivious to Brann's bleak stare, and said casually, 'Of course it would. It is a finely crafted vessel, and I am sure it sails well. And, most of all, it would be a pity for all those who are far from home who would be stranded without a means of return.' He turned to lock eyes with Brann. 'It would be tragedy for those for whom this ship is the only link back to their families, their friends,' he said in a steady, even voice. 'It would be a great shame for such as those, would it not, Brann?'

Brann's eyes changed. Where they had been cold, bleak and distant, a look of pleading now filled them, a show of confusion and despair that he was unable to disguise or restrain. Tears welled up with force, and he began to tremble. He had the torch in a tight, double-handed grip and Hakon moved smoothly to take hold of his wrists, ostensibly in calming reassurance – but also to steady the flaming brand as it shook uncomfortably close to the rope.

'I know,' he said, his voice soothing. 'I understand.'

Brann swallowed hard. 'Help me, Hakon,' he begged, his ragged stuttering contrasting with Hakon's measured tones. 'I cannot let go of it. Take it from me.'

Slowly, Hakon took hold of the shaft of the torch. It was not without some effort that he managed to ease it free of Brann's fingers but, once he had done so, he casually tossed it into the water where, with a brief hiss, the danger was extinguished.

Brann put his head in his hands, his fingers grasping his hair. His shoulders jerked spasmodically as he was wracked by silent sobs. Without any awkwardness, Hakon moved to put an arm around his shoulders and, for a few long moments, they sat, an unlikely pair locked in silence.

Brann gathered his shuddering breath. 'What do you know, Hakon? What do you understand? Do you know that I saw my brother, born less than a year before me and with me every day of my life, murdered for no reason when we were as close as you and I are now? Do you know that, one minute we were laughing together and the next a crossbow bolt hammered into his head, and he was gone? Do you understand what it feels like to turn from that horror and watch your family cut down and burned in their own home? Do you understand what it is like to be dragged from everything you have known, with no warning, no goodbyes, nothing but the knowledge that you are helpless to change any of it?' With the breaching of Brann's barriers, his anguish poured forth in a torrent. 'Do you know what it is like to be bullied, to be humiliated, to be attacked by a berserk madman, to be brought to the other side of the sea where home is so far away that it seems like a dream, only to face those screaming sub-humans in the mountains when the worst adversary you have had before is another boy in a

411

stupid game with a bundle of rags? Do you know what it is like to have to pretend that you are something you are not, when you are really locked in a reality that you hate and fear?' He turned and gripped the larger boy's arms fiercely, his voice rising almost to a ragged shout. 'Do you know, Hakon? Do you know I am a slave?'

He stood and stared down into the still water, his breath hissing between clenched teeth and tears smearing across his face. Appearing stunned as much by the passion as by the content of Brann's outburst, Hakon looked at the anguished figure at the dock's edge.

'I had guessed the last part, though it wasn't my place to question the circumstances,' he said quietly. 'The rest, I must admit, comes largely as a shock, although it explains much.'

Brann turned to face him. 'How long have you known?' His voice was hoarse, almost a whisper.

Hakon smiled gently. 'I first suspected only during this conversation, no earlier than that. No one else knows.'

Konall's voice from behind caused them both to jump. 'Although that is a miracle considering the volume at which you chose to announce it.'

'Oh, by the gods, I am dead,' Brann gasped. 'If Sigurr and Ragnarr do not execute me for deceiving them, Einarr will have my head for revealing it.'

Konall's eyebrows twitched conspiratorially. 'Only if I tell them. And why would I? I have suspected it for some time, and have said nothing before.'

Brann stared at him. 'You knew? How?'

Konall was looking around as his spoke, scanning the area around them rapidly. 'Why would a noble like my cousin take a miller's boy, with no training even remotely useful to the duties of a page and not even the beginnings of schooling in combat, to be his page? In fact, why would the captain of a ship-for-hire take a page at all?' He shrugged. 'But it matters not to me. I do not believe in slavery, so you are not a slave to me. You are merely a mill boy who I would prefer to be standing behind – well behind – when he is lining up a bow shot.'

At the mention of that, Brann's thoughts turned to a moment in the mountains, when a similar melancholy had gripped him. *If only you knew how true that is.* He looked at the two boys. 'I'm sorry. I get these feelings every now and again, but I can usually push them back down. This time it all seemed to be too much.'

Hakon put a large hand on his shoulder. 'Enduring what you have, and carrying the secrets that you do, creates great pressure. Perhaps pushing it down has let it grow ever stronger. This was one time too many. But this, tonight, may release the pressure a little. And now there are two others who can share your secret at least, and one of us may also be sympathetic to it.'

Konall glanced around until his gaze settled on a pile of crates, nets and ropes a short distance from them. 'This is all very touching but at this moment, it is secondary to the fact that we need a place of concealment. Someone approaches and I do not believe it would be respectable for the heir to the seat of Ravensrest to be seen in the docks at night.' He moved quickly to the cover he had identified. 'Here. Hurry.'

As they moved to follow, Brann whispered to Hakon, 'He does not believe in slavery? Then how does that explain the way he treated Grakk and Gerens on the hunting trip?'

Hakon murmured, 'That was how he treated all servants. Remember, he did go back for them, too, not just for me. And he has improved more than a little since then, has he not? Comparatively speaking, of course.'

'Quiet!' Konall hissed, and they slipped down beside him, disturbing a mangy cat that slunk away to find alternative shelter against a nearby pile of empty sacks. Brann picked up the sound of the footsteps that Konall's acute hearing had noticed, and held his breath. He was still trembling from the emotion of the past minutes, and the tension of listening to the approaching footsteps – a brisk, purposeful clacking of expensive boot heels – was not helping him to calm down. He was, however, surprised to find that the depression that had swamped him had lifted with his revelations. He was unsure what had helped: sharing the burden of his secrets, no longer having to live a deception, or the pair's supportive reaction. Probably all of them, he decided, but ultimately he did not care. He was just relieved to be free of the oppressive, near-suicidal feelings that had engulfed him, even if it did proved to be only a respite until they struck again. He would enjoy the respite.

His thoughts were interrupted by Konall's sharp intake of breath and he wriggled around to emulate the other two in peering through the slats of the crates. In mid-turn, his foot brushed against a rotting bucket lying beside him. At the sound of wood scraping on stone, the footsteps stopped abruptly. Konall snatched up a small pebble and adroitly skimmed it across the few yards that separated them from the previously disturbed cat. The unfortunate creature was struck on the rump and, not surprisingly, it squealed in surprise and pain and scuttled away with a malevolent backwards glare. Satisfied, the owner of the expensive boots resumed his progress.

The figure was past them by the time that Brann, more carefully, had completed his manoeuvre but, even from behind, the cause of Konall's reaction was clear: Loku. Simultaneously,

Brann and Hakon – on either side of the noble boy – placed a restraining hand on his arms.

Konall waited until the treacherous ambassador was further down the dockside before whispering, 'Calm yourselves. I am learning. I do not think my father and uncle would be overjoyed if I decapitated him and disrupted whatever plans they are hatching.'

'I do think we should follow him, though,' Brann suggested.

'I see no harm in that,' Hakon agreed.

Konall was already on his feet. 'I feel it would be remiss of us not to do so,' he observed. He looked pointedly at Brann. 'If we can all manage to avoid kicking any debris we happen to pass.'

Brann made an obscene gesture native to his homeland but which translated well. Konall chose to ignore it with aristocratic aplomb.

Loku had turned sharply up a side street and they hurried to regain sight of him as he moved into a part of the town even less reputable than the docks.

Konall grunted. 'He is on no official business, that is for sure, if he is headed in that direction.'

Brann frowned. 'He is not exactly hiding, though, is he? Surely, if he is up to no good, he would be trying to conceal himself more.'

'Sometimes,' Hakon explained lightly, 'you attract more attention if you skulk in the shadows than if you move confidently and with purpose, as if you have no care who sees you. And no one will question a man of such obvious importance as to where he is going, even in this quarter.'

'So why are we skulking in the shadows, then, among the muck and the rubbish?' Brann objected.

Pulling his hood forward to hide his face and, more importantly, his distinctive, long, white-gold hair, Konall said in a low tone, 'We are not hiding from onlookers; we hide from Loku. The streets will stay fairly quiet until the inns stop serving for the night. It would look a touch suspicious if he saw us behind him for any appreciable distance.'

Brann shrugged his acceptance, and hugged the wall closer.

As if Loku had heard Konall's words, however, he wheeled suddenly and stared directly at them. They had two options: freeze and hope that the shadows would conceal them, but risk being seen and looking suspicious; or be so conspicuous that they (hopefully) would dispel any suspicion – but in doing so, losing their secrecy if Loku had not, in fact, spotted them at all in the darkness.

Either way, Konall made the decision for them. Roaring in rage, he dragged Hakon into the middle of the street as if they had spilled from a doorway.

In a surprisingly coarse voice, he bellowed, 'That is one time too many you will insult her honour!' and swung a wild punch at his page's stomach. Fortunately, Hakon had the presence of mind to realise what was happening and doubled over the blow, looking as if the wind had been smashed out of him but absorbing the punch in his hunched position. He dropped to the ground, coughing roughly.

Brann pulled Konall by the arm, growling as loudly as he could, 'Come, Mad Dog, before his friends appear.' He started to drag the taller boy towards Loku and, as he had hoped, the ambassador had no wish to encounter such miscreants and turned and hurried on his way.

'Mad Dog?' Konall said, with more than a hint of amusement in his voice.

Brann shrugged. 'I could not think of any of your people's names quickly enough, so I went for a nickname. I think it quite suits you, actually.'

He could not see properly in the gloom, but he was sure that Konall came close to smiling.

'Come on, Mad Dog and Mad Pup,' Hakon's voice said behind them. 'He has turned down another street and we are in danger of losing him.'

They hurried to the junction and Konall peered around the corner. 'We just got here in time,' he said quietly. 'He slipped down an alleyway as I looked. If we had been a moment later, we would have had no idea where he had gone.'

'Hurry up, then,' Hakon said urgently. 'He is getting away.'

Brann tugged him back by the sleeve. 'Do not be so hasty. He may be waiting there to see if he is being followed.'

Konall nodded. 'That would make sense. I think it is time for the return of Mad Dog and his little helper.'

'What about me?' Hakon objected. 'Do not think you are leaving me out of this.'

'You will do what you are told,' Konall growled.

Brann stepped in. 'There is a simple solution. If Hakon keeps to the shadows, it will look as if he is following us, as if he is seeking revenge. That way, if Loku spots Hakon, he will think he is trailing us, not him, and there will be a reason, therefore, for all three of us to be there.'

'Enough talking,' Konall said abruptly. 'Get moving.'

He pulled his hood further down over his face and hunched forwards in an attempt to disguise his build. Placing an arm around Brann's shoulders as if he drunkenly needed support, he half-dragged him forward and the pair staggered ahead, with Konall grumbling incoherently – and surprisingly convincingly. Brann fought hard not to giggle, an urge that grew stronger as they neared the corner. When they drew level with the alley, Konall started a decidedly unhealthy coughing fit that was violent enough to wheel him around to face down the narrow lane. He sank his head into Brann's shoulder.

'He is not there,' he breathed into Brann's ear. He stiffened. 'Something moved behind that pile of rubbish. It may be a rat or it may be...'

'I will check,' Brann whispered. Konall held him back briefly, and he felt something cold and hard slip up his sleeve.

'Take my long knife,' he said. 'Just in case.'

Brann grinned weakly. 'In case it is a rat, you mean? I would more happily face a man than one of them.'

'Big woman,' Konall chided him. Brann did not answer but instead spluttered theatrically and spun away unsteadily.

'Going to be sick,' he moaned frantically and loudly and, hand over mouth, he ran at the pile – and startled a wizened, wrinkled beggar who sprang up, wide-eyed, from behind it.

It was unclear who was the more startled of the two. Konall was, however, less hesitant and was at the old man in a blink, pinning him against the building's wall with the edge of his boot knife resting against the dishevelled character's throat, the long fingers of his free hand gripping his captive's wrists and pinning them against the crumbling surface of the stonework above his head.

'I do not think he is in any state to run away,' Brann objected.

'Do not question me unless you have a better plan,' Konall hissed in anger. 'And unless you know what you are talking about. I am not worried about him running *away*, but about him running,' he nodded at a low opening in the wall behind the debris, 'in there.'

Feeling foolish, Brann nodded his acknowledgement just as Hakon joined them. Konall immediately sent him back to watch the street from the mouth of the alley and positioned Brann to one side of the hole in the wall.

'If anyone looks out, stick your knife in their face,' he growled.

His tone brought home to young boy how much more serious the situation had quickly become. No longer were they almost light-heartedly following a figure in the dark; now they were in a highly charged, uncertain situation that could prove instantly fatal for any of them – and the gods only knew how many others, if Loku was plotting some atrocity somewhere inside the building.

His nerves on edge, Brann tried to stare intently into the dark opening – but could not stop himself watching Konall with the old beggar. The tall boy pressed his blade harder against the man's grey-stubbled throat and, his face aggressively close, snarled, 'A noble went through that hole, did he not?'

In a quavering voice from a throat tightened by terror, the old man shrilled, 'I saw no such man, my lord. I am just a poor beggar who had found a place to sleep.' His eyes, however, betrayed his voice – darting calculatingly in search of any advantage he might gain.

Konall's eyes, staring directly into those of his captive, widened in anger. 'We both know that is not true, so stop wasting time,' he hissed. 'We both know you are a lookout for this viper's nest, and we both know they will kill you if you betray them. But they will have to find you to kill you. And that is if they survive what we bring to them. Whereas if you do not betray them, I will kill you now, for I have no more time to waste on you. So you have a choice to make, and a quick one: die now or take your chance to run, hide and survive.'

The grimy beggar's eyes narrowed and fixed on Konall. 'Then there is no choice,' he rasped, the fear dropping from his tone in an instant. 'What would you know, my lord?'

'Who entered just now?'

'Loku.'

'How many are in there?'

'Eight, and Loku. One guarding the door to their room, the rest inside if it be the same as the other times.'

'How many other times?'

The beggar shrugged. 'Six, maybe seven, since this time last year.'

'Why do they meet?'

He shrugged again. 'I do not know.' Konall pressed the knife harder and trickle of blood oozed from the grimy skin. 'Why would they tell me?' He opened one hand slightly to reveal a couple of small coins. 'I am just paid to sit here each time they get together.'

Konall's voice was low with contempt. 'You would betray your lord, and your people, for that?'

The beggar's contempt matched Konall's. 'Why not? Makes no difference to me either way. Now, do you need any more, or can I go now?'

Konall shook his head. 'I need no more.' The beggar relaxed in readiness to leave, and Konall made as if to start turning away. Abruptly, he tensed and sliced his knife across the old man's throat. Blood, dark in the shadows, gushed from the wound as he dropped, lifeless, to the hard ground.

Stunned, Brann found it hard to comprehend what he had seen. Konall's callous savagery shocked him. Why was he involved in this, when one side seemed as brutal as the other? Before he could think further, a harsh voice grumbled from the darkness within the building.

420

'Keep the noise down, you old fool. I can hear you talking to yourself from down the corridor.'

A large face bearing a tattered eye-patch appeared in the hole in the wall. In panic, Brann stabbed out with the knife, by pure chance ramming it into the hapless guard's good eye. It only entered a short way, but the man's embryonic scream was cut short by Konall, whose hand hammered against the hilt of the weapon, smashing it into the victim's brain and killing him instantly.

Konall followed the falling body into the building, dropping the few feet to the lower level of floor and, with a nauseating sound, retrieved the weapon and wiped it on the guard's tunic. Brann threw up violently. In a matter of seconds, two men had died in the most brutal of manners and, worse, he was a part of it. Whatever his distaste, he was as bad as Konall.

'Good reactions,' Konall observed, handing back the knife. 'The use of the knife, that is, not the vomiting.'

He turned back into the room. Unable to follow, Brann could not stop staring at the weapon in his open palm. Hakon moved beside him. He reached across and closed Brann's fingers around the hilt.

'You kept yourself alive. That is all. No more,' he said quietly. 'Now put those thoughts you have aside, and we will talk later. If you want to survive the next time as well, you must live in each moment alone for the next while, simple as that.'

'But the old man,' Brann said bleakly. 'There was no reason for him to die. Konall is as bad as they are. And now, so am I.'

Hakon turned him by the shoulders, and stared into his eyes. 'Yes there was a reason, no Konall is not, and no you

421

are not. But we have not the time to discuss it now. It comes down to this: do you want to die?' Brann shook his head. 'Good. Do you trust me?' Brann nodded, surprised at how readily he did so. 'Then do this, for I do not want you to die either – and neither does my sister.' Mention of Valdis brought Brann back slightly to his senses.

Hakon continued speaking rapidly. 'Fix your mind totally on what you have to do, in each second as it comes. Konall and I are with you. We are, the three of us, a team. These are hard men in here, and we must help each other, and work as one, if we are to come out of it alive. Bury all emotion, and do whatever you have to do, automatically.' He slapped Brann's shoulder. 'Now let's go. I will be right behind you.'

Konall was crouching in the gap in the wall. He had returned to hurry them on, but had stopped on hearing Hakon's words.

He looked at his page. 'You have much of your father in you.' Without further ado, he turned back into the dark room. Hakon, Brann was sure, was blushing as he nudged the smaller boy towards the gap. It was unevenly edged, as if it had originally started to crumble from poor workmanship and the effects of the weather, and had then been roughly enlarged once the opportunity had presented itself for an entrance other than the front door. It led into a small room that lay around four feet below ground level with, Brann noticed as he dropped onto the basic, earthen floor, light entering from a doorway to the right.

Without looking down, he stepped hesitantly around the body on the floor – then jumped as, with a soft thud, Hakon dragged the old man's corpse in from the alley. The taller boy gently propelled him towards Konall's waiting figure at the doorway.

'Sorry to startle you,' he murmured. 'It just was not wise to leave such an obvious sign of our entry lying in the street.'

'But what about, you know, what I did?' Brann asked awkwardly. 'You know: what I left lying on the ground out there.'

Hakon grinned. 'At last, you are thinking things out again – thank the gods. You have your moments away from us, but you always seem to come back. That is good.' Brann was not so sure if it was, indeed, so good, but Hakon was continuing. 'Do not worry about leaving your lunch out there. It is not that unusual a sight around here.'

Konall glanced at them. 'If you ladies have finished gossiping, would you like to proceed?'

The pair nodded, and after a quick glance from Konall into the corridor, they slipped from the room. Brann felt as if they left Hakon's small amount of levity in the room: strangely, despite the two dead bodies within it, there had been an irrational sense of security about that room. Now that they were moving deeper into the building, he had an acute sense of not belonging, and such a strong feeling of danger that it was almost as if he could taste the threat in the air.

A single lantern burned low in the corridor, bringing more shadow than light. There were two doorways. The first with a rotted door lying open, was revealed by a quick glance to be a dingy storeroom bereft of stores. The second was clearly their goal. Better lit than the corridor, it spilled light through a door that was shut, but barely in better condition than that of the storeroom.

More important than the light coming out from it was the possibility it offered through it. If they did have to charge into a room filled with murderers and cut-throats, as Brann envisaged them, at least they would not be so blinded by ignorance and guesswork as to what awaited them.

Konall edged up to the door, the thick dust on the floor masking any scrape his boots may inadvertently have made. Conscious that old floorboards have a tendency to creak, he placed his feet slowly and carefully. Brann, however, was not so worried about noisy floorboards: a broken section of the planks as they had entered the corridor had revealed that it had been constructed cheaply, the wood having been laid directly upon the earthen floor beneath rather than suspended on joists above it. The point soon became immaterial in any case, as the volume of voices from the room increased as several men began talking over each other. Konall eased his head to look through a crack in the door, then hurriedly waved Brann past him to reach the other side of the doorway while the animation of the occupants distracted them from any possible movement in the corridor, however fleeting it may be. It would have only taken one man within the room to be looking in the direction of the rickety door to see a shape passing by, and their advantage of surprise would be lost.

Brann flattened himself against the wall, breathing hard from the tension more than any exertion, before following Konall's lead and slowly rolling his head around to peer through the nearest crack. A group of men were gathered around a rough table that was only marginally in a better state than the door through which they were looking. Most of them were sitting but one was standing, a stool lying on its side behind him, his hands on the table as he leant forwards, red-faced and shouting. Two other men were bawling back at him, one of whom also rose to his feet as he found himself increasingly unable to contain his anger. As far as Brann could tell amid the raucous confusion, they were arguing over the apportioning of blame regarding plans having to be changed and brought forward. Brann counted quickly; the old beggar – his stomach lurched again at the thought of the old man's demise – had not lied in that respect, anyway. Seven men were present, including Loku, who sat impassively watching the argument and waiting, presumably, for the best moment to intervene. Most of the men looked of similar build as the guard lying dead in the other room: bruisers, but quick enough of movement to give a heightened sense of danger and with a liberal enough collection of scars and inflicted deformities to suggest an ability to survive situations that those who had given them the wounds had not possessed.

The look of them and the manner of the arguing also conveyed an impression that these men were more than just common criminals, although they displayed none of the quality of clothing, jewels or weapons that would be expected of leaders of the underworld. That would probably suit Loku best, Brann guessed: they would be more reliable than the most basic level of street thugs in respect of both carrying out plans and keeping confidence, and would be less ambitious and cunning – and less liable to double-cross Loku to their own ends – than those at the top of the tree.

One man was different: a lean, hard and opulent man sat to one side of Loku, lounging back in his chair with an air of indifference betrayed by the disdain in his eyes for those before him. He could have been a leading underworld figure, but Brann had a strong feeling that he was a nobleman, and of high rank.

Konall glanced across and caught Brann's attention. He gestured that they should listen and watch, then leave the way they had come. Brann acknowledged him. He liked the thought that, perhaps, it had been his influence that had curbed the more impetuous side of a future leader in this land. In any case, Konall's decision made sense: they had more to gain in the long run by giving Sigurr the plotters' precise plans and letting the lords decide how to use the information most effectively – the alternative (charging into the room, swords swinging) seemed, in light of the imbalance in numbers, to be one of suicidal folly.

He returned his attention to the room. The argument had heated more and the hand of one of the men strayed to the hilt of his knife. Loku noticed the movement and, judging that he could afford to wait no longer to intervene, stood in a measured movement that was enough in itself to prompt the raised voices to peter out abruptly.

'Gentlemen,' he said in a form of address that, given his audience, could not be further from appropriate. His deep, smooth tone contrasted sharply with the clamour it replaced. 'We are wasting time debating fault. It matters not, now, who – if anyone – is to blame or if anyone has or has not done their job properly: it will have no effect on what we do next.'

The hulking man who had initiated the argument picked up his stool and sat down, prompting his opponent to follow suit. His face still flushed, he growled, 'So what do we do next?'

'That was what I was trying to tell you before you became a little over-excited,' Loku purred. 'As I said, the plans have changed. Why, is of no consequence. My master has decreed it and that is enough reason for me. If you are fond of life, it will be enough for you, also.' The silence around the table was eloquent agreement. 'Our new orders are simple: the lords must die. Both of them, and their sons, to prevent any accession. Their women, also, in case they are pregnant, and any female personal servants – I do not want any bastards appearing in years to come, just when we have got the population subdued.'

426

The three boys looked at one another in shock. They did not know what was worse – the horrific plan unfolding before them, or the calm way in which it was being accepted by those in the room, as if it were perfectly normal to discuss the imminent genocide of a land's rulers. Brann made to move: they must warn the lords immediately. Konall's raised hand and Loku's voice stopped him, however. He took a breath and urged himself to calm down. They must glean as much of the plans as possible to give the nobles the best chance of thwarting the assassination attempt.

Loku's tone became intense, his eyes compelling as his words gripped everyone within and outwith the room. 'You must remember, this is not a single act. This is the beginning of a new era, and the few of us in this room will play an important part in its formation over the years to come.' Brann seriously doubted that this were true for anyone other than the well-dressed man and Loku himself, but the others in the room were rapt. The ambassador continued, 'We are further ahead with the same process across the water,' Brann caught his breath, 'and we know from that experience that what we are about to do here is crucial. The existing regime must be wiped out in one swift act, and replaced with the new order,' he slapped the man beside him on the shoulder, 'before the people are aware of it. Then, we can tell them what we want to explain it, and they will have no option but to believe it. In any case, they will soon have too much to worry about in staying alive and with their families to cause any trouble – the most effective and efficient way of using people and keeping them where you want them is through fear, as I am sure you will all agree,' there were nods around the table, and several dark smiles, 'and if there is one thing we are good at, it is fear. If you doubt me, take a trip across the sea.

'Once we have these lands under our control, the same tactics can be used in the next, and so on. As our power grows, it will move quicker – the need for subterfuge will grow less as our combined might becomes enough to persuade other warlords to accede to us, or enough to crush them if they do not agree. Eventually, this will become one country, as it should always have been, under one king, my master.

'Once we combine it with the islands over the water, we have the beginnings of a very rapidly assembled empire. All from our actions that we start in this room tonight. Now. That is the destiny, the history, that we are creating.'

He paused, letting the drama hang in the air. There was no dissent. Brann was eager to go, and knew Hakon and, particularly, Konall would be even more so. But they had to force themselves to wait to hear the actual plans for assassination. Fortunately, their impatience on that score was matched by one of the men at the table.

'That's all very well,' he said, 'but how is it to be done? With poison you might miss some of them and that stronghold is too tough to storm and, even if we slip a band of us in there, it is too well-filled with warriors to ensure that our knives would do the business in time before we are swamped by them.'

'Very true, very true, my astute friend,' Loku said smoothly. 'But you are forgetting that I am privy to knowledge of the movements and actions of the esteemed nobles, as I am living among them – especially when those movements are suggested by myself. I have suggested to the nobles that they ease their current tension with a brief break for an outdoor banquet that I have prepared for them in gratitude for the hospitality they have shown me. As such efforts have been made by a guest as high ranking as an ambassador, it is impossible for them to refuse.

428

'I have dictated the location for the pleasantries, so I know the route they will be taking. And I have nearly a hundred of my men from the hills who have been living in holes and bushes along that route for the last few days – do not worry about them, they are used to such conditions.' None of those present looked concerned for them anyway.

Konall made to leave, but Brann frantically caught his attention. 'When?' he mouthed.

The tall boy nodded once, then turned his attention back to the room. Hakon stood, white-faced, behind him, listening but also watching the corridor to avoid being surprised by any late-comers or messengers.

'But who are "your men from the hills"? How can we trust them?' one man said in a hoarse voice that was explained, Brann concluded, by the wide scar across his throat.

'You cannot trust them,' Loku smiled, then held up a hand to hush the murmur that ran around the room, 'but I can. They look on me as their master, their saviour, for I have given them a life, a community, an identity. They are wasters, the lowlifes, the scum of the streets, who have no respect for others and even less for themselves. Most importantly, they have one quality above all that I have sought in gathering them, and that is a quality that I have nurtured and developed into obsessive levels, for I have given them a religion based upon it. That quality is the enjoyment they find, for whatever reason, in the pain and suffering of others, and through the power of a religion that glorifies that enjoyment and indulges it, through blood-soaked ceremonies and a culture of torture and dismemberment as public entertainment, I have created an army of savages, capable of – even desiring – atrocities and horror beyond anything you or I could commit ourselves. Religion is a powerful tool. But especially so when enhanced with certain rather useful herbs found in certain regions in the Empire. Herbs that, once a person indulges, a craving is born. And, most usefully to us, herbs that if taken in a certain combination, creates an ever-increasing need to release energy, a frustration that produces a frenzied fury.' The atmosphere in the room was still, heavy. Loku looked slowly around the men before him. 'Well might you look uneasy. Well might you feel nervous. This combination of religion, the frenzy of the herbs and their natural cruelty means that these are not people you would want to be among. But,' he shrugged, 'as high priest of their religion and source of the herbs, I have absolute power over them. Which, for all your distaste, makes them highly effective shock troops. And they, above all, will be our tool of fear when we need it. Already we have been raiding villages, sowing the seeds. Once we have power, we will, as across the sea, use them very effectively to make sure the people live in the climate of obedience we would desire. We only have around one hundred of them here tonight, for it would have been hard to move and hide more than that, but that is enough to ensure there will be very little left of the aristocratic party. And I mean very little. But I have several communities, spread throughout the mountains. There are more than enough to maintain appropriate terror throughout the lands when our time comes.'

He smiled, coldly. 'So, my friends, you will not be called upon to do the dirty work: my savages will take care of that for you. I will ensure our next warlord,' he gripped the man beside him by the shoulder, 'is in place in the seat of power to quell the panic that will ensue as news filters in of the tragic demise of Lord Sigurr and his family at the hands of a raiding party of wildmen. And your job is to pass among the common people, spreading the news through your own men to the masses that Lord Balki, here, has stepped into the breach to fill the gap and has vowed to hunt down the marauders and ensure the attacks on this town never return – a brave and commendable gesture by a minor noble, I'm sure we all agree.' He laughed. 'I, will, of course, ensure that the attacks do stop to entrench his position and ensure the trust of the people until our regime can begin in earnest.

'But we must move urgently, for...' The boys made ready to leave quickly – here, surely, was the crucial detail of the timing of the attack. Brann was already thinking that they should arrange the two bodies in the other room to make it look as if they had fought, and killed, each other – however unlikely that outcome may seem, the men in the room before them would probably have so much of greater importance on their minds that they would not care or wonder too much about the exact circumstances of the pair's deaths.

Loku was continuing, '... for we strike tonight.' The trio looked at each other. *Tonight!* They must reach Sigurr at once. But Loku was not finished. 'You must go now to organise your own men. I have a man on the roof, ready to give a signal. The banqueting party will be leaving any time now, expecting to meet me at the destination they will never reach. At my man's signal, the mountain men will move to the ambush site in time for the warlord's passing.' He laughed, a chilling sound. 'My only regret is that I will not be there to see it.'

The men stood, but looked hesitant to leave. One of them growled, 'What about our pay? You said you would have it tonight, and it looks as if things will get very confused and busy from now on. I want my money now, so I know I've got it.'

'Oh, I am disappointed,' Loku said grandly. 'I had thought that helping to create history and receiving a place in the new order would have been reward enough for you.' Before they could react, he continued smoothly, 'Panic not. I merely jest.' He produced a small, but apparently heavy, sack from beneath the table. 'I will divide this, then you can be on your way and I will see my man on the roof.'

Brann glanced across at his companions. They nodded – they all knew that they had no option, that they must reach Loku before he could reach the roof. The clinking of coins revealed that the disbursement of the payment was beginning. Konall attracted Brann's attention. He was proffering a sword – Brann realised he had taken it from the guard they had killed.

He shook his head and indicated Hakon. He felt that the page, with his weapons training, would find it far more useful. Hakon, however, peered around Konall and, grinning, showed him that he had brought a sword with him – in his misery earlier, and with the rapid progression of events, Brann had not noticed that Hakon was armed. It was unusual for a page to walk around town with a sword on his belt – except, he mused, after dark when it was probably more prudent.

He held out his hand for the weapon. Konall started to toss it over to him, then, remembering Brann's dismal catching ability, changed his mind. His eyes narrowing in brief amusement, he held the sword by the blade and reached it across to the waiting boy. Brann took hold of the hilt – it was a short sword, probably the weapon of choice of many criminal figures because it could be hidden more easily and was more practical in confined spaces, a factor that could prove helpful very soon. He hefted it experimentally, finding it, to his untrained eye, to appear of fairly good quality and well maintained – certainly far better than the decrepit weapons found on the bandits on the mountains.

Further examination was not possible. Catching him by surprise with the suddenness of his move, Konall took one step back and slammed his boot sole in the door. Amazingly, the wood held, but the latch did not, and the door crashed back against the wall. Konall threw himself into the room with Hakon close behind and bellowed, 'In the name of the warlord, throw down your weapons! Two men, follow me – the rest wait in the corridor and watch the exits.'

Caught by surprise, Brann had been left momentarily outside the room. Taking a deep breath, he launched himself after the other two, remembering just in time to avoid careering into the back of them. But there was little chance of that happening. Years of warrior training kicked in and the two boys in front of him barely paused before falling into a routine that was born of countless hours of practice. They split right and left to pick their targets, but stayed close enough together to avoid becoming isolated. The men they faced may have been common criminals, but they were hardened enough to react almost instantly to the sudden invasion of their room. They did not, as Konall had optimistically ordered, give up their weapons – rather they drew them and, with a growl of rage at being threatened in their own environment, turned upon the intruders. Whether or not they believed Konall's orders to his imaginary squad of men was irrelevant: their sole intent was to swat away the immediate threat in front of them in the form of three young boys. One of them up-ended the table and, as it fell, it pushed across the room, forming a low barrier that split the area in two; on the nearside, four of the men faced the boys, while the other half of the room held Loku, Balki and a wiry man with a dark moustache and a calculating darkness in his eyes.

Without a pause, Konall and Hakon fell upon the men in front of them. Konall, to Brann's right, faced two, each of whom seemed twice his width without a trace of fat in sight, while Hakon, to his left, was engaging a man with more scars than skin on his twisted face. In the centre, the fourth man – the hulk who had initiated the earlier argument – either did not notice Brann or rated him inconsequential. He directed his attention, and a heavy murderous cudgel, at the side of Hakon's head in a killing blow that would have mashed his skull into pulp.

Brann hesitated – it had been one thing reacting instinctively as survival instincts took over as had happened with Boar or in the mountains – it was another prospect entirely to cold-bloodedly try to stick a blade into another person with conscious forethought.

But the man taking an enormous back-swing, however, meant that Brann's hesitation was only momentary. Galvanised into action by the prospect of Hakon's death – and with the memory of Callan still burning painfully in his mind – he screamed, 'Not again!' and thrust the short sword into the man's unguarded side. The man arched his back in pain and his agonised bellow roared above the din of ringing metal, shouts and grunts that already filled the room.

Brann's blow stopped the huge man's arm in mid-swing but, to the boy's horror, it did not kill him. Moreover, with his rage over-riding the pain, it did not seem to incapacitate him, either, as he swung round to face Brann.

An initial lurch of discomfort and fear at being the object of attention fell away as the man viciously swung the club at him. An almost abstract calmness slipped over him, leaving him conscious only of each second as it passed and seeing everything before him with an unusual clarity.

He jumped backwards rather than ducking under the swing, and then blessed his luck as he saw that the club had been aimed at his torso for a blow that would have crushed his ribs – had he ducked, it would have caught his head instead. His heel brushed against the wall and he knew that the backwards option was no longer open to him. The massive man saw this also, and began a back-handed swipe with a maniacal look of glee. As the swing started, Brann crouched, and in the same movement, dived headlong to the right of his attacker. The force of the man's swing through fresh air turned him side on and Brann landed behind his massive legs. He slashed Konall's knife across the back of the man's knees and, as the hamstrung man's legs gave way, Brann rolled to his feet and swung his body, arm and sword in one movement to slam the edge of the blade into the man's throat, almost decapitating him.

Breathing so heavily that it almost drowned out the din in the room, he turned to see Hakon kill the man before him with a hammer-blow of a cut with his sword. In the seconds that the conflict had taken so far, Konall had managed to wound both of the men before him, one seriously and the other with merely a gash on his left arm. As Hakon moved to engage the latter, Konall was able to deftly finish off the already dying man before him but, as he was turning to the other brute to help Hakon, there was a sudden movement from the other side of the table. Konall cried in pain as a throwing knife embedded itself in his left arm, close to the top. Had he not been in the act of turning, it would have struck him in the back, probably squarely between the shoulderblades.

Brann grabbed a stool and hurled it at the moustached man as he drew back his arm for another cast. The throw, clumsy as it was, managed to clatter the heavy wooden stool into the man's chest, knocking him back a few steps and, more importantly, causing him to drop the knife. Hakon's adversary saw a glimmer of a chance in the confusion and hurled himself at the two tall boys – only to embed himself on two sword-points as both youths thrust simultaneously.

From either side of the table, each trio faced the other, the air laden with tension and the only noise the heavy breathing of the boys and the slow scrape as the moustached criminal abandoned his dropped knife and drew his sword – a short-bladed one similar to that inherited by Brann.

It was eerie, the pause. The sudden change from raucous madness to silence left Brann edgy, his heart still pumping wildly but with no physical outlet for his twitching muscles and mind.

Loku spoke. 'So, what now, boys?' he said, the sound of a voice strange in the fraught atmosphere. 'It is clear now that there are no men outside – not that it was ever believable, as what warriors would let a lord enter such a room with only two boys to help? You have just killed four men.' He exuded sarcasm. 'Oh, well done. They were little better than base criminals who had fulfilled their usefulness. At least you have saved me the cost of their pay. The only one of them with brains made sure he stayed on this side of the table until you had tired yourselves out. For, let us face it, that is what you have done: you are fatigued, you are wounded,' he nodded at the knife still protruding from Konall's shoulder, 'and you are facing three fresh men. So, I ask you again: what now, boys?'

Balki hefted his sword as if eager to be in action. 'I will tell you what happens now, Loku. Now we start what will be finished by the ambush: I will take great pleasure in personally starting the eradication of the ruling family with its youngest member.' He glanced at the two men beside him. 'Do you hear that? The pup is mine.'

'Pity,' the lean, moustached man smirked. 'I like to finish what I start. But, in this case, I will make an exception, in deference to my future warlord. It should not take us long, anyhow.'

Balki, barely able to contain his eagerness, stepped forward, his sword twitching. 'You go on upstairs to your man on the roof, Loku,' he growled. 'We will take care of this.'

In contrast, Konall was deadly still. His eyes never left those of Balki. He pointed his sword down and rammed it, point-first, into the earthen floor so that it stood, quivering.

His gaze still fixed on Balki, he reached across with his right hand and grasped the knife protruding from his shoulder. Slowly, and deliberately, he pulled the blade, bit by agonising bit, from his flesh. Brann winced, almost feeling the pain himself, but Konall's gaze never flickered.

He laid the knife in his hand. 'Normally I would finish what someone else has started with me, but this time I, too, will make an exception.' The tone of the conversation contrasted dramatically from one side of the table to the other: sneering disdain from the traitors was met by the deep-rooted fury and menace of Konall. The young noble continued, his voice quiet and cold. 'The traitor will have his wish to face the pup. Hakon,' he tossed the knife sideways and his page plucked it from the air adeptly, 'stick this in that scumbag for me, will you?'

'With the greatest of pleasure,' Hakon grinned as Konall, in one movement, snatched his sword and, hooking his boot over the table, slammed it upside down, leaving no barrier between the groups.

Sword swinging, Balki charged with an eager roar at Konall who met him head on but swung his impetus to the side, clearing the way between Brann and the door at the far side through which Loku was rapidly disappearing.

'Get after him, Brann,' he grunted, deflecting Balki's murderous swings. 'Do what you can to stop him until we can catch up to help you.'

Brann obeyed, still astonished at his companions' casual approach in prelude to the current mêlée. He darted to the doorway, wondering if he would ever see the other two alive again, and realised that he would most likely have to stop Loku – and whoever else was on the roof – alone.

How he would attempt that, he had no idea, but he concentrated for now on following Loku as fast as he could: at all costs, he could not let the signal be issued to the hiding mountain men. He guessed that he need not worry about rushing headlong into an attack by the scheming ambassador as he climbed the steep, winding stairs that led from the basement room – as far as Loku knew, all three boys were tied up in combat downstairs, and his main consideration would be to issue the signal as a matter of urgency.

He could hear Loku's heavy, expensive boots pounding the wooden stairs ahead of him… and getting rapidly closer. By contrast, his own lighter body weight and softer footwear ensured that his progress was not only quieter in itself but was also masked by the louder noise of Loku's footsteps.

He realised that this was not a good thing after all. He seemed unlikely to reach Loku before he gained the roof and, if Loku was unaware that there was anyone closing in on him, there would be no reason for him to check his progress. The stairway straightened in its final stretch before reaching a door – presumably onto the roof area – and Brann's assessment was proved correct: Loku was already too-thirds of the way up the flight and there was no way he could catch him before he reached the door.

In desperation, Brann yelled, 'Loku! I have got you now!' Whether it was convincing or not, he would never know, but Loku's surprise at someone being behind him caused him to turn to assess the danger.

He had lost his momentum. Brann, who had continued his rush up the stairs, managed to scramble the remaining distance between them. Realising he still had Konall's knife in his left hand he reversed the blade and, with a flailing lunge, dived forward and stabbed it down into the top of Loku's foot. The man screamed and slashed down wildly with his sword, but the stairway was narrow, confining his swing, and Brann managed to rear back and avoid the blade as it splintered the wood inches in front of him.

Loku, in a violent rage, began to rain blows down on top of him. Thankful that his short sword was not too long to fit sideways across the passage, all that Brann could do was to desperately ward off the blows as he was forced back down the stairs.

He almost stumbled as he reached a small square landing at the foot of the straight stretch of stairs before the rest of the steps coiled back down towards the lower levels. With a blood-curdling screech, Loku launched himself at him from the bottom of the stairway. Brann threw himself to one side to avoid the wild blow and crashed through a door that he had not even realised was there. A middle-aged woman, obviously accustomed to hearing men in dispute outside her door but not to sword-swinging maniacs bursting through it and into her room, sat up in bed, screaming wildly.

Brann had no time to pay her any more attention as Loku came at him without hesitation. The man was experienced where Brann knew nothing; he was broad, powerful and supple where Brann was undersized and weaker; but he was limping heavily and the wound in his foot was seriously affecting his mobility, giving Brann a slight advantage. He knew he should be trying to devise a strategy to exploit Loku's wound, but it was all happening so fast it was all he could do to dodge the man's blows.

He was tiring fast, and he knew he would have to close with the man and offer something with his own blade, otherwise it would be a mere matter of time before Loku managed to land a blow. Taking a deep breath, he stepped forward instead of back, throwing himself into it before he had time to think – or to hesitate.

The move caught Loku by surprise and, as Brann slashed his sword up and across towards his jaw, he had to fling his own weapon up to deflect the blow, the uncultured and instinctive move upsetting the ordered movements of a man used to sparring with seasoned warriors who fought to a set routine born of years of training. Loku's parry saved him from death, but the force of the meeting of the two blades sliced the edge of his own sword into his cheek, opening up a long gash from temple to jaw – and jarred Brann's sword from his own grasp, sending the weapon spinning over Loku's head towards the door.

In triumph, with one side of his face a terrifying, bloody mask, Loku cried with glee and swept his sword down and across towards the side of Brann's neck. In fright, Brann dropped to one knee under the swipe – and stabbed Konall's long knife as hard as he could into the side of Loku's thigh.

With both legs wounded, the man fell to the floor, but the movement pulled the knife from Brann's hand. He lurched the few yards to retrieve his sword but, as he reached it in the doorway, Loku threw open the shutters on the window and began to yell to the man on the roof. Brann knew that, even if he re-engaged Loku, the ambassador could continue to shout as they fought. The boy's priorities had changed: he must reach the man above and stop him, and in his current state, Loku would be unable to catch him. He grabbed his sword and ran up the stairs. As he reached the door at the top, he snatched at the latch – and felt a sharp pain across the left side of his wrist. A throwing knife clattered into the door in front of him. As he jerked in pain, his sword fell from his slippery grasp and slid down the steep stairs behind him. He ignored Loku's cry of triumph and, grabbing the knife from the step in front of him, thanking the gods that it had struck side-on rather than with the point of edge of the blade, he put his shoulder to the door, half-falling onto the roof.

A scruffy man with a longbow was slouched beside a glowing brazier. Relief swept over Brann as he realised that Loku's cries from the window had not been heard on the rooftop and had not set off the signal... yet.

Loku's voice roared up the stairs as the man leapt to his feet at Brann's surprising appearance. 'The signal! Give the signal, man!'

The man grabbed an arrow and thrust its tip into the brazier. A rag on the end immediately caught fire and, in a fluid movement, he nocked the arrow to the bowstring. As he drew back the bow, Brann instinctively and desperately flung the knife. It hammered, purely by chance, point-first into the centre of the man's chest. He arched backwards but, as he fell, his fingers – dead or dying – loosed the arrow. Blazing brightly in the darkness, it soared high into the night sky. Brann sank to his knees with a moan of despair. He had failed. The ambush would go ahead, and men and women would be savaged by Loku's wildmen.

The thought slammed his thoughts into the present. If there was any way that they could be warned, it must be done. If Konall and Hakon were still alive, he must reach them. He scrambled back to his feet and ran to the door, dragging it open. He flung himself back as the thought struck that if Loku had managed to drag himself to the bottom of the stairs – and he had – then he could have managed to reach the top of them while Brann had been on the roof... and be waiting on the other side of the door. There was no one there, however, and he started more cautiously down the steps, spotting his sword lying at the bottom.

As he bent to pick up the weapon, footsteps thundered up the steps from below. To his relief – both at seeing his friends alive and at the fact that he was not about to face another fight – Konall and Hakon battered into view, swords raised, eyes blazing and chests heaving.

'Did you get him?' Konall shouted. 'Did you get Loku?'

'I did enough to let me get to the bowman: the man with the signal. But Konall,' his face, and voice, were stricken, 'I am so sorry. The signal went up. We have failed. I have failed.' He slumped on the bottom step, dejected, his head in his blood- and grime- and sweat-smeared hands.

'Where is Loku?' Konall said grimly. 'I am right here,' the deep voice said, causing the three boys to jump. They rushed to the doorway of the room where Brann and Loku had fought. The treacherous ambassador, drenched in blood and clearly fighting to keep his legs strong enough to remain upright – an impressive feat in itself – was standing on the sill of the tall window, facing them. 'And I have heard what

I wanted to know. The consequences of that signal are in motion, boys, and there is nothing that can stop them. You,' he nodded at Konall, 'would be well advised to run now while you can and thank the gods for the extra chance they have given you to live, unlike the rest of your family. Under the regime about to take power, you will be caught and killed very shortly. No one will shelter you when they see the atrocities performed upon those who are even vaguely suspected of assisting you, and there will be many examples made of innocent people to reinforce that impression. You would be well advised to leave this country and never return if you want to live out your days, although I strongly suspect – and hope – that you will not be able to manage to reach the shore. You,' his cold gaze locked on Brann, 'I have unfinished business with. We will meet again, I will see to that. And it will be finished.

'But for now, I must take my leave.'

Konall had snatched a knife from his boot and his movements were a blur as he hurled it at the man. Loku, however, had taken a step backwards and dropped from sight an instant before the missile streaked through the space he had filled.

Konall strode across the room. He noticed the shocked woman, still sitting wide-eyed and bewildered in her bed. 'Madam,' he acknowledged her, with a nod.

Brann and Hakon hurried after him. Brann turned to the woman. 'My apologies about, well, about...' What, exactly, was he sorry about? The mess? The carnage? The disturbance of her sleep? The shock of seeing two people burst into her room and attempt to butcher each other? He had no idea. All he did know was that, whatever he said, would be hopelessly inadequate. 'My apologies about all of this,' was all he could lamely repeat. She whispered something inaudible in reply.

He hurried to the window to join the other two. 'Where is he?' he asked.

Hakon shrugged. 'Gone. A river runs through this city to the fjord and has been channelled into several canals to control its route. It seems that one of them passes directly behind this building. So he had a safer landing than we expected.'

'That was lucky for him,' Brann observed.

Still staring down into the darkness, Konall said, 'I would guess that the position of the canal for the purpose that you have just witnessed is one of the reasons why this building was chosen by the conspirators.' He turned to Brann. 'Were you responsible for all of that damage to him?' Brann nodded. 'Impressive. He is considered to be a formidable swordsman.'

'I think I was a bit unorthodox for him. I just made it up as I went along, and I do not think he knew what to expect because of that.'

Hakon slapped him on the back as they made their way to the door. 'Good lad!' he said enthusiastically. 'Long may you do so. Now let us go and do more of the same to those madmen from the mountains.'

As they rushed to the stairs, Brann said to Hakon, 'How can you two be so matter of fact, even cheerful, when all these people are about to be wiped out? And what can we do to stop it? There are only three of us.'

Hakon grinned. 'But if we can get to Lord Sigurr's party before they are attacked, the mountain men lose the surprise but do not know they have lost it and we can turn the ambush to our advantage. As for the first question, we are always cheerful – well, as cheerful as my Lord Konall ever gets.'

Konall's reply, cast over his shoulder, was extremely rude. Hakon continued, 'That is, we are cheerful when we feel we can do something about a problem, especially when our solution involves giving someone a good thrashing. It is just a pity that we do not have time to reach the garrison on the way, but they are billeted up beside the warlord's hall. We could give the scum a real thumping, then.'

They had reached the room in the basement (they had decided to leave the building by the way that they had entered, rather than try to negotiate what was often, in these buildings, a warren of corridors to reach the main entrance) and the sight of the two bodies – Balki's with a savage wound from the side of his neck extending diagonally a hand's span into his chest, and the moustached criminal with the throwing knife embedded in the centre of his chest – Hakon had stayed true to Konall's instruction – had caused Hakon's words to sink in slightly slower than normal.

Brann skidded to a halt as realisation struck him. 'But we can get help,' he started, but was cut off as Hakon slammed into his back. He picked himself up as Konall wheeled around. 'What?'

'The slaves. The galley slaves and crew from Einarr's ship. If they are held near here, and one would expect that they would have been accommodated close to the docks, surely we could use them.'

Hakon looked at Konall. 'Are they?'

Konall nodded. 'They are.'

Hakon grinned. 'Could we?'

Konall, to Brann's shock, smiled. 'We could.'

Chapter 12

As ever, he sensed the knock at the door before it came. Except that, this time, it never came.

The door opened and, unannounced, the servant entered. Older than the normal; much older. At closer glance, even older than he. One he had not seen before. He did not like unanticipated change.

Still, while she performed the same few duties, setting down the pitiful amount of food that now satisfied his mid-day appetite and replacing his ewer with a fresh one, it made no difference. It was safe to say that she was not so pleasant on the eye as those who normally came; it was safe to say that he was equally not so pleasant on the eye, but he could choose not to look at his own image; but it was also safe to say that his days of finding personal use for a woman pleasant on the eye were long past.

But he did not like change, when he knew not the reason for change.

'It is customary to knock before entering these chambers,' he said.

His voice was as dusty as the floor, and she moved to pour him water. 'For what purpose? Do you have the speed of *your youth to react in the moment betwixt knock and entry?'*

Her voice was as dry as his and he surprised himself by offering her his goblet. She shook her head. 'I have acquired years beyond even yours, old man, when a mountain lake could not ease the croak in my throat.'

His ire rose again. 'Know you whom you address, servant?' he barked.

Unconcerned, she turned away, as if to go. 'Would I be here if I did not?'

'So why are you here?' He was irritated, but this time with himself. His self-control and subtlety had vanished with the question, blurted before his mind could keep pace.

She looked deep into his eyes. 'For the same reason you are here. Fates are intertwining, as they do beyond the power and ken of man.'

He caught at her arm. 'Do I know you?'

She lifted away his fingers. 'If you want it, then it has been so.'

'Speak clearly that I may understand.'

'In this moment, you need know this: I am here...' she left the door ajar '...once again.'

He moved to the doorway, but dropped his hand from the latch. For a reason he found himself unable to explain, he could not close the door on her.

****

'I don't know what to say.' Brann looked up at the towering figures of Konall and Hakon for inspiration. 'Why should they listen to me?'

'It has to come from you.' Hakon was adamant, as he had been on their run over to the warehouse that was a temporary home for the crew and galley slaves. 'Say what you feel.'

Konall nodded. 'A man who is forced to fight will never truly fight. He is already dead. It can only be their choice. Say it how it is. Give them the choice.'

Brann looked at them then, without further discussion, turned to the men who had fallen silent at the sight of the three blood-spattered boys crashing through the doors. He drew a breath deep into his chest.

'I am just a boy. I haven't seen what you have seen, and I haven't done what you have done. I haven't sat beside you on the rowing benches for long, but I have sat beside you long enough to know the sort of men you are.

'There are men out there who are attempting an atrocity. I...' he looked at the two boys beside him '...*we* have seen what they are capable of, what they have done, and it is beyond the understanding of people like us.

'The Captain and these warriors with you did not make you slaves. They do not treat you as other masters have treated you. The people of this land did not make you slaves, and they have treated you all with respect since we came here. They have given you food and ale and housed you in comfort. Were you a crew of free men, in all honesty what more could their hospitality have provided?'

'Women!' came a cry from the back. Laughter rolled around the room. Hakon coughed pointedly and nudged Brann, but he ignored him and seized the moment.

'That omission was a hospitable gesture to you as well – the women here are beautiful, there's no denying it, but they are so formidable that you would soon be at their bidding more than to any slavemaster,' he grinned, to more amusement among the men. His tone became serious. 'But there

448

is a throng of these inhuman monsters of men moving now on the leaders of these people, leaders who are hopelessly unaware and outnumbered. Should they be massacred, the ordinary people of this place, people who have done nothing to deserve this fate, men like us and women,' he smiled, 'more formidable than us would be in the thrall of the engineers of horrors we cannot imagine. It is not right. If we could stop it, surely we would.'

He looked around their faces. 'But we can. We have weapons here. If these men are willing,' he looked at Cannick, who nodded without hesitation, 'we can move as one group to help these people. We can do the right thing. Alone or with any of you who are willing, we three will go to do what we can. But a friend told me that a man who is forced to fight will never truly fight, so I can only ask.

'So I ask: will you come with us? Will you fight with us? I...' The reality of talking to these hardened men swept over him and he felt small and exposed. He spread his hands. 'I would be grateful.'

There was no resounding roar, no stamping of feet or pounding of fists. But in the silence, one man stood, stepped forward and nodded. Another followed, and several more before Brann was suddenly aware that every man was on his feet. And looking at him.

He turned to Cannick. 'I think we need to look out some weapons.' Cannick's grin was all the confirmation his men needed.

The ship's stores, of all kinds, had been transferred for security reasons to the upper storey of the building and with the help of the two guards from Yngvarrsharn's militia who had been left with the ship's company, the arming of the slaves was finished quickly. Konall looked at Brann.

449

'What do you propose? How will we use them?'

As Brann gathered his thoughts, Cannick coughed politely for attention. Without acknowledging the incredulous sight of the local warlord's nephew relying on a youthful galley slave for advice on how to approach a military situation, he said, 'If I may suggest one thing, young lord, we might be better to discuss our approach as we move, given the urgency of the situation.'

Konall's eyes blazed. It had not been easy for him to alter an entire childhood's attitude towards dealing with people, and he just managed to stop himself from snapping a furious retort at the veteran warrior. Then the fire in his gaze subsided. He nodded.

'You are right. Let us leave.' He checked the padding strapped to the wound where he had pulled the knife from his shoulder, swept his cloak behind him dramatically, and strode out through the doorway.

Brann smiled.

As the party moved from the warehouse at a fast jog, Konall moved beside Cannick. 'You do not find it odd that I should ask a slave for advice?'

Cannick's eyes widened in a good show of astonishment. 'Lord Einarr's page: a slave?' He saw the look on Konall's face, and grunted, 'You know, then. And if you are asking him for advice, despite knowing his true position, then clearly it matters not that you know.' He ran a heavy, calloused hand over his close-cropped grey hair. 'And, no, I do not find it particularly odd. Every good commander has learned early on to use all of the talents and strengths at his disposal, no matter what – or who – they may be.'

Konall nodded. 'I was taught that lesson in the mountains earlier this month.' He looked at Cannick. 'By the one whose advice I would now seek.' He looked ahead again, and took a deep breath, as if launching into something he found hard to say. 'I would also welcome any suggestions you may have, should you feel our actions are folly.'

Cannick's eyes were also fixed on the road ahead. 'If you, as the highest ranking noble commanding this party, issue orders, regardless of who supplied the logic for those orders, I will obey without question. To do otherwise would be to destroy the cohesion and the ability to act quickly of a military unit.' As a student of such matters, Konall nodded his agreement. 'If, however, something occurs to me that may assist you in your decision, and if the time is suitable for such a suggestion, I will be happy to offer it to you.'

Konall nodded. 'Appreciated,' he said, and moved forward to join Brann at the front of the rapidly moving column. Hakon moved to follow him, but paused beside Cannick. 'Very carefully put,' he observed. 'You should think about a career as a diplomat once you grow too old for all this running about.'

Cannick's reply left him in no doubt about his view of diplomats, and dispelled the possibility of that career move. He did, however, stare thoughtfully at the small figure ahead of him.

Konall had reached that small figure. 'You have had time to think. Tell me.'

Brann spoke between heavy breaths. He was not a natural runner, and the exertions of the night and the lack of sleep were taking their toll.

'As far as I can see,' he started, 'there are two parts of this – our approach to the place where it will all happen, and what will happen when it does all happen, if you see what I mean. As far as getting there is concerned, speed is the important bit. There is no need for quiet, as the mountain men may be moving anyway and unlikely to hear us, and if they are already in position and do hear us, it may distract them and give the warlord's party some extra time or warning, either of which would be good. So we should try to get there as fast as we can – to be honest, I think too much time has already passed to reach them before the attack begins. So we have to arrive as soon afterwards as we can, for obvious reasons.'

Konall nodded. 'If we do get there before any attack, we will be at the disposal of the warlord, so we do not need to worry about what we do in that case. But what if we do not?' He held up his hand to pause Brann. 'Wait. I want someone else to hear this.' He waved Cannick forward, then gestured for Brann to continue.

Slightly nervous in front of this growing, and more knowledgeable, audience, Brann forced himself to resume. 'If we try to hit them hard and fast from, as much as we can, the opposite side from the warlord's party's position, they will not know which way to turn.' Konall nodded, and moved to speak to Cannick, but Brann spoke again. 'No, wait. There is more. If we hit them as a single bunch – I am sorry I do not know the military term for it...'

'No matter, carry on,' Konall grunted.

'If we hit them all together it will be effective, but I think it will be effective because of the surprise, because they will not know which way to turn, and because they will be attacked together, but not because of our numbers. So it might be just as effective if we use fewer people to do it.'

Konall was confused. 'Why not just hit them with all we have got and hammer them?'

'Because we could split our lot into two groups – one can hit them like I said, and the other can either help defend the warlord's party if they need it or hit the mountain men from yet another angle, causing even more confusion and less chance of manoeuvring for them.'

Cannick cleared his throat in what was becoming apparent was his way of respectfully indicating he had a contribution to make. Konall nodded, and the experienced warrior said, 'It seems a good idea, youngster, but it is always a risk to split yourselves too many ways. It can overly weaken your forces, and make it difficult to co-ordinate each section of your, er, bunches, as you would say, especially the way situations can change quickly in battle.'

Brann flinched. 'In battle'. The words seemed so ominous, making what was about to take place so much more than just launching a rescue bid to save a party of aristocrats on their way to an outdoor banquet. Yet what they were proposing was a battle – a small one, but a battle nonetheless. He wished Cannick had never used the words.

He shook his head in an effort to concentrate on the whole of what Cannick suggested, rather than just those two words. 'If we were talking of attacking normal warriors, properly trained, I think you would be right.' He flushed. 'Well, I mean, I know you would be right. But I have...' He looked at Konall and Hakon. 'We have seen these men in action. They fight like wild animals, like the lowest order of vicious street criminals, and nothing like trained warriors. They overwhelm you with their numbers and their wild attacks, with no tactics other than their desire, their urgent desire, to rip you apart. And I mean, really rip you apart.' He shook his head again. He was nearly crying as the attack on Konall's hunting party flooded his memory. 'But that is an advantage, too: because they fight like animals, they will react like animals. If we surprise them, and confuse them, and turn them so they do not know where to expect the next danger, they will panic. Each one will care only about his own survival, and they will cease to operate as one force, which is their only real advantage. We might be splitting our total resources into three smaller, er, bunches – but I think we can split them into a hundred bunches of one.

'Then we can chase them off, or hem them in and destroy them.'

Konall snorted. 'There is only one option there, then.' He looked at Cannick. 'What do you think?'

The old warrior was breathing even more heavily than Brann. 'I think,' he panted, 'that I find it hard to believe that a farm boy thinks like that. It is simple, flexible, and makes sense. All you can ask for.'

Hakon grinned. 'He seems to have a knack for it. Well, that and hitting with a sword. Oh, and it is better not to call him a farm boy. He is a touchy little mill boy.'

Cannick smiled. 'So, what is your secret, boy? Father used to be a soldier? Uncle served as a mercenary? Where did you get it from?'

Brann shrugged. 'I really do not know. It is just what seems right, that is all. To be honest, I keep expecting my luck to run out, it terrifies me.'

The veteran slapped him on the back, almost knocking him to the ground as he ran. 'Stay that way, boy. It will stop you being complacent. I can show you plenty of complacent warriors – they are the dead ones.'

Without slowing their advance, Konall called the two local warriors forward, and sent Cannick back to spread the word among Einarr's men about their plans and to organise the party into two groups as they ran. Those who would attack the mountain men from the outset would be led by Cannick: Konall reckoned that he knew them better than anyone and that they would respond to his leadership – and that, as by far the most experienced warrior present, he was quite simply the best man for the job. The second group, to either reinforce Lord Sigurr's party or attack separately, would be headed by Konall, with Hakon and Brann at his side. Brann felt that the two boys felt obliged to keep him close because they were worried about him, but he was not insulted. Rather, he felt comforted, and relieved that they would be beside him. It did not, however, relieve his fear. He reflected that his recent life seemed to involve him lurching from one situation of terror to another.

Just then, the warriors that Konall had called to the front to act as guides indicated that they were nearing their destination. Konall raised a hand to halt them and take stock of the situation. As they paused, and the sound of their running dispersed, they became aware of clamour in front and behind them: the sounds of battle ahead and, to the rear, the shouts of confusion and concern from the residents who had been wakened and alarmed by a large group of armed men thundering past their homes.

Brann sank to one knee to catch his breath and relieve his aching arms. Despite the strength he had built up as a rower it had not taken long for the unaccustomed weight of a shield on one arm and a long sword in his other hand – the sword had been lying loose and there had been no time to find a scabbard – to take its toll. And the ill-fitting helmet that had been dumped onto his head kept slipping backwards and forwards, both irritating him and worrying him that it would fall over his eyes at a crucially bad moment.

'You will catch your breath better if you stand up,' a familiar voice said above him.

Brann jumped up in surprise – and alarm. 'Gerens! What are you doing here? You are in no state for this.'

His rowing partner's dark gaze never altered. 'I will be fine, chief. I would have worried too much about you if I let you do this alone. And I am not the only one.' He nodded to his side to direct Brann's attention to Grakk who, quiet as ever, was a few yards behind them.

Brann smiled. 'Good to see you both. Although Grakk looks a little overdressed.'

Grakk pulled uncomfortably at the long, sleeveless, woollen waistcoat that was all that covered his wiry, tattooed torso.

'I am far from happy,' he grumbled. 'This country is far too cold. One requires far too many clothes. It is not convenient and surely cannot be healthy.'

'You should have seen the struggle we had getting him to wear even just that,' Gerens confided. 'He only cheered up when he found those two curvy swords.'

Grakk scowled. 'Scimitars, you ignorant boy. These are true swords, not the sharpened clubs that you people use. One requires skill to use these – would you like me to demonstrate for you?'

The offer was half in humour, but Gerens considered it seriously, and nervously. 'It is fine, I believe you. But I think we will have plenty of chances for you to demonstrate for the men from the mountains, instead. We all have a few scores to settle with them.'

That thought cheered up Grakk immediately. 'Indeed,' he grinned. 'Many scores can be settled today.'

Hakon appeared beside them. 'Ah, my erstwhile comrades in captivity! Are we ready to show our appreciation to our former hosts for the treatment we received?'

'Funnily enough,' Brann smiled, 'they were just talking about that.'

'Well, very soon you will have a chance to do more than talk,' Hakon replied, indicating behind them. 'Here comes Konall – we must be all sorted out now, and from the noises ahead, we cannot waste any time.'

Konall jogged up, and glanced around their little group. 'Are you ready?' Four grim faces and nearly thirty more behind them nodded at him. He spoke tensely, his voice coming in a clipped rush. 'We will move out slightly behind Cannick's group, so we can judge how best to use ourselves as the others hit the enemy.' He looked at Brann and Gerens. 'I am assuming that the two of you have no experience or knowledge of what you are going into, so you should work with Hakon, me,' he nodded towards Grakk, 'and him as a group of five. The other two know what they are doing and while I can't move my shield arm properly, the shield itself will give me enough protection on that side to let me work my sword. You two stay close to us.'

Brann interrupted. 'I do not want to be a hindrance to you.'

'Be quiet,' Konall snapped. 'There is no time for being considerate. We work as a group, no argument. Many, if not all, of the others will be doing the same to some extent or another. There will be no time or opportunity for you to watch others and learn, so listen now. I will keep it brief: watch each other's backs as much as you can and, when you are facing a man, deal with him the quickest and simplest way possible. Once he is down, check all around you – especially behind – for the nearest and most immediate danger.'

The last of the other group had just finished moving away. Konall raised his hand and swept it forward in a clear signal to the men with him. 'Stick together,' he said to the four around him as they moved forward. Then, astonishingly, he grinned. 'And enjoy yourselves!'

Stunned, Gerens looked at Brann as they broke into a trot. 'Did I just see him smile?' he asked incredulously – an ironic question, Brann thought, coming from him.

'Not only that,' Brann said, pushing his helmet back from his eyes, 'but that is the second time in a matter of hours that he has done it. These sort of situations seem to bring out the best in him. Or the worst.'

Gerens grunted. 'While he is on our side, I will call it the best.'

They were climbing a shallow rise, and Brann watched as Cannick's party spread out into a wide line as they approached the crest of the slope. Nausea lurched through him and his knees buckled slightly as he forced forward limbs that had suddenly become heavy with fear.

'You all right, chief?' Gerens asked.

'Not really,' Brann said, his voice sounding distant and detached to him. 'I am scared witless. I feel like I just want to turn and run away from here as fast as I can.'

'Thank the gods,' the other boy replied. 'I thought I was the only one feeling that way.'

Grakk's voice came from close behind. 'All men feel this way before battle. Time to think is not helpful at a time like this. You will feel better when you start fighting. No time to think then.'

'I hope so,' Brann said faintly, using his forearm to push his helmet away from his eyes yet again. 'And it had better be soon, or I think I will be sick. Or wet myself. Or both.'

'Me, too,' Gerens said with his usual simple honesty. 'At the warehouse I could not wait to get at these people... Now it seems... different.'

Hakon appeared beside them and jovially slapped Brann on the back, the jolt tilting his helmet over his eyes yet again.

458

'Worry not, lads – we are about to start.' He pointed ahead. 'There go the first lot.'

As the other party had crested the ridge, Cannick had swept his sword down from on high and, with a roar that startled Brann both in terms of its volume and its abrupt start, they launched themselves towards the chaos below.

'Here we go,' Hakon continued cheerfully as Konall waved them forward, up the slope. He reached across and pushed Brann's helmet back. 'That looks a bit loose – you had better watch it doesn't fall over your eyes.'

The thought passed through Brann's mind of telling Hakon where exactly the helmet was in danger of being rammed, but the words stuck in his throat. He felt detached, almost surreal, as they broke into a trot towards the crest of the shallow hill. His breathing was shallow, but loud in his ears. His stomach was knotted and his legs were leaden and harder to lift with each successive step. He was so scared that he felt on the verge of fainting. And he desperately wished he was anywhere else but here.

They were nearing the low summit, and some of the men started to spread out. With a quick wave Konall stopped them.

'Keep tight,' he shouted over the noise that was filling the air from the other side of the hill. 'We do not know yet where we will strike. Wait to spread out until we charge – that way we will hit them as a broad arrowhead and punch into them. Follow my lead and my signal.'

The men crowded together again and, as they crested the hill, Konall said to Brann, 'Stay close to me. I may want your opinion on where to hit them.'

As the scene of desperate and frantic fighting opened up in front of them, it was instantly apparent that there was no question as to where they were most needed. The warlord's party, beset on all sides, were defending themselves ferociously but looked as if they could be over-run at any instant, such were the relentless numbers throwing themselves upon them with an eagerness for blood that was obvious even at a distance. The first party of reinforcements was wreaking havoc and confusion at the rear, but the sheer number and fanaticism of the wildmen prevented them from having any effect on the struggle around the nobles' party.

'To the warlord! Follow me!' Konall roared, and set off at a sprint. The others hurried to catch him, and with a visible and urgent objective now clear rather than just the general imaginings of anarchic and brutal conflict that had gone before, Brann forgot his fear. Pounding across and down the slope, trying to keep up with Konall's longer legs, he focused on the point at which they would slam into the side of the wildmen attacking the warlord's party and forced himself as hard as his legs would carry him towards it.

Below them, blood and sweat stinging his eyes and plastering his long hair to his face, Einarr glanced up as movement on the hillside caught the edge of his vision. The party knew that they had been reinforced, but could not see by whom, and they had quickly realised that the help would soon be insufficient to save them. In an action that had already been repeated countless times, Einarr slammed an attacker's weapon away with a two-handed swing of his heavy sword, and killed the man with the return swing in the opposite direction, the effort dragging a grunt from him that was becoming more of a shout with every blow. As another opponent leapt to take the dead man's place with a scream of bloodlust, he risked wiping a sleeve across his eyes and snatched a quick look again at the hillside. His surprise almost cost him his life, and his astonishment froze him for an instant. Years of training and survival instincts born of countless life-threatening situations kicked in however and he dealt with his next opponent as efficiently as the last, although weariness seemed slightly less in evidence than before.

'By all the gods, it is the slaves,' he gasped, his voice cracking with relief and unexpected emotion.

'What is that, boy?' his father roared beside him, swinging a large, double-headed axe that he had plucked from the hands of a lifeless warrior, with lethal ease as if it were a switch, the tattoo of a dragon on one massive bicep seeming to writhe with every movement.

'Tell the others,' Einarr shouted back between swings, 'we only need to hold out for a few moments more. We are about to receive some help.'

As Brann and those with him closed on the position, they noticed that the small party was fighting with increased vigour.

'Come on!' Hakon bellowed, unable to contain himself. 'They are going to hang on enough for us to reach them!'

Their speed and the downwards slope carried them head-long like a battering ram into the flank of the wildmen at one side of the beleaguered party. They had been concentrating so hard on getting there before it was too late that, to a man, they had never thought of roaring a challenge as they charged, and their near-silent approach saw them crash deep into the mass of the enemy before it was even known that they were coming.

Brann found himself heading for a tall, skinny man with a rusty pike. Catching his foot on the leg of a corpse left behind as the warlord's party had slowly been forced backwards by the initial assault, before they had become surrounded, he

461

stumbled and his helmet fell, predictably, over his eyes. In fury and frustration, he skidded to a halt, rammed his sword point-first into the hard earth, and wrenched the helmet from his head. He swung it directly at the unsuspecting man, catching him squarely on the side of the head. Grabbing his sword, he followed the direction of the helmet.

The man was stunned for only an instant, but a wild slash of Brann's sword ensured that he never lived beyond that moment. Remembering Konall's advice, he did not dwell on his small success but immediately swung around, just in time to see a snarling foe with a short spear lunging at him. Too late to take the thrust directly on his shield, he swayed to his left and brought the shield down hard, turning his arm over so that the top edge forced the spear downwards and the point into the ground. Pivoting his shoulders, he swung his shield back round and his sword arm forward, taking the wildman square in the chest. The man's eyes widened – not in surprise, but in fury – before they balled and he slumped to one side.

Trapped between the man's ribs, Brann's sword was twisted from his grasp. In a panic, he leapt upon the lifeless body and, one foot on its chest, wrenched the weapon from its gruesome sheath. Eyes wild, he swung round and back again, seeking danger.

There was movement to his right. He flung his sword around, desperately. Hakon jumped back in alarm.

'Easy, little wolf,' he said. 'Save it for the bad people.'

The familiar voice jerked Brann back to reality. He paused long enough to hear Konall shout, 'Get back here, you short-legged idiot. You cannot take them all on by yourself.'

Calmed slightly, Brann looked quickly round him. The force of their charge, and its surprise factor, had carried them into the mass of the mountain men slightly behind the enemy's front two ranks. Those two rough lines of wildmen were isolated as a result, and the party of nobles had been able to cut through them before the remainder of the enemy, who had been rocked back by the sudden and unexpected entrance of the reinforcements, could assist their companions. Konall's men were now able to protect that side of the warlord's party, allowing the nobles to turn their full force on the wildmen who had circled behind them, originally surrounding them, but were now cut off themselves. In seconds, they had been slaughtered.

Hakon took advantage of the fleeting respite as the majority of the wildmen adjusted to the developments in the fight. To respond to Konall's cry of 'Get him back here, now!' he grabbed Brann by the back of his tunic and dragged him at a run to the rest of his companions.

'This time, we stick together like I said,' Konall instructed.

'I am sorry,' Brann stammered. 'I have no idea how it happened.'

His momentum must have carried him into the throng until he came across an opponent and, by chance, his path must have opened up further before him than anyone else's had. But, before he could expound his theory to Konall, the mountain men were upon them once more.

The little band of five formed into a loose group, far enough apart to have some room to fight, but close enough to support each other. A leering, bearded man, the top half of his face concealed behind one of the demonic masks favoured by the wildmen, came at Brann with a cleaver held high above his head. As he started his downward swing, however, Brann pre-empted his move by darting forward and poking the tip of his sword into the man's throat. He jumped to the side as the body, and weapon, crashed towards him.

He had deliberately, this time, thrust his weapon only far enough to be effective without carrying on and trapping it but, before he could congratulate himself, another man was upon him, carrying a long-handled axe with more worn notches than straight edges along the blade. Brann deflected the blow with his shield, but not without jarring his arm almost to the point of numbness. Falling forwards, he thrust out his sword to steady himself – and by chance stabbed in through one of his foe's ragged-booted feet. The man screamed, pausing as he raised his weapon for another almighty blow, and Brann thrust his sword into his heart. The killing blow, by necessity, had to be deeper than that delivered to the previous man's throat but he remembered to pull his sword back quickly before the body fell, and he was able to stand ready for the next attack.

Hakon grunted beside him as he almost decapitated an opponent. 'You could try swinging that thing now and again. I have never seen anyone so determined to stick it straight into people. These swords are really made for cutting, you know.'

Like Brann, he was casting about for another opponent, but the emphasis seemed to have moved away from their side of the group for the moment. His eyes opened wide in alarm as movement caught his attention, and he slammed his sword, point-first, into the throat of the wildman who had fallen beside Brann. The thrust by Brann must have failed to find his heart properly and the man had retained just enough life, and fury, to try to thrust a rusty knife up at the boy standing over him. Hakon's sword-tip had, however, finished what Brann had started.

'I will admit, however,' the tall boy added, 'that this poking thing does sometimes have its merits.'

The wildmen had started to panic as their advantage and seemingly easy victory had vanished under the combined fightback of the nobles and their reinforcements. Falling back had taken them away from Brann and Hakon's side of the group, explaining the pair's sudden lack of opponents, and Brann glanced about to find another position where he could be more helpful.

The other three were somewhat busier. Konall was using his sword with his usual assured efficiency; to his left, Gerens was swinging his axe with an effectiveness that was probably surprising even himself; and, to Konall's right, Grakk was engaged in what appeared to be a macabre dance with as many opponents as he could find, the two scimitars weaving shining patterns as he twisted, turned, crouched and spun in a mesmeric flow of movement.

Brann moved to help them and, as he did so, saw a large bearded man aim an unnoticed blow at Konall's side. The young noble was in the process of despatching another foe and had no idea that the unseen man was delivering an overhand thrust with a heavy spear. In desperation, Bran threw himself forward and flung his sword up blindly. The blade, by good fortune, smacked against the spear shaft, knocking it upwards, but Brann's dive had taken him onto one knee, directly in front of the mountain man – with his back to him. Without time to rise or turn, he let go of the handle of his shield (it was still attached to his forearm by a heavy strap) and, reversing his sword, he grasped the hilt with his left hand. With his right palm against the pummel, he shouted hoarsely with the effort and thrust the blade backwards under his left shoulder, driving it into the stomach of the nauseatingly stinking man and up under his ribs and into his chest. The man fell forwards onto Brann, forcing the boy's chest almost onto his knee and making him retch at his stench. Konall, who had finished his opponent in time to notice Brann's intervention, used his boot to push the corpse from the smaller boy and Brann, with a savage grunt that contrasted with the mask of calm, almost serenity, that had oddly settled over his face, twisted slightly to help retrieve his blade as the body slumped backwards.

Brann never saw the blow coming. Konall watched, almost mesmerised by horror, as a drooling, cackling wildman leapt on top of his dead comrade's body and swung a high looping downwards swing directly at the crown of the smaller boy's unprotected head, just as Brann started to look up at Konall with a smile of gratitude.

For a long second, watching as the movement seemed to unfold in slow motion, Konall hesitated, watching the death of his friend. Comprehension of Brann's mortal danger kicked him back to reality and, in desperate panic, he lashed out with his sword.

The movement was so quick that Brann could not realise what was happening until he felt a dull thump above and behind his left ear. It felt more like a punch than the strike of a weapon, and he started to rise to confront the culprit.

Konall knew otherwise. His sword had managed to deflect the wildman's broad-bladed weapon, but not enough to force it completely away from Brann. The edge of the blade smacked into Brann's head exactly where he had felt it but, rather than cleaving his skull as it would have done had it struck him squarely on the crown, it instead and, to Konall's astonishment, bounced off Brann's head, ricocheting wildly to one side.

Perhaps the angle caused it to rebound rather than chop into his skull. Perhaps the movement of Brann as he had looked up had made the difference. Perhaps he had unusually thick bone there. Konall did not care. And, this time, he did not hesitate. Pushing Brann's head down with his left hand, feeling the slick wetness of the boy's blood, he swung a savage blow which not only cut into the man's thigh, but knocked his legs from under him. He leapt past Brann and, with a bellow of rage and relief, plunged his sword downwards with lethal effect.

Brann had known something was wrong as Konall's flippant thanks had died on his lips and his expression had frozen. He had not had time to react – and no knowledge of the form of danger to react to – and had merely seen a flash of movement as Konall had thrown his own blade forward. He guessed that Konall had saved him from further injury following the blow to his head, but before he could say anything to the boy, Konall had turned to face the increasingly frenzied mountain men whose panic had turned to the furious offence of cornered animals after they had been forced back enough to realise that they were caught between two forces.

The blow had stunned Brann slightly, and that, added to the increasingly desperate ferocity of the mountain men, saw the battle, for him, descend into a hazy repetitious sequence of deflecting blows and striking out at the nearest exposed part of any man in front of him at any given moment. He even swung his sword, occasionally.

The two groups of warriors and slaves had slowly converged, grounding the savage mountain men between them. The enemy's main advantage – their savage and wild bloodlust – had worked well when they believed they had the upper hand and that slaughter was a formality. When the tide had turned, however, they had lost their one asset and, trapped between the vice of their opponents, their resistance had evaporated.

The battle had descended into grim and methodical carnage as the wildmen were systematically butchered. Fury and disgust combined to create a passion for wiping out the savages and ensuring they would never be unleashed on anyone again. The warriors knew that there must be more of them in the mountains, and that destroying this band would not solve the problem. But, to these men, the wildmen before them had come to symbolise the horrors beyond human comprehension of which they had heard in gruesome tales from the few, the very few, survivors.

And then, without warning, it was over.

The small groups that most of the men had formed had become bigger as the noose of steel tightened around the mountain men, and as those intent on destroying them came closer to achieving that aim. Such was the intensity of the fighting, however, that the two halves of the combined forces of locals and slaves met, with no foe left between them, before they had realised just how close they had become.

Brann felt like collapsing to the ground in exhaustion and relief at finding himself still alive, but noticed that the others were still upright and guessed that it was not a warrior-like course of action to follow. What little was left of his strength and, mainly determination, kept his knees from buckling as the boys found themselves faced by the nobles – the two small groups had merged but the youngsters, immersed in fighting for survival, had been oblivious to all around them unless it was a threat or a target.

Lord Sigurr leant on a long, two-handed sword and smiled warmly. 'I do not know who exactly to thank yet, but I suspect that the answer lies somewhere immediately before me. In any case, my deepest gratitude goes to all who risked their lives and, in some cases, gave them, to save ours.'

'My gratitude also,' beamed Lord Ragnarr, whose grin shone large in the midst of his beard. 'For a while there, I did not think it was going to be as much fun as it turned out to be. My thanks for showing up, boys.'

The words were becoming more distant to Brann with each passing sentence. His spinning head felt as if it had been pumped full of smoke – with more constantly being added – and his vision had darkened to a tunnel that was narrowing rapidly. However, he forced himself to remain erect, breathing deeply and – to his own ears – loudly as he gently swayed.

'Einarr,' Ragnarr called to the tall, black-clad figure who was directing a small group of warriors in pursuit of the last surviving wildmen – an equally small group who had managed to squeeze out of the battle on one flank as the two converging lines had closed in. 'Your page looks exhausted. Do you not keep him fit enough for a little exercise like this?' He turned to Brann. 'At least you look like you got involved, little one. Is that your blood or theirs?'

Brann tried to speak, but his words were slurred and unintelligible. Concerned, Konall took him by the arm to steady him. 'Probably much of it is his, father. He took a sword blow to the head and the blade just bounced off. It was the strangest thing.'

Ragnarr looked curiously at his son, who was full of concern for this small foreign boy. He grunted, 'Many strange things happen in battle, some that cannot be explained in any way other than that the gods were not ready to receive a man in the next life at that time.' He laughed, beamingly. 'And he must have a damned hard skull, too!'

Einarr strode up. Ragnarr nodded over at Brann, 'You always had a knack for treating wounds, nephew,' the bear-like noble said. 'Perhaps you should take a look at your page's head. He seems to think it is a good means of stopping a sword blow.'

Einarr frowned as he caught sight of Brann. 'Gods, he looks awful,' he gasped, moving quickly to the boy. He smoothed back the blood-soaked hair to examine the wound. The sharp pain caused Brann to suck in his breath, but he felt that to complain would be ungrateful to the man who was trying to help him – and he did not, in any case, want to show any weakness in front of such hard men.

'Give me some water. Quickly,' Einarr snapped. The women who had been with the nobles' party – and who had been protected by the relentless defence of the men around them – had joined them, and one immediately handed Einarr a canteen. He drenched the wound, clearing enough of the blood and grime to allow him to see the extent of the damage and forcing another hiss from Brann as he sharply inhaled.

Einarr cursed as he saw the severity of the wound. 'It has cut into the bone,' he said, alarmed. 'Even if the sword did not cut through to his shoulders, his skull should have, at least, been cracked. You should thank the gods for giving you such a thick head, boy.' He knelt before Brann, taking his head between his hands and looking into the unresponsive eyes. The boy had smiled faintly at the last comment, but there was little other comprehension evident.

Sigurr was standing behind his son. 'He looks out on his feet. I have no idea how he is still standing.'

'Yet he was still swinging his sword to the end,' Konall pointed out. 'I had to stop him when it was all over. He knew little of what was going on around him, but he kept going. He does not give up, that is for sure. Similar to when he went after Loku.'

The older men looked at him sharply. 'He went after Loku? You have much to tell us, Konall,' his father growled.

Konall nodded. 'More than that. They fought. And he nearly killed him.'

'It shows,' Ragnarr grunted. 'Look at the state of the poor lad.'

Konall was still supporting Brann, who was aware of the noise of their words but not their meaning. 'No, father,' the blond boy said in a low voice. 'Brann nearly killed Loku.'

There was a stunned silence. Einarr gently stroked a strand of hair from Brann's brow. 'There seems to be more to this little one,' he said quietly, 'than we would have expected. Our Lady hinted at it in riddles, and it seems we are seeing a little of what she spoke.' He pulled up each of Brann's eyelids with his thumb and peered into his eyes. 'Right now, however, he needs attention. And a lot of it.'

Although he could not hear the words, Brann responded right on cue. Darkness swept softly over him like a welcoming quilt on a cold night, and his legs, at least, gave way. He did not feel Ragnarr's arms catch him as he fell and carry him from the field. He did not hear the sobs of the women at the sight of the slight figure, made to seem all the more vulnerable and small in the grasp of the huge warrior. And he never heard the warlord's snapped command: 'Get that boy help. He has priority over all. And tell the healer that if he dies, he will join the boy in the afterworld.'

Chapter 13

Brann awoke in an atmosphere so idyllic that he assumed he was dead and in some dreamlike afterworld. Warm sunlight enveloped him and the bed beneath him was firm and comfortable. A damp and soothing cloth was stroking across his brow and the sound of it being dipped occasionally in water was heavenly in its ordinariness.

His eyes, heavy, had to be forced open. They took a few moments to focus, but he felt as if there was no rush. As they cleared, his gaze found Valdis smiling gently as she wrung out the cloth. At the very least, he thought, this must be a dream. Feeling that there was no need, therefore, to keep his eyes open again, he let the lids sink back down.

Valdis's lilting tones drifted down to him. 'That is good, keep them closed,' she murmured. 'The longer they think you are still asleep, the longer they will leave you alone.'

He lay with his eyes closed, enjoying the soothing attention, while he adjusted to the contrast between the horror of the battlefield where he had lost consciousness and the dreamlike serenity of the room where he had reawakened.

After several contented minutes, he began to feel guilty at lapping up the intimate care deceptively and, opening his eyes, he pushed himself up on his elbows.

'What are you doing here?' he said. 'I thought I was dreaming.'

Valdis frowned coquettishly. 'What sort of a greeting is that? Really, a girl sails all the way down here and she is not sure if the first words she hears from you are an insult or a compliment.'

Brann's face coloured. 'A compliment. It was definitely a compliment,' he stammered.

'I know,' Valdis smiled gently. 'I am just teasing you.'

Brann was a picture of relief. 'Thank the gods for that. I have had enough of violence for a while.'

'So I hear,' Valdis said, fetching a towel from the other side of the room. 'You are quite the little heroes, you, Konall and even my brother. You are the talk of the town you know.'

Brann blushed once more. 'I did not do much. I just tagged along with the other two.'

The girl laughed. Brann sank back, closed his eyes, and wished he could listen to the sound for ever. 'That is not what the other two are saying,' she said. 'And do not pretend you are not pleased to hear it. You cannot fool me, boy.'

'Well, maybe I did a little,' he admitted – then was jolted from his reverie by the bunched towel hitting him squarely in the face.

'Come on, you,' Valdis chided, her words following closely in the wake of the towel. 'Get out of bed before they come looking for you. If they can do without you for a week, they can manage for a little longer.'

'A week?' Brann stopped in the act of pulling off an undershirt that he seemed to have acquired since losing consciousness. 'What do you mean: a week?'

Valdis patted his cheek affectionately. 'Eight days, to be precise. You were slumbering for a while. You took quite a knock on the head, so it has taken you a while to recover.'

He lifted a tentative hand to investigate, and found a bandage, but no pain. And no hair.

His eyes widened. 'I am bald! In the name of all the gods, I have gone bald!'

Valdis smiled and placed a reassuring hand on his arm – which, in itself, partially made up for the loss of hair. 'Do not worry, it did not fall out. It was just easier to work on the wound if they shaved your head. It is quite common with scalp wounds, and it always grows back.' She grinned mischievously. 'Well, almost always.'

Brann looked alarmed. Highly alarmed. The girl continued before he could take her joke too seriously. 'You were lucky, you know. The doctor here has worked a lifetime treating battle wounds, and he gets plenty of practice, believe me.' Having seen the carefree glee with which Konall and Hakon had approached conflict, Brann believed her. 'Anyway, I am assured that your wound will heal quickly, although it has taken a lot out of you. That was why you slept so long, that and the potions they gave you to aid the healing: they tend to knock you out a bit.'

Brann felt around the most tender part of his head, where he guessed the wound must be. 'I can only agree that he knows what he is doing if the lack of pain is anything to go by.' He flexed his right arm. 'I wish I could say the same for my arm. It does not half nip. It was all so frantic that I must not have noticed being wounded there also.'

'Well, I would not say you were wounded, exactly,' Valdis said, slightly coyly. 'And not exactly during the battle.'

'Not during it?' Brann repeated, almost absently, as he lifted the wide neck of his shirt to peer down inside the sleeve.

His eyes widened again, even more violently than before. 'What is all of heaven and hell is that?' he yelled.

'That,' Valdis said primly, 'is an honour.'

Brann tore off the shirt. Inked in black into his skin was a design stretching from his shoulder to his elbow, dominated by a mighty dragon and with a band bearing runic emblems encircling his arm.

He stared at it in silence for a long moment. At last, he said, 'How long does it last before it fades?'

Valdis spoke quietly, and intently. 'It lasts as long as you do. As I said, this is an honour, one of the greatest you could have been paid by my people.'

Her tone conveyed the reverence she felt for the deep-rooted beliefs and traditions of her land, and Brann felt that to say any more would be seen as offensive. No matter the level of shock he was feeling, he could not bring himself to contemplate offending Valdis.

'Can I wash it?' he asked, moving to a bowl in the corner.

'Of course,' she smiled. 'In fact, it is recommended to prevent infection.'

He splashed water over his arm, then his face, using the shock of its coldness to try to focus his thoughts away from their fixation on his arm. He stared into the water, watching the drips from his face ripple his bizarre-looking reflection.

Eventually, he grinned. 'So,' he said, without looking up, 'I am brought among your people, I try to help where I can, I take a thump on the head from the gods know what sort of a weapon, and what do I get in return? A bald head and a drawing on my arm. Is there anything else that has been done to me that I should know about?'

Noticing his change of attitude, she smiled playfully. 'Not yet, boy, not yet. But any more grumpiness like that and you may find you have a few more war wounds.' She took the towel and gave his face a quick rub. 'Now move it. Get a tunic on and we will get out of here. We are more likely to find peace for a little longer down in the garden, and there I will fill you in on what has been happening while you were lazing in bed.'

She demurely turned her back as Brann pulled off his shirt and dived into a fresh tunic, then dragged him from the room, before he could don the warm cloak he had been in the act of grabbing. He did manage, however, to pull the cloak around him as the giggling girl led him at speed through the corridors and downstairs, darting between corners and peering around them in a way that reminded Brann vividly of passing, with Konall, along the trail through the ravine on their way to the wildmen's village – and in a way that contrasted more than favourably with the first occasion.

They reached the garden with much giggling and without incident. Brann found the laughter a welcome release from the tension of the previous few days that he could remember and, moreover, the childishness of their actions was a welcome change from the adult world he had been thrust into.

The garden was more workmanlike than decorative, used for growing vegetables for the kitchens rather than pretty flowers or shrubs. Still, its high wall that provided shelter for the vegetables from the salt-laden sea winds also provided shelter for the young pair from prying eyes as they walked on narrow paths among the orderly rows of carefully tended greenery.

Valdis brought Brann up-to-date on the aftermath of the battle – it did not take her long as there was not a great deal to tell: none of the wildmen had survived; there had been casualties on their side, but none was serious among the noble hierarchy, thanks to the intervention of the reinforcements;

the nobles had been closeted away while they discussed their next move; and Einarr had, as well as freeing the slaves, instructed his crew to overhaul his ship in readiness of returning to sea.

Brann stopped abruptly in his stride. 'Wait there,' he said. 'He freed the slaves?'

Valdis shrugged. 'He could hardly leave them as slaves after all that they did. Maybe other cultures would, but not here.' Brann moved with her as she started walking again. 'In any case, from what I overheard of a conversation between my father and Lord Ragnarr, Lord Einarr's heart was never really in that business. It seems that he and his crew were forced into that line after "inheriting" their ship, and its rowers, from some pirates who sank his ship but lost their lives as a result of that misguided attack. They said that Lord Einarr's ship had been of the normal type for our people – similar to the warlord's that you saw on the way here – and was no match for it in a sea battle for the one he now has. So Lord Einarr and his men abandoned their ship as it sank, boarded the pirate vessel and disposed of the pirates. As their own cargo had sunk with the ship, they were forced into continuing the pirates' slaving until they could raise funds to return to a more pleasant form of trade: it was either that or risk destitution and starvation for not only them, but for the rowing slaves that they had taken on also, and for whom they now also had responsibility. After all, they had lost everything, and could not even afford to free the rowers or, by the law of seafaring nations, they would then have had to pay the rowers, which would have been difficult since everything they had owned was now at the bottom of the sea. It was not feasible at first for them to pick up one type of cargo here and another there and so on, and since

477

there were some slave boys gathered already in the hold, their only feasible option was to continue that trade, no matter how distasteful it may be for them, until they had enough money to both set themselves up in more acceptable business and take on the rowers as paid help.'

She paused and placed a hand on his arm, a gesture he was enjoying more each time it was made. 'I know it is scant consolation to you – we know now of your true background – but it seems it did not sit well on Lord Einarr's shoulders or those of many of his men.'

Despite enjoying the physical contact, Brann felt awkward at her compassion, as if he were imposing worry upon her. 'Do not be concerned about me,' he countered lightly. He looked into her eyes. 'There have been certain advantages to the way my life has gone.'

She poked him in the chest with one finger. 'You do not fool me, boy. No one gets much sympathy around here, so take it when you can get it. And do not think that your compliments will get you anywhere, either.' But she could not hide the blush in her cheeks, or the smile in her eyes.

'You seem to have heard a great deal about Einarr's, er, Lord Einarr's story,' he observed.

She smiled. 'It is amazing how nobles forget who can hear what they are saying when they relax at mealtimes and there is a serving wench behind them.'

'Perhaps that is why they use trusted families in these capacities,' Brann pointed out.

She laughed, and his heart jolted. 'Perhaps it is. Anyhow, our Lord Einarr seems to think a lot of you so you could do worse than forge a living with him, if that was to your taste. Mind you,' she poked his tattooed arm, 'a few people seem to think highly of you, so you might have options.'

478

Having overcome his surprise at finding the tattoo (though not yet accustomed to it) he began to be interested in the design itself. He pulled his arm from his sleeve and pulled up his tunic to allow him to examine it.

The dragon, its folded wings enclosing it, sat atop a shield bearing the emblem of a bird. Without taking his eyes from it, he said quietly, 'Tell me about it. What does it mean? Not just the design itself; what does it mean to have this put on you?'

She led him to a nearby bench against the stone wall of the garden. 'Sit here, and I will tell you. To answer your second question first, it is a great honour for courage in conflict, but also if that courage has done a service to this land or the people in it; it does not denote merely bravery for the sake of bravery itself. Only the warlord himself can grant it, and he decrees the basis of the design: the beast denotes his regard for your actions.'

'So there are different levels to it?'

She nodded. 'It starts with the bear: a fierce and strong opponent. Greater than that is the wolf – not as strong as the bear, but more cunning, on its own or with others, and so a more dangerous foe. And the dragon,' she traced it with her finger, raising goosepimples along his arm, 'is the highest there is: the most formidable beast of lore, granted to signify an act by the bearer of the design that was considered by the warlord to be of the greatest benefit to our people and that is far beyond what would be expected of any ordinary individual. Konall and Hakon had their wolves bestowed publicly, but unfortunately you were still slumbering under the influence of your medication when this was done.'

He looked at her in surprise. 'Their wolves? But they did as much as I did. In fact, they talked me through much of it. It is not fair that they were given only wolves.'

'I would not say that to anyone else,' she chided him. 'To receive any of these is regarded as a true honour, and one rarely bestowed, so do not diminish that by referring to them as "only wolves". There are many fine warriors who show great bravery over years of loyal service who are not awarded this, and the two boys were overcome to receive such acclaim. In your case, Lord Sigurr was impressed by the fact that you have come to this land against your will and yet you have repeatedly faced danger to help people from here, when you have no obligation at all to do so. And my brother and Konall disagreed with your assessment of what you did. I may be wrong, but I think the fact that it was you who faced, and saw off, Loku – they were impressed by that, by the way – and the fact that it was your plan that saved the warlord's life, in fact the lives of the whole of his family, and saved his domain from falling under an evil and murderous rule, and the fact that you nearly died doing your utmost in carrying out that plan – I think that all of these may have had something to do with you receiving the dragon.'

Brann laughed. 'You make it sound very grand. All I did was be forced into situations where I had to react or die. But I suppose it had a good outcome. And I understand now the enormity of this huge picture on my arm, so I do feel quite honoured, I must admit.' He looked at the design with renewed interest. 'So tell me about this.'

She smiled, contentedly, tracing the lines with her finger as she described each part. At the feeling he smiled even more contentedly, then forced himself to listen to her words.

'Apart from the beast itself, each design is unique to the individual. Hakon and I created it for you. The raven emblem is the banner of our home town, and the hammer the dragon is holding in its tail is the symbol of Rakor, the blacksmith of the heavens and our god of war, who I pray will watch over you.' She smiled. 'I think it is quite nice, really.'

Brann stared at it, still trying to become accustomed to it. 'I suppose so,' he admitted. 'So what does the writing say?'

Valdis stood up, brushing her skirt into shape. 'You will have to ask my brother about that. It is just something to remember us by.'

'Remember you by? I am not going anywhere soon.'

'That is what you think, little wolf,' said Hakon who had approached unseen by the enraptured Brann. 'Lord Einarr's ship is being provisioned as we speak, and his Lady will soon be aboard. His father has commissioned him to take a cargo of goods to the market in Sagia, so he is a reputable merchant once more – although I suspect he is also travelling as an emissary to the Emperor to discuss his stance on these matters that good old Loku has brought to our attention.' He slapped Brann on the back with such gusto that the smaller boy almost fell forward. Oblivious to the dazed vision and spinning head that he had caused, he continued, 'Anyhow, I am off to pack – and I suggest you do, too. These things tend to happen all of a sudden and we may not have much time. A couple of the former slaves have accepted offers of land from the warlord to start a new life here, but the rest have remained as crew members, either to serve as seamen under Lord Einarr or as a means of passage on their way back to their homes. Some of the local men have also signed up to fill the places of those who died in the fight, so that side of things is taken care of. I would guess we will sail as soon as the provisions and cargo have been stowed.'

He grinned. 'It is just as well you wakened this morning – you may have opened your eyes for the first time while at sea – without having been able to say your fond farewells.'

He looked mischievously at this sister, winked at Brann and sauntered off.

'What does he mean: "we"?' Brann asked, ignoring Hakon's parting comments.

'He means that he is one of the locals joining the crew,' Valdis said simply, starting to lead him towards the building.

Brann was surprised by her acceptance of the fact. 'Are you not upset? Will you not miss him?'

She stopped. 'Our people are different from yours: the women must learn to fight in case they are needed alongside the men. Fighting with bears is a doorway to manhood, and our men all feel the urge at some point to take to the sea. We are used to it – in fact, we expect it.' She paused. 'But I will miss him, of course.' She added pointedly as she started walking again, 'I will miss you both.'

Blushing, Brann blurted, 'I know I will miss you.'

She spun gracefully, and dropped into a light-hearted curtsy. 'I am flattered, young sir, but you will have my brother to remind you. And this.' She traced her fingers down his arm where his sleeve covered the tattoo once more. 'And this.' She bent forward and lightly kissed his cheek. For a moment her face became uncharacteristically serious, her expression poignant, her fingertips lightly brushed the spot she had kissed. Then she spun on her heel.

'Now come on – you heard Hakon. You had better pack.'

'What's the rush?' he objected. 'I have no possessions to take.'

'You would be surprised,' she called over her shoulder. 'The warlord was very grateful, and Lord Einarr also felt that, now that you are officially his page – until you get home at least – you should look the part.'

Back in his room, he discovered the truth of her words. Directed by the girl to a chest in the corner, he found clothes, including a heavy cloak and pair of leather gauntlets. What caught his eye above all, however, was, lying across the top of the clothing, a scabbarded short sword, plain in design but well-balanced in his hand when he drew it experimentally.

'That is from the warlord,' Valdis explained. 'Made by his own blacksmith. The clothes were sent by Lord Einarr, and Lord Konall left you a boot knife. He said it was always good to have something in reserve. And my brother insisted you had this.' She lifted the cloak with a quizzical look. 'Though why a new one would not have been better, I don't know. This one has even been ripped, here at the hem. Look, you can see the stitches.'

Brann took it from her, his fingers unerringly finding the repair. He smiled but, before he could say anything, shouts echoed through the corridor outside his door, urging all who were travelling to meet in the main hall immediately. Hurriedly, Valdis helped him to store the clothes in a canvas bag that had been left beside them. He strapped on the sword and swung the heavy cloak around his shoulders – it was quicker than trying to cram it into the bag.

He hesitated before they left the room. Valdis looked back at him urgently, her expression urging him on.

'It just seems so quick,' he said faintly. 'There does not seem to be a chance to say goodbye properly.'

To his embarrassment, he felt tears welling up in his eyes.

'I know,' she said seriously. 'But I said my goodbye in the garden. And my thoughts and prayers will go with you whether we take three breaths or three days to bid each other farewell.'

He smiled. 'Should I not take a favour as a token from a beautiful lady?'

Her eyes smiled back at him. 'My favour you will take with you wherever you go, whether you like it or not. It is here,' she touched his arm, 'in the words around your arm.'

He started to ask her again what the runes said, the lettering being different from that used in his homeland, but he was drowned out by fresh, more urgent, shouts in the passageway.

Grabbing his hand, she dragged him and they set off at a run to the hall, where they found Konall and Hakon among those gathering. The large room was almost filled, the former slaves having been brought up from their billet, and with those who were bidding farewell to the local crew members adding to the numbers in the room.

Above the hubbub, Brann thanked Konall for the knife.

His face as straight as ever, the tall boy said, 'I was going to give you a bow, but I thought it would be safer for your companions if you had a knife instead. As long as you do not try to throw it, that is.'

Gerens and Grakk pushed through the crowds to join them but, before they could speak, the warlord – flanked by Einarr and Ragnarr – swept into the room, prompting a hush to fall over those assembled.

'It seems,' Sigurr said, his voice quiet but clear in every corner, 'that no sooner has my son returned to me than he is leaving again. But his absence will lend more time to repair relations with our neighbours in anticipation of his next return. And at least he brought us a little excitement while he was here.' Laughter rippled around the crowded room. 'I do not intend to keep you long here, for the water is calm and you will be eager to make the most of that while it lasts, but I would like to say that it pleases me greatly that, during your visit, I saw enslaved men freed – and deservedly so. Having witnessed you in battle, and speaking as a warrior, I am glad and relieved that you are on our side.

'In that respect, as I bid farewell to my son, my nephew,' he looked across at Konall, and Brann started in surprise at

484

the realisation that he, too, would be sailing with them, 'and to those others of my people who are choosing to leave here for this voyage, I do so knowing that they are in the company of the finest of men.

'I bid you a safe voyage and look forward to your return.'

A resounding cheer rocked the room, and Brann found himself infected with the emotion of the moment. Valdis quickly hugged him and her brother before ushering them to join the others leaving the room. They made their way to the harbour, the streets lined with cheering crowds and windows filled with those seeking a better vantage point. Brann grinned at the group around him.

'I almost feel important,' he shouted above the noise.

'Enjoy it – it will be quiet enough at sea by comparison,' Gerens pointed out.

Konall could be seen working his way back to them from the head of the procession. Brann had not been the only one who noticed the young noble's significant decision to stand within the body of the men in the hall, rather than, as would previously have been the case, at the side of his father as Sigurr made his speech. However, he had been signalled to take his place with the other nobles at the head of what was almost a ceremonial parade to the docks.

Konall reached them. 'My uncle would like a quick departure once we get to the ship. All has been safely stowed already, so it will be a matter of getting on board and starting to row straight away.

'There will be more crew than there are rowing places, though, so you'll be split into teams of three and put on a rota. Cannick is working his way back, informing everyone of who they are with and who will be rowing first.

'Around here, we are all sailors so everyone will play their part at the oars. I am told that Einarr, Cannick and myself will be excused rowing, but I intend to remedy that once we are at sea – the inactivity would drive me insane otherwise.'

Without waiting for a reply, he headed back towards the front of the column. By the time they reached the ship, each man knew what was expected of him; Brann, to his delight, had been teamed with Gerens and Hakon and, through happy coincidence – or perhaps through Cannick's design – he was back on his old familiar bench. Grakk was with another former slave on the bench in front of them, the pair having been chosen to partner a local man who, like Hakon, was perhaps an experienced sailor but who had never before sat on a three-man rowing bench. Brann was quietly amused that he himself was now considered experienced.

Even as they were settling into their seats, the ship was untied and pushed from the jetty. Feeling strange at the lack of chains around his ankles, Brann advised Hakon to follow his lead as the order was given to release the oars. Within seconds, the ship was sweeping around to face up the fjord and pulling away through the dark, deep and calm water.

Brann had stared intently at the crowd as they turned and had been rewarded with a sight of the girl in the long green dress. The vision was fixed in his mind as he pulled at the oar beside her brother, and reminded him that Valdis had directed his final query about his tattoo to towards Hakon.

Hakon glanced at him. 'Interesting rowing style,' he observed, referring to Brann's use of the box that Grakk had arranged to be fixed to the floor for him to brace his feet against as he half stood and pulled at the oar. 'Not trying to attract anyone's attention in particular, are you?'

Brann grinned. 'It is the only way you can do it when you do not have the approved length of legs. And, on the subject of your sister: she said you would tell me what the words are that my arm is forced to bear.'

'Oh, that,' Hakon said, feigning indifference. 'It is nothing much, just something she said you should remember. I cannot really remember.'

'Tell me or you will find yourself at the other end of the oar,' Brann growled.

'All right, I relent,' Hakon conceded. 'It should mean much to you: it meant much to my sister, and you seem to mean much to her.

'It says: "Dare to dream. Trust your heart. Let your soul fly."'

Brann smiled faintly. As the words repeated in his mind, he saw Valdis's lips forming them.

Dare to dream. Trust your heart. Let your soul fly.

He knew not where he was headed. He knew not what awaited him. He knew not how he would cope with it. But, as he pulled himself closer to it with every sweep of the oar, he knew that what he took with him was a dream he could cling to, could nurture. And could return to.

* * * *

He awoke with a start. The angle of the glare through the window spoke of noon.

He jumped once again as he turned to see her standing there, staring into his soul.

The voice as dry as the desert rasped.

'He is coming.'

487

Epilogue

The storyteller drew breath. His piercing eyes swept around the chamber, the torchlight dancing on the rapt faces of the villagers.

'Now you know. Now that story is told. Now you know *the beginning*. But I am not so young in years as once I was, and my strength is not the strength of my youth. If some kind soul will fetch me a supper, I will retire for the moment.

'While I am finished for this night, however, the tale goes on.

'You have heard how the hero was born. If you would hear more, return with me on the morrow. Return with me, and hear him grow.'

Acknowledgements

We all have dreams, and sometimes we get lucky and one of them comes true.

I got lucky.

Lucky to have come across the people who could make it possible.

My wife, Valerie, who always believes in me, even when I don't. Especially when I don't. And who inspires me in more ways than she knows, or ever will know.

My family, Martyn, Johnny, Melissa, Nicky, Adam and Nathan, who delight me and keep my feet firmly on the ground in equal measure – the first being wonderful and the second essential (and inevitable, where offspring are concerned).

My parents, Ian and Diane, who gave me the genes to achieve this and the encouragement to let the dream grow into reality, and my brother, Gordon, whose relentless irreverence and ready support never cease to make me smile from the other side of an ocean.

My grandpa, Frank Hales, whose gift of *The Lord of the Rings* took a very small but voracious reader from Enid Blyton and Capt. W. E. Johns and introduced him to the concept of epic and heroic fantasy, something that never left its grip on that young boy's imagination.

All at Harper *Voyager* who have taken my story and turned it into a book. That one sentence covers a multitude of jobs and more expertise than I even know exists, but in particular deep gratitude to: Natasha Bardon, who discovered this book and took it on with an enthusiasm that was as delightful as it was unexpected; to Rachel Winterbottom, who edited it with perception and an understanding of the characters and story that was reassuring to a first-time novelist and invaluable to the quality of the finished tale; to Eleanor Ashfield, for calming advice just when I needed calming and advising; and to Ben Gardiner and Cherie Chapman, for a cover design that, magically, just seemed perfect from the first moment I saw it.

Margaret Shaw, who laboured with indefatigable cheer and willingness over a keyboard to type the very first draft of this story, and Anne-Janine Nugent, who somehow produced publicity photos of quality and warmth despite being lumbered with history's most uncomfortable model.

And Brann, who dragged me into a world of excitement and wonder on and off the page, on a journey that has had a magical and breathless beginning.

Yes, 'beginning'. There is indeed more for Brann to face, endure and try to survive. And you are cordially invited to come along for the ride.